Steam™

To our beloved cat Arlo who blessed so much of
our studio time with his magical presence.

—Duane & Eva

For Kiki & Lolo

—Drew

Steam™

written by
DREW FORD

art and lettering by
DUANE LESLIE

colors by
EVA DE LA CRUZ

Dark Horse Books

President & Publisher
MIKE RICHARDSON

Editor
SHANTEL LAROCQUE

Assistant Editor
BRETT ISRAEL

Designer
SKYLER WEISSENFLUH

Digital Art Technician
SAMANTHA HUMMER

Special thanks to Brendan Wright.

Neil Hankerson Executive Vice President • Tom Weddle Chief Financial Officer • Randy Stradley Vice President of Publishing • Nick McWhorter Chief Business Development Officer • Dale LaFountain Chief Information Officer • Matt Parkinson Vice President of Marketing • Vanessa Todd-Holmes Vice President of Production and Scheduling • Mark Bernardi Vice President of Book Trade and Digital Sales • Ken Lizzi General Counsel • Dave Marshall Editor in Chief • Davey Estrada Editorial Director Chris Warner Senior Books Editor • Cary Grazzini Director of Specialty Projects • Lia Ribacchi Art Director • Matt Dryer Director of Digital Art and Prepress • Michael Gombos Senior Director of Licensed Publications • Kari Yadro Director of Custom Programs • Kari Torson Director of International Licensing • Sean Brice Director of Trade Sales

Published by Dark Horse Books
A division of Dark Horse Comics LLC
10956 SE Main Street
Milwaukie, OR 97222

DarkHorse.com

To find a comics shop in your area, visit ComicShopLocator.com.

First Dark Horse edition: May 2020
ISBN 978-1-50671-726-5

1 3 5 7 9 10 8 6 4 2

Printed in Korea

Library of Congress Cataloging-in-Publication Data

Names: Ford, Drew (Andrew), writer. | Leslie, Duane, artist. | De la Cruz, Eva, colourist.
Title: Steam / written by Drew Ford ; art and lettering by Duane Leslie ; colors by Eva De La Cruz.
Description: First Dark Horse edition. | Milwaukie, OR : Dark Horse Books, 2020. | Audience: Ages 10+ | Summary: Arlo escapes his abusive guardians on Earth through an intergalactic portal to the steam-powered planet of Pother where he joins a group who work to protect the planet's resources, giving Arlo a chance to discover his own self-worth.
Identifiers: LCCN 2019050413 | ISBN 9781506717265 (trade paperback) | ISBN 9781506717272 (epub)
Subjects: LCSH: Graphic novels. | CYAC: Graphic novels. | Science fiction. | Life on other planets--Fiction. | Environmental protection--Fiction. | Self-esteem--Fiction.
Classification: LCC PZ7.7.F67 St 2020 | DDC 741.5/973--dc23
LC record available at https://lccn.loc.gov/2019050413

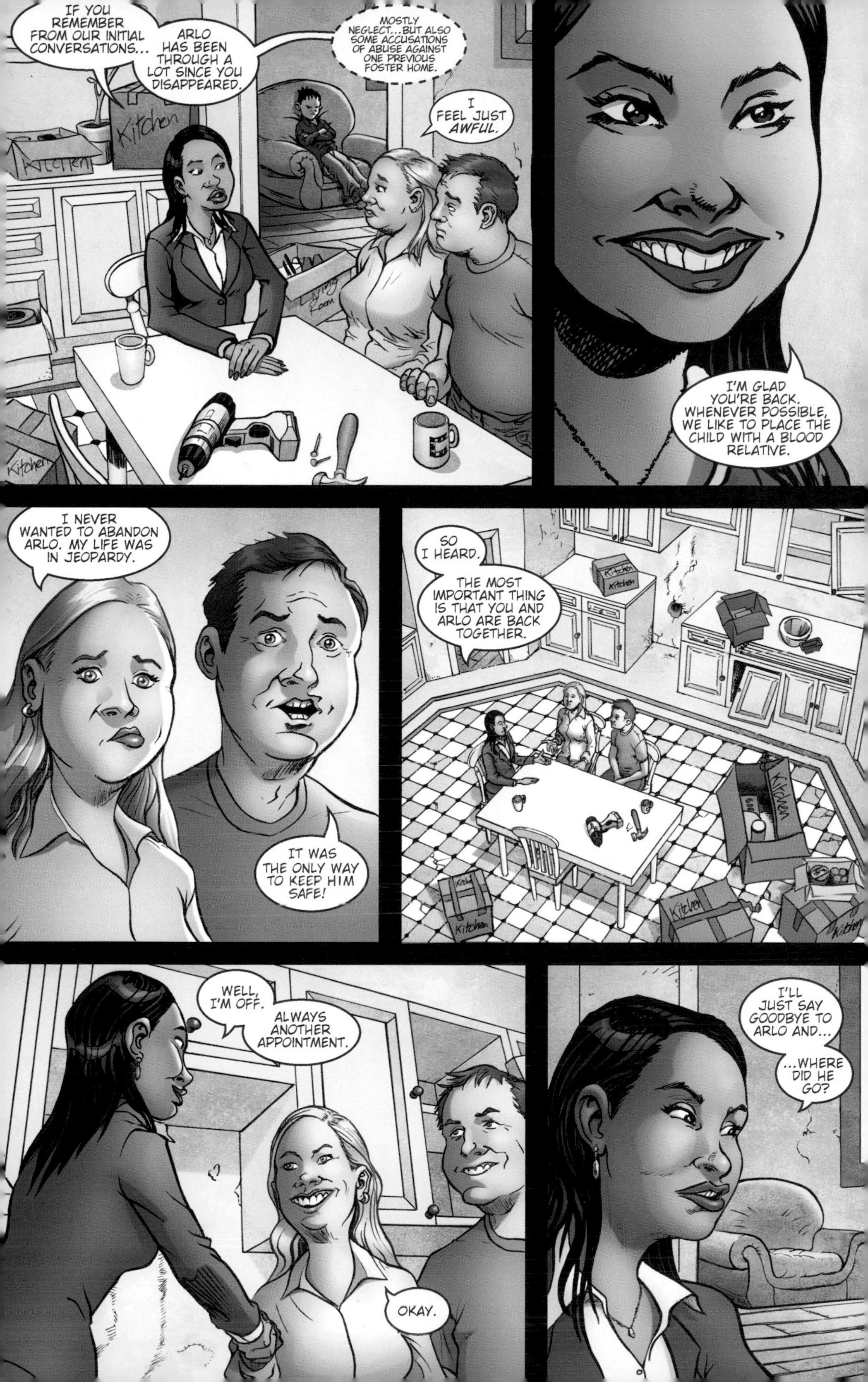
IF YOU REMEMBER FROM OUR INITIAL CONVERSATIONS...
ARLO HAS BEEN THROUGH A LOT SINCE YOU DISAPPEARED.
MOSTLY NEGLECT...BUT ALSO SOME ACCUSATIONS OF ABUSE AGAINST ONE PREVIOUS FOSTER HOME.
I FEEL JUST AWFUL.
Kitchen
Kitchen
Living Room
Kitchen
I'M GLAD YOU'RE BACK. WHENEVER POSSIBLE, WE LIKE TO PLACE THE CHILD WITH A BLOOD RELATIVE.
I NEVER WANTED TO ABANDON ARLO. MY LIFE WAS IN JEOPARDY.
IT WAS THE ONLY WAY TO KEEP HIM SAFE!
SO I HEARD.
THE MOST IMPORTANT THING IS THAT YOU AND ARLO ARE BACK TOGETHER.
Kitchen
Kitchen
Kitchen
Kitchen
Kitchen
Kitchen
WELL, I'M OFF.
ALWAYS ANOTHER APPOINTMENT.
OKAY.
I'LL JUST SAY GOODBYE TO ARLO AND...
...WHERE DID HE GO?

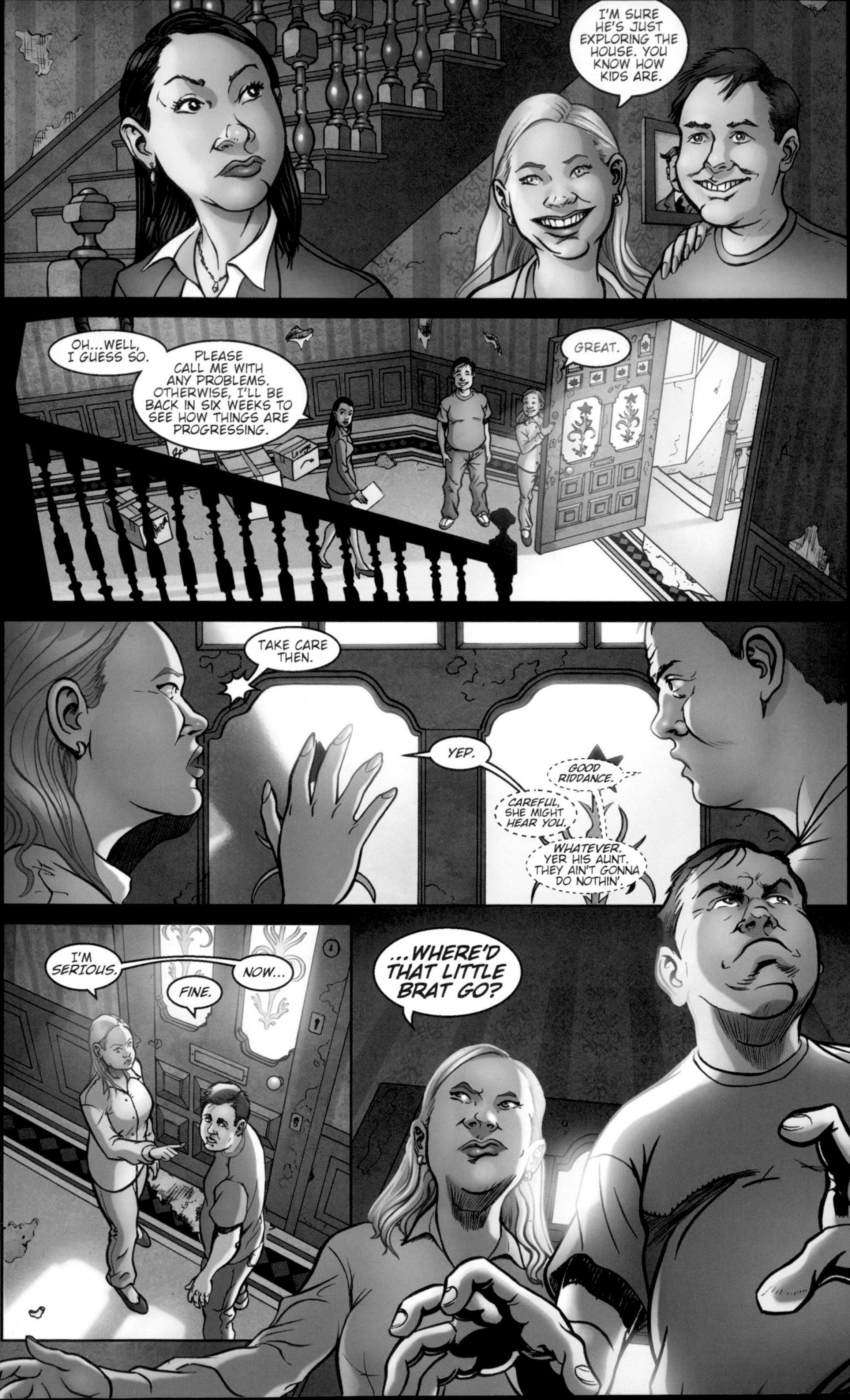
I'M SURE HE'S JUST EXPLORING THE HOUSE. YOU KNOW HOW KIDS ARE.
OH...WELL, I GUESS SO.
PLEASE CALL ME WITH ANY PROBLEMS. OTHERWISE, I'LL BE BACK IN SIX WEEKS TO SEE HOW THINGS ARE PROGRESSING.
GREAT.
TAKE CARE THEN.
YEP.
GOOD RIDDANCE.
CAREFUL, SHE MIGHT HEAR YOU.
WHATEVER. YER HIS AUNT. THEY AIN'T GONNA DO NOTHIN'.
I'M SERIOUS.
FINE.
NOW...
...WHERE'D THAT LITTLE BRAT GO?

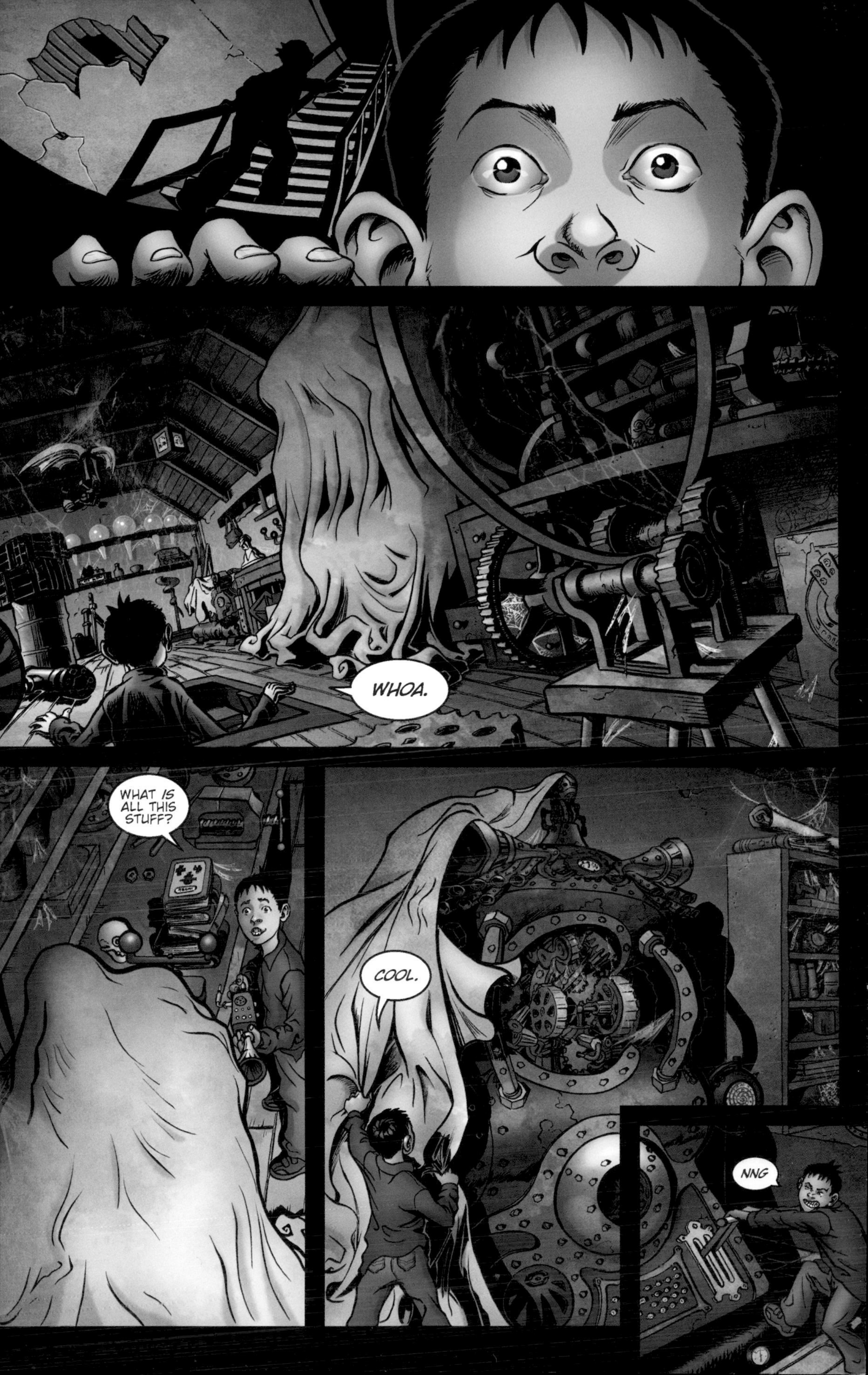
WHOA.
WHAT IS ALL THIS STUFF?
COOL.
NNG

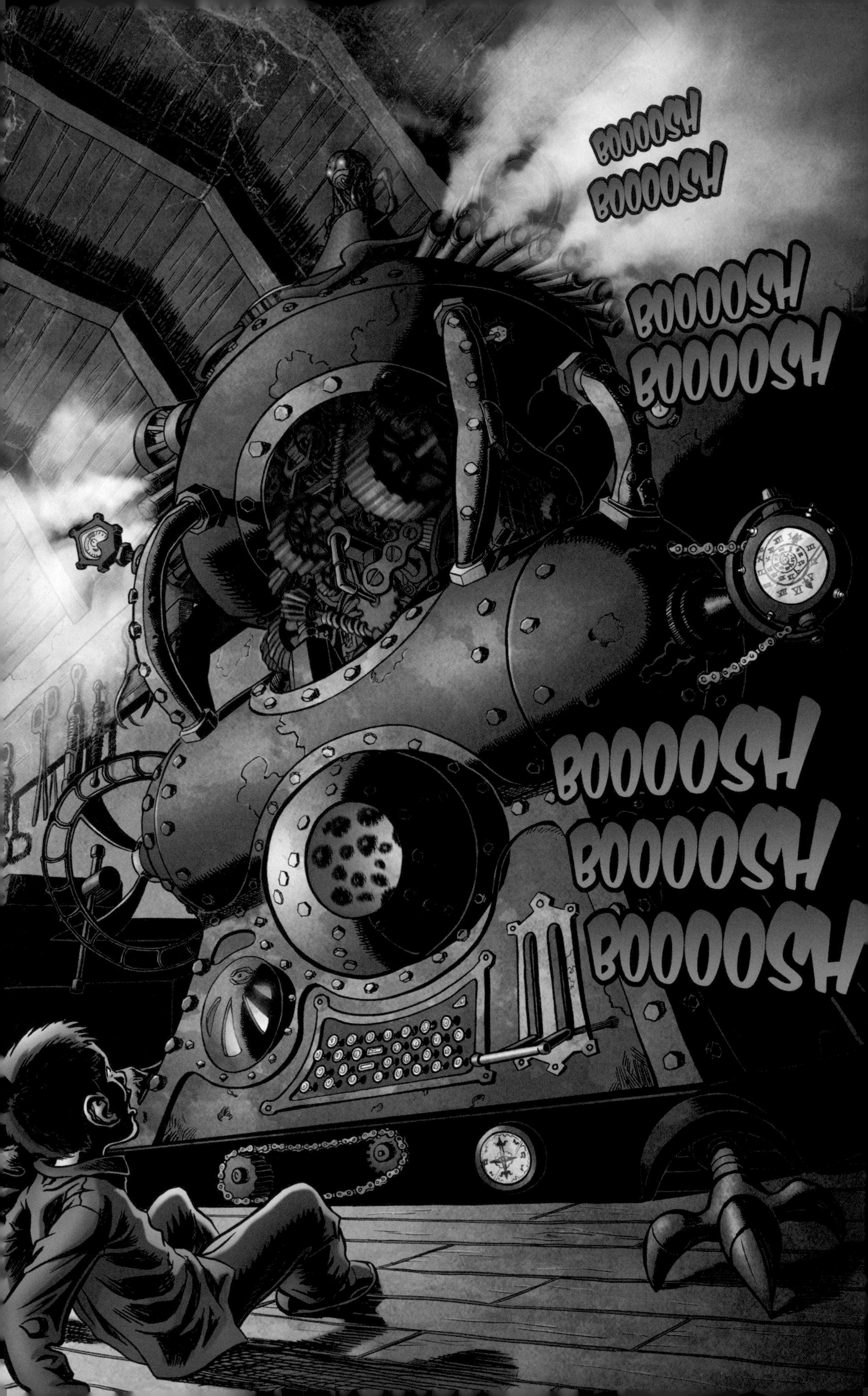
BOOOOSH
BOOOOSH
BOOOOSH
BOOOOSH
BOOOOSH
BOOOOSH
BOOOOSH

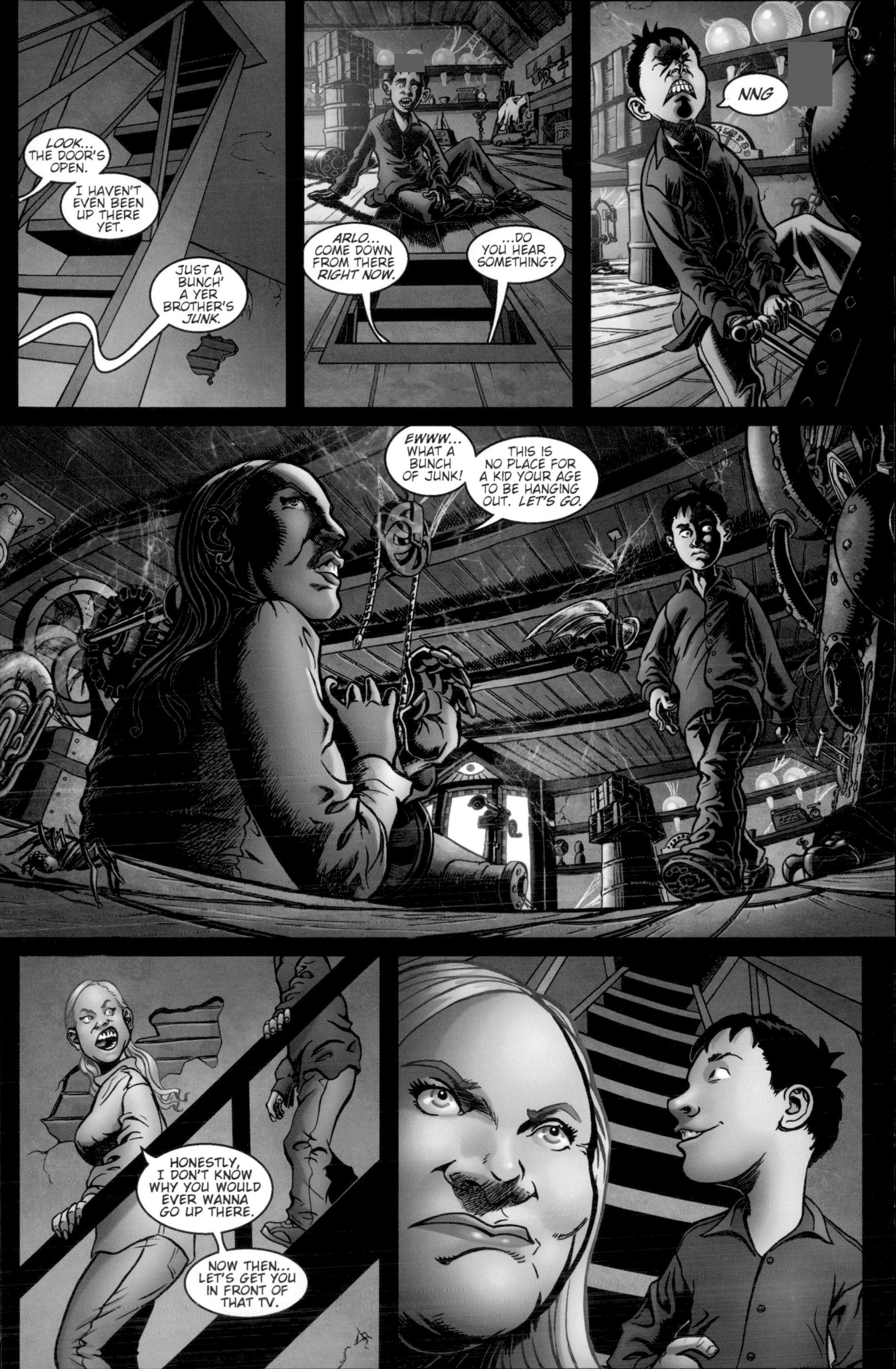
LOOK... THE DOOR'S OPEN.
I HAVEN'T EVEN BEEN UP THERE YET.
JUST A BUNCH' A YER BROTHER'S JUNK.
ARLO... COME DOWN FROM THERE RIGHT NOW.
...DO YOU HEAR SOMETHING?
NNG
EWWW... WHAT A BUNCH OF JUNK!
THIS IS NO PLACE FOR A KID YOUR AGE TO BE HANGING OUT. LET'S GO.
HONESTLY, I DON'T KNOW WHY YOU WOULD EVER WANNA GO UP THERE.
NOW THEN... LET'S GET YOU IN FRONT OF THAT TV.

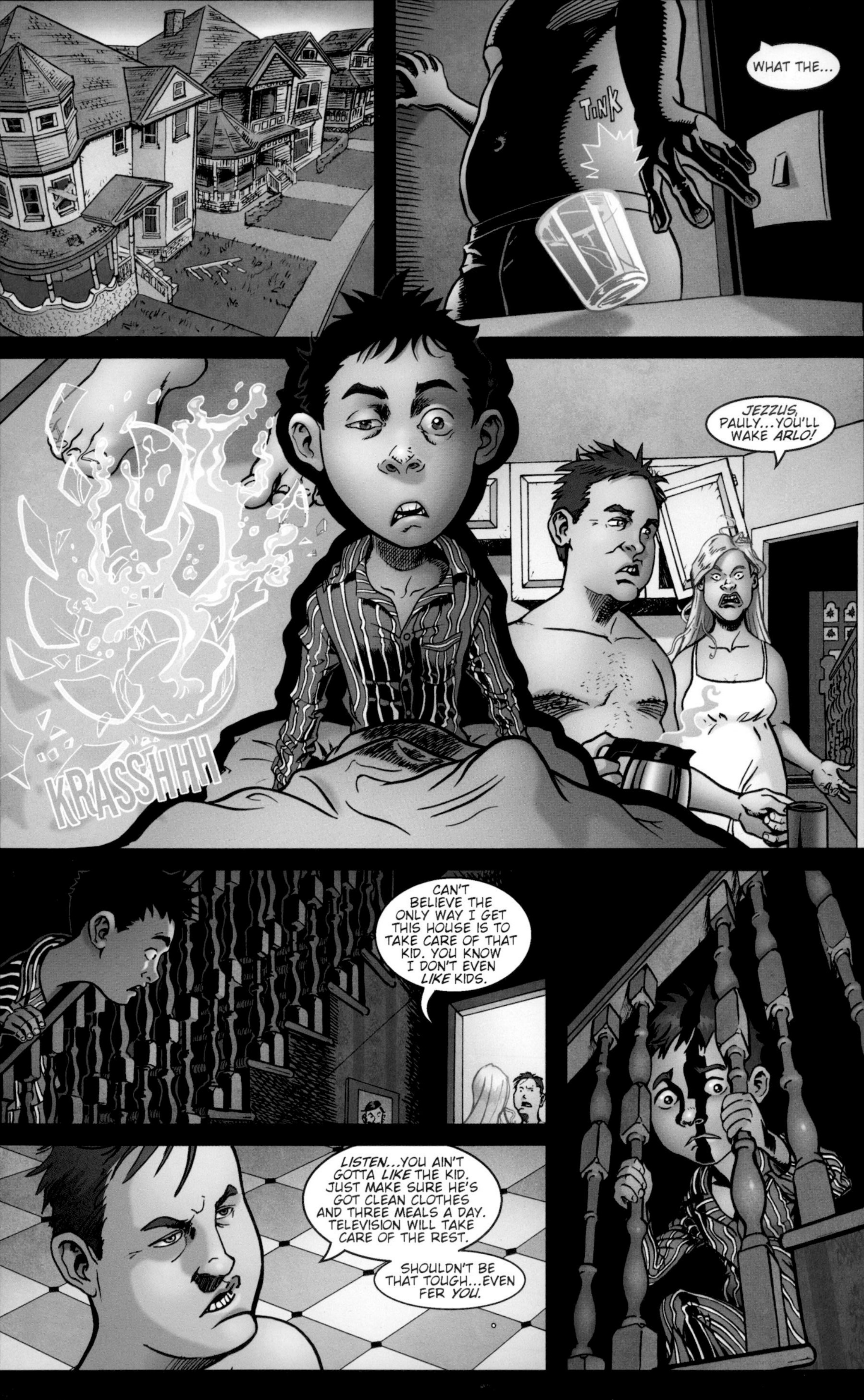
WHAT THE...
TINK
KRASSHHH
JEZZUS, PAULY...YOU'LL WAKE *ARLO*!
CAN'T BELIEVE THE ONLY WAY I GET THIS HOUSE IS TO TAKE CARE OF THAT KID. YOU KNOW I DON'T EVEN *LIKE* KIDS.
LISTEN...YOU AIN'T GOTTA *LIKE* THE KID. JUST MAKE SURE HE'S GOT CLEAN CLOTHES AND THREE MEALS A DAY. TELEVISION WILL TAKE CARE OF THE REST.
SHOULDN'T BE THAT TOUGH...EVEN FER *YOU*.

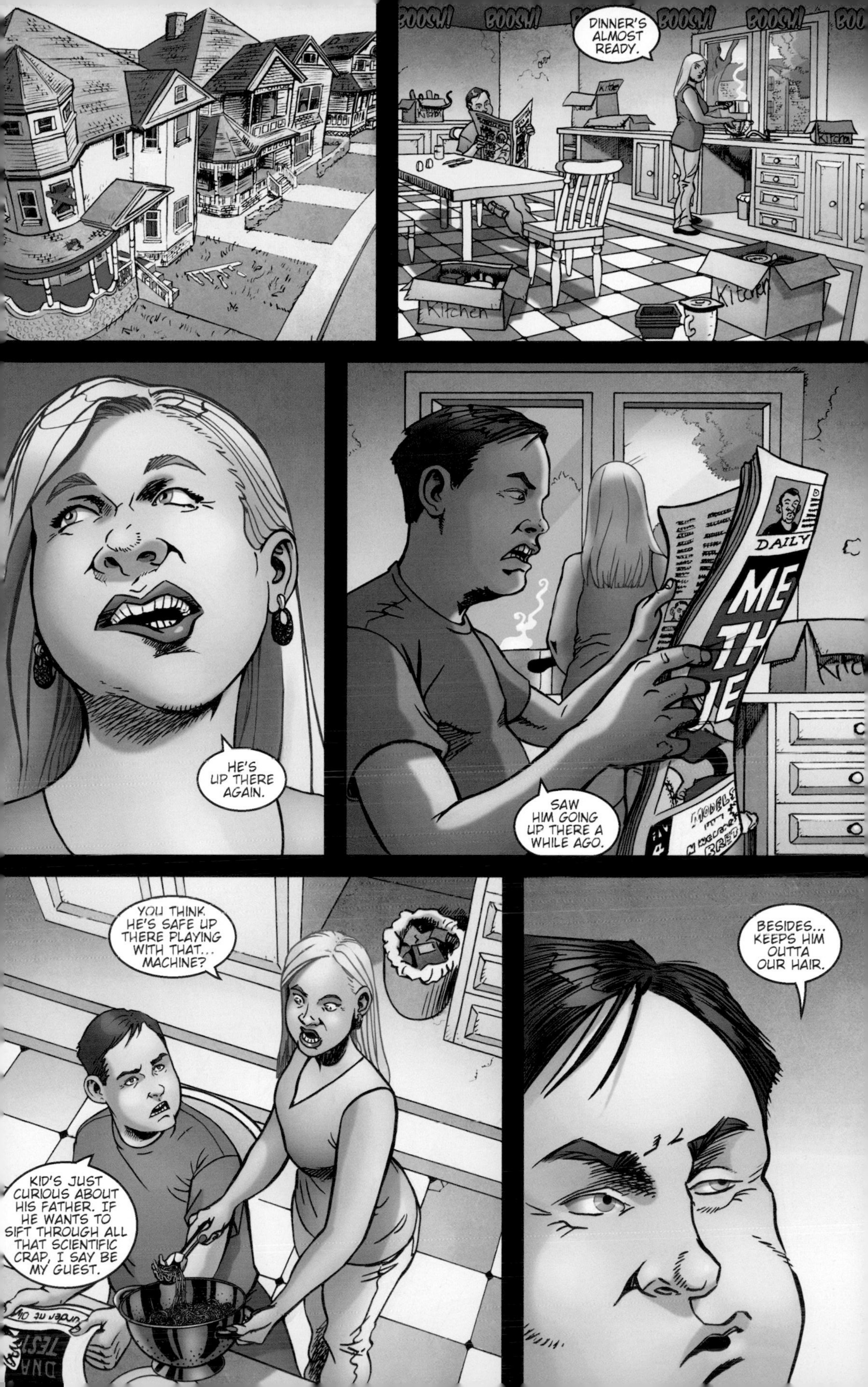
BOOSH! BOOSH! BOOSH! BOOSH!
DINNER'S ALMOST READY.
Kitchen
HE'S UP THERE AGAIN.
DAILY
SAW HIM GOING UP THERE A WHILE AGO.
YOU THINK HE'S SAFE UP THERE PLAYING WITH THAT... MACHINE?
KID'S JUST CURIOUS ABOUT HIS FATHER. IF HE WANTS TO SIFT THROUGH ALL THAT SCIENTIFIC CRAP, I SAY BE MY GUEST.
BESIDES... KEEPS HIM OUTTA OUR HAIR.

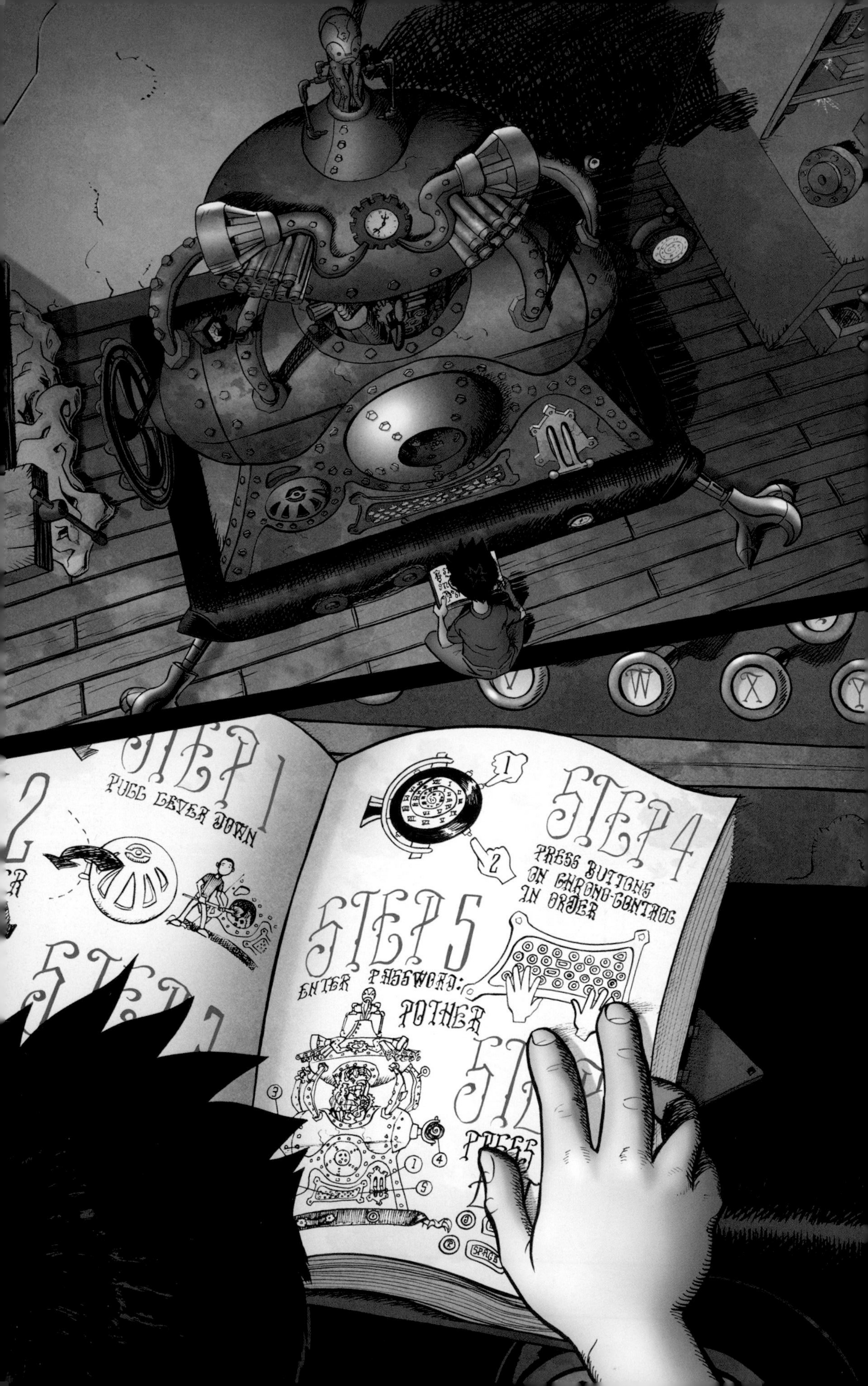
STEP 1
PULL LEVER DOWN
STEP 4
PRESS BUTTONS ON CHRONO-CONTROL IN ORDER
STEP 5
ENTER PASSWORD: POTHER
SPACE

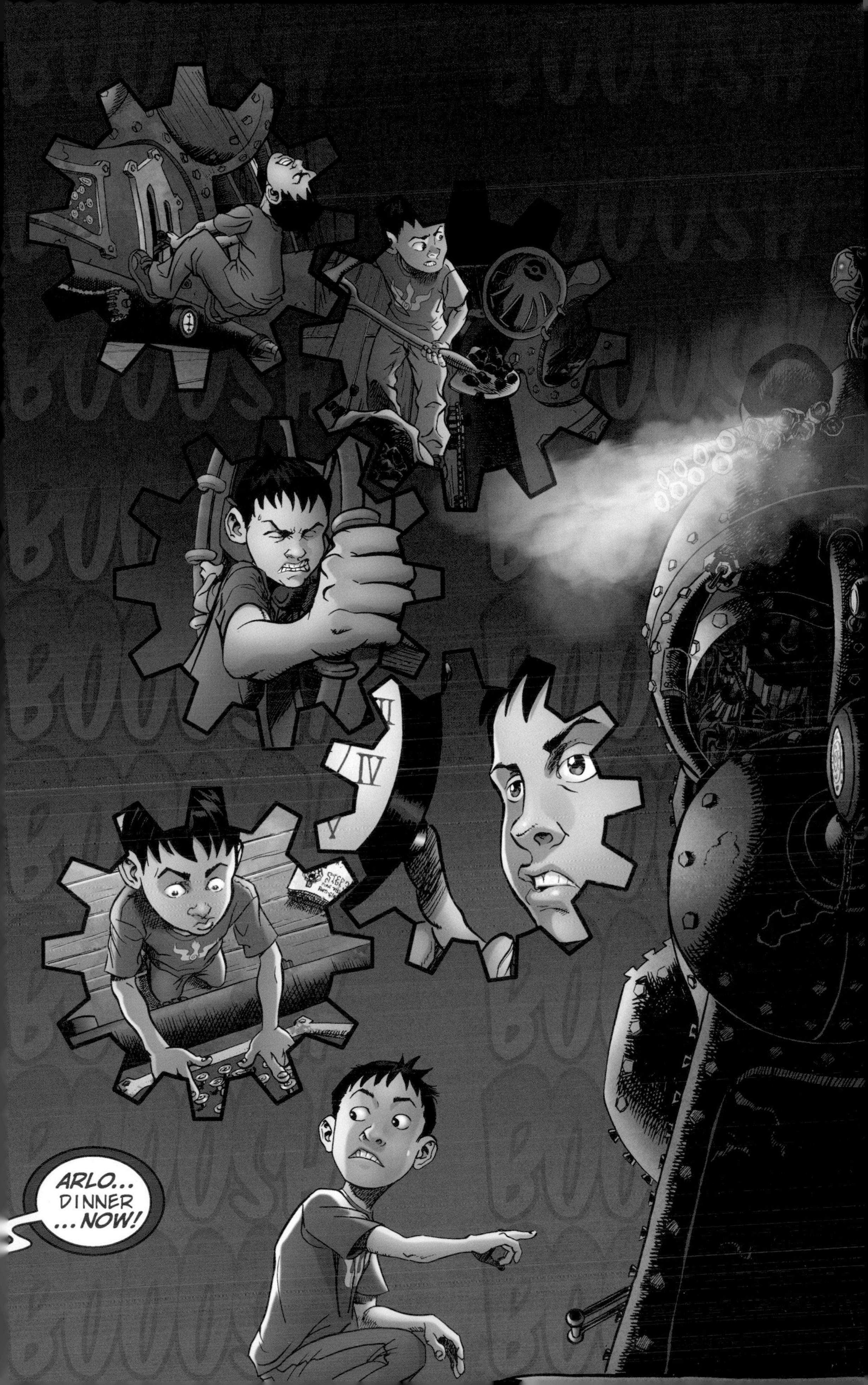
ARLO...
DINNER
...NOW!
BOOOSH

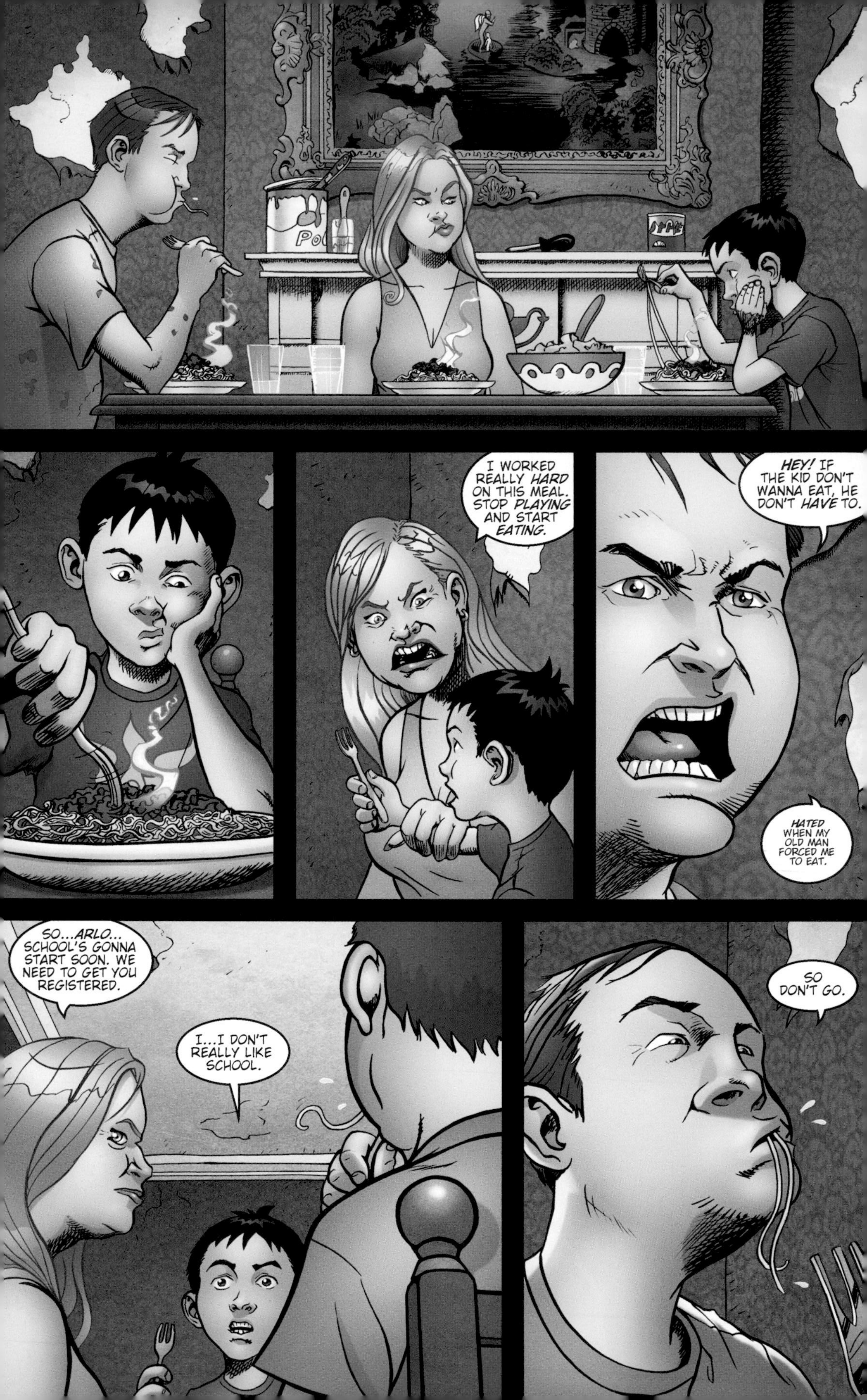
I WORKED REALLY *HARD* ON THIS MEAL. STOP *PLAYING* AND START *EATING*.
HEY! IF THE KID DON'T WANNA EAT, HE DON'T *HAVE* TO.
HATED WHEN MY OLD MAN FORCED ME TO EAT.
SO...*ARLO*... SCHOOL'S GONNA START SOON. WE NEED TO GET YOU REGISTERED.
I...I DON'T REALLY LIKE SCHOOL.
SO DON'T GO.

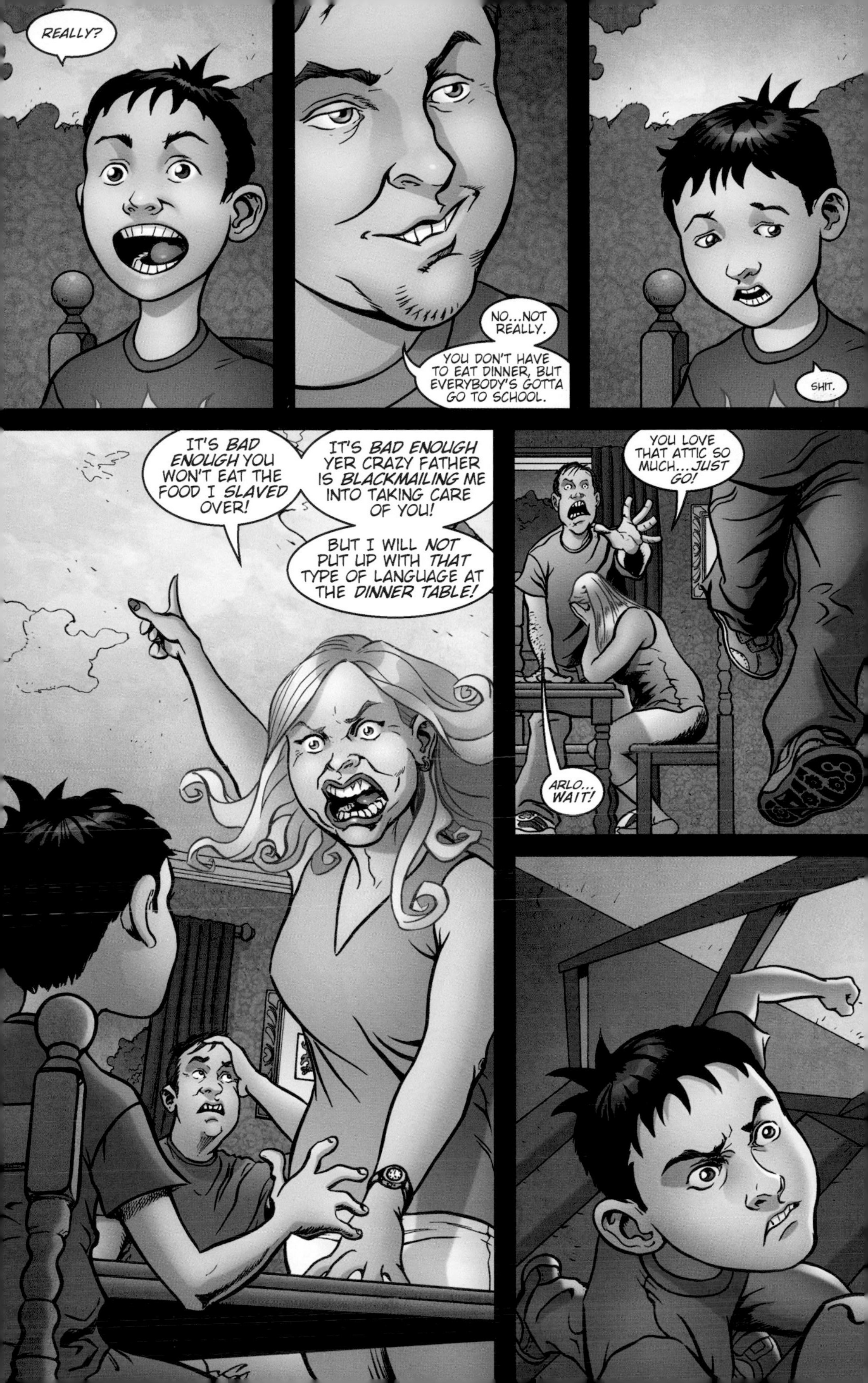
REALLY?
NO...NOT REALLY.
YOU DON'T HAVE TO EAT DINNER, BUT EVERYBODY'S GOTTA GO TO SCHOOL.
SHIT.
IT'S *BAD ENOUGH* YOU WON'T EAT THE FOOD I *SLAVED* OVER!
IT'S *BAD ENOUGH* YER CRAZY FATHER IS *BLACKMAILING* ME INTO TAKING CARE OF YOU!
BUT I WILL *NOT* PUT UP WITH *THAT* TYPE OF LANGUAGE AT THE *DINNER TABLE!*
YOU LOVE THAT ATTIC SO MUCH...*JUST GO!*
ARLO... *WAIT!*

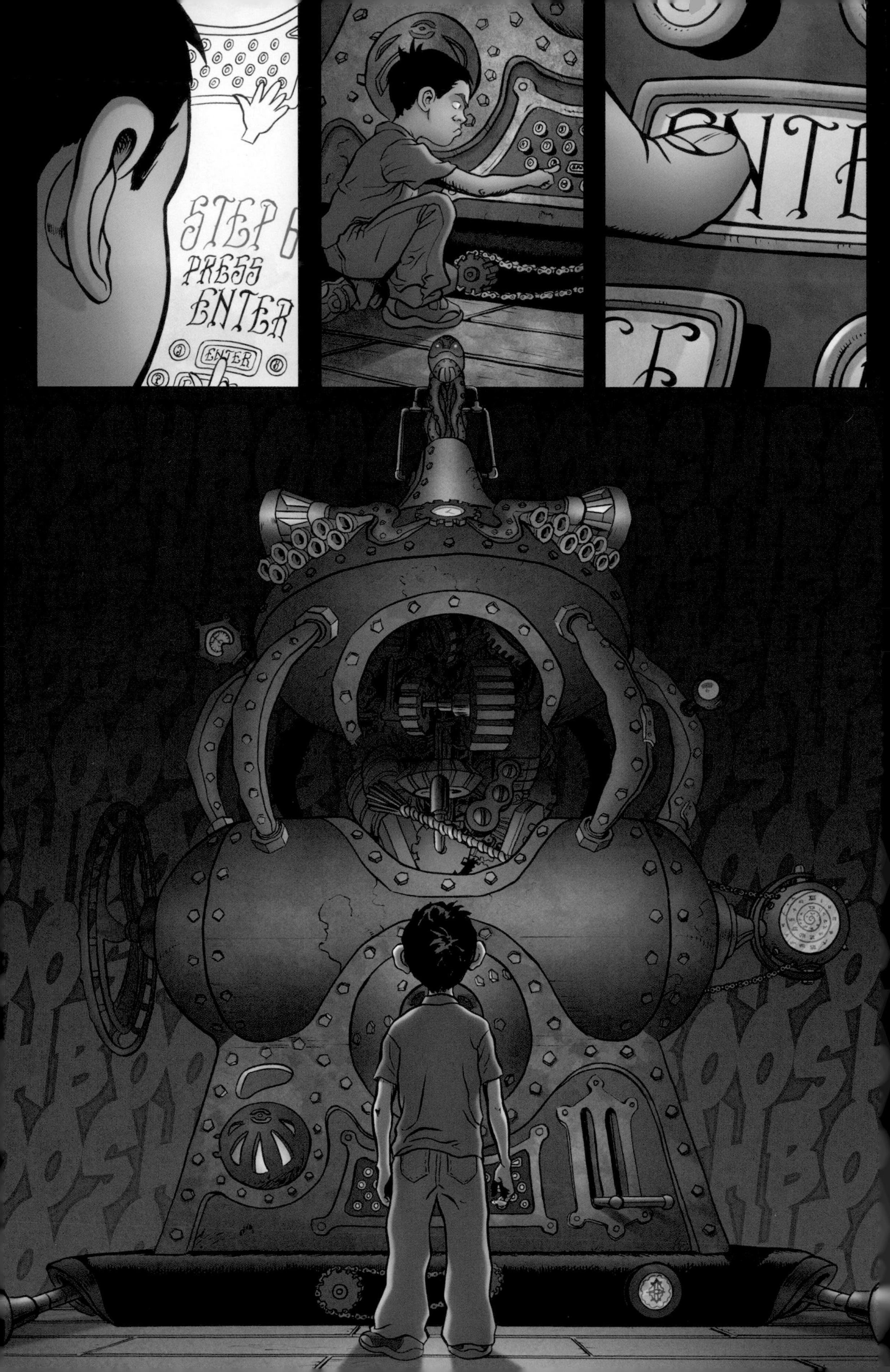
STEP 6
PRESS
ENTER
ENTER

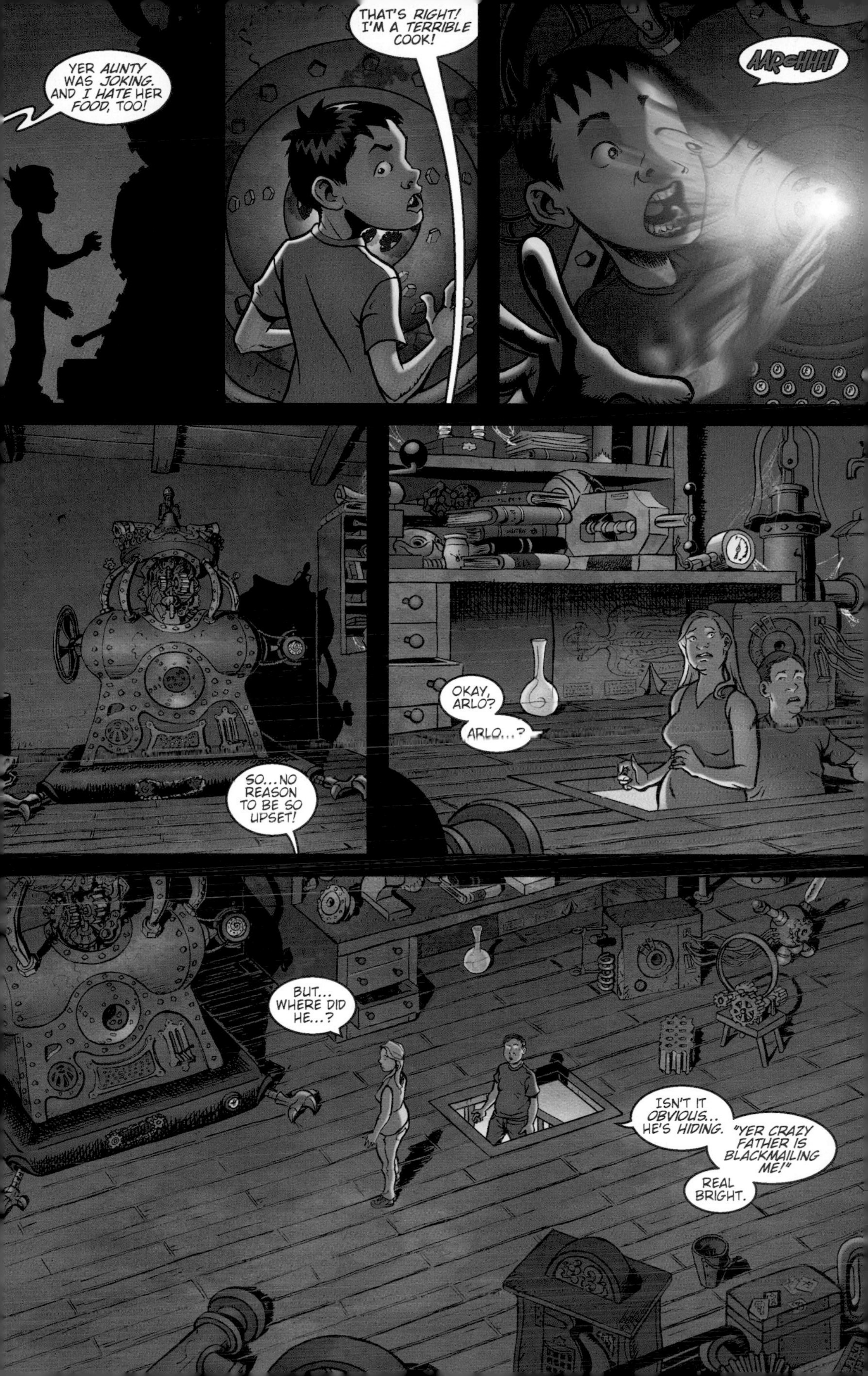
YER AUNTY WAS JOKING. AND I HATE HER FOOD, TOO!
THAT'S RIGHT! I'M A TERRIBLE COOK!
AARGHHH!
SO... NO REASON TO BE SO UPSET!
OKAY, ARLO?
ARLO...?
BUT... WHERE DID HE...?
ISN'T IT OBVIOUS... HE'S HIDING.
"YER CRAZY FATHER IS BLACKMAILING ME!"
REAL BRIGHT.

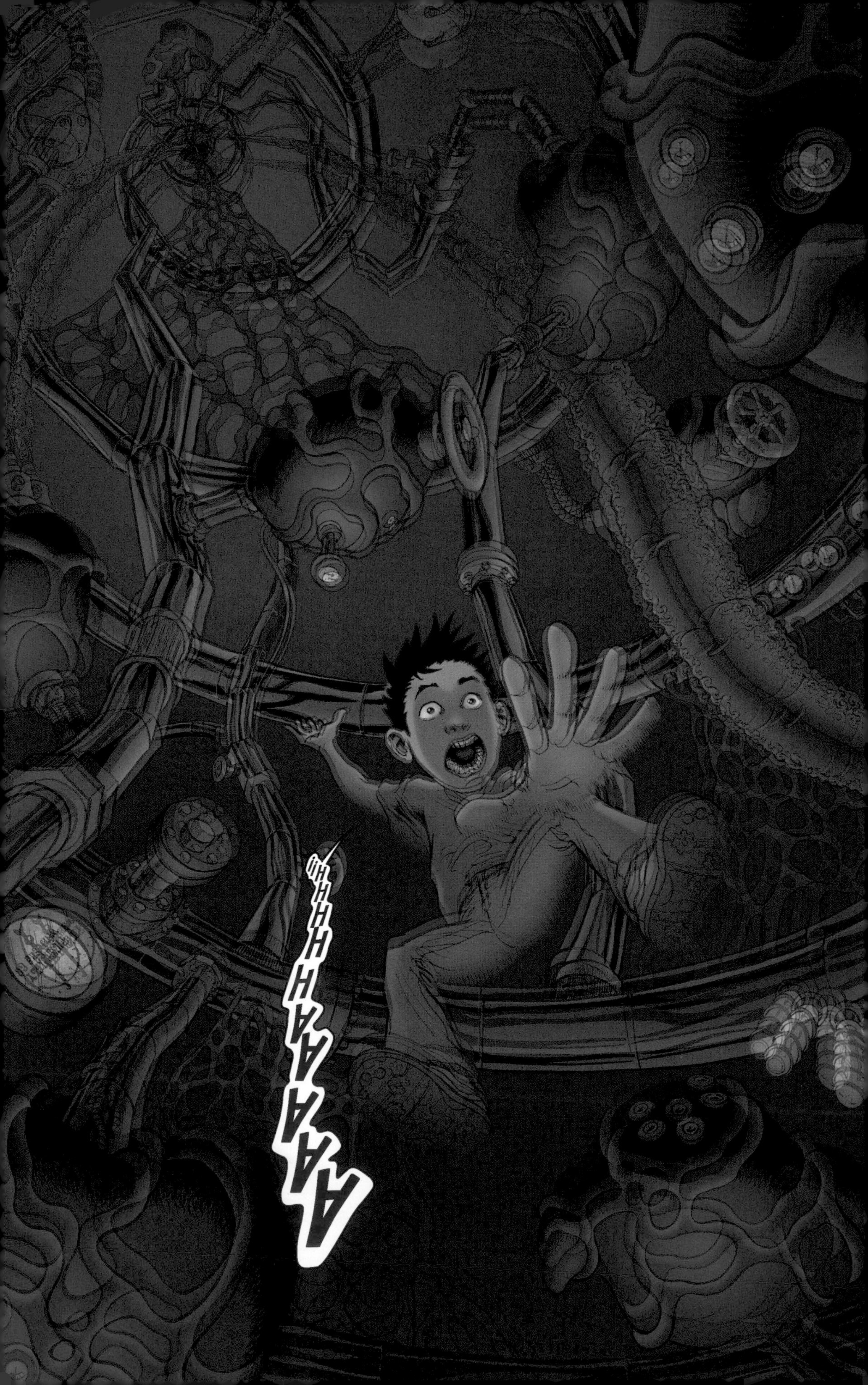
AAAAHHHHHHH!!

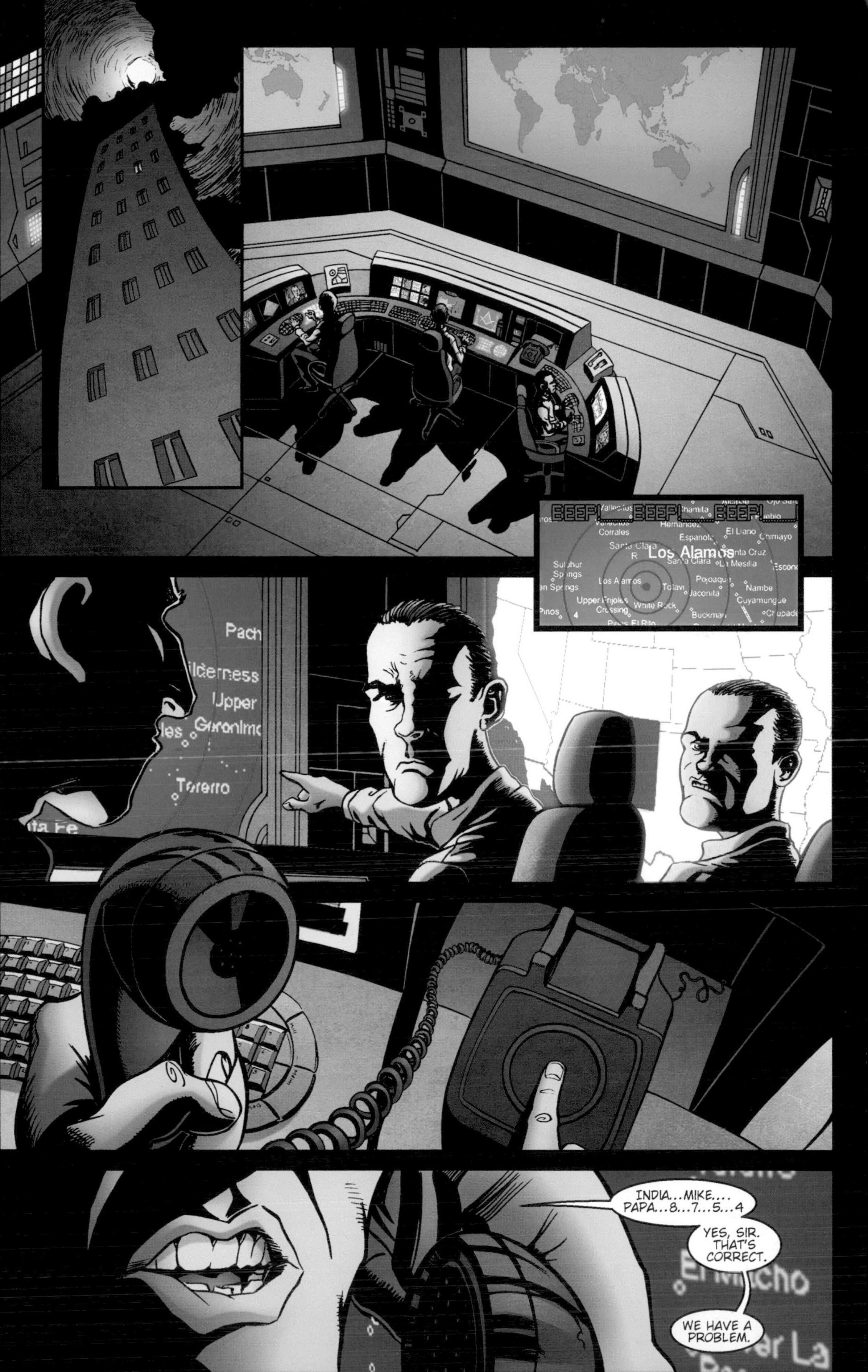
BEEP!... BEEP!... BEEP!
Los Alamos
INDIA...MIKE.... PAPA...8...7...5...4
YES, SIR. THAT'S CORRECT.
WE HAVE A PROBLEM.

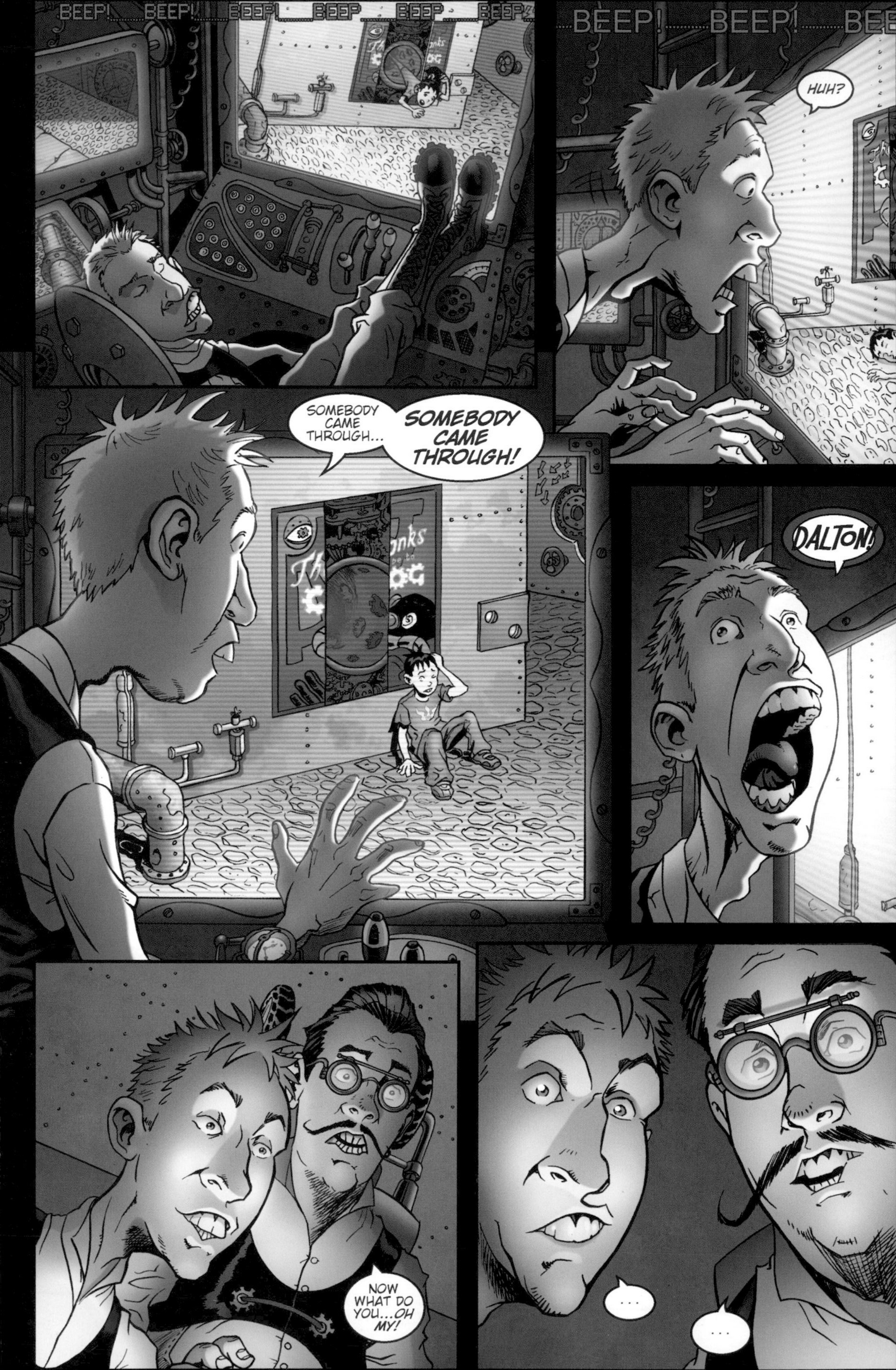
BEEP! BEEP! BEEP! BEEP BEEP BEEP
BEEP! BEEP! BEE
HUH?
SOMEBODY CAME THROUGH...
SOMEBODY CAME THROUGH!
DALTON!
NOW WHAT DO YOU...OH MY!
...
...

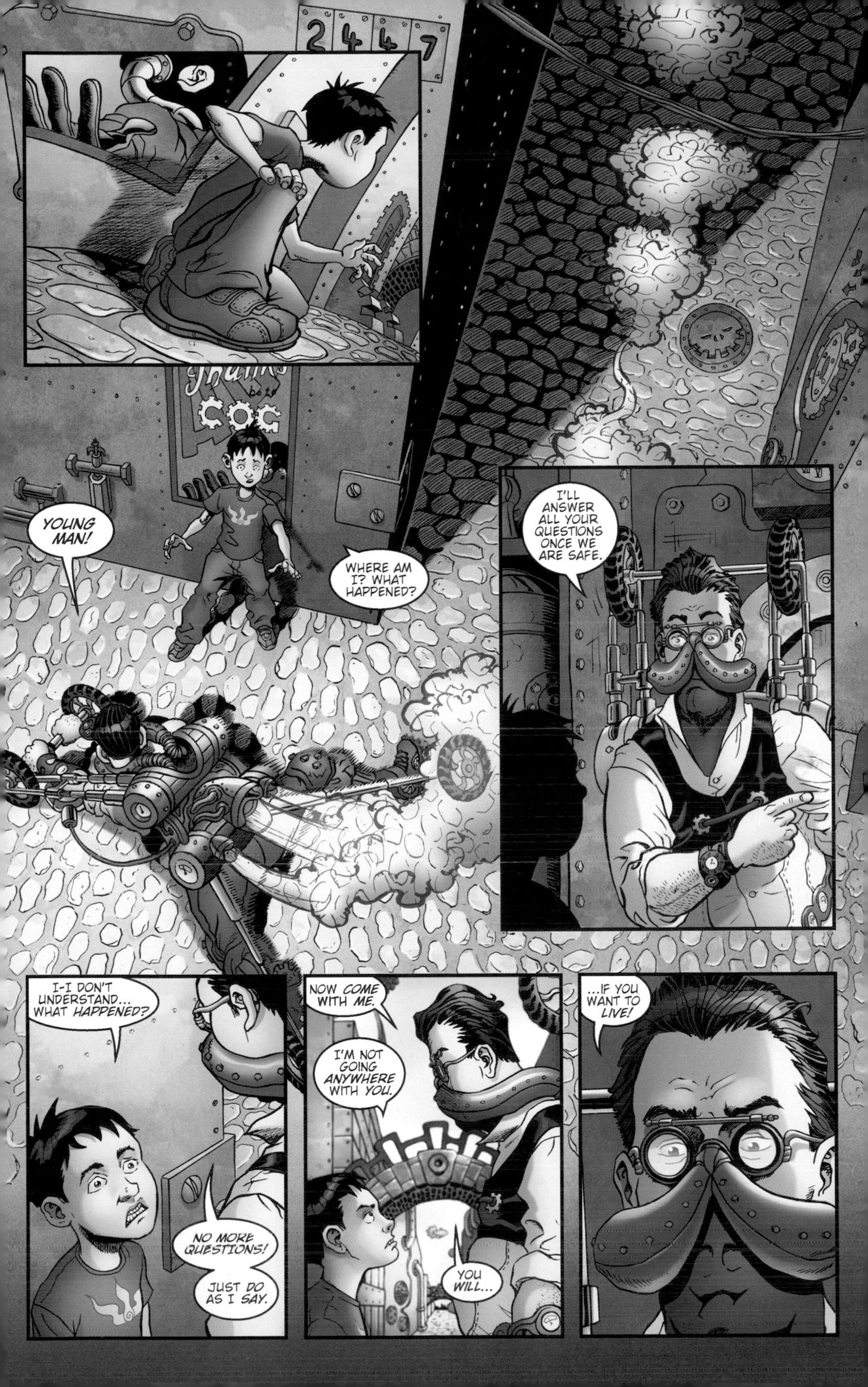
2447
Thanks to be to COG
YOUNG MAN!
WHERE AM I? WHAT HAPPENED?
I'LL ANSWER ALL YOUR QUESTIONS ONCE WE ARE SAFE.
I-I DON'T UNDERSTAND... WHAT *HAPPENED*?
NO MORE QUESTIONS!
JUST *DO* AS I *SAY*.
NOW *COME* WITH *ME*.
I'M NOT GOING *ANYWHERE* WITH *YOU*.
YOU *WILL*...
...IF YOU WANT TO *LIVE!*

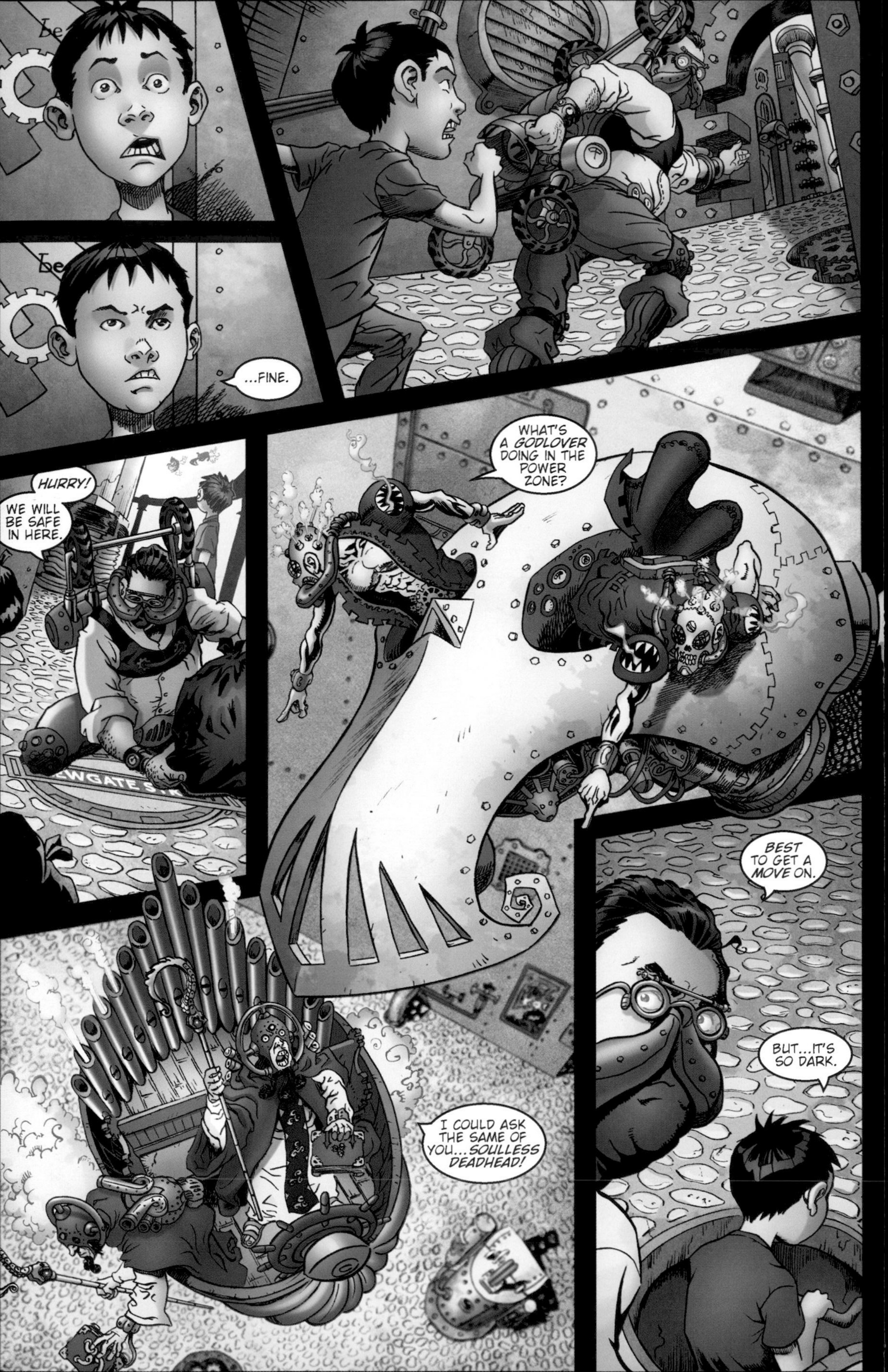
...FINE.
HURRY!
WE WILL BE SAFE IN HERE.
WHAT'S A *GODLOVER* DOING IN THE POWER ZONE?
I COULD ASK THE SAME OF YOU... *SOULLESS DEADHEAD!*
BEST TO GET A *MOVE* ON.
BUT...IT'S SO DARK.

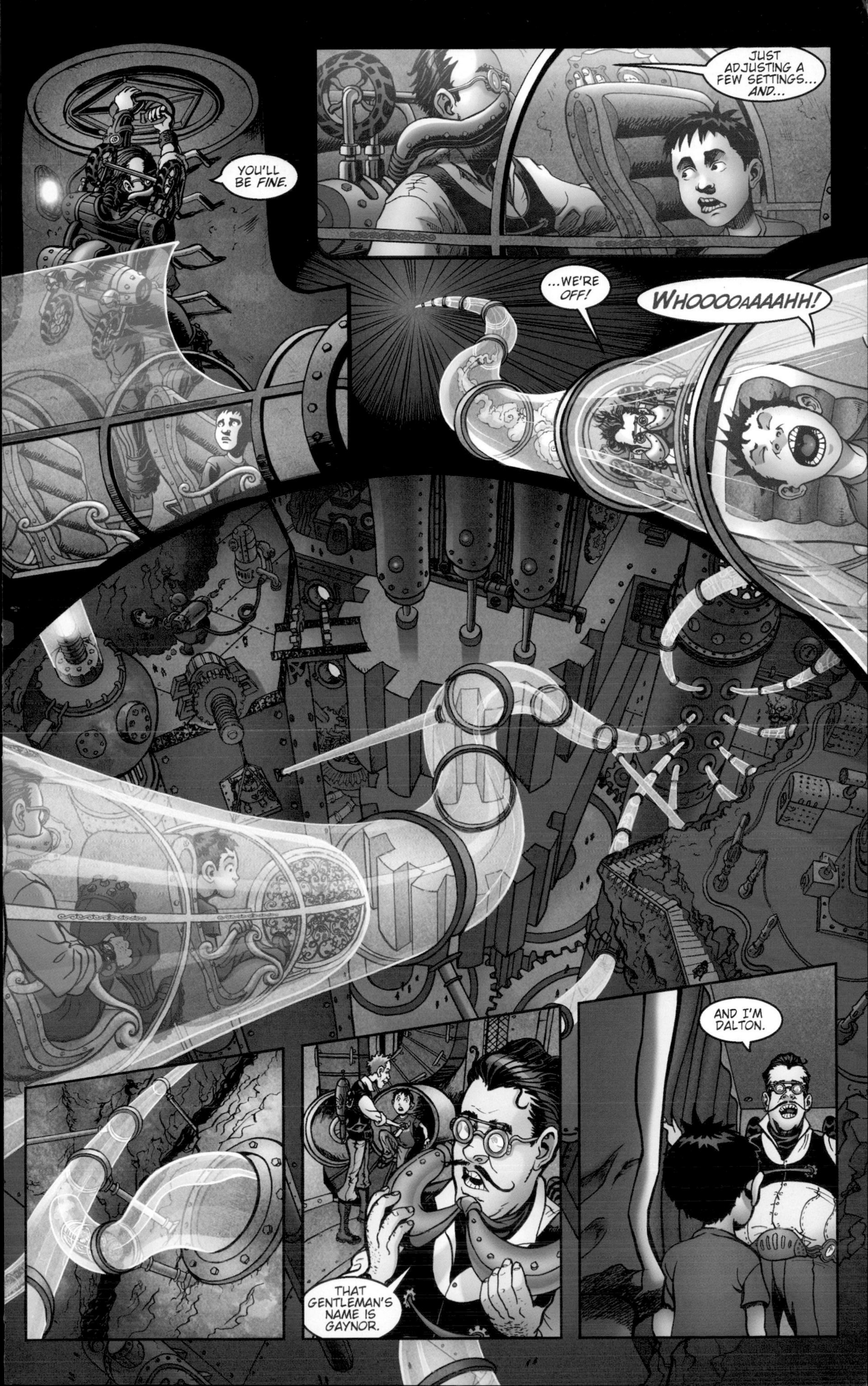
YOU'LL BE *FINE*.
JUST ADJUSTING A FEW SETTINGS... AND...
...WE'RE OFF!
WHOOOOAAAAHH!
THAT GENTLEMAN'S NAME IS GAYNOR.
AND I'M DALTON.

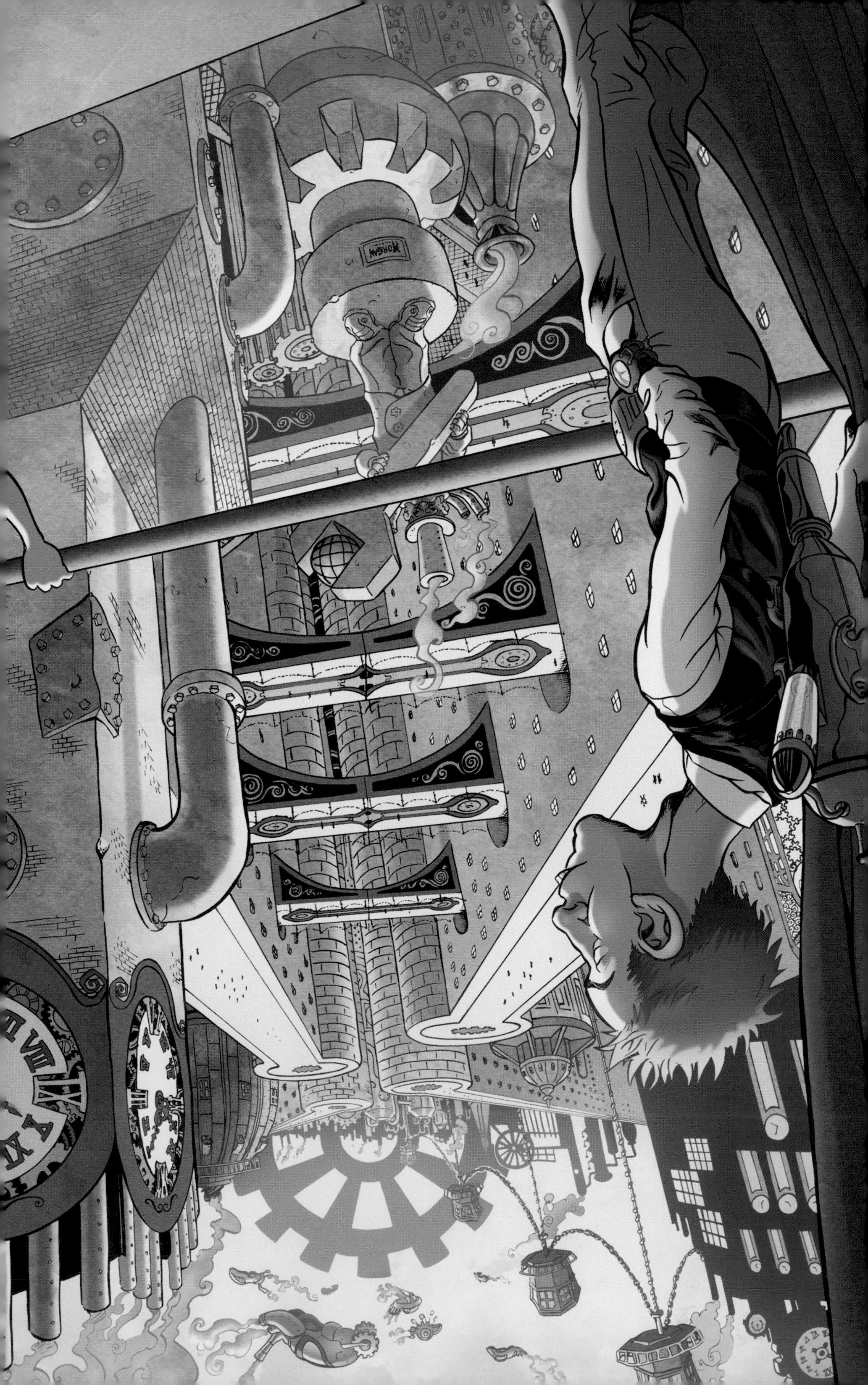

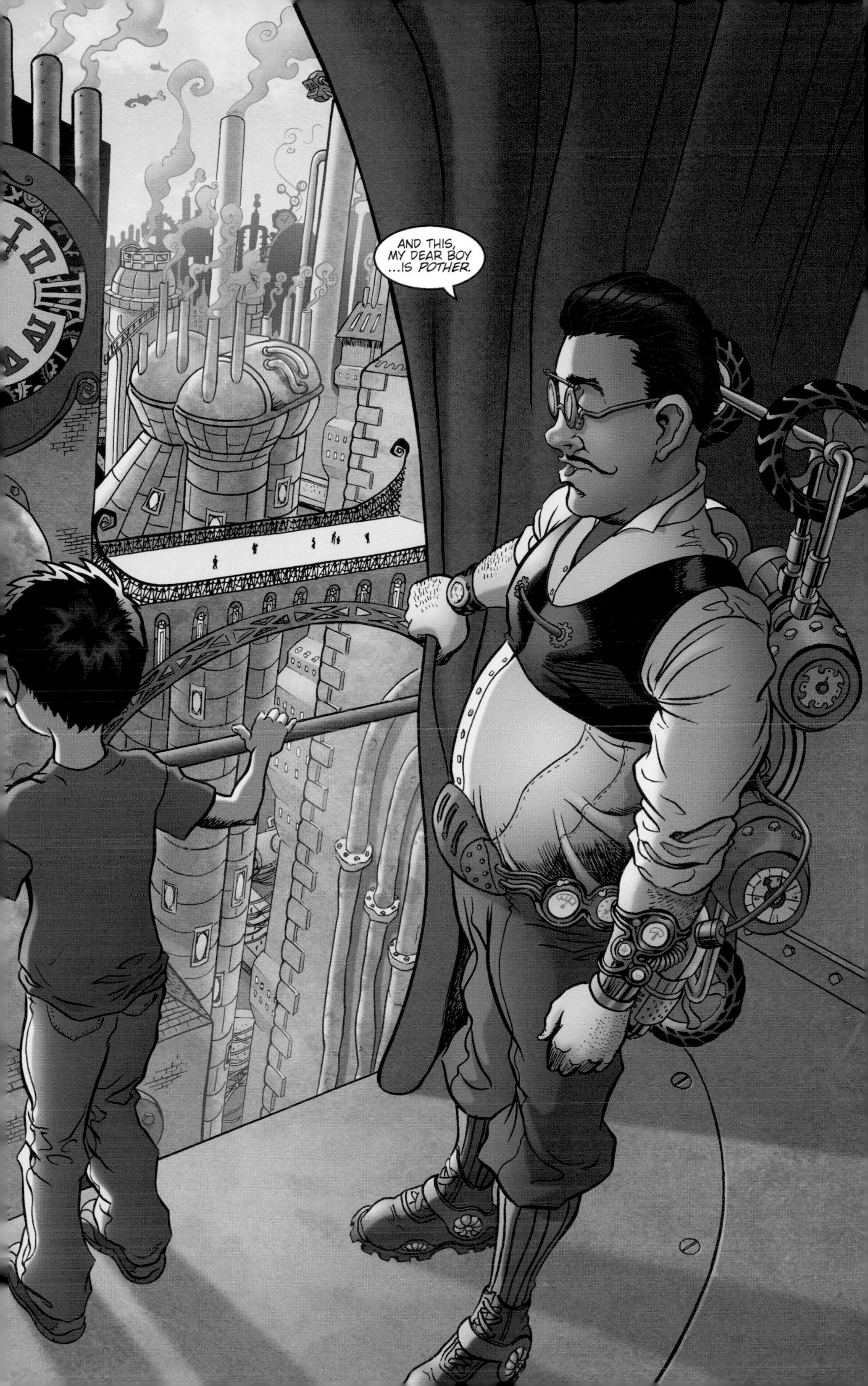
AND THIS, MY DEAR BOY ...IS *POTHER*.

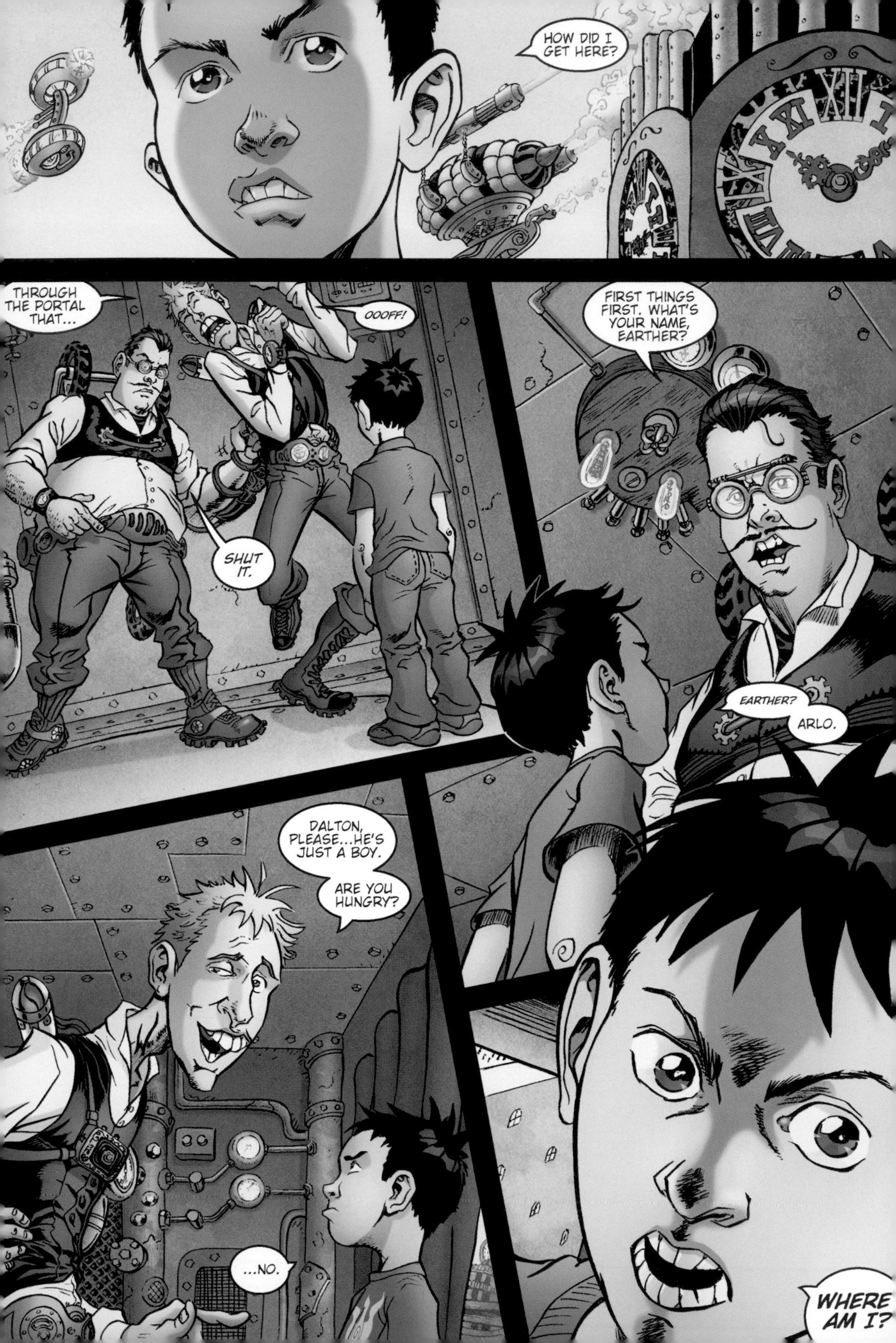
HOW DID I GET HERE?
THROUGH THE PORTAL THAT...
OOOFF!
SHUT IT.
FIRST THINGS FIRST. WHAT'S YOUR NAME, EARTHER?
EARTHER?
ARLO.
DALTON, PLEASE...HE'S JUST A BOY.
ARE YOU HUNGRY?
...NO.
WHERE AM I?

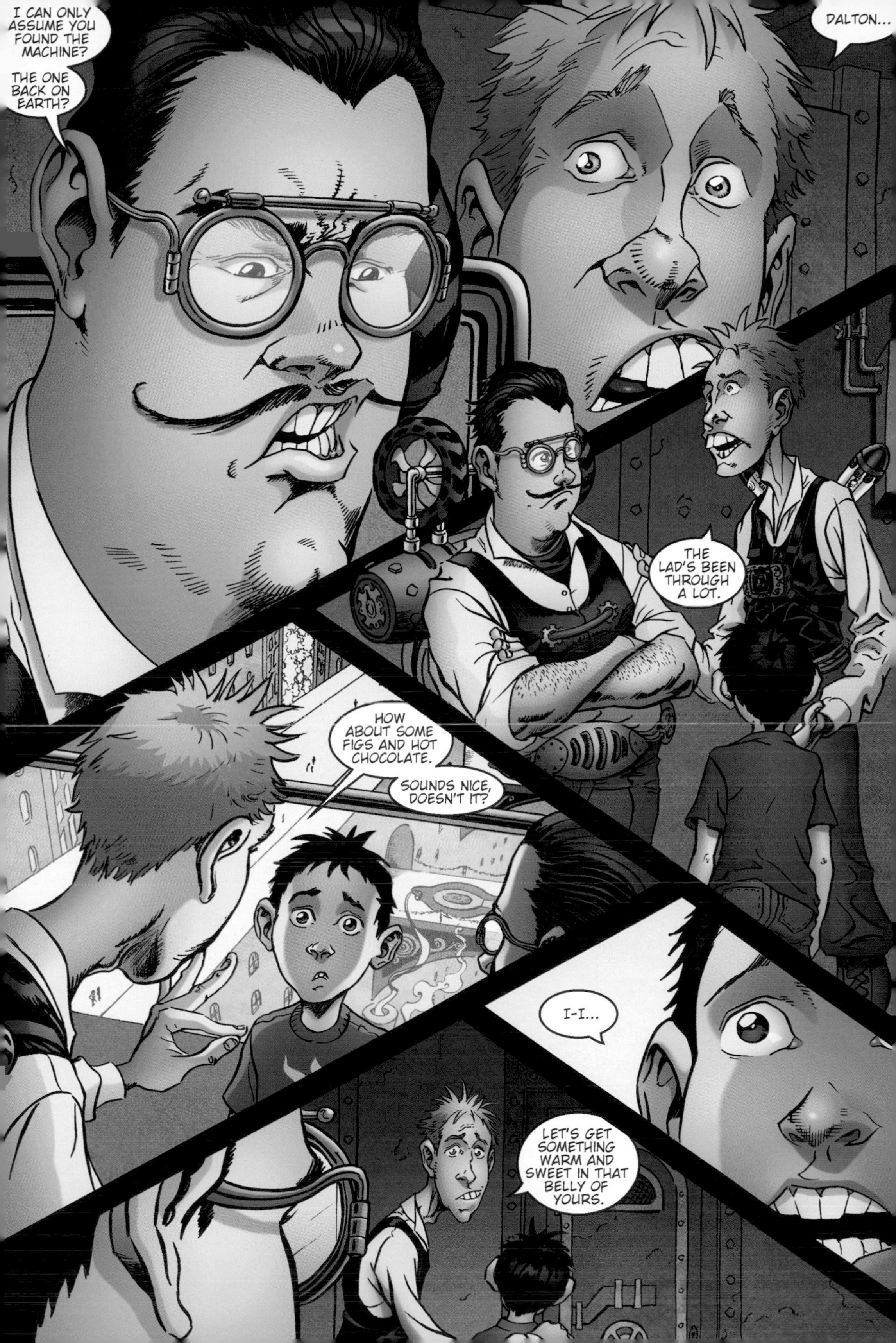
I CAN ONLY ASSUME YOU FOUND THE MACHINE?
THE ONE BACK ON EARTH?
DALTON...
THE LAD'S BEEN THROUGH A LOT.
HOW ABOUT SOME FIGS AND HOT CHOCOLATE.
SOUNDS NICE, DOESN'T IT?
I-I...
LET'S GET SOMETHING WARM AND SWEET IN THAT BELLY OF YOURS.

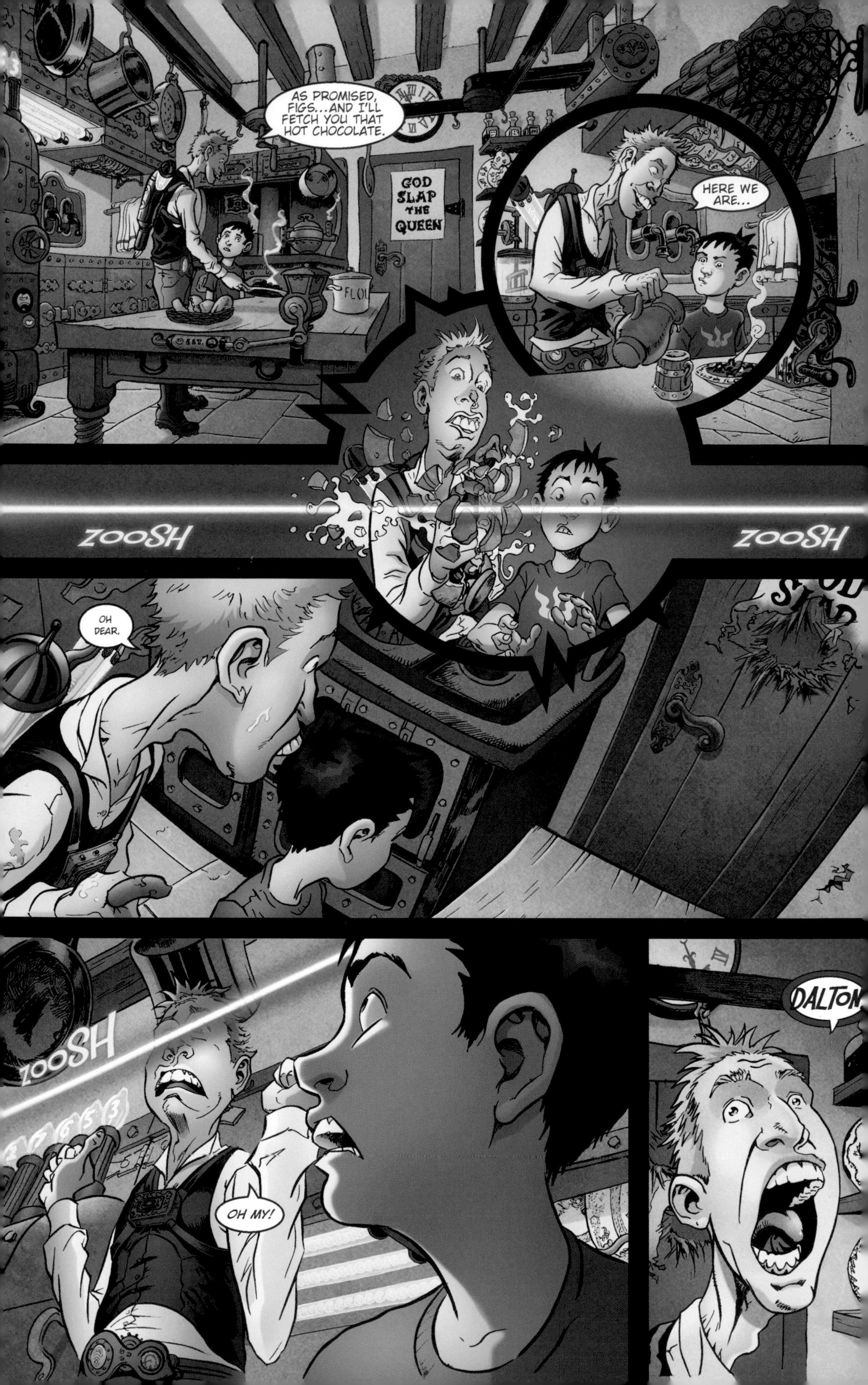
AS PROMISED, FIGS...AND I'LL FETCH YOU THAT HOT CHOCOLATE.
GOD SLAP THE QUEEN
HERE WE ARE...
ZOOSH
ZOOSH
OH DEAR.
ZOOSH
OH MY!
DALTON

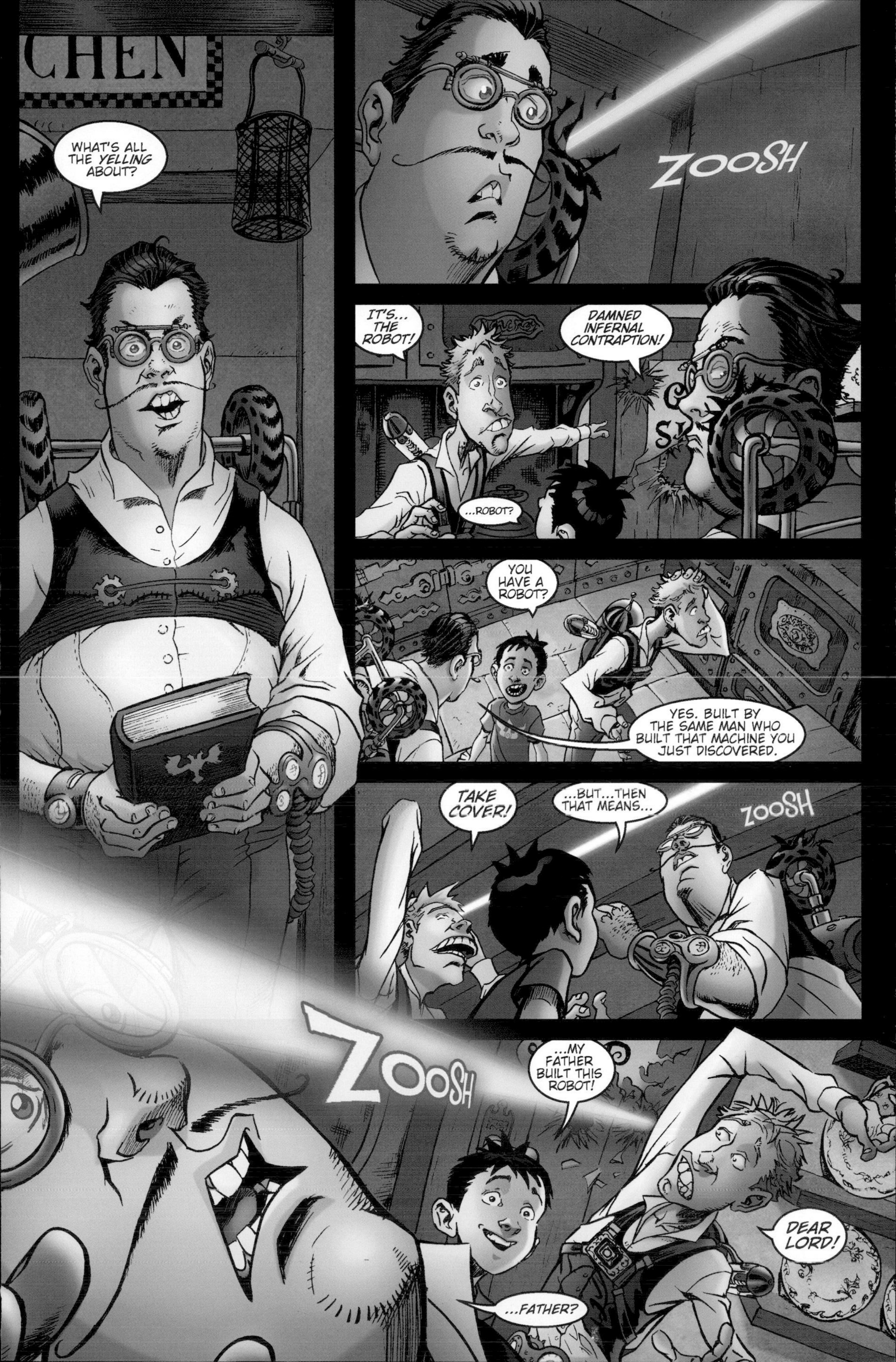
CHEN
WHAT'S ALL THE *YELLING* ABOUT?
ZOOSH
IT'S... THE ROBOT!
DAMNED INFERNAL CONTRAPTION!
...ROBOT?
YOU HAVE A ROBOT?
YES. BUILT BY THE SAME MAN WHO BUILT THAT MACHINE YOU JUST DISCOVERED.
TAKE COVER!
...BUT...THEN THAT MEANS...
ZOOSH
ZOOSH
...MY FATHER BUILT THIS ROBOT!
DEAR LORD!
...FATHER?

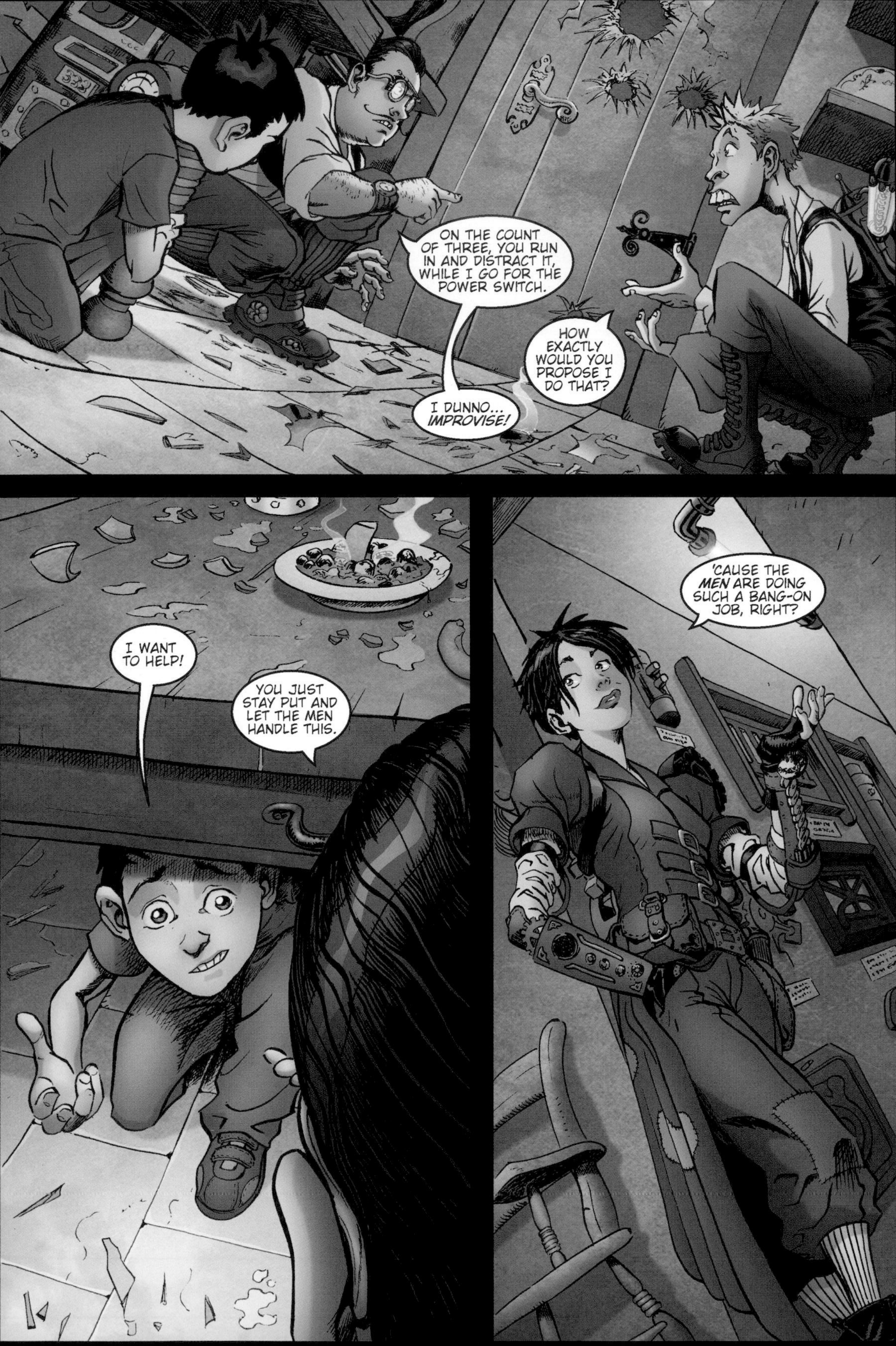
ON THE COUNT OF THREE, YOU RUN IN AND DISTRACT IT, WHILE I GO FOR THE POWER SWITCH.
HOW EXACTLY WOULD YOU PROPOSE I DO THAT?
I DUNNO... *IMPROVISE!*
I WANT TO HELP!
YOU JUST STAY PUT AND LET THE MEN HANDLE THIS.
'CAUSE THE *MEN* ARE DOING SUCH A BANG-ON JOB, RIGHT?

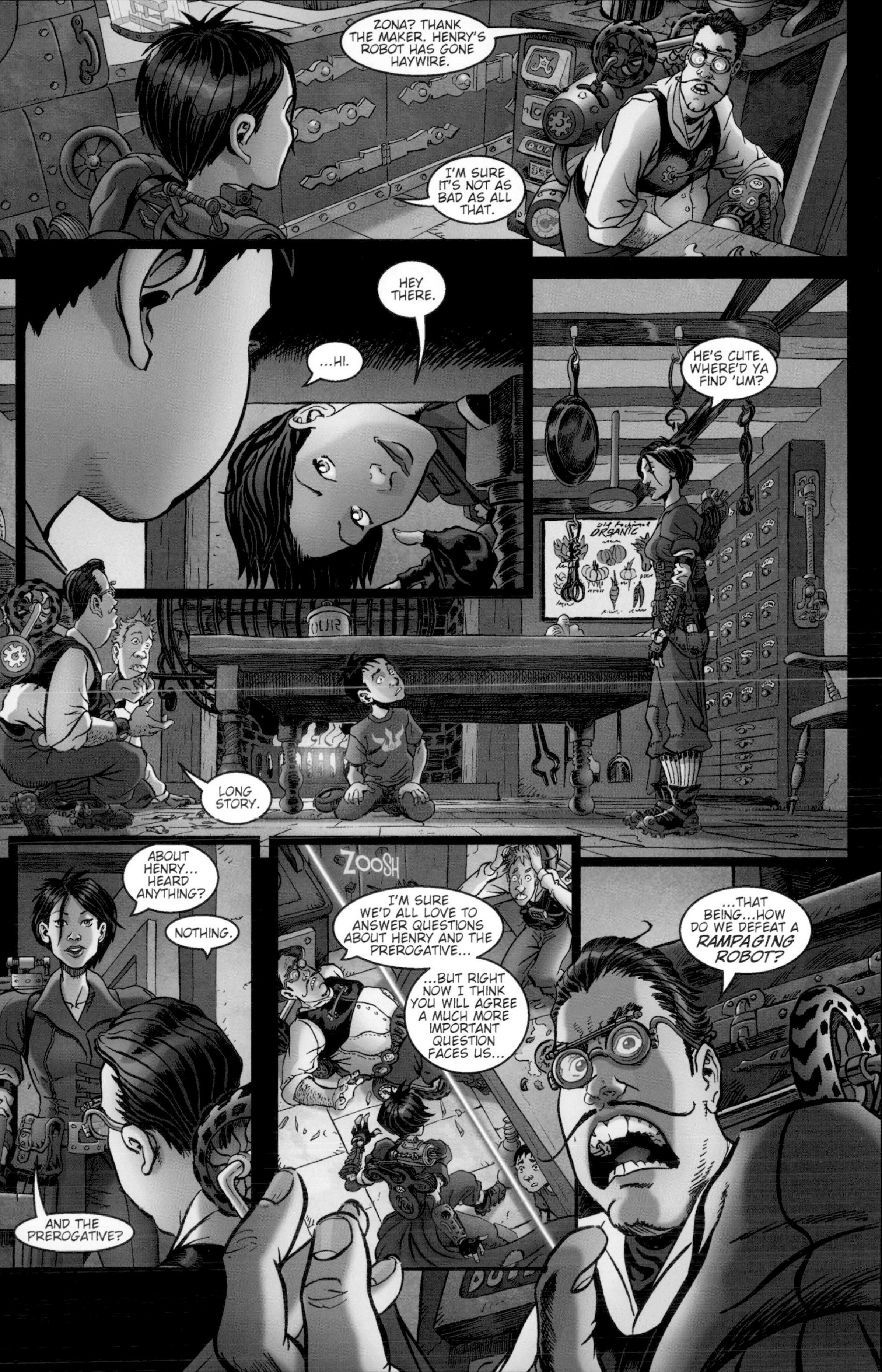
ZONA? THANK THE MAKER. HENRY'S ROBOT HAS GONE HAYWIRE.
I'M SURE IT'S NOT AS BAD AS ALL THAT.
HEY THERE.
...HI.
HE'S CUTE. WHERE'D YA FIND 'UM?
LONG STORY.
ABOUT HENRY... HEARD ANYTHING?
NOTHING.
AND THE PREROGATIVE?
ZOOSH
I'M SURE WE'D ALL LOVE TO ANSWER QUESTIONS ABOUT HENRY AND THE PREROGATIVE...
...BUT RIGHT NOW I THINK YOU WILL AGREE A MUCH MORE IMPORTANT QUESTION FACES US...
...THAT BEING...HOW DO WE DEFEAT A *RAMPAGING ROBOT?*

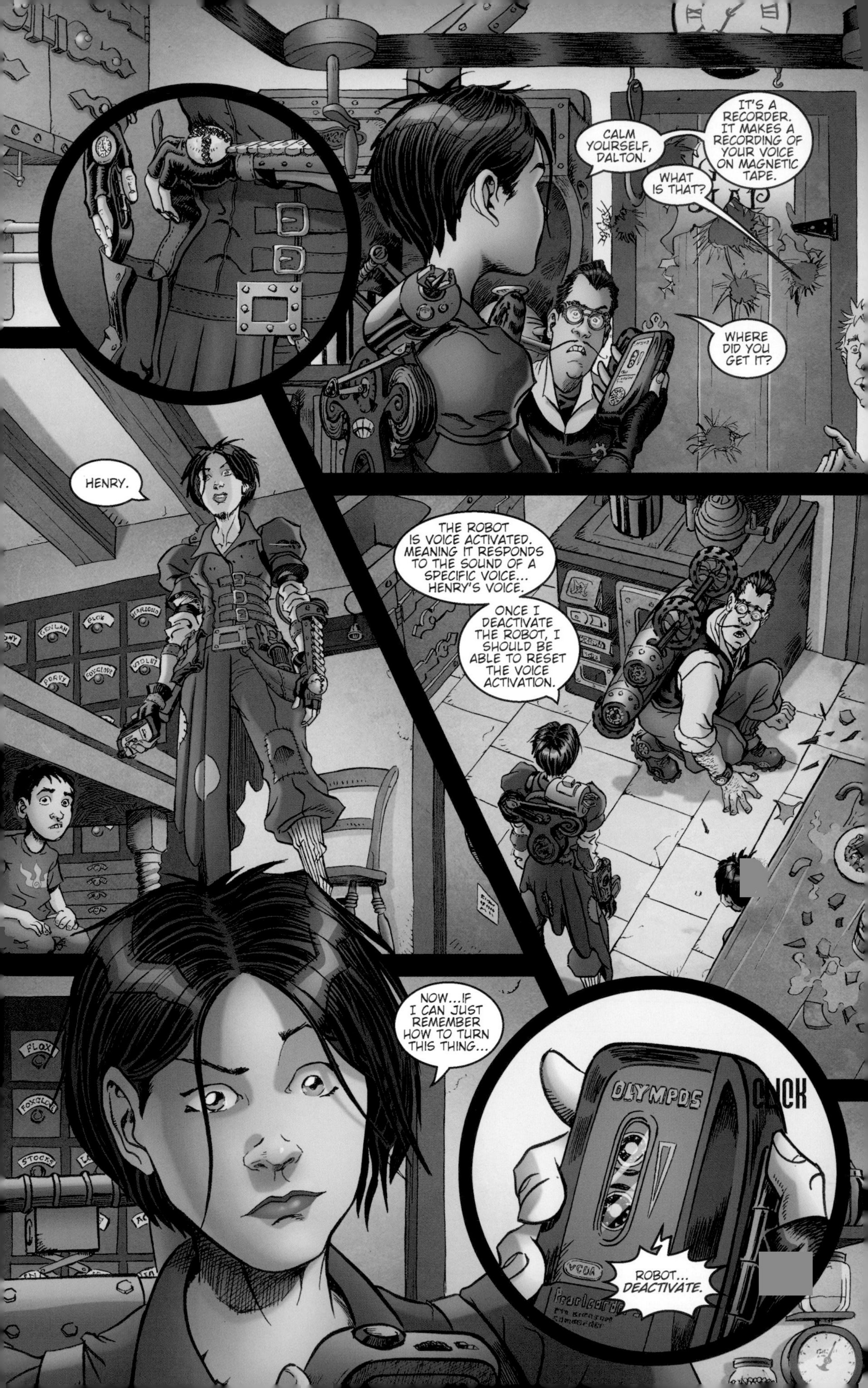
CALM YOURSELF, DALTON.
WHAT IS THAT?
IT'S A RECORDER. IT MAKES A RECORDING OF YOUR VOICE ON MAGNETIC TAPE.
WHERE DID YOU GET IT?
HENRY.
THE ROBOT IS VOICE ACTIVATED. MEANING IT RESPONDS TO THE SOUND OF A SPECIFIC VOICE... HENRY'S VOICE.
ONCE I DEACTIVATE THE ROBOT, I SHOULD BE ABLE TO RESET THE VOICE ACTIVATION.
NOW...IF I CAN JUST REMEMBER HOW TO TURN THIS THING...
OLYMPOS
ROBOT... DEACTIVATE.

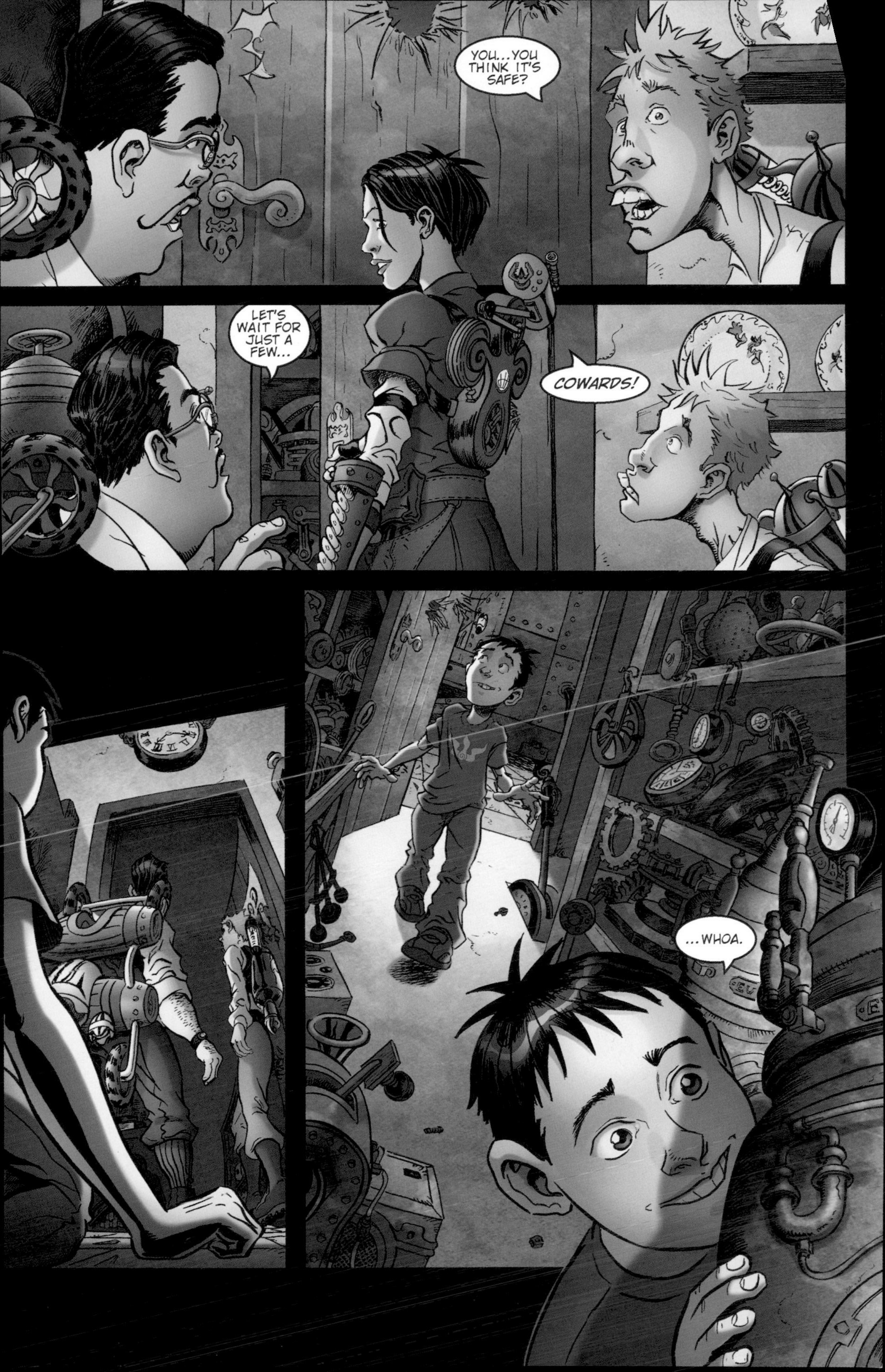
YOU... YOU THINK IT'S SAFE?
LET'S WAIT FOR JUST A FEW...
COWARDS!
...WHOA.

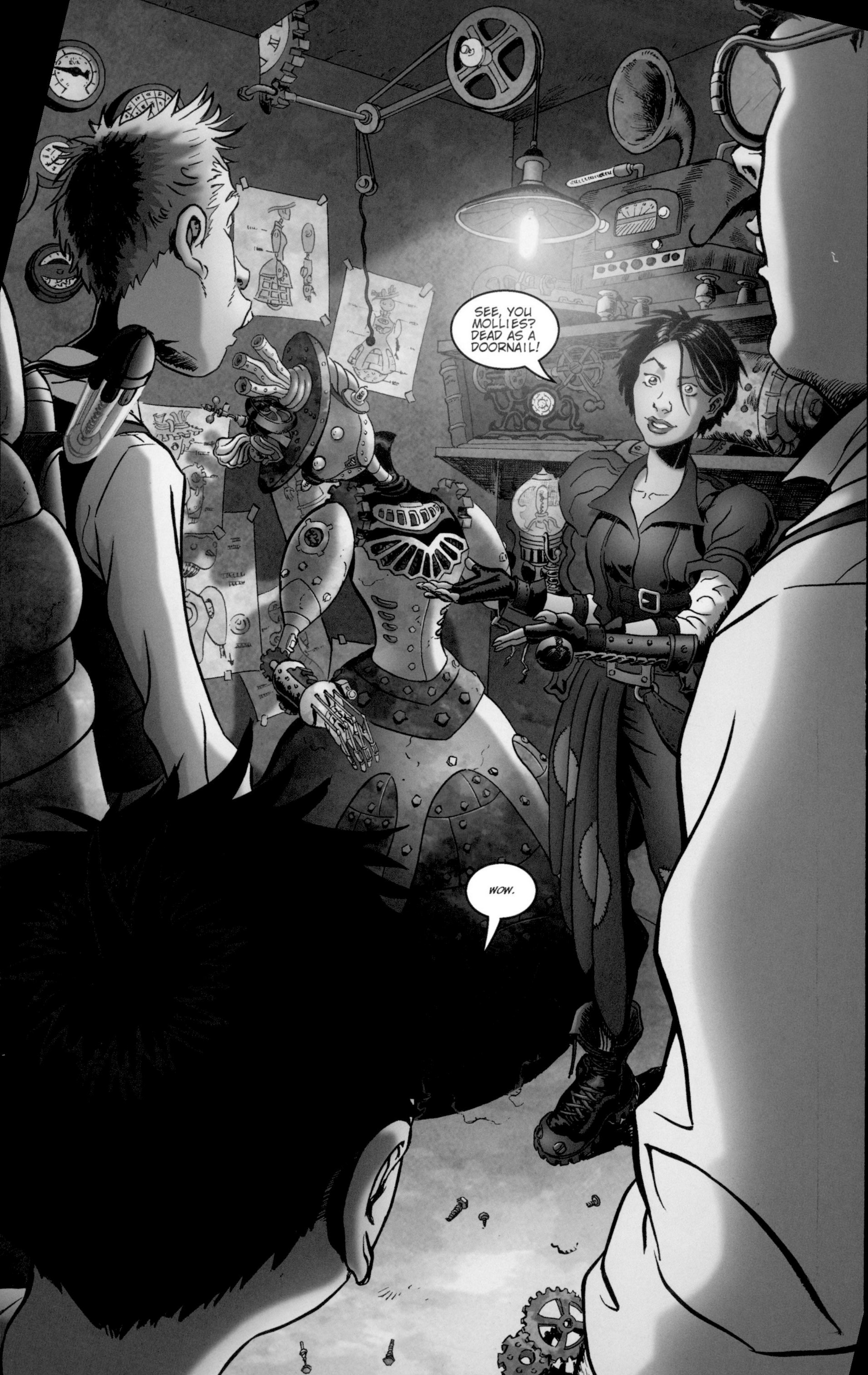
SEE, YOU MOLLIES? DEAD AS A DOORNAIL!
WOW.

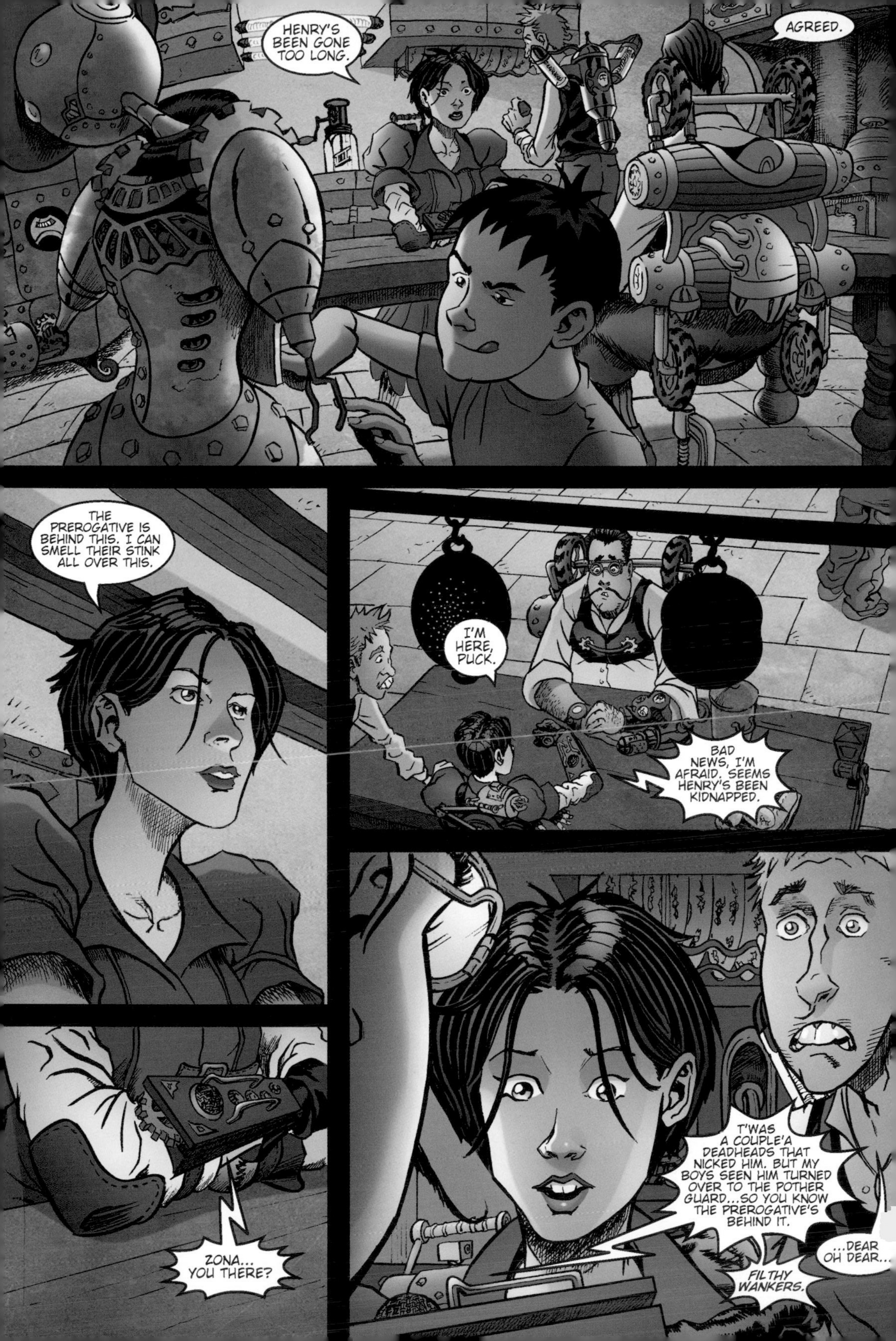
HENRY'S BEEN GONE TOO LONG.
AGREED.
THE PREROGATIVE IS BEHIND THIS. I CAN SMELL THEIR STINK ALL OVER THIS.
ZONA... YOU THERE?
I'M HERE, PUCK.
BAD NEWS, I'M AFRAID. SEEMS HENRY'S BEEN KIDNAPPED.
T'WAS A COUPLE'A DEADHEADS THAT NICKED HIM. BUT MY BOYS SEEN HIM TURNED OVER TO THE POTHER GUARD...SO YOU KNOW THE PREROGATIVE'S BEHIND IT.
FILTHY WANKERS.
...DEAR OH DEAR...

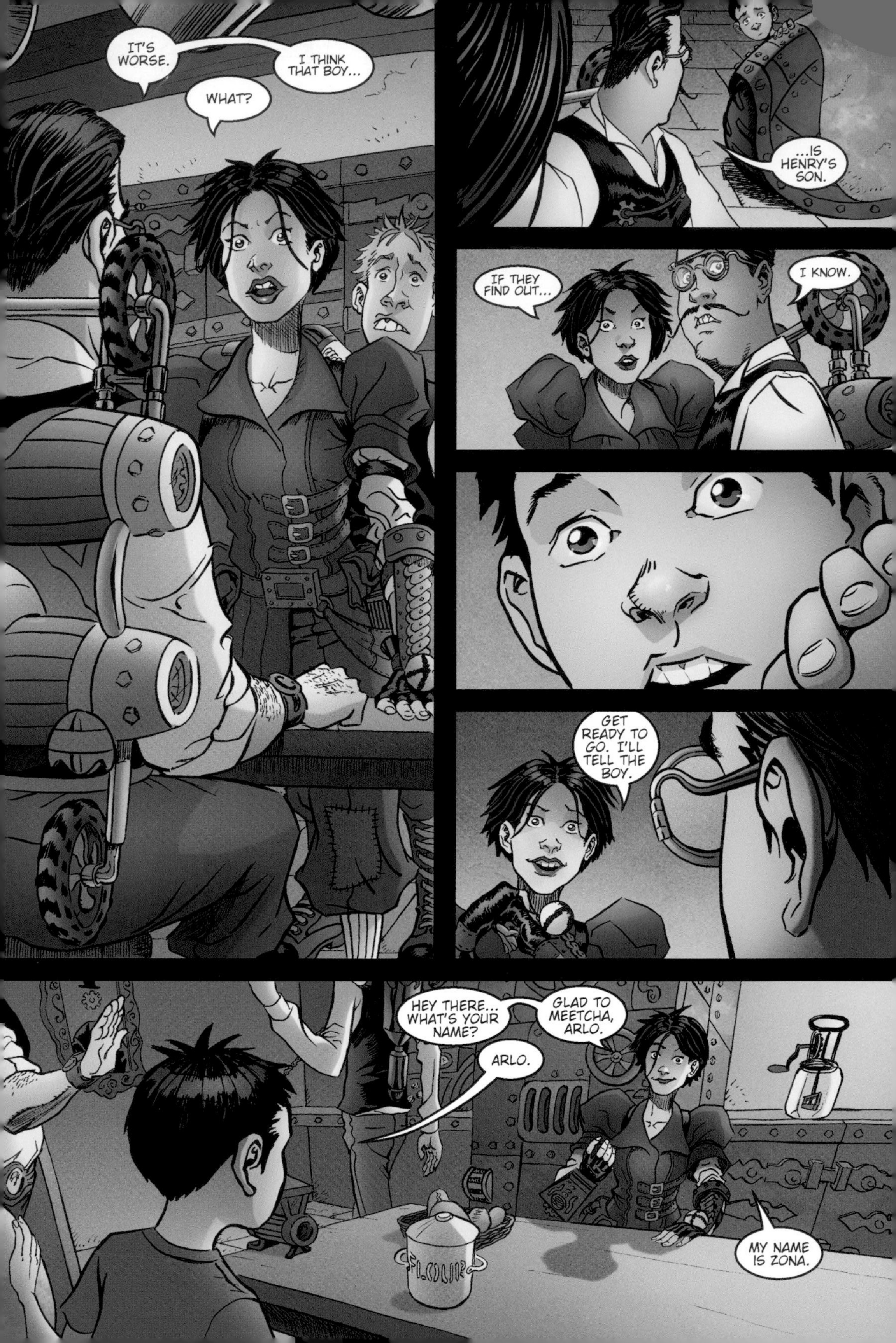

IT'S WORSE.
I THINK THAT BOY...
WHAT?
...IS HENRY'S SON.
IF THEY FIND OUT...
I KNOW.
GET READY TO GO. I'LL TELL THE BOY.
HEY THERE... WHAT'S YOUR NAME?
ARLO.
GLAD TO MEETCHA, ARLO.
MY NAME IS ZONA.
FLOUR

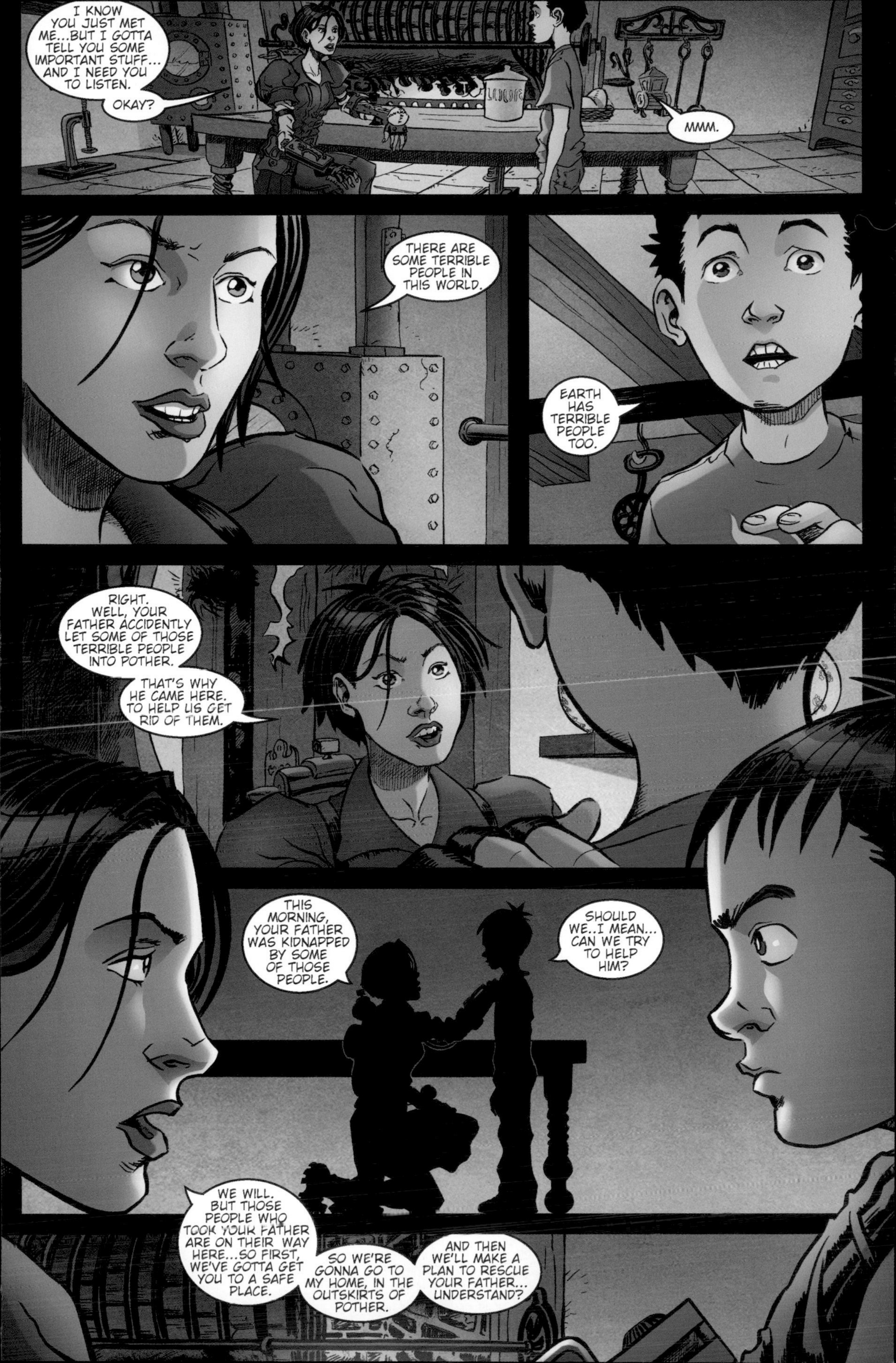
I KNOW YOU JUST MET ME...BUT I GOTTA TELL YOU SOME IMPORTANT STUFF... AND I NEED YOU TO LISTEN.
OKAY?
MMM.
THERE ARE SOME TERRIBLE PEOPLE IN THIS WORLD.
EARTH HAS TERRIBLE PEOPLE TOO.
RIGHT. WELL, YOUR FATHER ACCIDENTLY LET SOME OF THOSE TERRIBLE PEOPLE INTO POTHER.
THAT'S WHY HE CAME HERE. TO HELP US GET RID OF THEM.
THIS MORNING, YOUR FATHER WAS KIDNAPPED BY SOME OF THOSE PEOPLE.
SHOULD WE..I MEAN... CAN WE TRY TO HELP HIM?
WE WILL. BUT THOSE PEOPLE WHO TOOK YOUR FATHER ARE ON THEIR WAY HERE...SO FIRST, WE'VE GOTTA GET YOU TO A SAFE PLACE.
SO WE'RE GONNA GO TO MY HOME, IN THE OUTSKIRTS OF POTHER.
AND THEN WE'LL MAKE A PLAN TO RESCUE YOUR FATHER... UNDERSTAND?

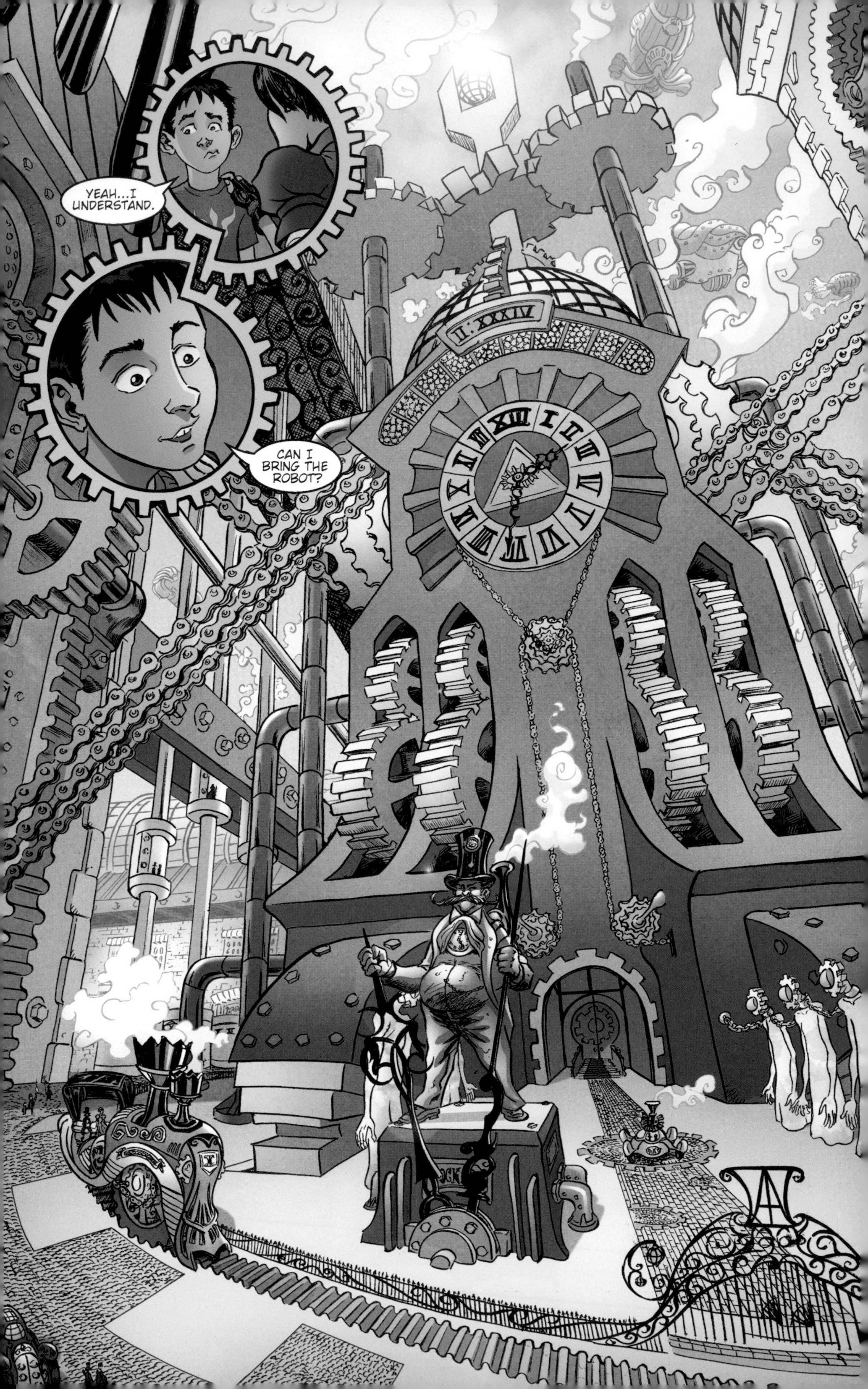
YEAH...I UNDERSTAND.
CAN I BRING THE ROBOT?
II: XXXIV

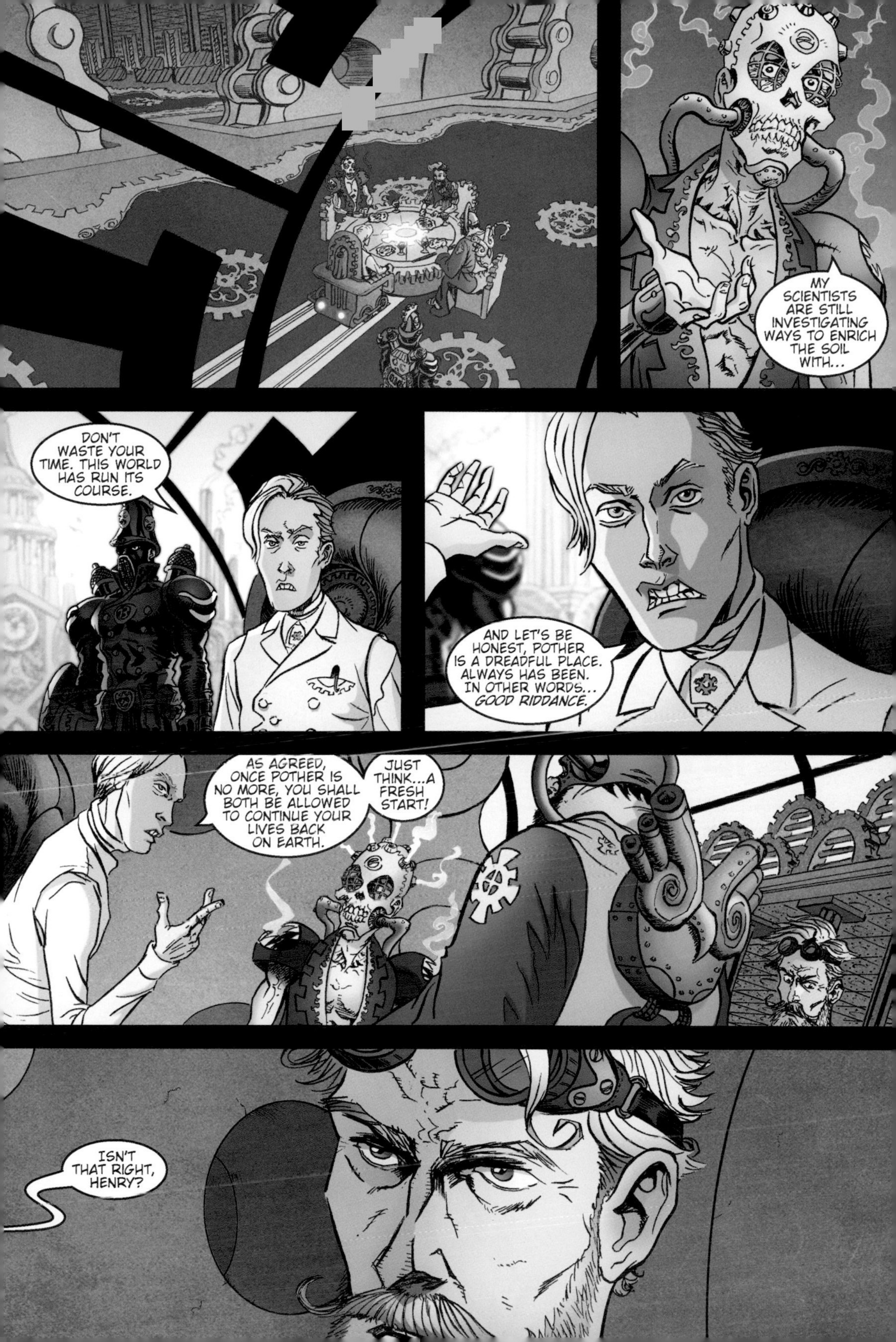
MY SCIENTISTS ARE STILL INVESTIGATING WAYS TO ENRICH THE SOIL WITH...
DON'T WASTE YOUR TIME. THIS WORLD HAS RUN ITS COURSE.
AND LET'S BE HONEST, POTHER IS A DREADFUL PLACE. ALWAYS HAS BEEN. IN OTHER WORDS... *GOOD RIDDANCE.*
AS AGREED, ONCE POTHER IS NO MORE, YOU SHALL BOTH BE ALLOWED TO CONTINUE YOUR LIVES BACK ON EARTH.
JUST THINK...A FRESH START!
ISN'T THAT RIGHT, HENRY?

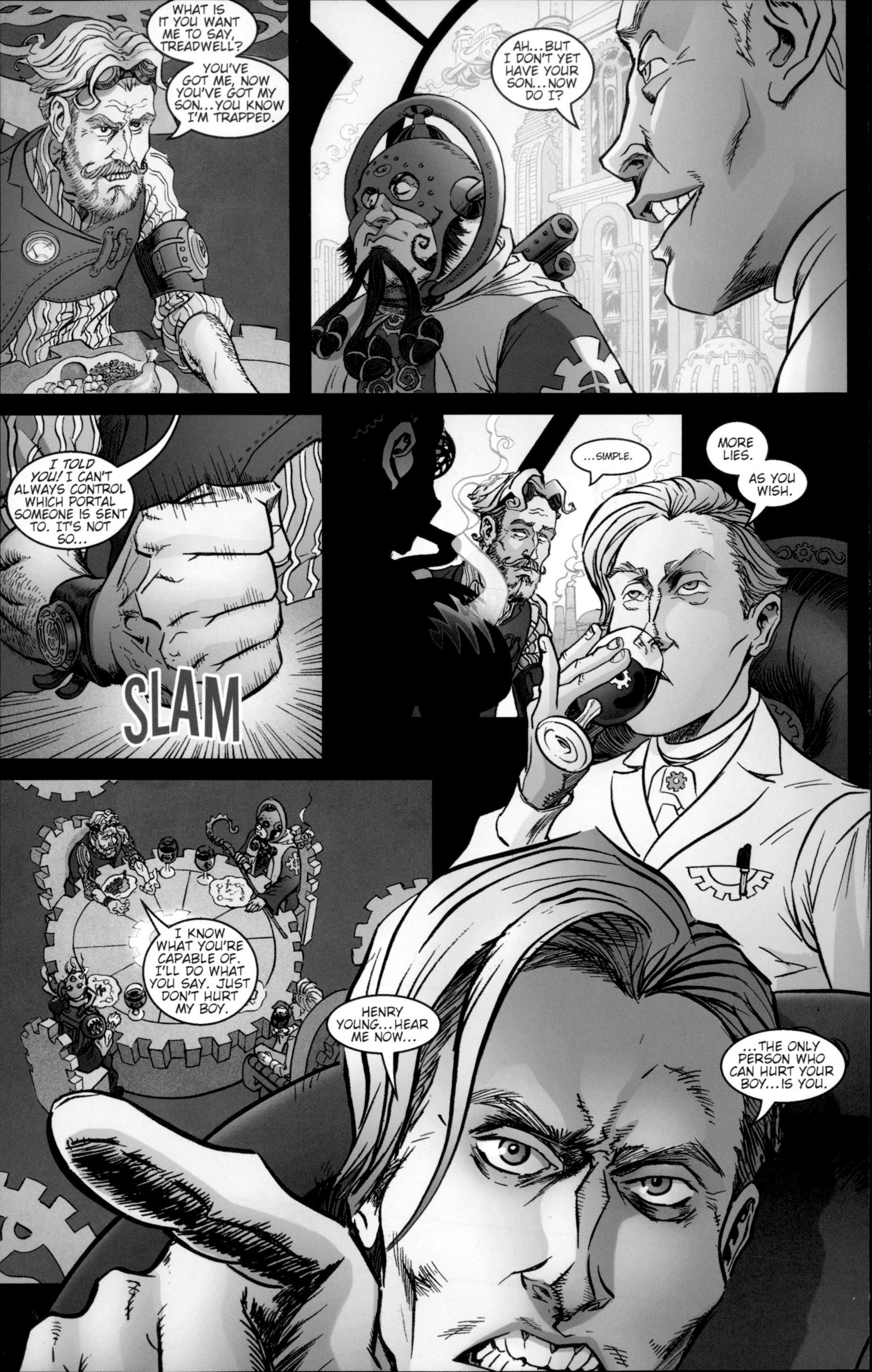
WHAT IS IT YOU WANT ME TO SAY, TREADWELL?
YOU'VE GOT ME, NOW YOU'VE GOT MY SON...YOU KNOW I'M TRAPPED.
AH...BUT I DON'T YET HAVE YOUR SON...NOW DO I?
I TOLD YOU! I CAN'T ALWAYS CONTROL WHICH PORTAL SOMEONE IS SENT TO. IT'S NOT SO...
SLAM
...SIMPLE.
MORE LIES.
AS YOU WISH.
I KNOW WHAT YOU'RE CAPABLE OF. I'LL DO WHAT YOU SAY. JUST DON'T HURT MY BOY.
HENRY YOUNG...HEAR ME NOW...
...THE ONLY PERSON WHO CAN HURT YOUR BOY...IS YOU.

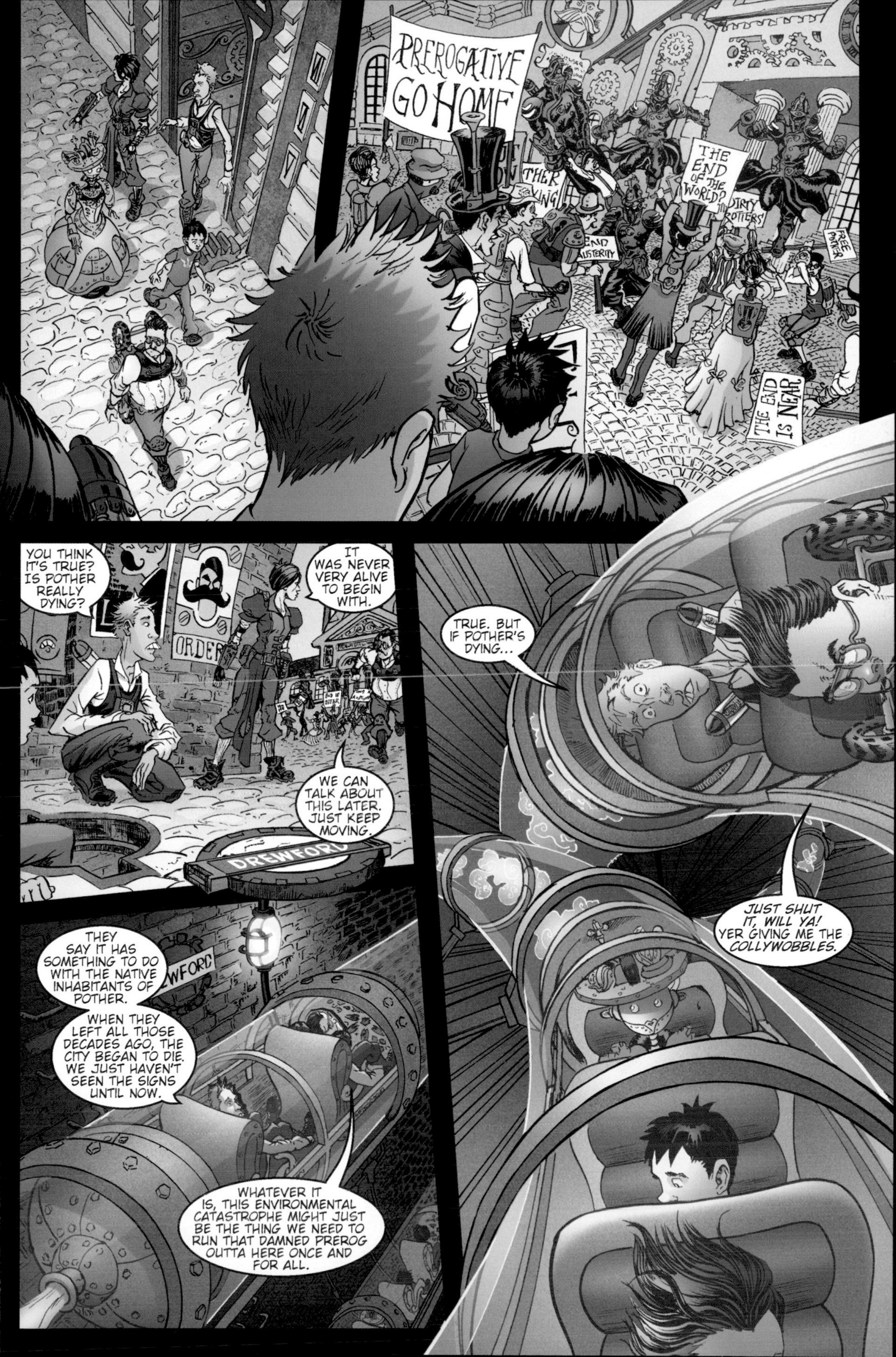
PREROGATIVE GO HOME
THE END OF THE WORLD?
END AUSTERITY
FREE POTHER
THE END IS NEAR
YOU THINK IT'S TRUE? IS POTHER REALLY DYING?
IT WAS NEVER VERY ALIVE TO BEGIN WITH.
WE CAN TALK ABOUT THIS LATER. JUST KEEP MOVING.
DREWFORD
THEY SAY IT HAS SOMETHING TO DO WITH THE NATIVE INHABITANTS OF POTHER.
WHEN THEY LEFT ALL THOSE DECADES AGO, THE CITY BEGAN TO DIE. WE JUST HAVEN'T SEEN THE SIGNS UNTIL NOW.
WHATEVER IT IS, THIS ENVIRONMENTAL CATASTROPHE MIGHT JUST BE THE THING WE NEED TO RUN THAT DAMNED PREROG OUTTA HERE ONCE AND FOR ALL.
TRUE. BUT IF POTHER'S DYING...
JUST SHUT IT, WILL YA! YER GIVING ME THE COLLYWOBBLES.

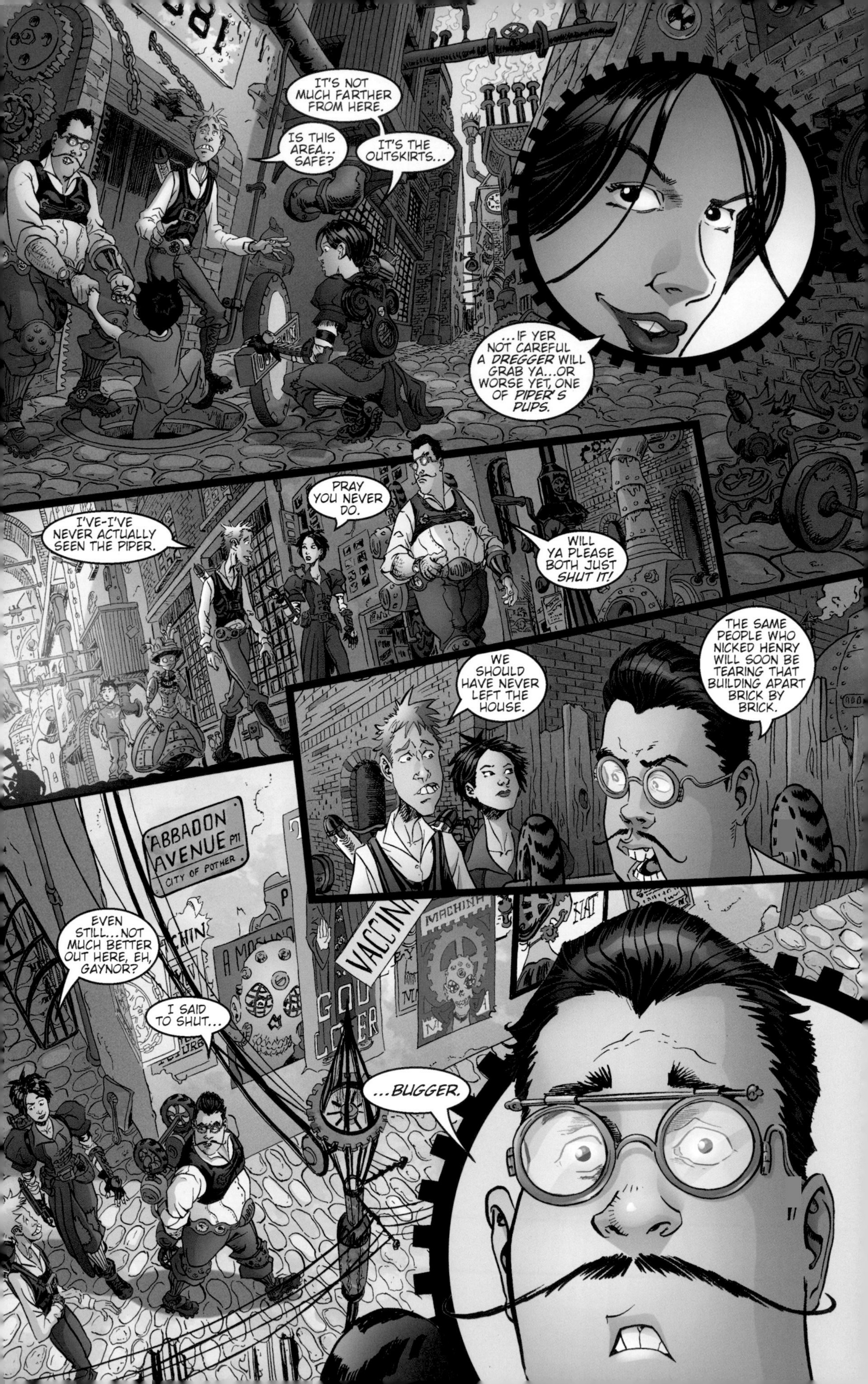
IT'S NOT MUCH FARTHER FROM HERE.
IS THIS AREA... SAFE?
IT'S THE OUTSKIRTS...
...IF YER NOT CAREFUL A DREGGER WILL GRAB YA...OR WORSE YET, ONE OF PIPER'S PUPS.
I'VE-I'VE NEVER ACTUALLY SEEN THE PIPER.
PRAY YOU NEVER DO.
WILL YA PLEASE BOTH JUST SHUT IT!
WE SHOULD HAVE NEVER LEFT THE HOUSE.
THE SAME PEOPLE WHO NICKED HENRY WILL SOON BE TEARING THAT BUILDING APART BRICK BY BRICK.
ABBADON AVENUE P11
CITY OF POTHER
EVEN STILL...NOT MUCH BETTER OUT HERE, EH, GAYNOR?
I SAID TO SHUT...
...BUGGER.

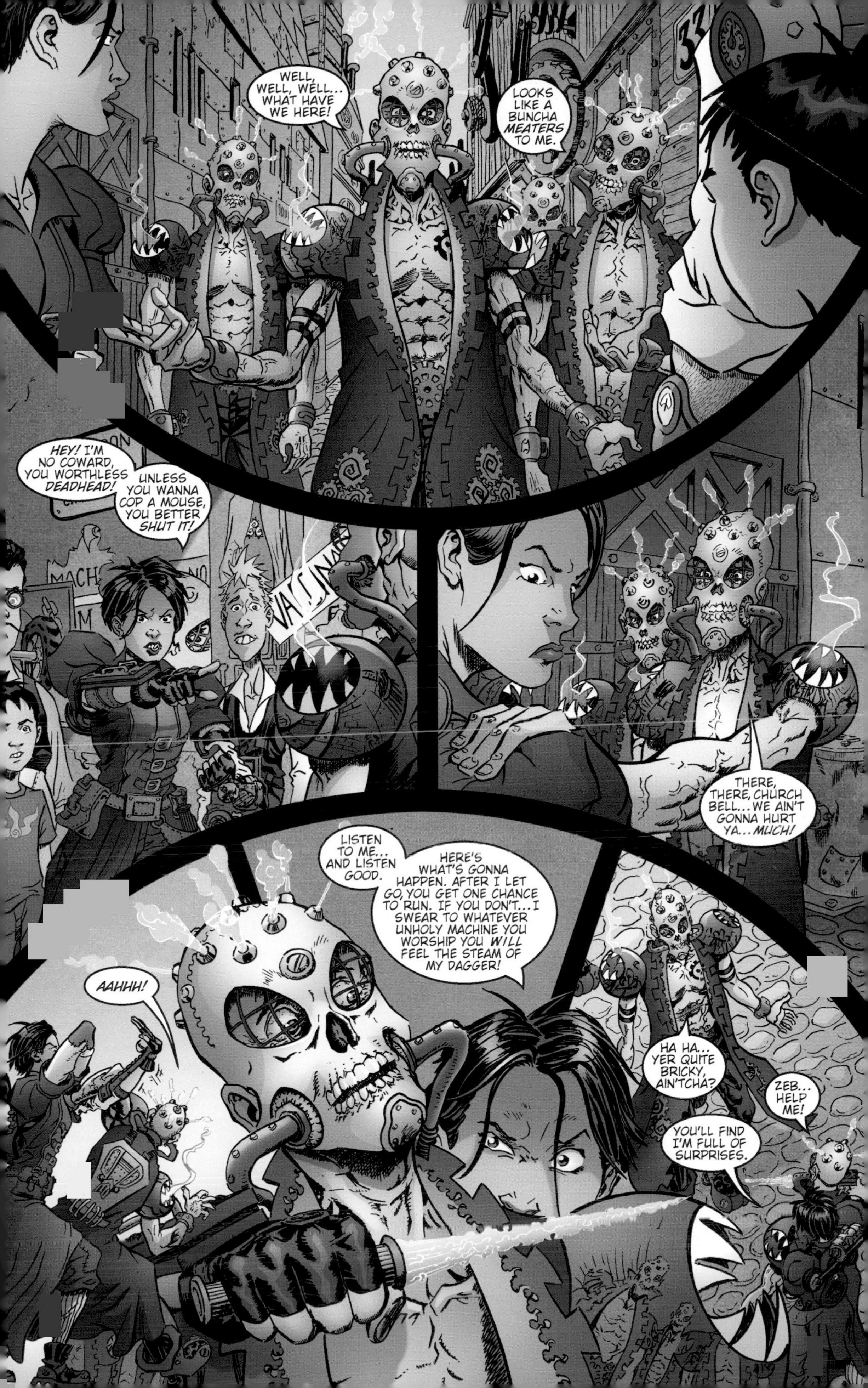
WELL, WELL, WELL... WHAT HAVE WE HERE!
LOOKS LIKE A BUNCHA MEATERS TO ME.
HEY! I'M NO COWARD, YOU WORTHLESS DEADHEAD!
UNLESS YOU WANNA COP A MOUSE, YOU BETTER SHUT IT!
THERE, THERE, CHURCH BELL... WE AIN'T GONNA HURT YA... MUCH!
LISTEN TO ME... AND LISTEN GOOD.
HERE'S WHAT'S GONNA HAPPEN. AFTER I LET GO, YOU GET ONE CHANCE TO RUN. IF YOU DON'T... I SWEAR TO WHATEVER UNHOLY MACHINE YOU WORSHIP YOU WILL FEEL THE STEAM OF MY DAGGER!
AAHHH!
HA HA... YER QUITE BRICKY, AIN'TCHA?
YOU'LL FIND I'M FULL OF SURPRISES.
ZEB... HELP ME!

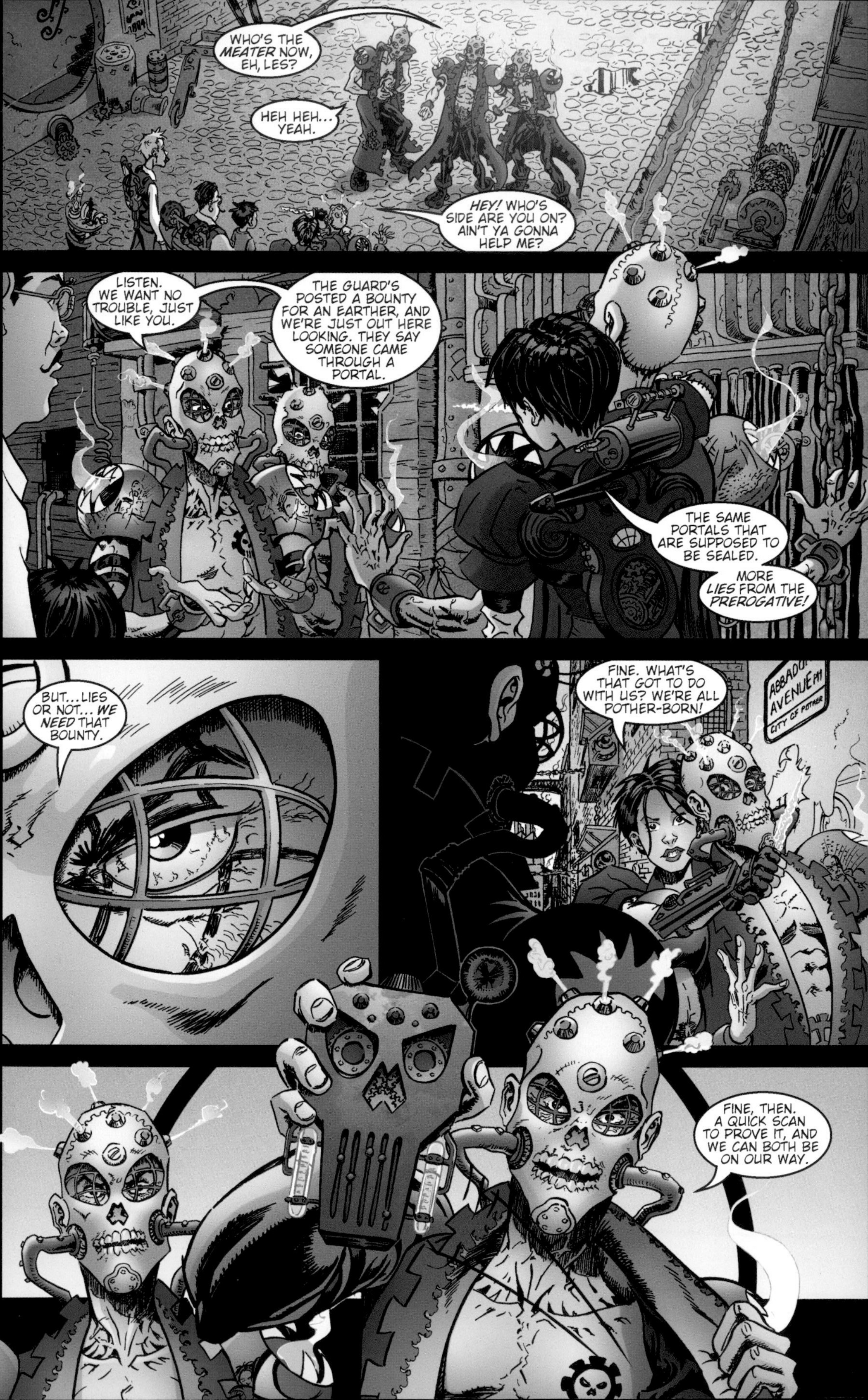
WHO'S THE *MEATER* NOW, EH, LES?
HEH HEH... YEAH.
HEY! WHO'S SIDE ARE YOU ON? AIN'T YA GONNA HELP ME?
LISTEN. WE WANT NO TROUBLE, JUST LIKE YOU.
THE GUARD'S POSTED A BOUNTY FOR AN EARTHER, AND WE'RE JUST OUT HERE LOOKING. THEY SAY SOMEONE CAME THROUGH A PORTAL.
THE SAME PORTALS THAT ARE SUPPOSED TO BE SEALED.
MORE *LIES* FROM THE *PREROGATIVE!*
BUT... LIES OR NOT... *WE NEED* THAT BOUNTY.
FINE. WHAT'S THAT GOT TO DO WITH US? WE'RE ALL POTHER-BORN!
ABBADON AVENUE
CITY OF POTHER
FINE, THEN. A QUICK SCAN TO PROVE IT, AND WE CAN BOTH BE ON OUR WAY.

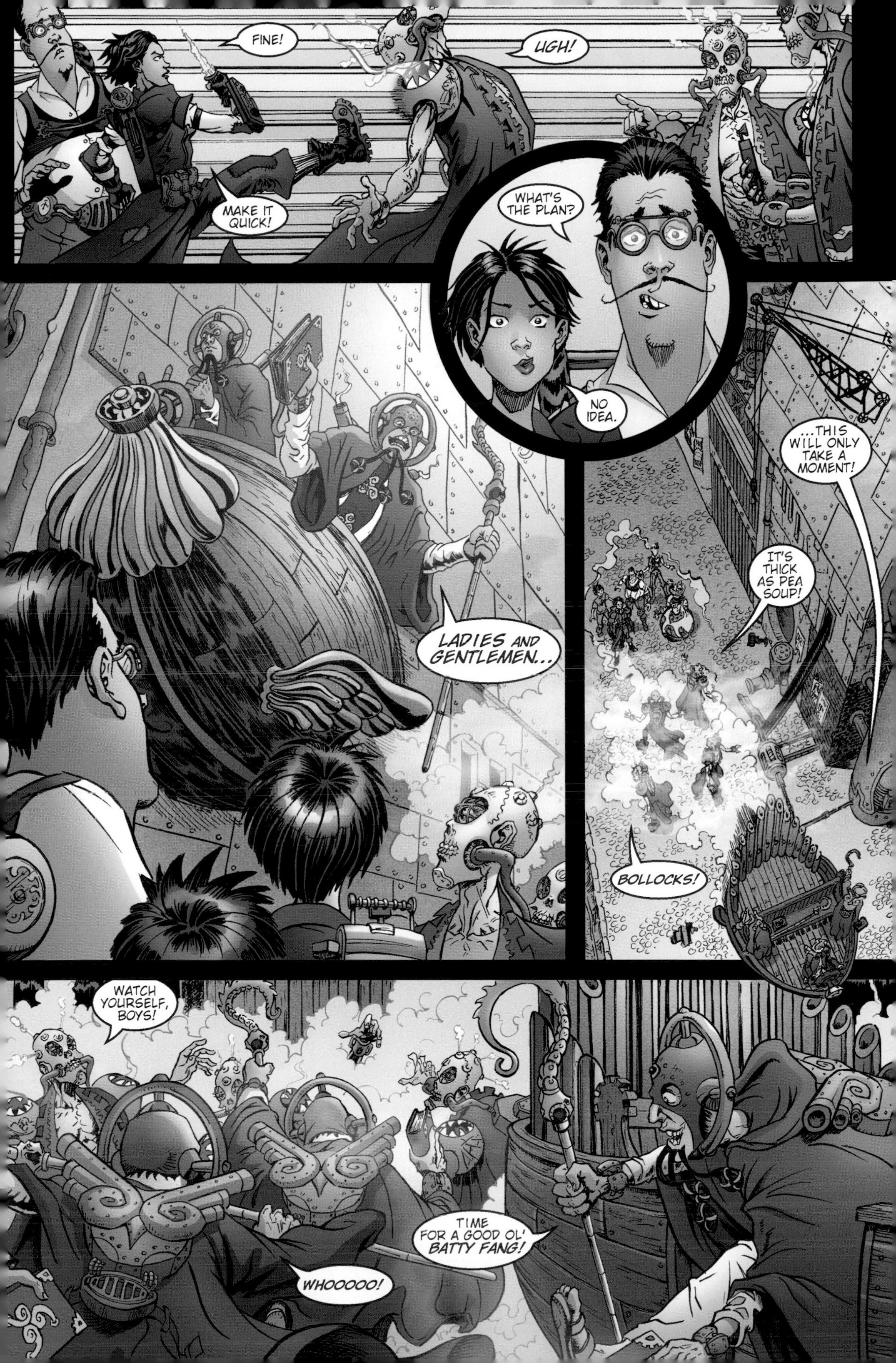
FINE!
UGH!
MAKE IT QUICK!
WHAT'S THE PLAN?
NO IDEA.
LADIES AND GENTLEMEN...
...THIS WILL ONLY TAKE A MOMENT!
IT'S THICK AS PEA SOUP!
BOLLOCKS!
WATCH YOURSELF, BOYS!
TIME FOR A GOOD OL' BATTY FANG!
WHOOOOO!

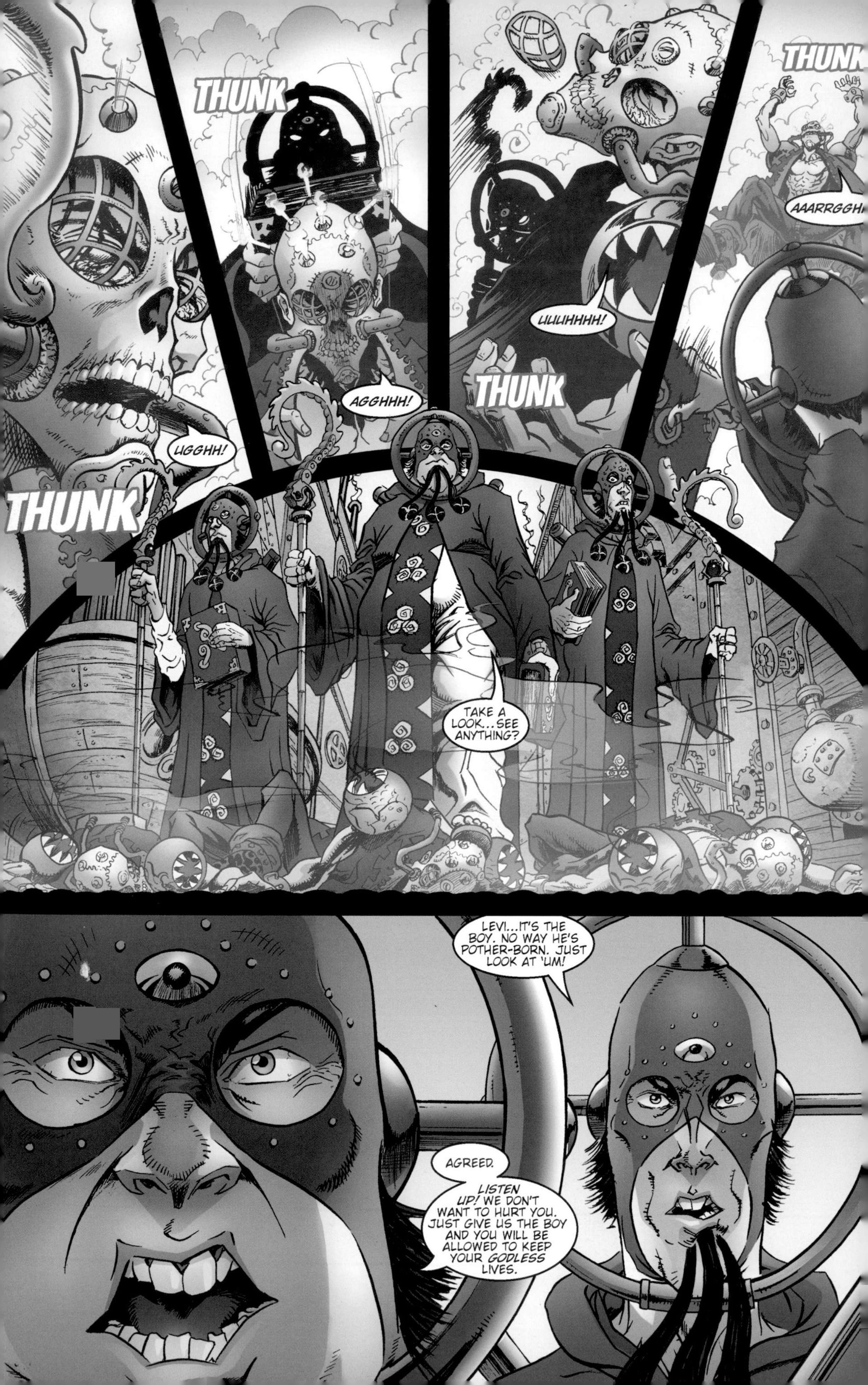
THUNK
UGGHH!
THUNK
AGGHHH!
UUUHHHH!
THUNK
THUNK
AAARRGGH!
TAKE A LOOK...SEE ANYTHING?
LEVI...IT'S THE BOY. NO WAY HE'S POTHER-BORN. JUST LOOK AT 'UM!
AGREED.
LISTEN UP! WE DON'T WANT TO HURT YOU. JUST GIVE US THE BOY AND YOU WILL BE ALLOWED TO KEEP YOUR GODLESS LIVES.

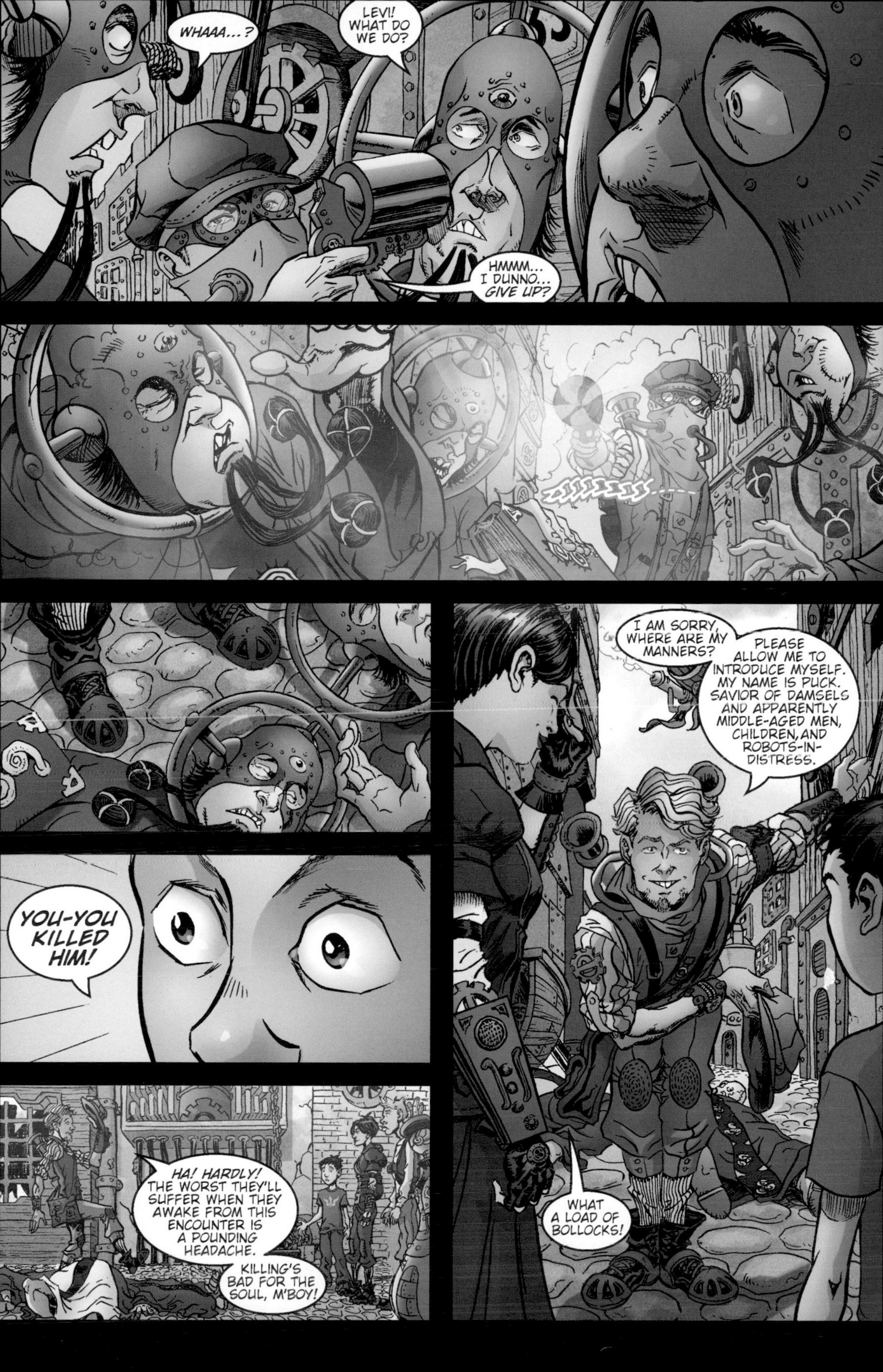

WHAAA...?
LEVI! WHAT DO WE DO?
HMMM... I DUNNO... GIVE UP?
I AM SORRY, WHERE ARE MY MANNERS?
PLEASE ALLOW ME TO INTRODUCE MYSELF. MY NAME IS PUCK. SAVIOR OF DAMSELS AND APPARENTLY MIDDLE-AGED MEN, CHILDREN, AND ROBOTS-IN-DISTRESS.
YOU-YOU KILLED HIM!
HA! HARDLY! THE WORST THEY'LL SUFFER WHEN THEY AWAKE FROM THIS ENCOUNTER IS A POUNDING HEADACHE.
KILLING'S BAD FOR THE SOUL, M'BOY!
WHAT A LOAD OF BOLLOCKS!

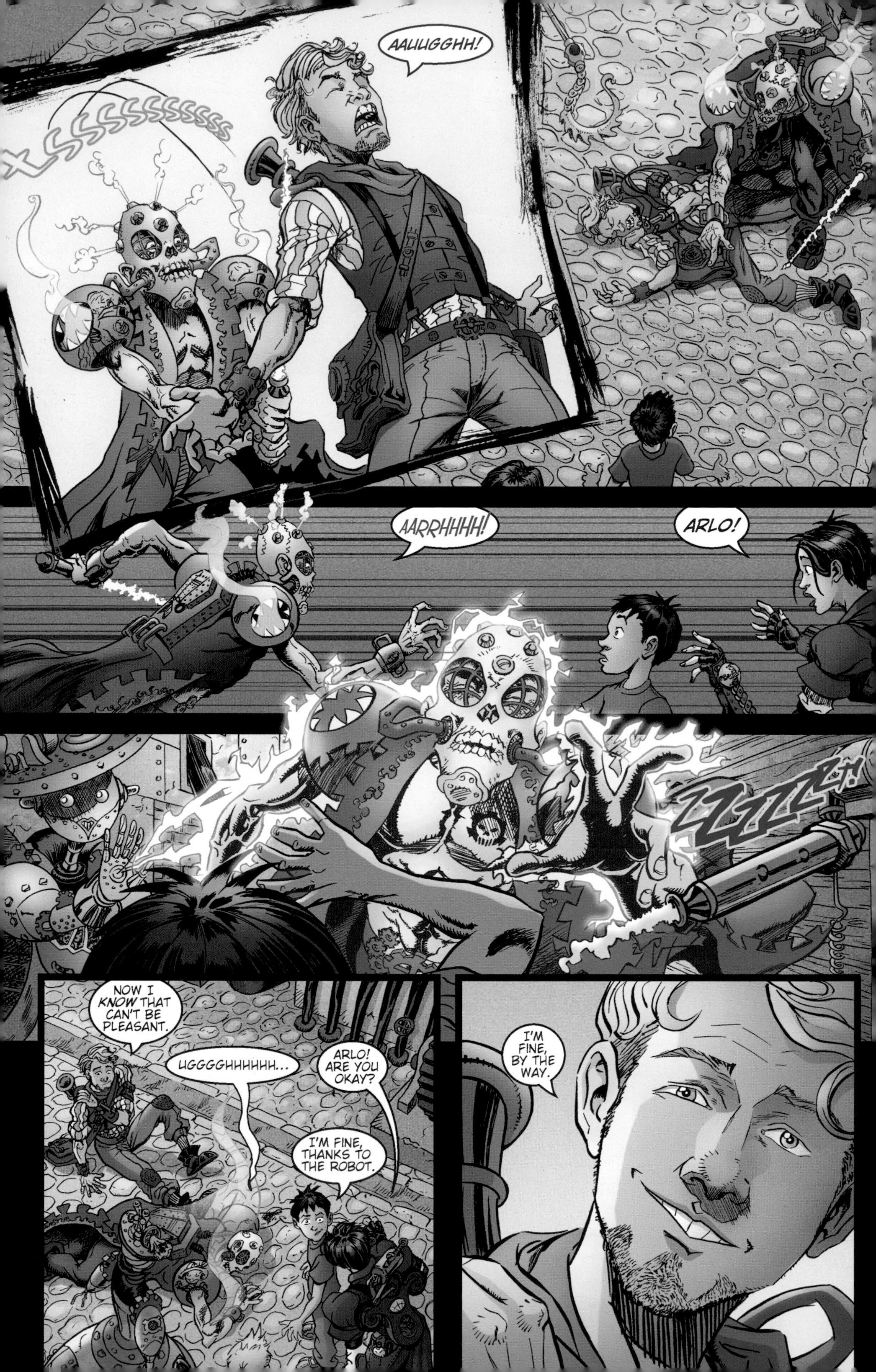

AAUUGGHH!
XSSSSSSSSSSS
AARRHHHH!
ARLO!
ZZZZZZT!
NOW I KNOW THAT CAN'T BE PLEASANT.
UGGGGHHHHHH...
ARLO! ARE YOU OKAY?
I'M FINE, THANKS TO THE ROBOT.
I'M FINE, BY THE WAY.

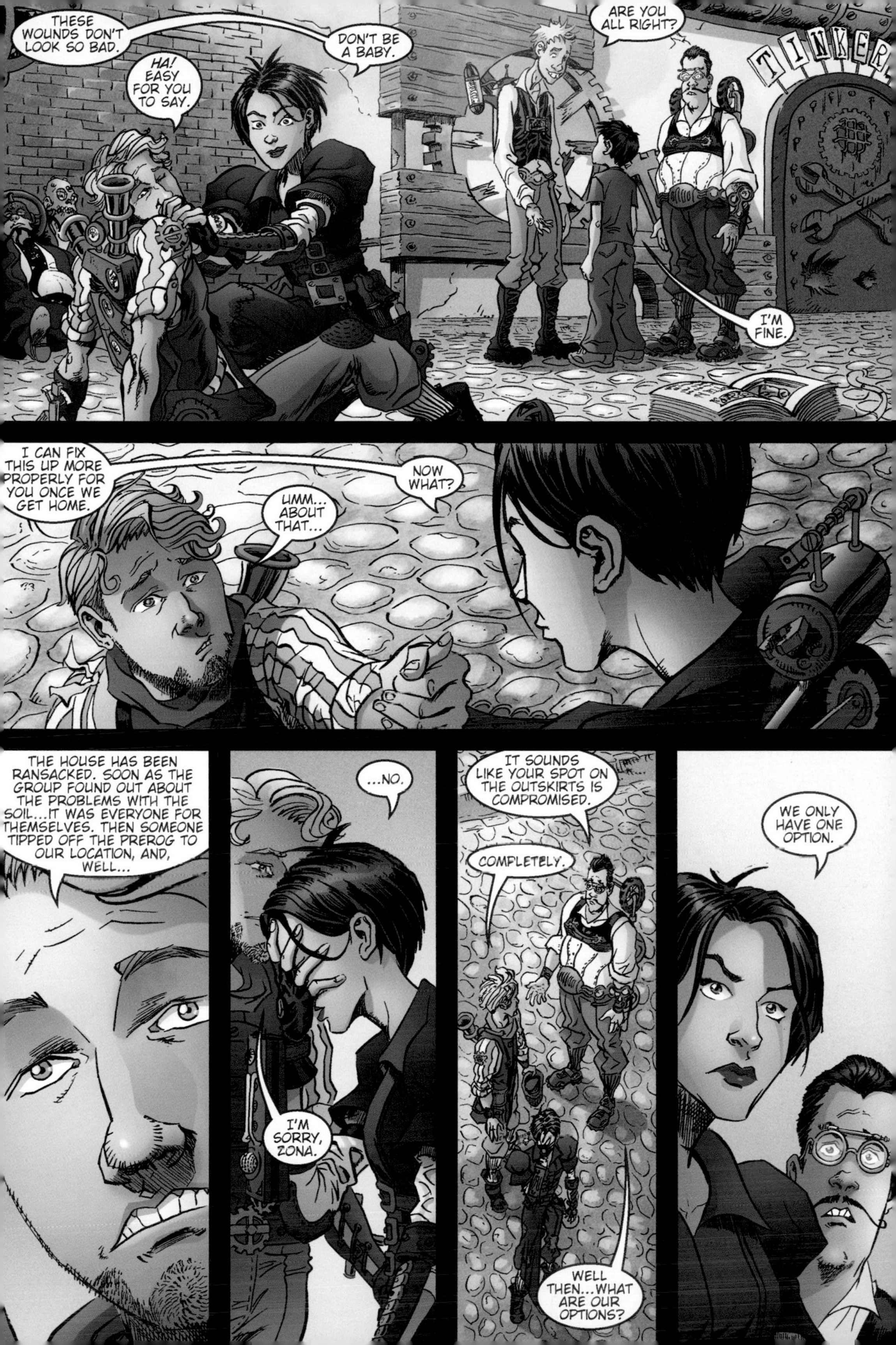
THESE WOUNDS DON'T LOOK SO BAD.
HA! EASY FOR YOU TO SAY.
DON'T BE A BABY.
ARE YOU ALL RIGHT?
TINKER
I'M FINE.
I CAN FIX THIS UP MORE PROPERLY FOR YOU ONCE WE GET HOME.
NOW WHAT?
UMM... ABOUT THAT...
THE HOUSE HAS BEEN RANSACKED. SOON AS THE GROUP FOUND OUT ABOUT THE PROBLEMS WITH THE SOIL...IT WAS EVERYONE FOR THEMSELVES. THEN SOMEONE TIPPED OFF THE PREROG TO OUR LOCATION, AND, WELL...
...NO.
I'M SORRY, ZONA.
IT SOUNDS LIKE YOUR SPOT ON THE OUTSKIRTS IS COMPROMISED.
COMPLETELY.
WELL THEN...WHAT ARE OUR OPTIONS?
WE ONLY HAVE ONE OPTION.

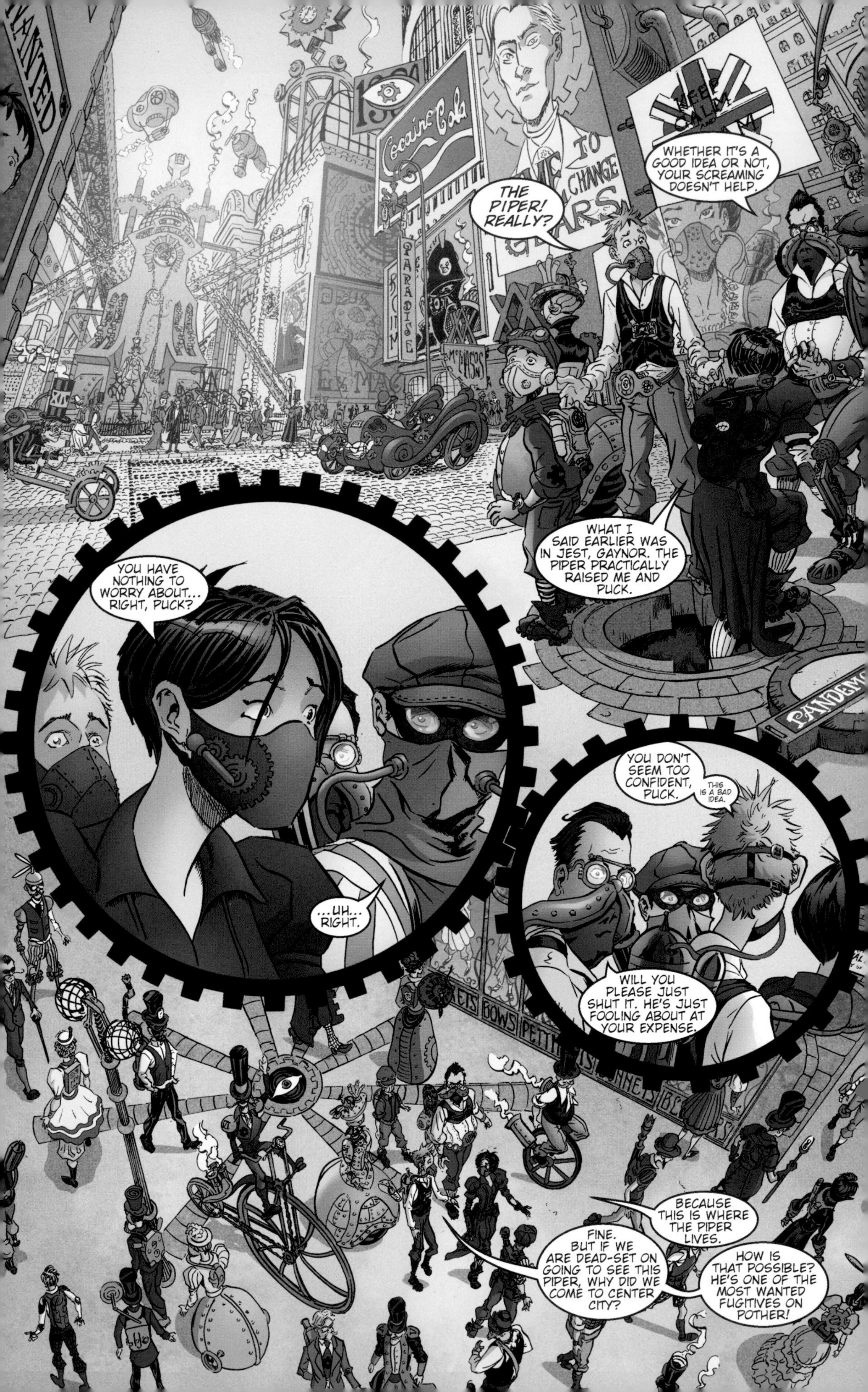
WHETHER IT'S A GOOD IDEA OR NOT, YOUR SCREAMING DOESN'T HELP.
THE PIPER! REALLY?
WHAT I SAID EARLIER WAS IN JEST, GAYNOR. THE PIPER PRACTICALLY RAISED ME AND PUCK.
YOU HAVE NOTHING TO WORRY ABOUT... RIGHT, PUCK?
...UH... RIGHT.
YOU DON'T SEEM TOO CONFIDENT, PUCK.
THIS IS A BAD IDEA.
WILL YOU PLEASE JUST SHUT IT. HE'S JUST FOOLING ABOUT AT YOUR EXPENSE.
BECAUSE THIS IS WHERE THE PIPER LIVES.
FINE. BUT IF WE ARE DEAD-SET ON GOING TO SEE THIS PIPER, WHY DID WE COME TO CENTER CITY?
HOW IS THAT POSSIBLE? HE'S ONE OF THE MOST WANTED FUGITIVES ON POTHER!

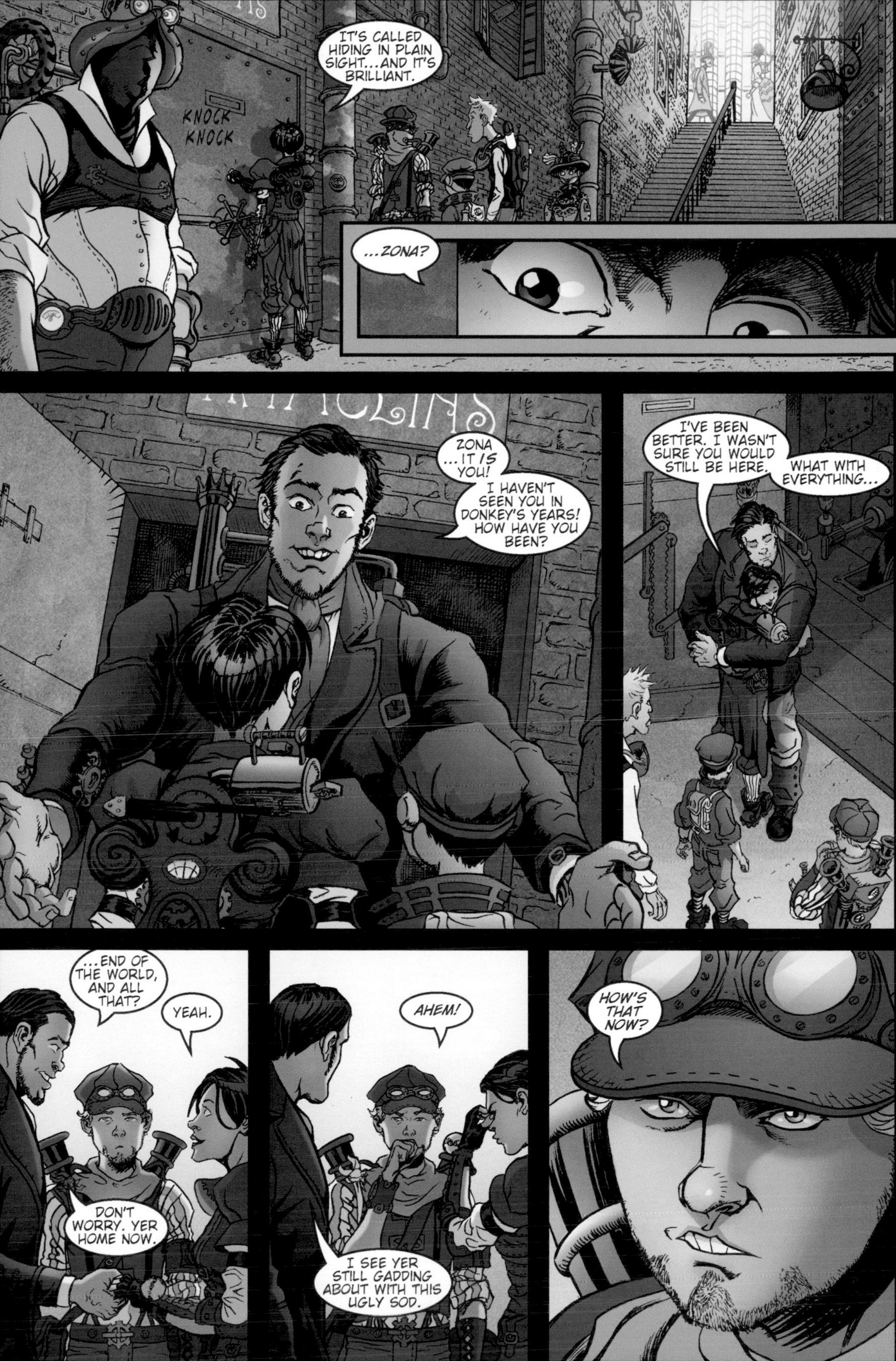

IT'S CALLED HIDING IN PLAIN SIGHT...AND IT'S BRILLIANT.
KNOCK KNOCK
...ZONA?
ZONA ...IT IS YOU!
I HAVEN'T SEEN YOU IN DONKEY'S YEARS! HOW HAVE YOU BEEN?
I'VE BEEN BETTER. I WASN'T SURE YOU WOULD STILL BE HERE.
WHAT WITH EVERYTHING...
...END OF THE WORLD, AND ALL THAT?
YEAH.
DON'T WORRY. YER HOME NOW.
AHEM!
I SEE YER STILL GADDING ABOUT WITH THIS UGLY SOD.
HOW'S THAT NOW?

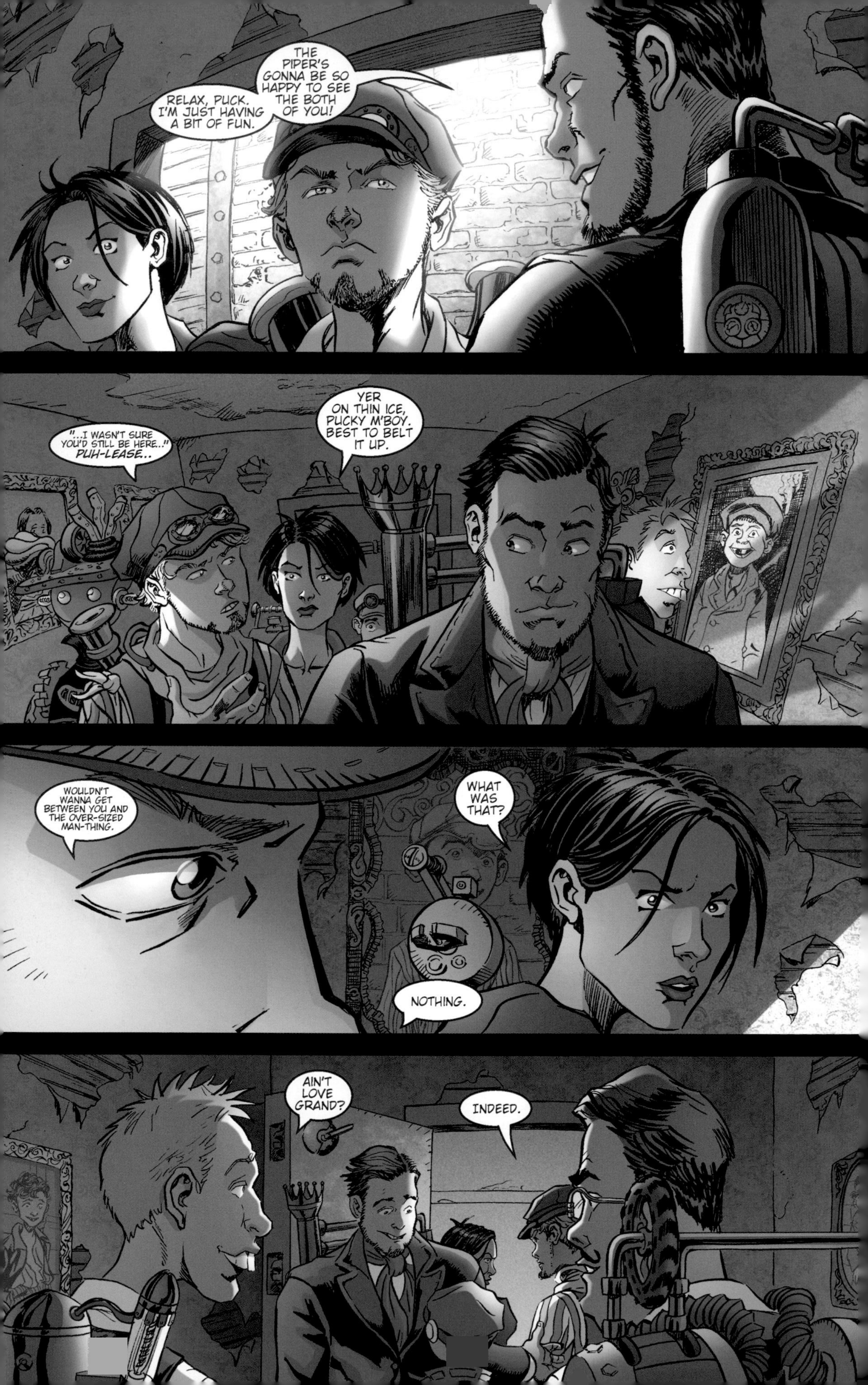
RELAX, PUCK. I'M JUST HAVING A BIT OF FUN.
THE PIPER'S GONNA BE SO HAPPY TO SEE THE BOTH OF YOU!
"...I WASN'T SURE YOU'D STILL BE HERE..." PUH-LEASE...
YER ON THIN ICE, PUCKY M'BOY. BEST TO BELT IT UP.
WOULDN'T WANNA GET BETWEEN YOU AND THE OVER-SIZED MAN-THING.
WHAT WAS THAT?
NOTHING.
AIN'T LOVE GRAND?
INDEED.

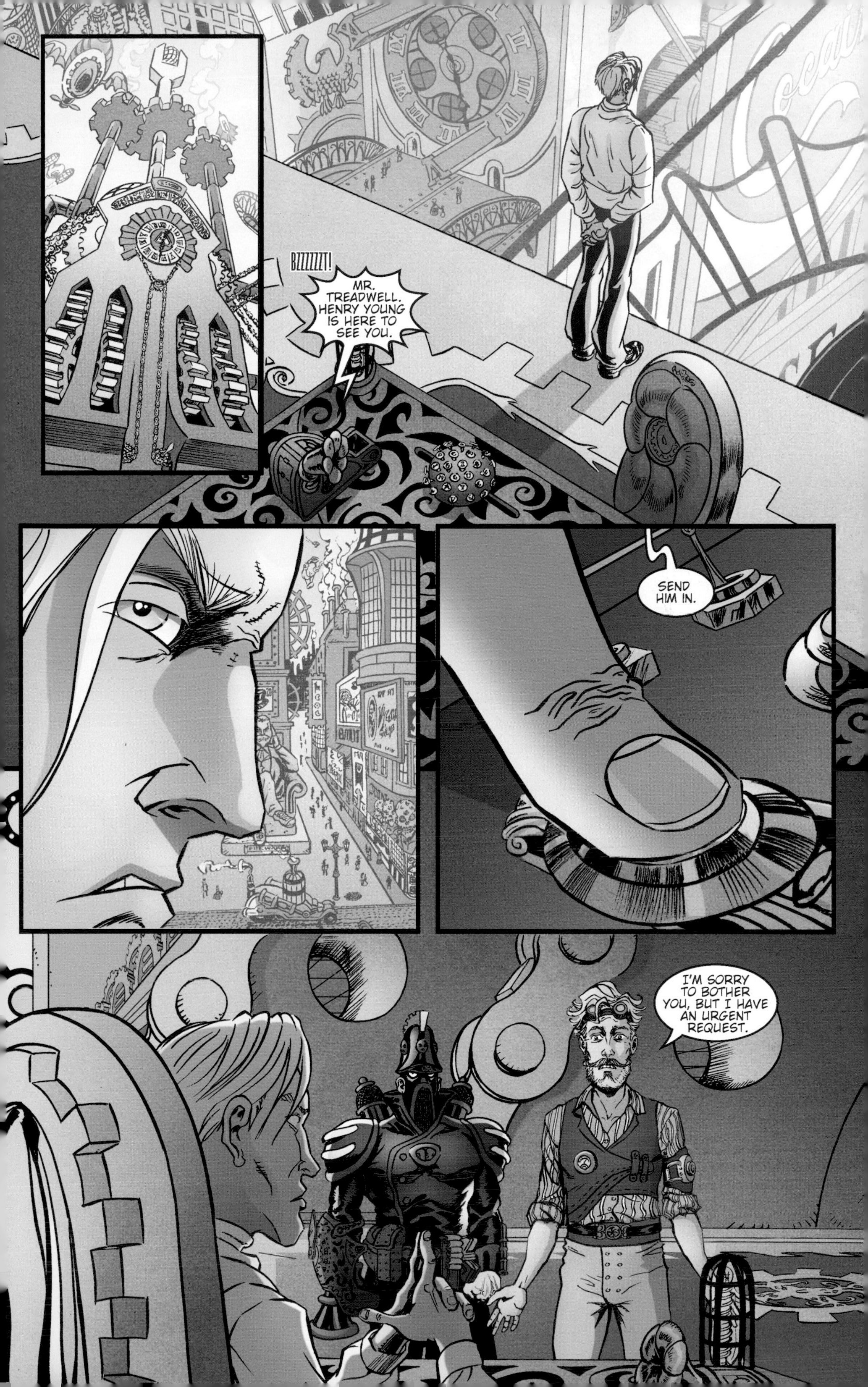
BZZZZZZT!
MR. TREADWELL. HENRY YOUNG IS HERE TO SEE YOU.
SEND HIM IN.
I'M SORRY TO BOTHER YOU, BUT I HAVE AN URGENT REQUEST.

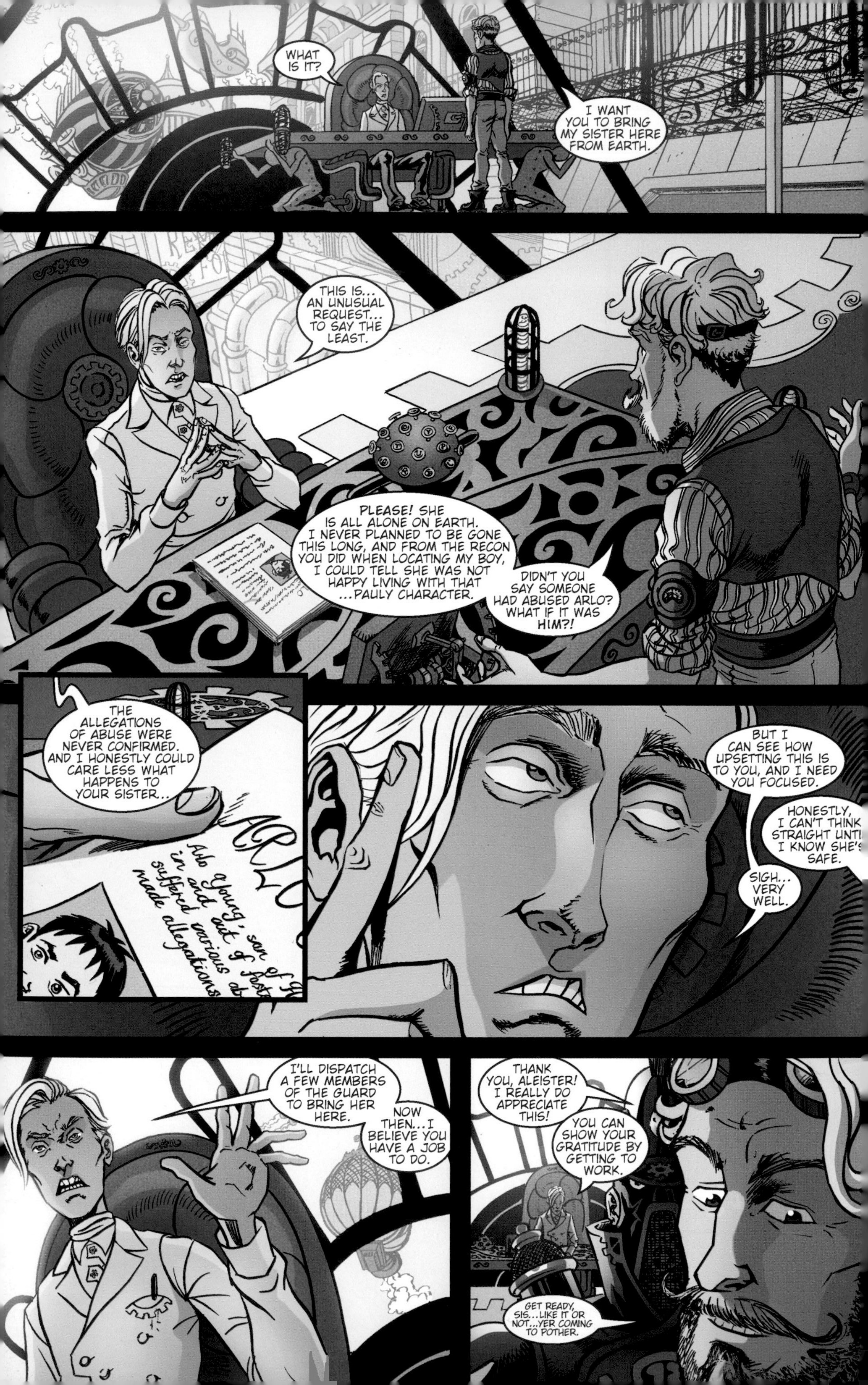
WHAT IS IT?
I WANT YOU TO BRING MY SISTER HERE FROM EARTH.
THIS IS... AN UNUSUAL REQUEST... TO SAY THE LEAST.
PLEASE! SHE IS ALL ALONE ON EARTH. I NEVER PLANNED TO BE GONE THIS LONG, AND FROM THE RECON YOU DID WHEN LOCATING MY BOY, I COULD TELL SHE WAS NOT HAPPY LIVING WITH THAT ...PAULY CHARACTER.
DIDN'T YOU SAY SOMEONE HAD ABUSED ARLO? WHAT IF IT WAS HIM?!
THE ALLEGATIONS OF ABUSE WERE NEVER CONFIRMED. AND I HONESTLY COULD CARE LESS WHAT HAPPENS TO YOUR SISTER...
BUT I CAN SEE HOW UPSETTING THIS IS TO YOU, AND I NEED YOU FOCUSED.
SIGH... VERY WELL.
I'LL DISPATCH A FEW MEMBERS OF THE GUARD TO BRING HER HERE.
NOW THEN... I BELIEVE YOU HAVE A JOB TO DO.
THANK YOU, ALEISTER! I REALLY DO APPRECIATE THIS!
YOU CAN SHOW YOUR GRATITUDE BY GETTING TO WORK.
GET READY, SIS... LIKE IT OR NOT... YER COMING TO POTHER.

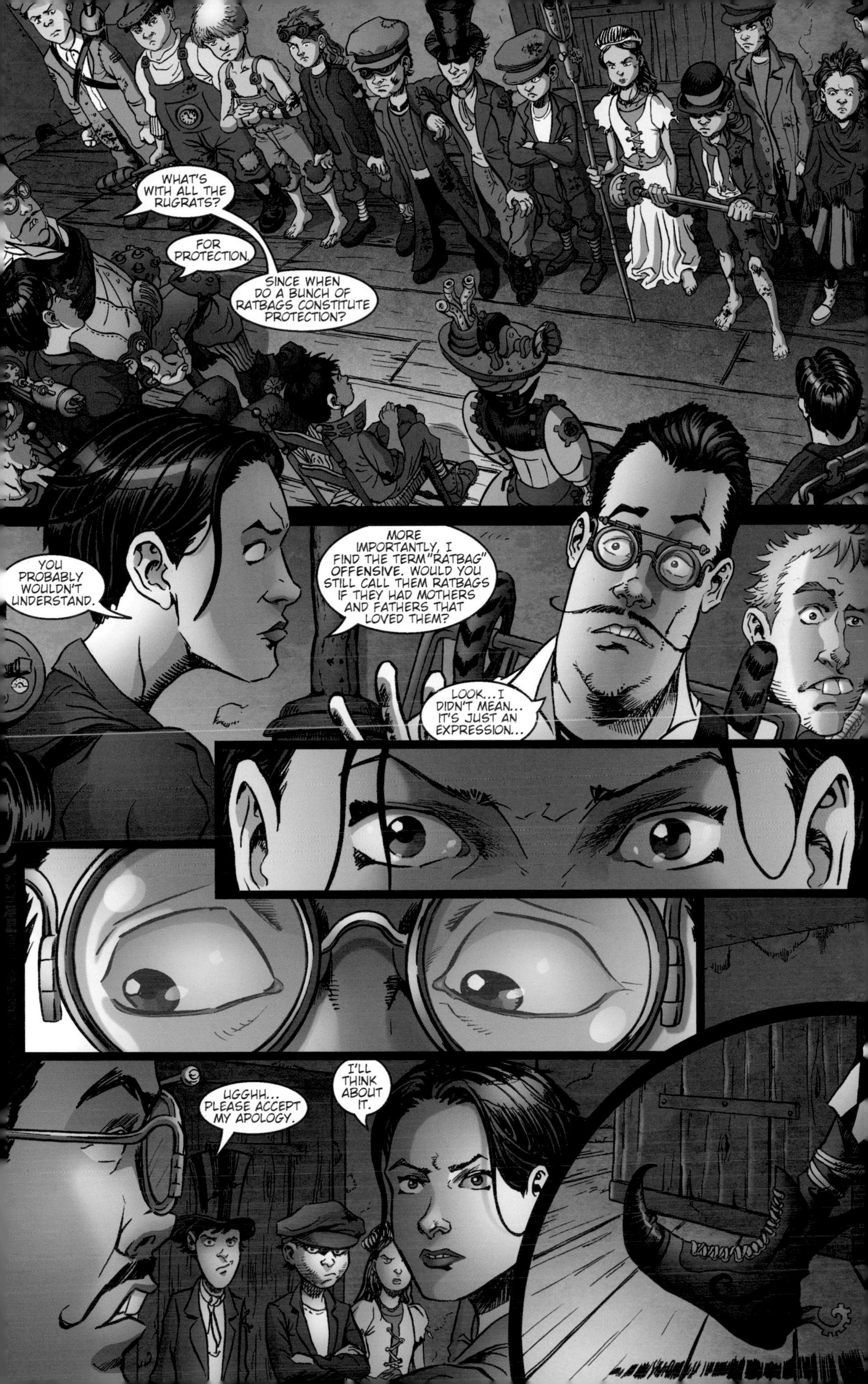
WHAT'S WITH ALL THE RUGRATS?
FOR PROTECTION.
SINCE WHEN DO A BUNCH OF RATBAGS CONSTITUTE PROTECTION?
YOU PROBABLY WOULDN'T UNDERSTAND.
MORE IMPORTANTLY, I FIND THE TERM "RATBAG" OFFENSIVE. WOULD YOU STILL CALL THEM RATBAGS IF THEY HAD MOTHERS AND FATHERS THAT LOVED THEM?
LOOK... I DIDN'T MEAN... IT'S JUST AN EXPRESSION...
UGGHH... PLEASE ACCEPT MY APOLOGY.
I'LL THINK ABOUT IT.

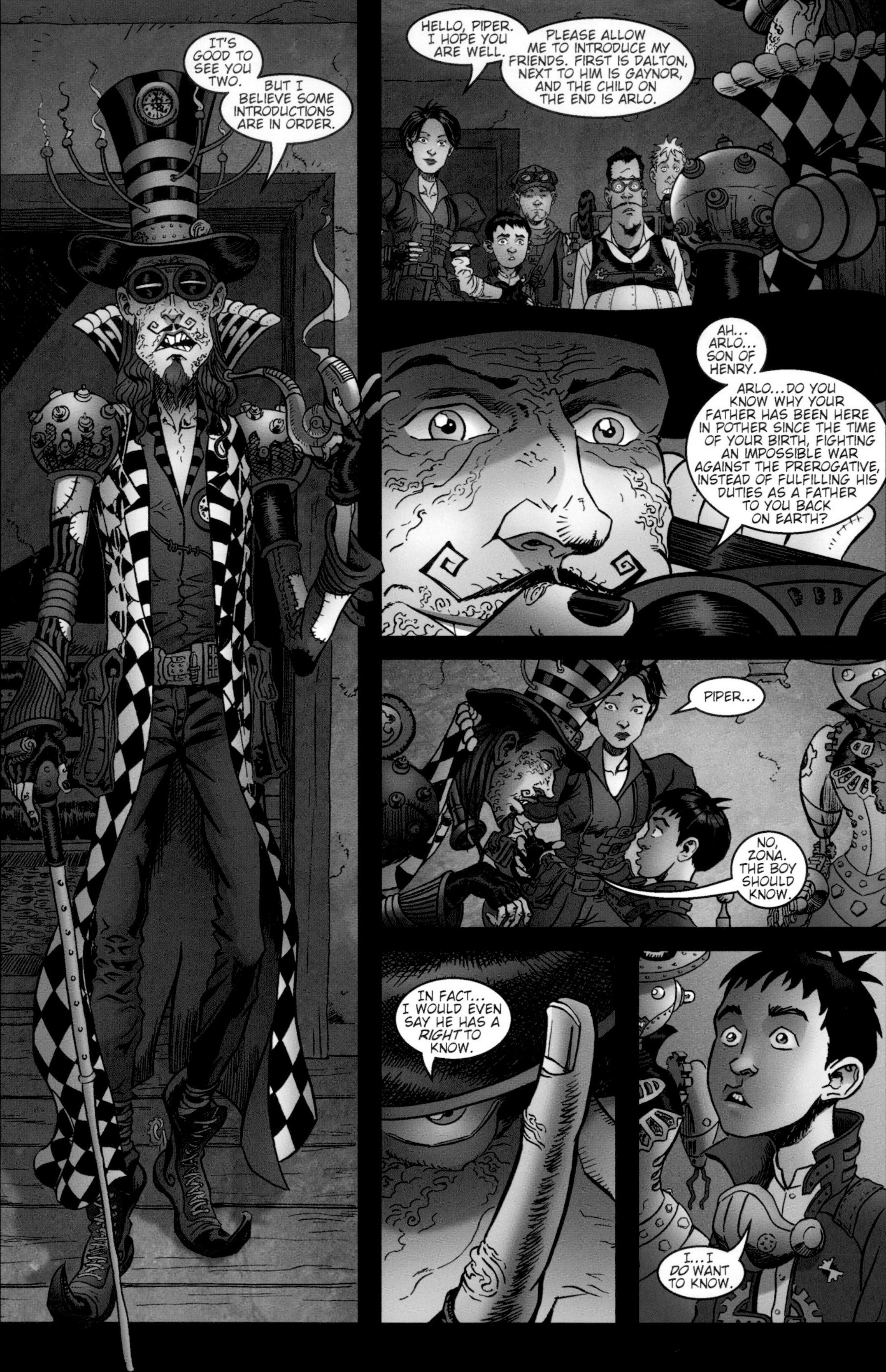
IT'S GOOD TO SEE YOU TWO.
BUT I BELIEVE SOME INTRODUCTIONS ARE IN ORDER.
HELLO, PIPER. I HOPE YOU ARE WELL.
PLEASE ALLOW ME TO INTRODUCE MY FRIENDS. FIRST IS DALTON, NEXT TO HIM IS GAYNOR, AND THE CHILD ON THE END IS ARLO.
AH... ARLO... SON OF HENRY.
ARLO...DO YOU KNOW WHY YOUR FATHER HAS BEEN HERE IN POTHER SINCE THE TIME OF YOUR BIRTH, FIGHTING AN IMPOSSIBLE WAR AGAINST THE PREROGATIVE, INSTEAD OF FULFILLING HIS DUTIES AS A FATHER TO YOU BACK ON EARTH?
PIPER...
NO, ZONA. THE BOY SHOULD KNOW.
IN FACT... I WOULD EVEN SAY HE HAS A RIGHT TO KNOW.
I...I DO WANT TO KNOW.

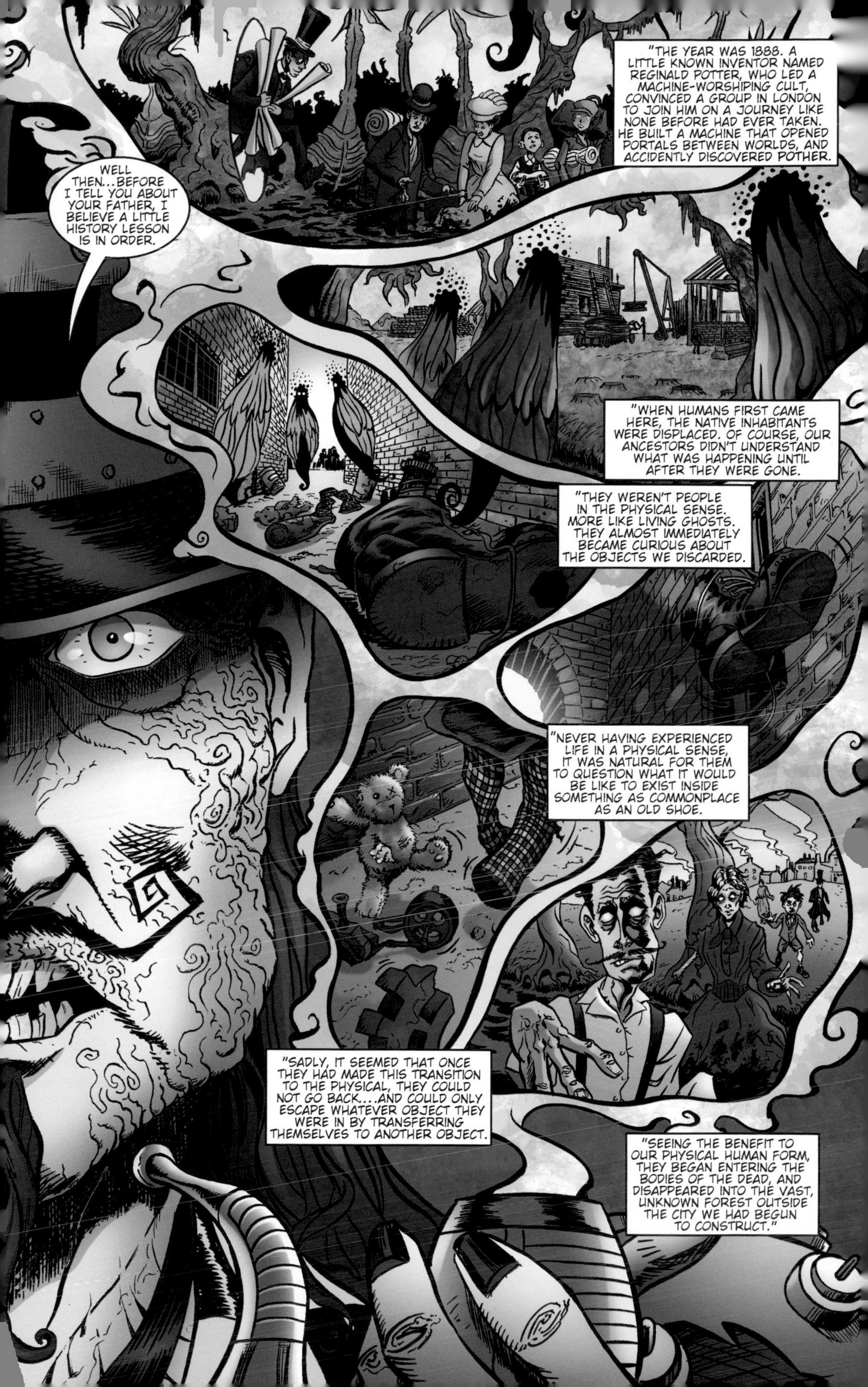
WELL THEN...BEFORE I TELL YOU ABOUT YOUR FATHER, I BELIEVE A LITTLE HISTORY LESSON IS IN ORDER.
"THE YEAR WAS 1888. A LITTLE KNOWN INVENTOR NAMED REGINALD POTTER, WHO LED A MACHINE-WORSHIPING CULT, CONVINCED A GROUP IN LONDON TO JOIN HIM ON A JOURNEY LIKE NONE BEFORE HAD EVER TAKEN. HE BUILT A MACHINE THAT OPENED PORTALS BETWEEN WORLDS, AND ACCIDENTLY DISCOVERED POTHER.
"WHEN HUMANS FIRST CAME HERE, THE NATIVE INHABITANTS WERE DISPLACED. OF COURSE, OUR ANCESTORS DIDN'T UNDERSTAND WHAT WAS HAPPENING UNTIL AFTER THEY WERE GONE.
"THEY WEREN'T PEOPLE IN THE PHYSICAL SENSE. MORE LIKE LIVING GHOSTS. THEY ALMOST IMMEDIATELY BECAME CURIOUS ABOUT THE OBJECTS WE DISCARDED.
"NEVER HAVING EXPERIENCED LIFE IN A PHYSICAL SENSE, IT WAS NATURAL FOR THEM TO QUESTION WHAT IT WOULD BE LIKE TO EXIST INSIDE SOMETHING AS COMMONPLACE AS AN OLD SHOE.
"SADLY, IT SEEMED THAT ONCE THEY HAD MADE THIS TRANSITION TO THE PHYSICAL, THEY COULD NOT GO BACK...AND COULD ONLY ESCAPE WHATEVER OBJECT THEY WERE IN BY TRANSFERRING THEMSELVES TO ANOTHER OBJECT.
"SEEING THE BENEFIT TO OUR PHYSICAL HUMAN FORM, THEY BEGAN ENTERING THE BODIES OF THE DEAD, AND DISAPPEARED INTO THE VAST, UNKNOWN FOREST OUTSIDE THE CITY WE HAD BEGUN TO CONSTRUCT."

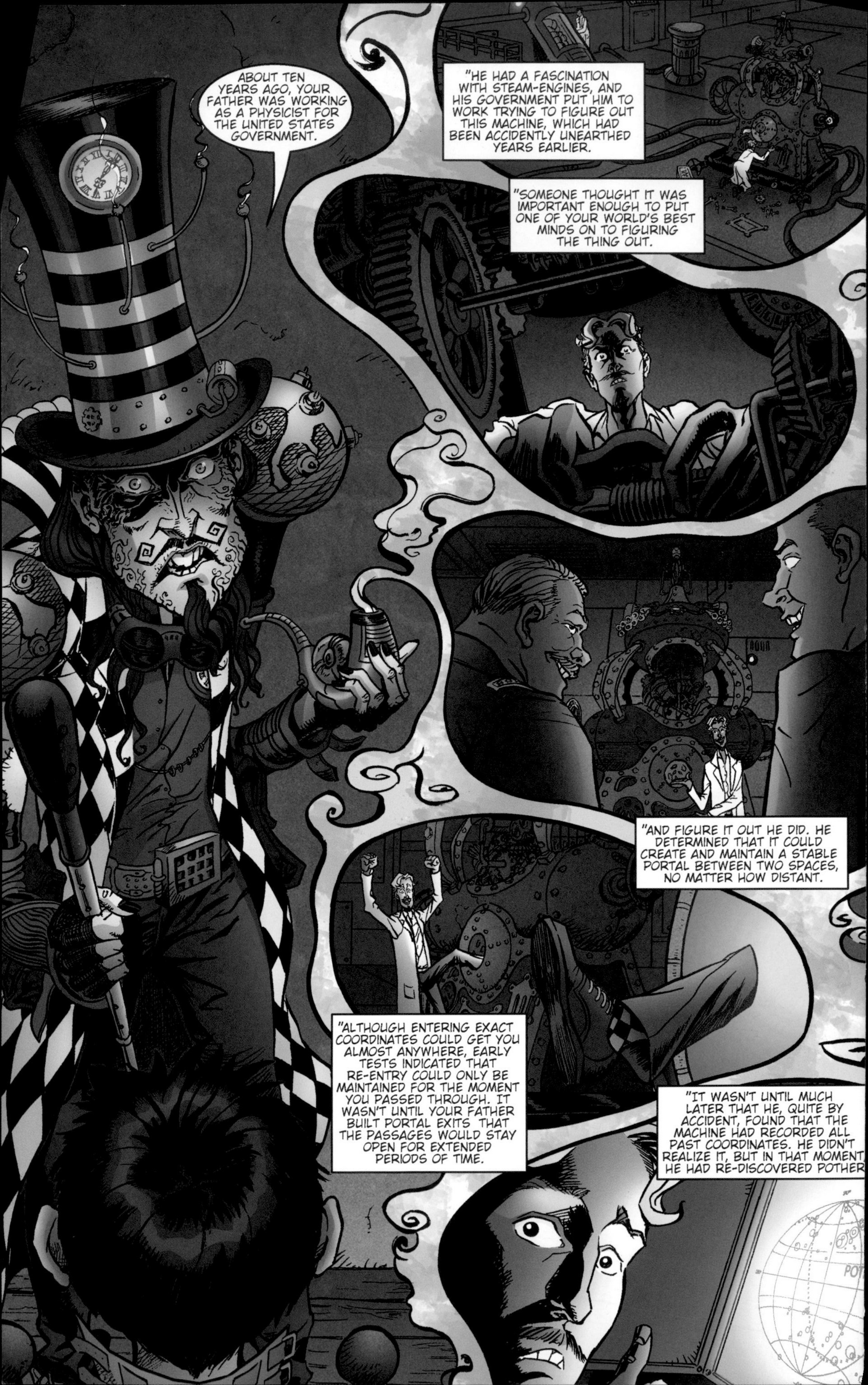
ABOUT TEN YEARS AGO, YOUR FATHER WAS WORKING AS A PHYSICIST FOR THE UNITED STATES GOVERNMENT.
"HE HAD A FASCINATION WITH STEAM-ENGINES, AND HIS GOVERNMENT PUT HIM TO WORK TRYING TO FIGURE OUT THIS MACHINE, WHICH HAD BEEN ACCIDENTLY UNEARTHED YEARS EARLIER.
"SOMEONE THOUGHT IT WAS IMPORTANT ENOUGH TO PUT ONE OF YOUR WORLD'S BEST MINDS ON TO FIGURING THE THING OUT.
"AND FIGURE IT OUT HE DID. HE DETERMINED THAT IT COULD CREATE AND MAINTAIN A STABLE PORTAL BETWEEN TWO SPACES, NO MATTER HOW DISTANT.
"ALTHOUGH ENTERING EXACT COORDINATES COULD GET YOU ALMOST ANYWHERE, EARLY TESTS INDICATED THAT RE-ENTRY COULD ONLY BE MAINTAINED FOR THE MOMENT YOU PASSED THROUGH. IT WASN'T UNTIL YOUR FATHER BUILT PORTAL EXITS THAT THE PASSAGES WOULD STAY OPEN FOR EXTENDED PERIODS OF TIME.
"IT WASN'T UNTIL MUCH LATER THAT HE, QUITE BY ACCIDENT, FOUND THAT THE MACHINE HAD RECORDED ALL PAST COORDINATES. HE DIDN'T REALIZE IT, BUT IN THAT MOMENT HE HAD RE-DISCOVERED POTHER

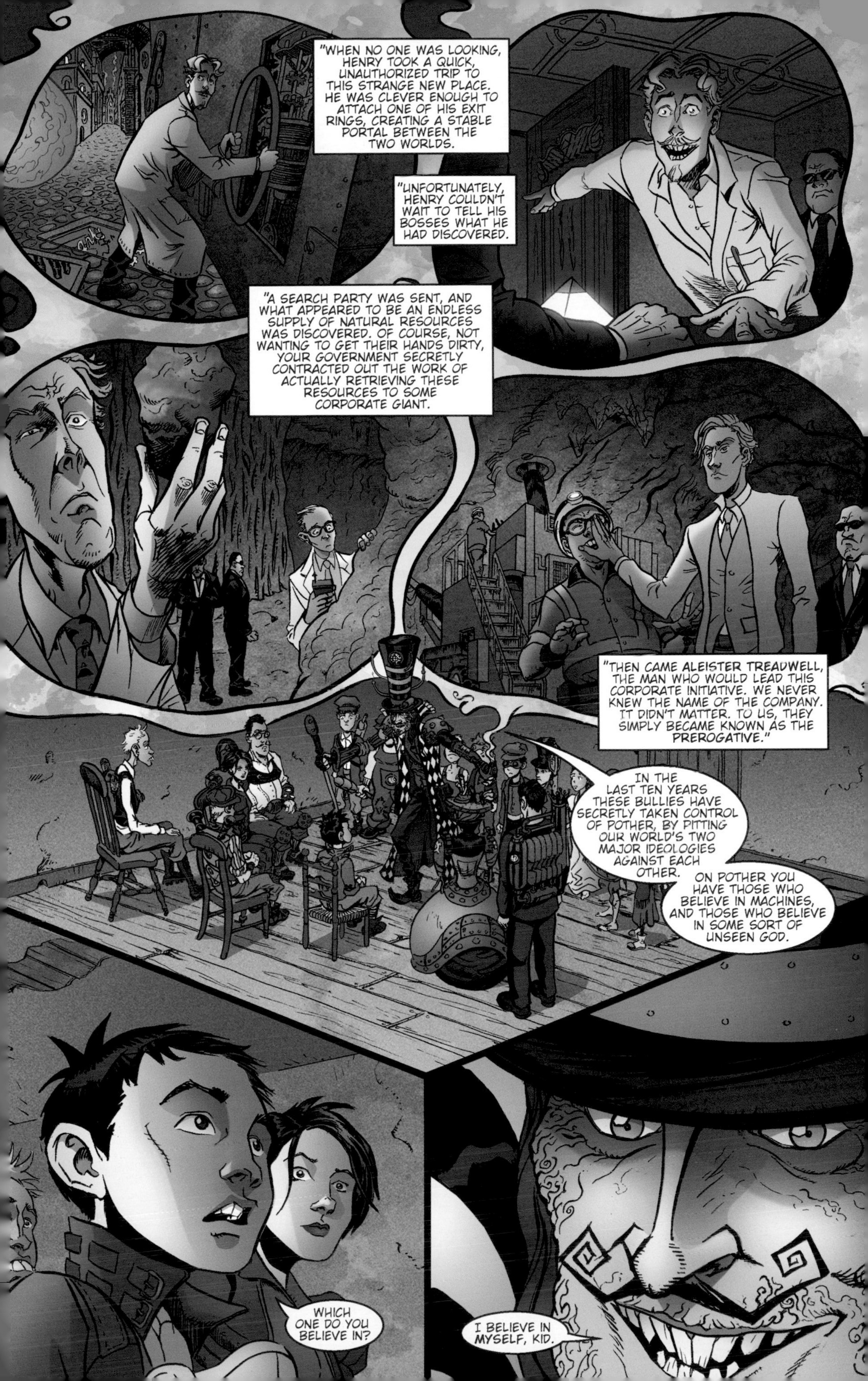
"WHEN NO ONE WAS LOOKING, HENRY TOOK A QUICK, UNAUTHORIZED TRIP TO THIS STRANGE NEW PLACE. HE WAS CLEVER ENOUGH TO ATTACH ONE OF HIS EXIT RINGS, CREATING A STABLE PORTAL BETWEEN THE TWO WORLDS.
"UNFORTUNATELY, HENRY COULDN'T WAIT TO TELL HIS BOSSES WHAT HE HAD DISCOVERED.
"A SEARCH PARTY WAS SENT, AND WHAT APPEARED TO BE AN ENDLESS SUPPLY OF NATURAL RESOURCES WAS DISCOVERED. OF COURSE, NOT WANTING TO GET THEIR HANDS DIRTY, YOUR GOVERNMENT SECRETLY CONTRACTED OUT THE WORK OF ACTUALLY RETRIEVING THESE RESOURCES TO SOME CORPORATE GIANT.
"THEN CAME ALEISTER TREADWELL, THE MAN WHO WOULD LEAD THIS CORPORATE INITIATIVE. WE NEVER KNEW THE NAME OF THE COMPANY. IT DIDN'T MATTER. TO US, THEY SIMPLY BECAME KNOWN AS THE PREROGATIVE."
IN THE LAST TEN YEARS THESE BULLIES HAVE SECRETLY TAKEN CONTROL OF POTHER, BY PITTING OUR WORLD'S TWO MAJOR IDEOLOGIES AGAINST EACH OTHER.
ON POTHER YOU HAVE THOSE WHO BELIEVE IN MACHINES, AND THOSE WHO BELIEVE IN SOME SORT OF UNSEEN GOD.
WHICH ONE DO YOU BELIEVE IN?
I BELIEVE IN MYSELF, KID.

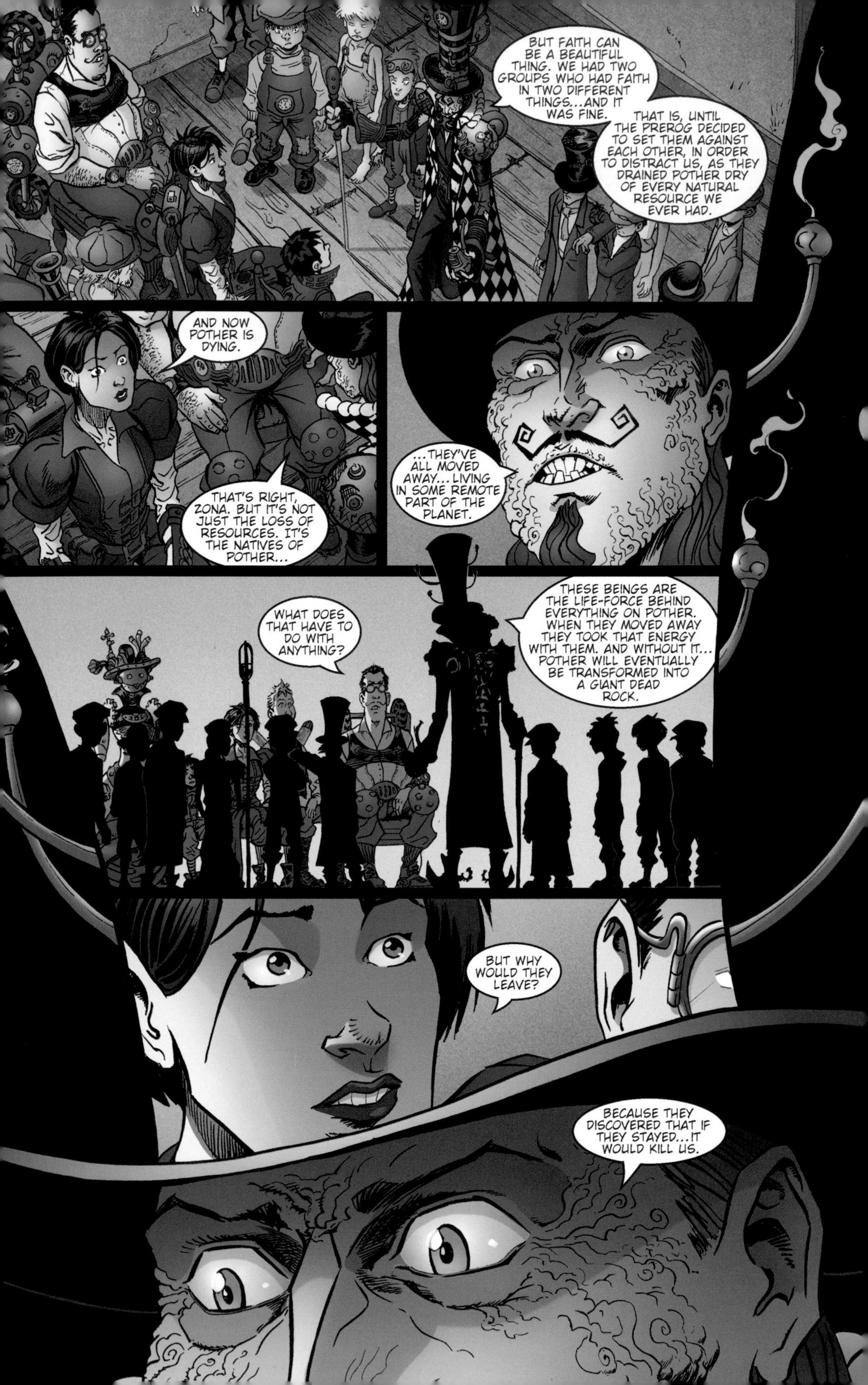
BUT FAITH CAN BE A BEAUTIFUL THING. WE HAD TWO GROUPS WHO HAD FAITH IN TWO DIFFERENT THINGS...AND IT WAS FINE.
THAT IS, UNTIL THE PREROG DECIDED TO SET THEM AGAINST EACH OTHER, IN ORDER TO DISTRACT US, AS THEY DRAINED POTHER DRY OF EVERY NATURAL RESOURCE WE EVER HAD.
AND NOW POTHER IS DYING.
THAT'S RIGHT, ZONA. BUT IT'S NOT JUST THE LOSS OF RESOURCES. IT'S THE NATIVES OF POTHER...
...THEY'VE ALL MOVED AWAY... LIVING IN SOME REMOTE PART OF THE PLANET.
WHAT DOES THAT HAVE TO DO WITH ANYTHING?
THESE BEINGS ARE THE LIFE-FORCE BEHIND EVERYTHING ON POTHER. WHEN THEY MOVED AWAY THEY TOOK THAT ENERGY WITH THEM. AND WITHOUT IT... POTHER WILL EVENTUALLY BE TRANSFORMED INTO A GIANT DEAD ROCK.
BUT WHY WOULD THEY LEAVE?
BECAUSE THEY DISCOVERED THAT IF THEY STAYED... IT WOULD KILL US.

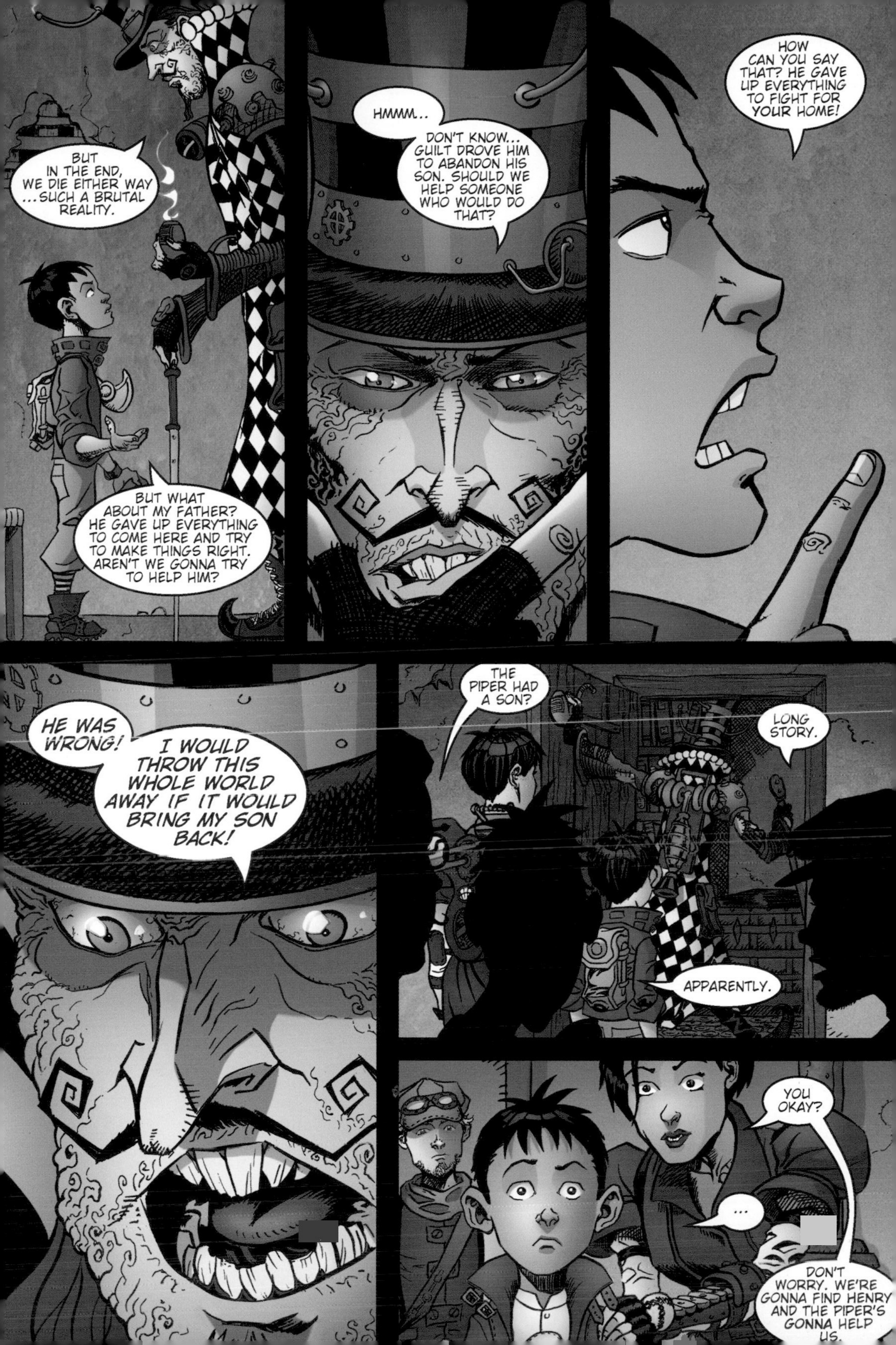
BUT IN THE END, WE DIE EITHER WAY ...SUCH A BRUTAL REALITY.
BUT WHAT ABOUT MY FATHER? HE GAVE UP EVERYTHING TO COME HERE AND TRY TO MAKE THINGS RIGHT. AREN'T WE GONNA TRY TO HELP HIM?
HMMM...
DON'T KNOW... GUILT DROVE HIM TO ABANDON HIS SON. SHOULD WE HELP SOMEONE WHO WOULD DO THAT?
HOW CAN YOU SAY THAT? HE GAVE UP EVERYTHING TO FIGHT FOR YOUR HOME!
HE WAS WRONG!
I WOULD THROW THIS WHOLE WORLD AWAY IF IT WOULD BRING MY SON BACK!
THE PIPER HAD A SON?
LONG STORY.
APPARENTLY.
YOU OKAY?
...
DON'T WORRY. WE'RE GONNA FIND HENRY AND THE PIPER'S GONNA HELP US.

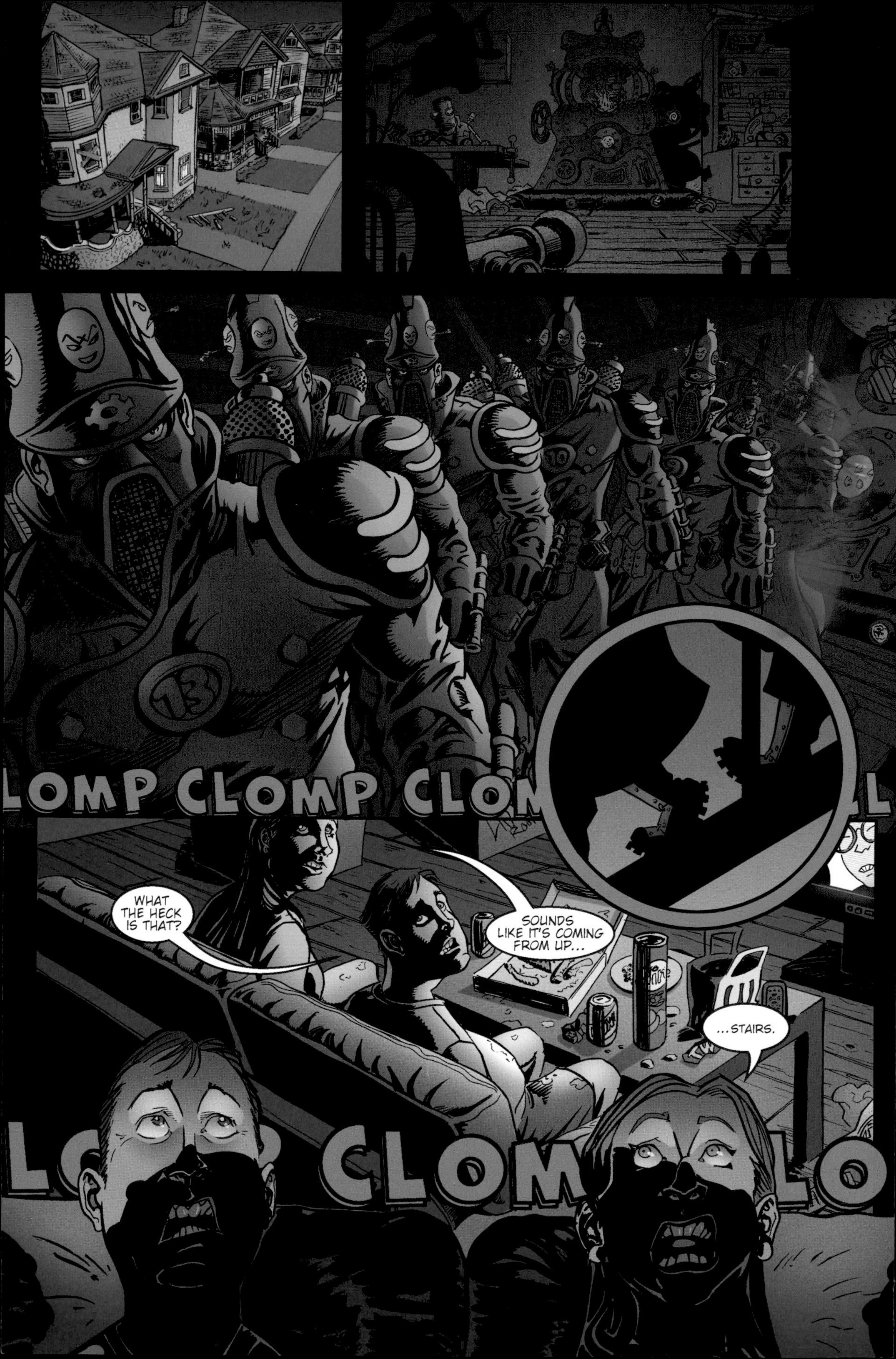
LOMP CLOMP CLOM
WHAT THE HECK IS THAT?
SOUNDS LIKE IT'S COMING FROM UP...
...STAIRS.
CLOM

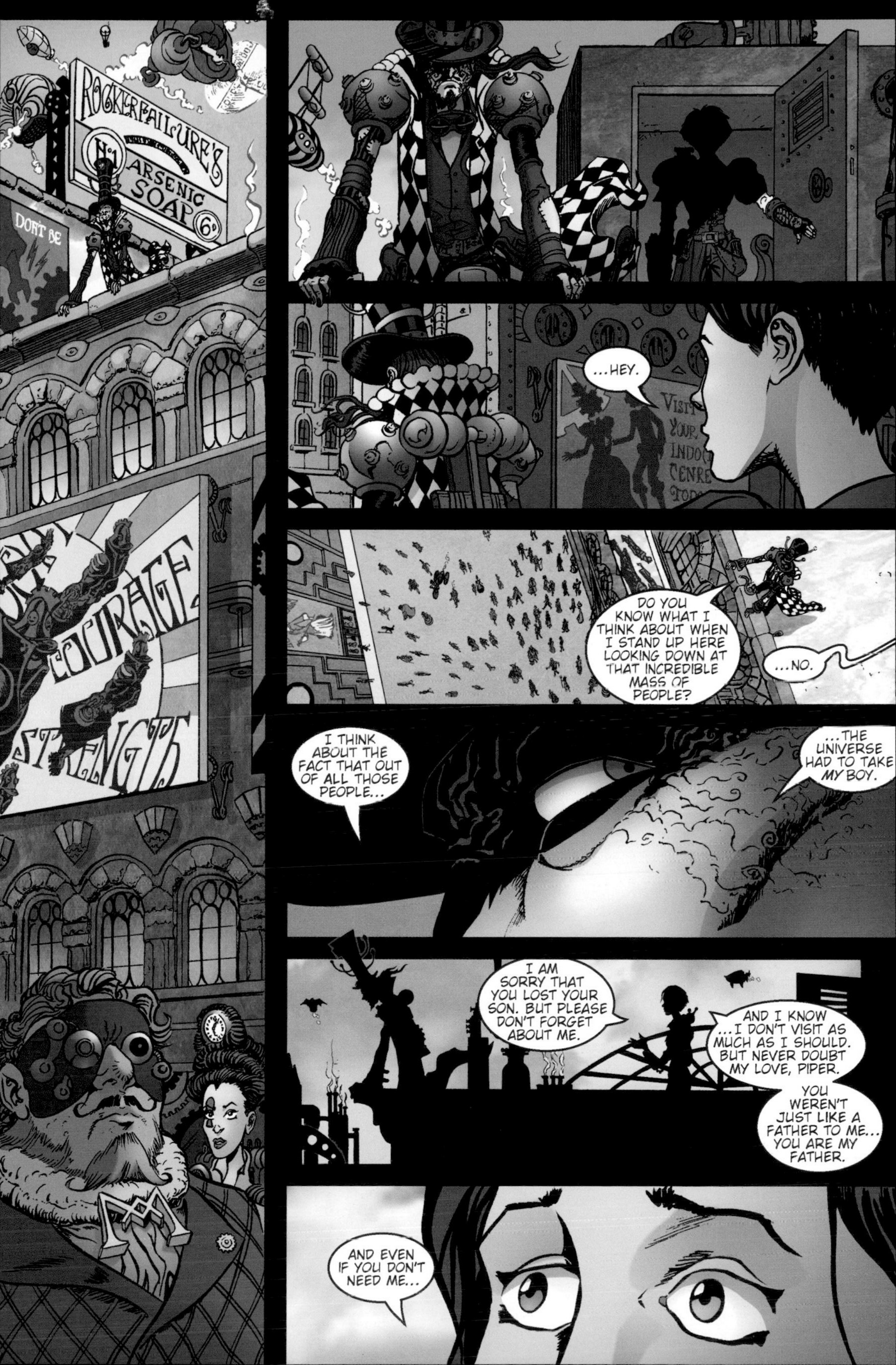

ROCKERFAILURE'S
Nº1
ARSENIC
SOAP
6D
DON'T BE
COURAGE
STRENGTH
...HEY.
VISIT
YOUR
INDO
CENTRE
DO YOU KNOW WHAT I THINK ABOUT WHEN I STAND UP HERE LOOKING DOWN AT THAT INCREDIBLE MASS OF PEOPLE?
...NO.
I THINK ABOUT THE FACT THAT OUT OF ALL THOSE PEOPLE...
...THE UNIVERSE HAD TO TAKE MY BOY.
I AM SORRY THAT YOU LOST YOUR SON. BUT PLEASE DON'T FORGET ABOUT ME.
AND I KNOW ...I DON'T VISIT AS MUCH AS I SHOULD. BUT NEVER DOUBT MY LOVE, PIPER.
YOU WEREN'T JUST LIKE A FATHER TO ME... YOU ARE MY FATHER.
AND EVEN IF YOU DON'T NEED ME...

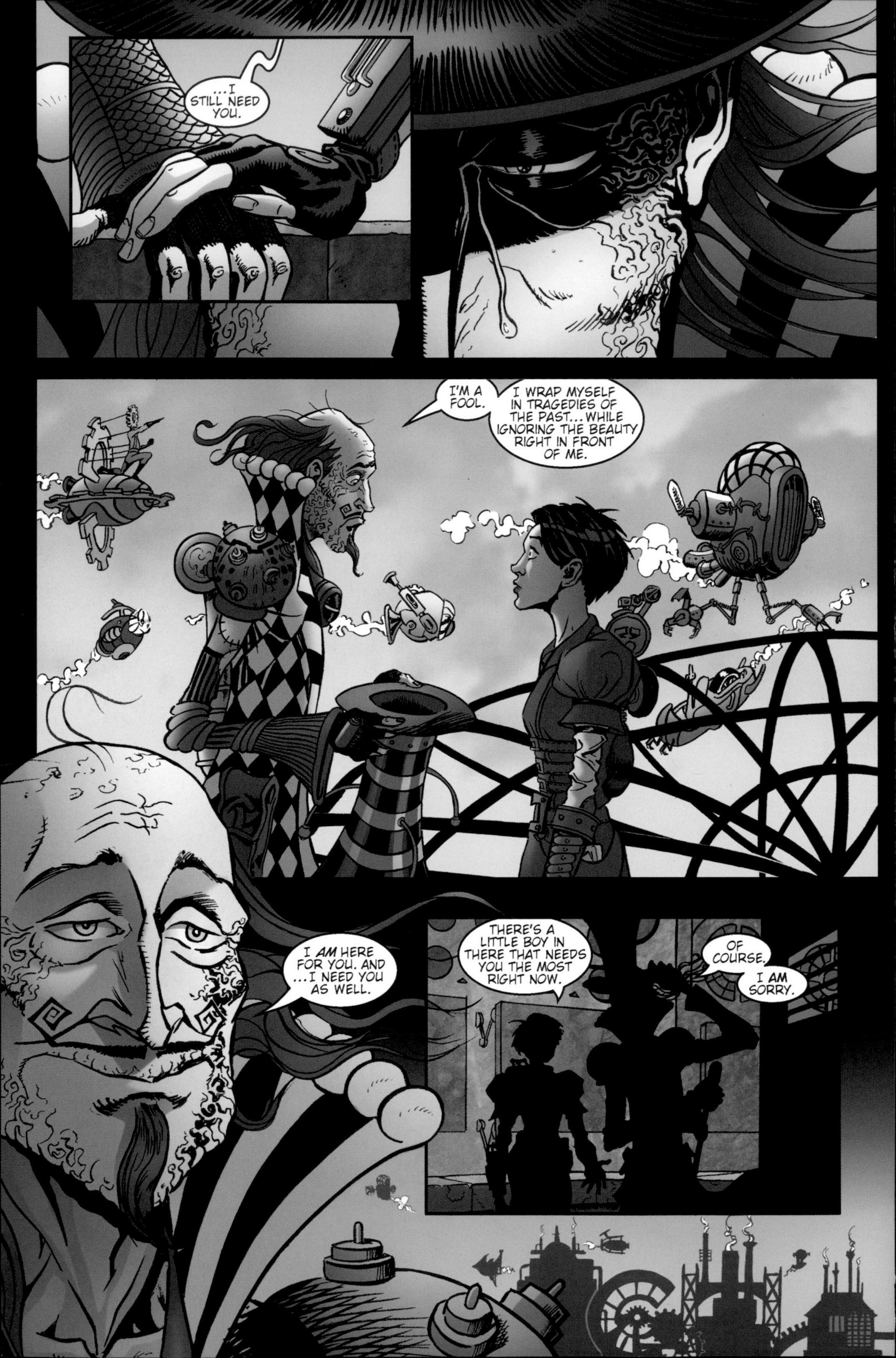
...I STILL NEED YOU.
I'M A FOOL.
I WRAP MYSELF IN TRAGEDIES OF THE PAST... WHILE IGNORING THE BEAUTY RIGHT IN FRONT OF ME.
I *AM* HERE FOR YOU. AND ...I NEED YOU AS WELL.
THERE'S A LITTLE BOY IN THERE THAT NEEDS YOU THE MOST RIGHT NOW.
OF COURSE.
I *AM* SORRY.

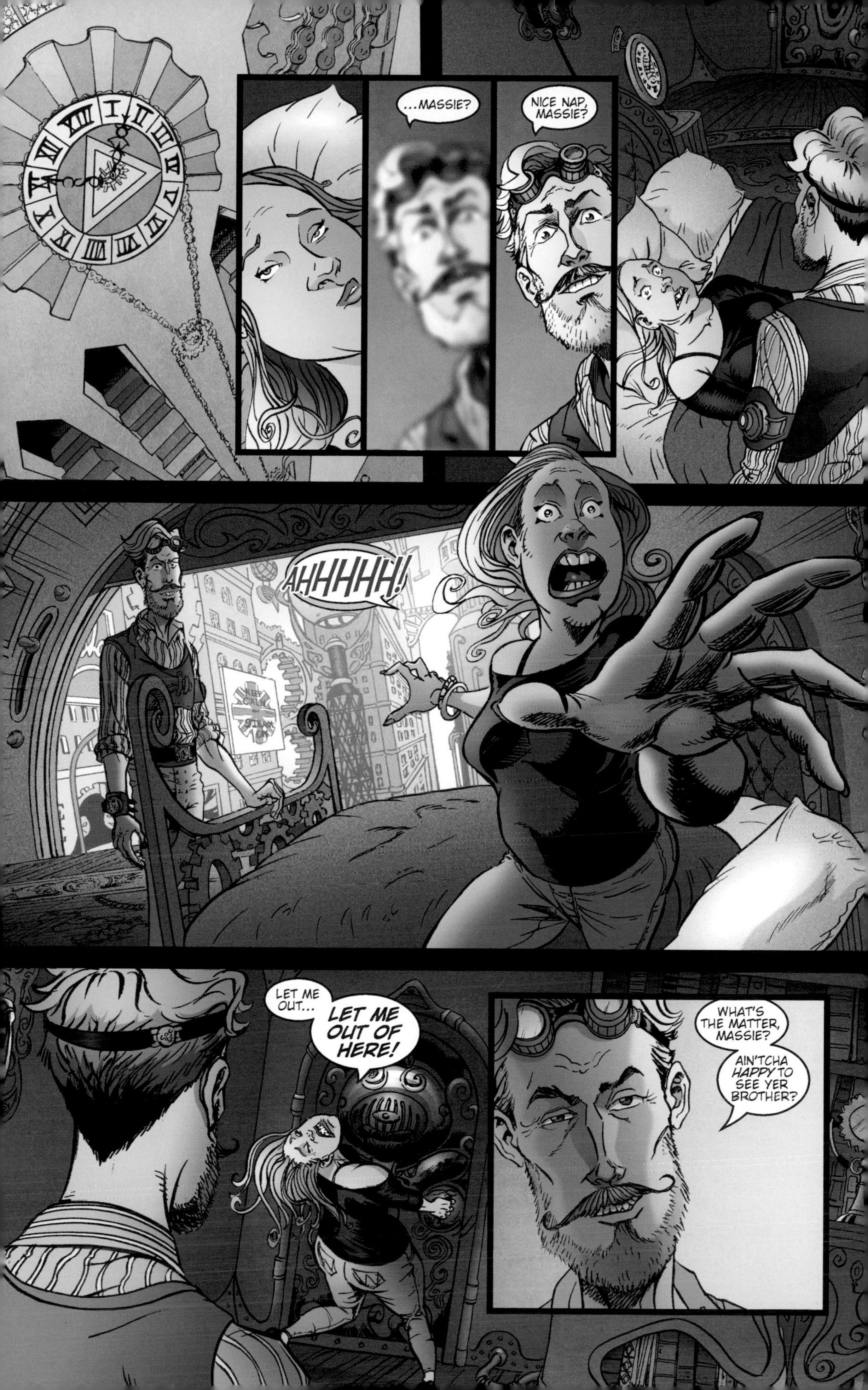
...MASSIE?
NICE NAP, MASSIE?
AHHHHH!
LET ME OUT...
LET ME OUT OF HERE!
WHAT'S THE MATTER, MASSIE?
AIN'TCHA HAPPY TO SEE YER BROTHER?

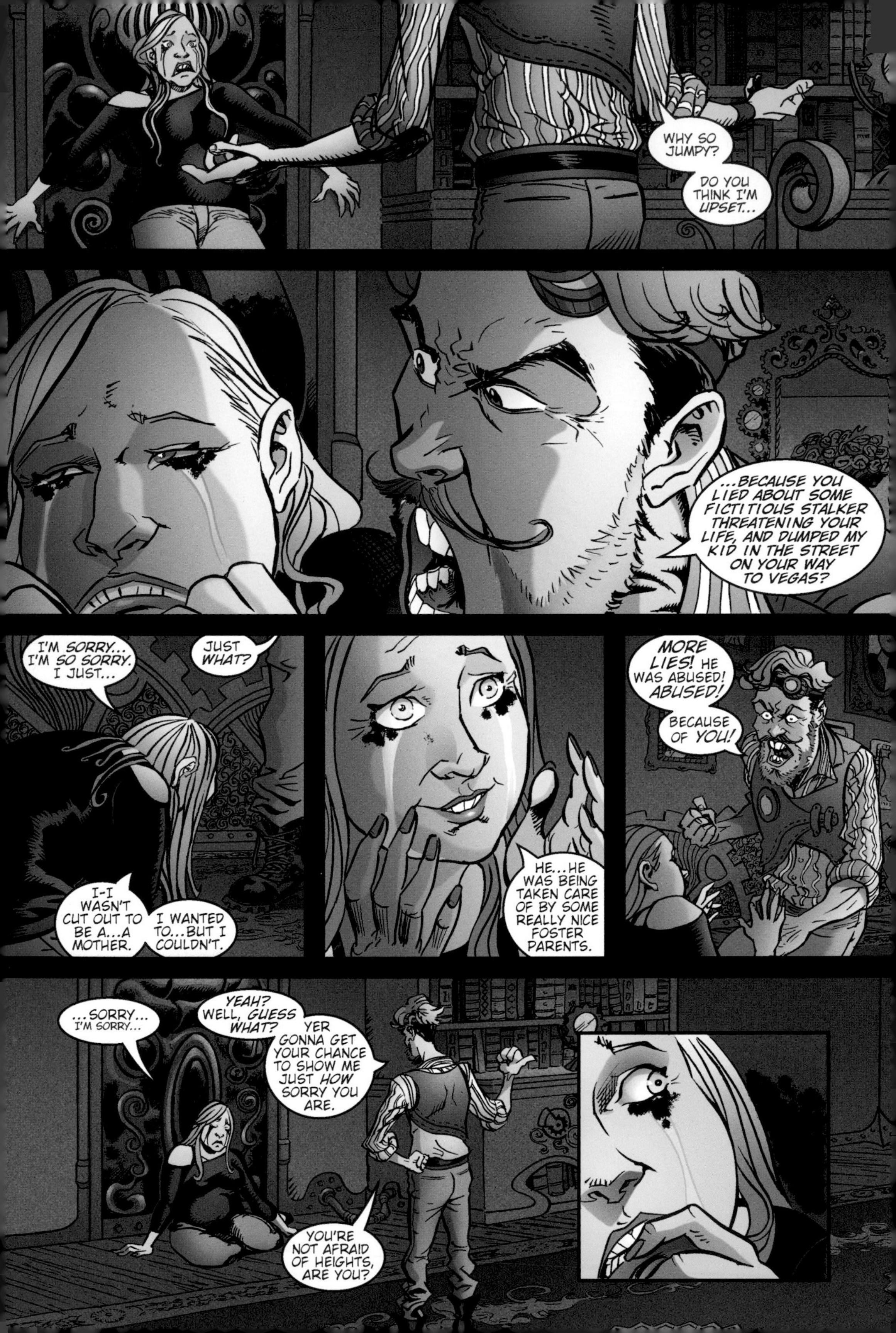
WHY SO JUMPY?
DO YOU THINK I'M *UPSET*...
...BECAUSE YOU LIED ABOUT SOME FICTITIOUS STALKER THREATENING YOUR LIFE, AND DUMPED MY KID IN THE STREET ON YOUR WAY TO VEGAS?
I'M *SORRY*... I'M *SO SORRY*. I JUST...
JUST *WHAT?*
I-I WASN'T CUT OUT TO BE A...A MOTHER.
I WANTED TO...BUT I COULDN'T.
HE...HE WAS BEING TAKEN CARE OF BY SOME REALLY NICE FOSTER PARENTS.
MORE LIES! HE WAS ABUSED! *ABUSED!*
BECAUSE OF *YOU!*
...SORRY... I'M SORRY...
YEAH? WELL, *GUESS WHAT?*
YER GONNA GET YOUR CHANCE TO SHOW ME JUST *HOW* SORRY YOU ARE.
YOU'RE NOT AFRAID OF HEIGHTS, ARE YOU?

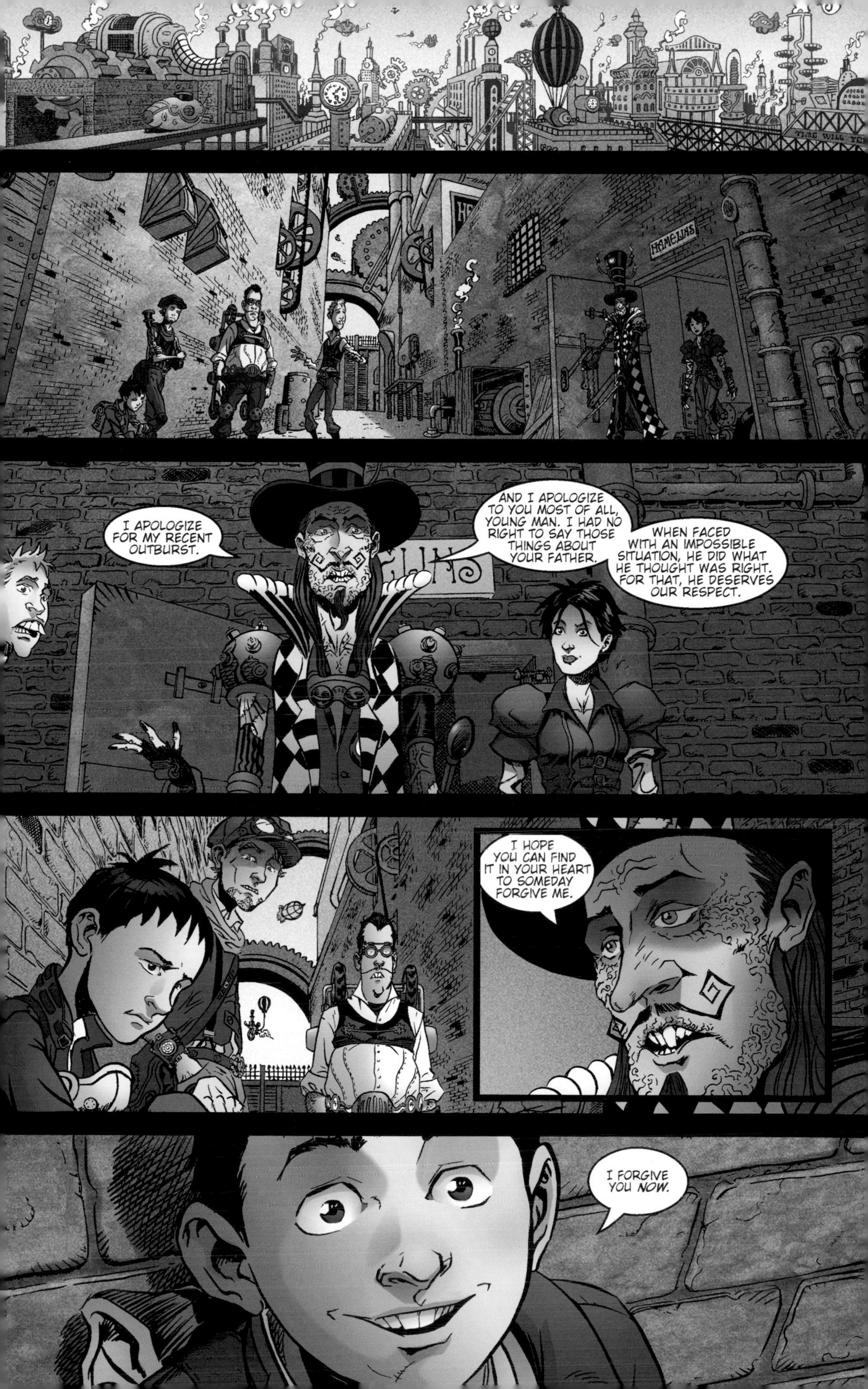
TIME WILL TE
HAMELINS
I APOLOGIZE FOR MY RECENT OUTBURST.
AND I APOLOGIZE TO YOU MOST OF ALL, YOUNG MAN. I HAD NO RIGHT TO SAY THOSE THINGS ABOUT YOUR FATHER.
WHEN FACED WITH AN IMPOSSIBLE SITUATION, HE DID WHAT HE THOUGHT WAS RIGHT. FOR THAT, HE DESERVES OUR RESPECT.
I HOPE YOU CAN FIND IT IN YOUR HEART TO SOMEDAY FORGIVE ME.
I FORGIVE YOU *NOW*.

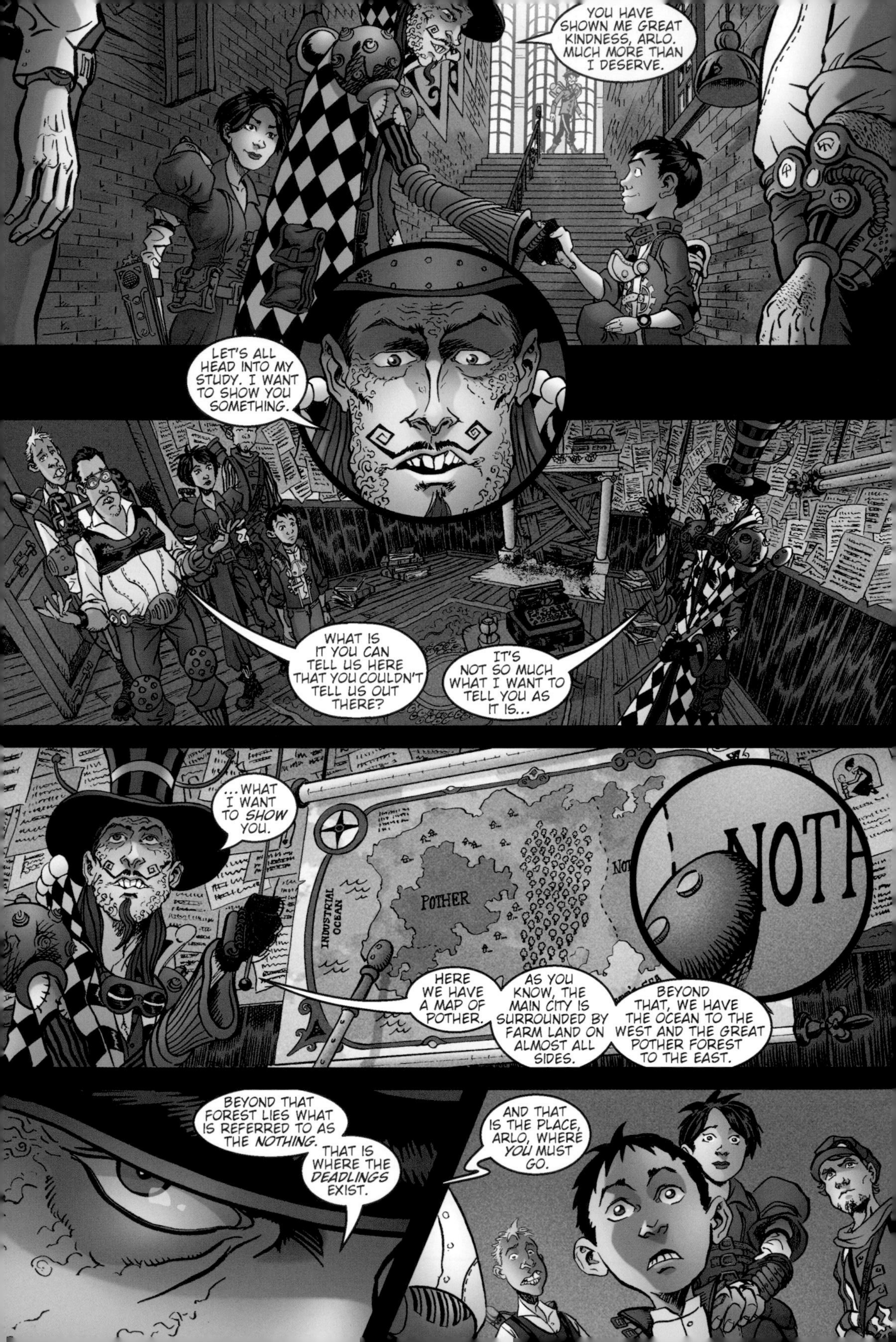
YOU HAVE SHOWN ME GREAT KINDNESS, ARLO. MUCH MORE THAN I DESERVE.
LET'S ALL HEAD INTO MY STUDY. I WANT TO SHOW YOU SOMETHING.
WHAT IS IT YOU CAN TELL US HERE THAT YOU COULDN'T TELL US OUT THERE?
IT'S NOT SO MUCH WHAT I WANT TO TELL YOU AS IT IS...
...WHAT I WANT TO SHOW YOU.
POTHER
INDUSTRIAL OCEAN
NOTH
HERE WE HAVE A MAP OF POTHER.
AS YOU KNOW, THE MAIN CITY IS SURROUNDED BY FARM LAND ON ALMOST ALL SIDES.
BEYOND THAT, WE HAVE THE OCEAN TO THE WEST AND THE GREAT POTHER FOREST TO THE EAST.
BEYOND THAT FOREST LIES WHAT IS REFERRED TO AS THE NOTHING.
THAT IS WHERE THE DEADLINGS EXIST.
AND THAT IS THE PLACE, ARLO, WHERE YOU MUST GO.

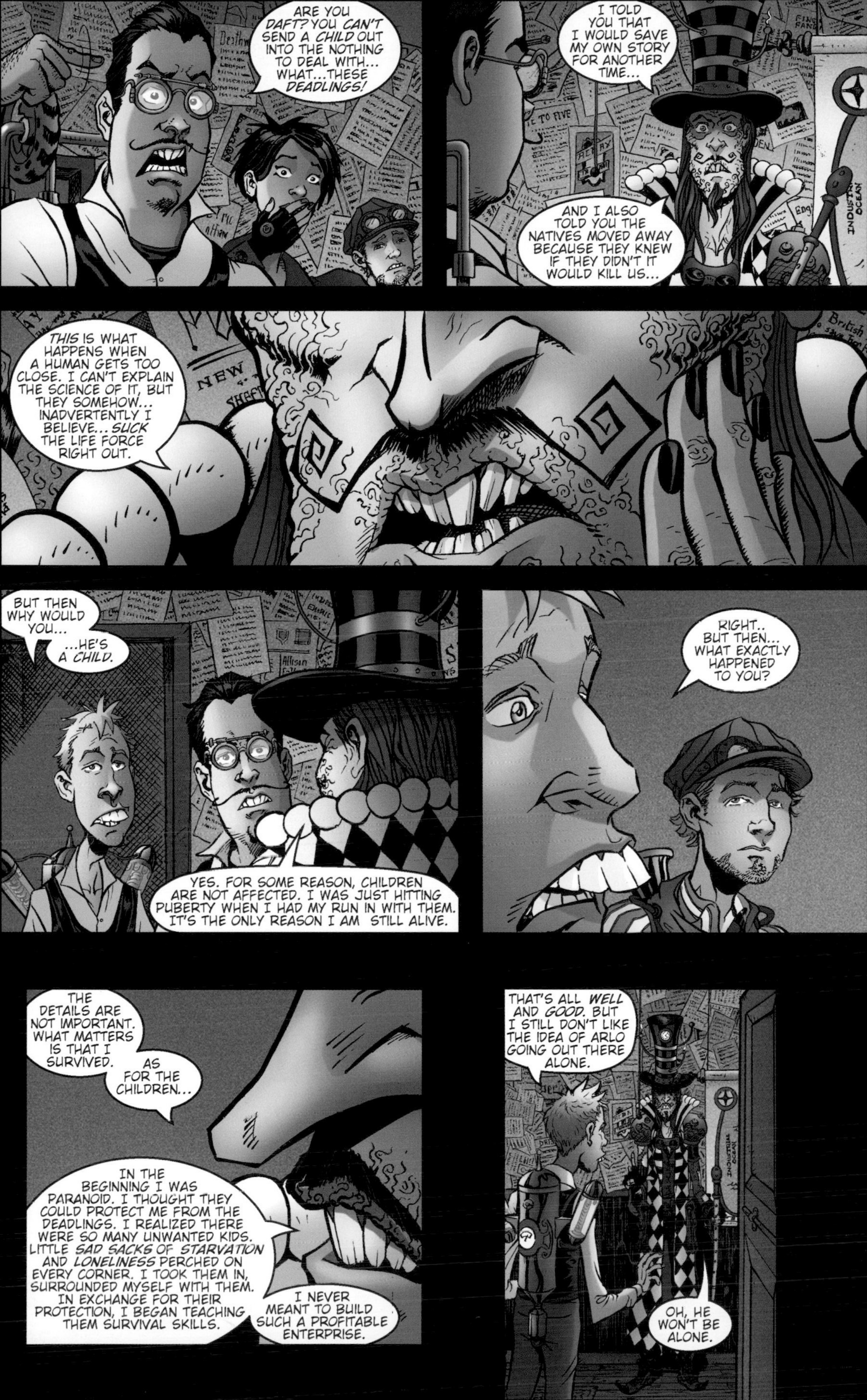
ARE YOU DAFT? YOU CAN'T SEND A CHILD OUT INTO THE NOTHING TO DEAL WITH... WHAT...THESE DEADLINGS!
I TOLD YOU THAT I WOULD SAVE MY OWN STORY FOR ANOTHER TIME...
AND I ALSO TOLD YOU THE NATIVES MOVED AWAY BECAUSE THEY KNEW IF THEY DIDN'T IT WOULD KILL US...
INDUSTRIAL OCEAN
THIS IS WHAT HAPPENS WHEN A HUMAN GETS TOO CLOSE. I CAN'T EXPLAIN THE SCIENCE OF IT, BUT THEY SOMEHOW... INADVERTENTLY I BELIEVE... SUCK THE LIFE FORCE RIGHT OUT.
BUT THEN WHY WOULD YOU...
...HE'S A CHILD.
YES. FOR SOME REASON, CHILDREN ARE NOT AFFECTED. I WAS JUST HITTING PUBERTY WHEN I HAD MY RUN IN WITH THEM. IT'S THE ONLY REASON I AM STILL ALIVE.
RIGHT.. BUT THEN... WHAT EXACTLY HAPPENED TO YOU?
THE DETAILS ARE NOT IMPORTANT. WHAT MATTERS IS THAT I SURVIVED.
AS FOR THE CHILDREN...
IN THE BEGINNING I WAS PARANOID. I THOUGHT THEY COULD PROTECT ME FROM THE DEADLINGS. I REALIZED THERE WERE SO MANY UNWANTED KIDS. LITTLE SAD SACKS OF STARVATION AND LONELINESS PERCHED ON EVERY CORNER. I TOOK THEM IN, SURROUNDED MYSELF WITH THEM. IN EXCHANGE FOR THEIR PROTECTION, I BEGAN TEACHING THEM SURVIVAL SKILLS.
I NEVER MEANT TO BUILD SUCH A PROFITABLE ENTERPRISE.
THAT'S ALL WELL AND GOOD. BUT I STILL DON'T LIKE THE IDEA OF ARLO GOING OUT THERE ALONE.
OH, HE WON'T BE ALONE.

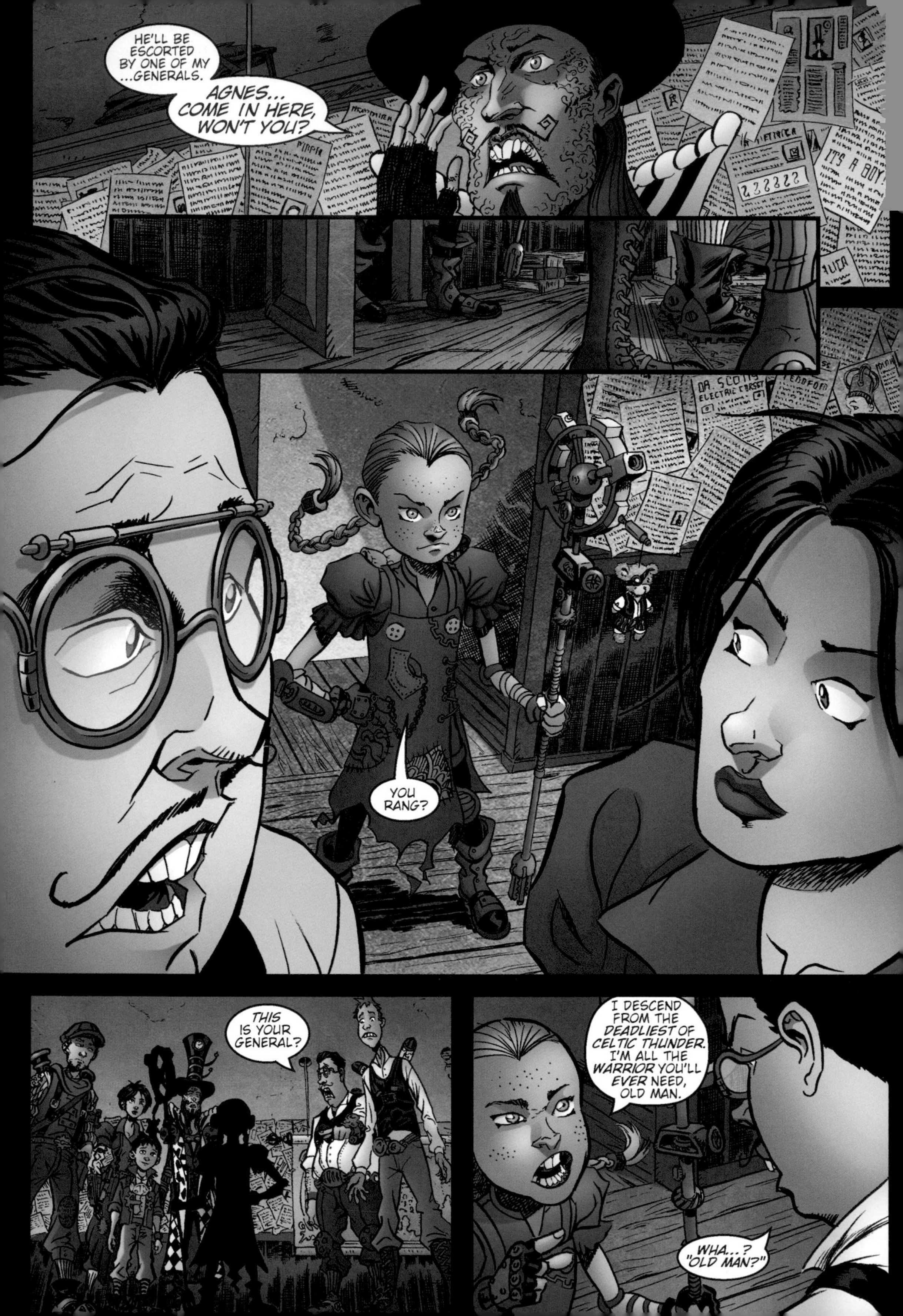
HE'LL BE ESCORTED BY ONE OF MY ...GENERALS.
AGNES... COME IN HERE, WON'T YOU?
YOU RANG?
THIS IS YOUR GENERAL?
I DESCEND FROM THE DEADLIEST OF CELTIC THUNDER. I'M ALL THE WARRIOR YOU'LL EVER NEED, OLD MAN.
WHA...? "OLD MAN?"
IT'S A BOY!
DR. SCOTT'S ELECTRIC CORSET

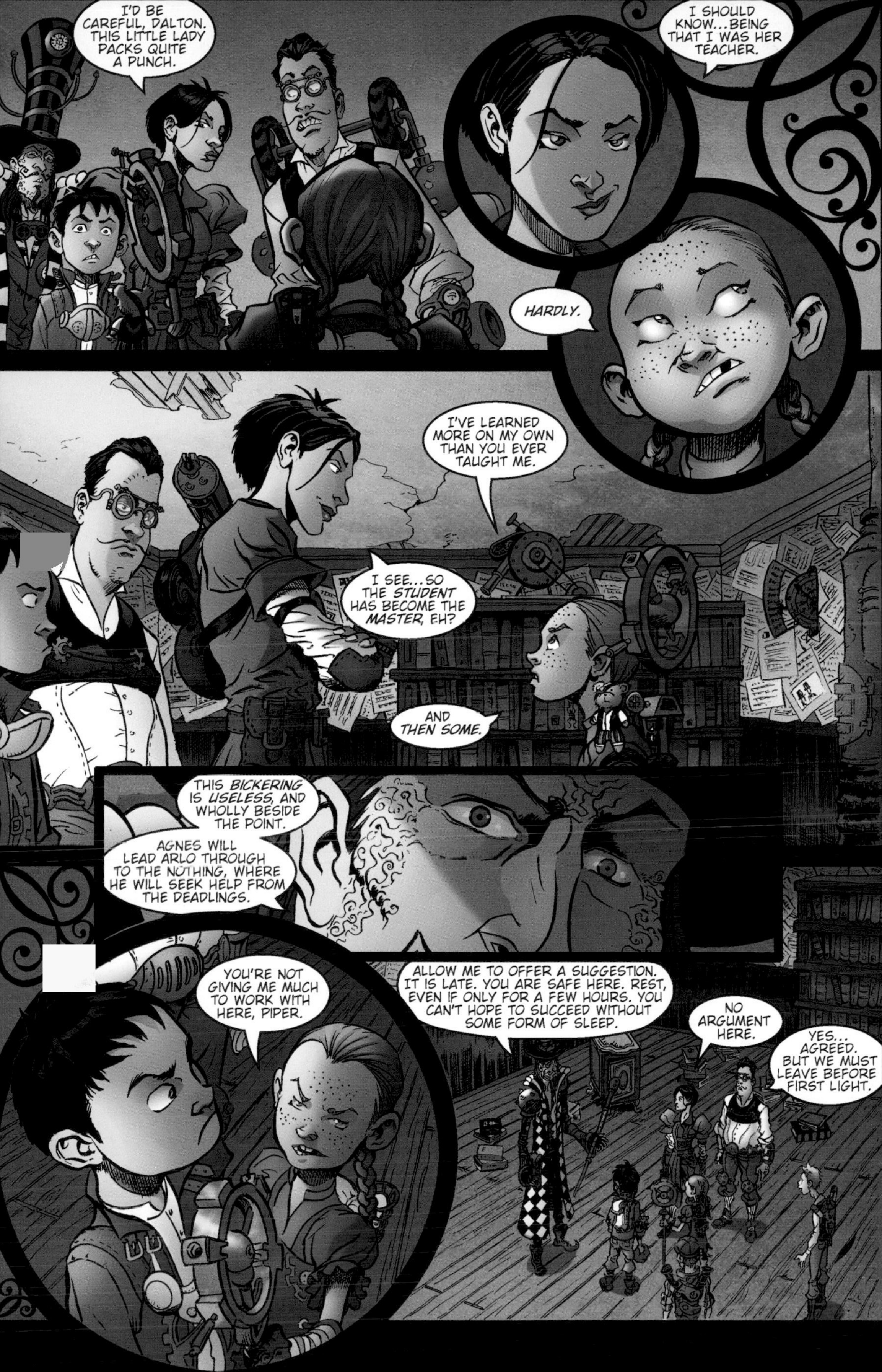
I'D BE CAREFUL, DALTON. THIS LITTLE LADY PACKS QUITE A PUNCH.
I SHOULD KNOW...BEING THAT I WAS HER TEACHER.
HARDLY.
I'VE LEARNED MORE ON MY OWN THAN YOU EVER TAUGHT ME.
I SEE...SO THE STUDENT HAS BECOME THE MASTER, EH?
AND THEN SOME.
THIS BICKERING IS USELESS, AND WHOLLY BESIDE THE POINT.
AGNES WILL LEAD ARLO THROUGH TO THE NOTHING, WHERE HE WILL SEEK HELP FROM THE DEADLINGS.
YOU'RE NOT GIVING ME MUCH TO WORK WITH HERE, PIPER.
ALLOW ME TO OFFER A SUGGESTION. IT IS LATE. YOU ARE SAFE HERE. REST, EVEN IF ONLY FOR A FEW HOURS. YOU CAN'T HOPE TO SUCCEED WITHOUT SOME FORM OF SLEEP.
NO ARGUMENT HERE.
YES... AGREED. BUT WE MUST LEAVE BEFORE FIRST LIGHT.

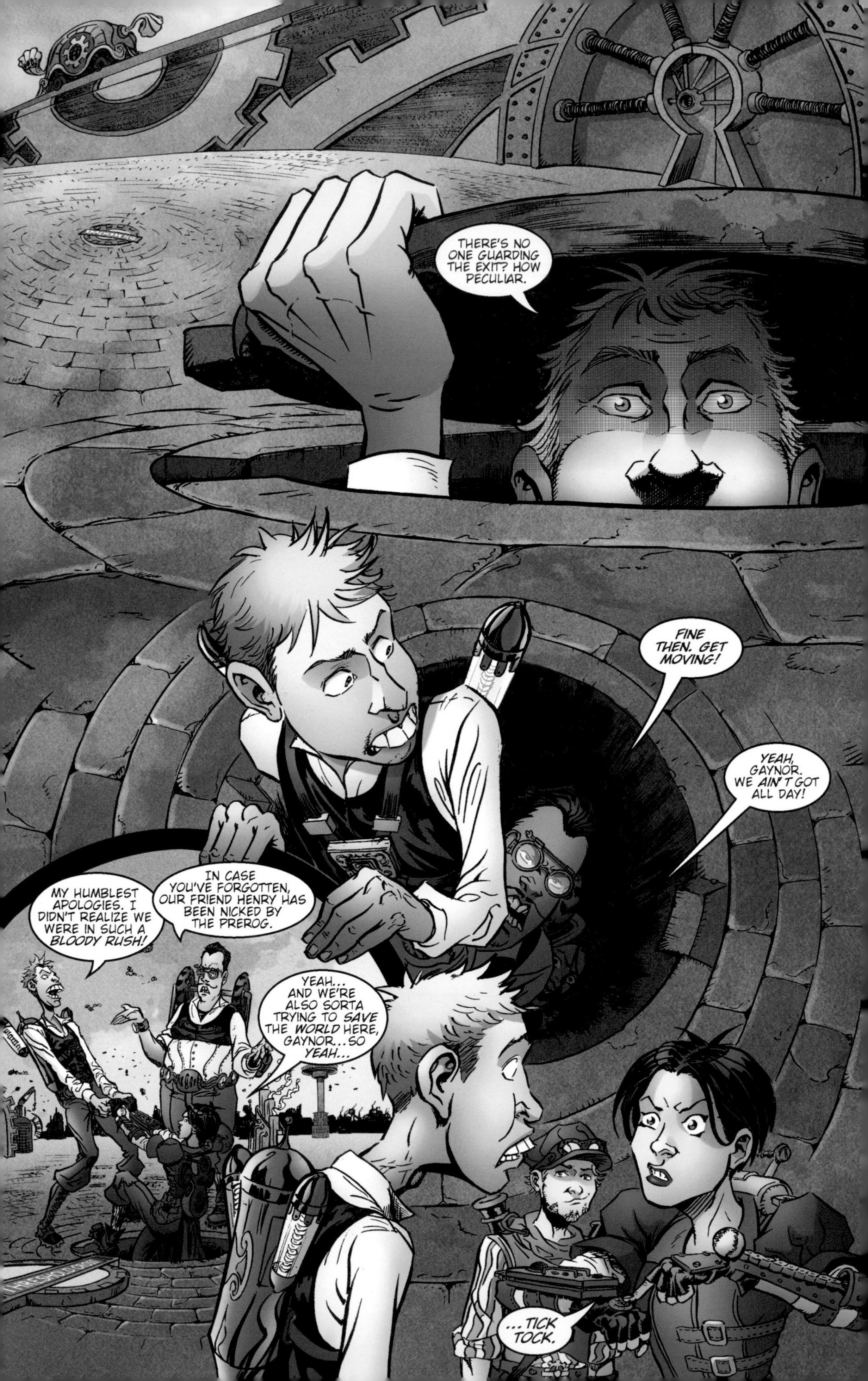
THERE'S NO ONE GUARDING THE EXIT? HOW PECULIAR.
FINE THEN. GET MOVING!
YEAH, GAYNOR. WE *AIN'T* GOT ALL DAY!
MY HUMBLEST APOLOGIES. I DIDN'T REALIZE WE WERE IN SUCH A *BLOODY RUSH!*
IN CASE YOU'VE FORGOTTEN, OUR FRIEND HENRY HAS BEEN NICKED BY THE PREROG.
YEAH... AND WE'RE ALSO SORTA TRYING TO *SAVE* THE *WORLD* HERE, GAYNOR... SO *YEAH...*
...TICK TOCK.

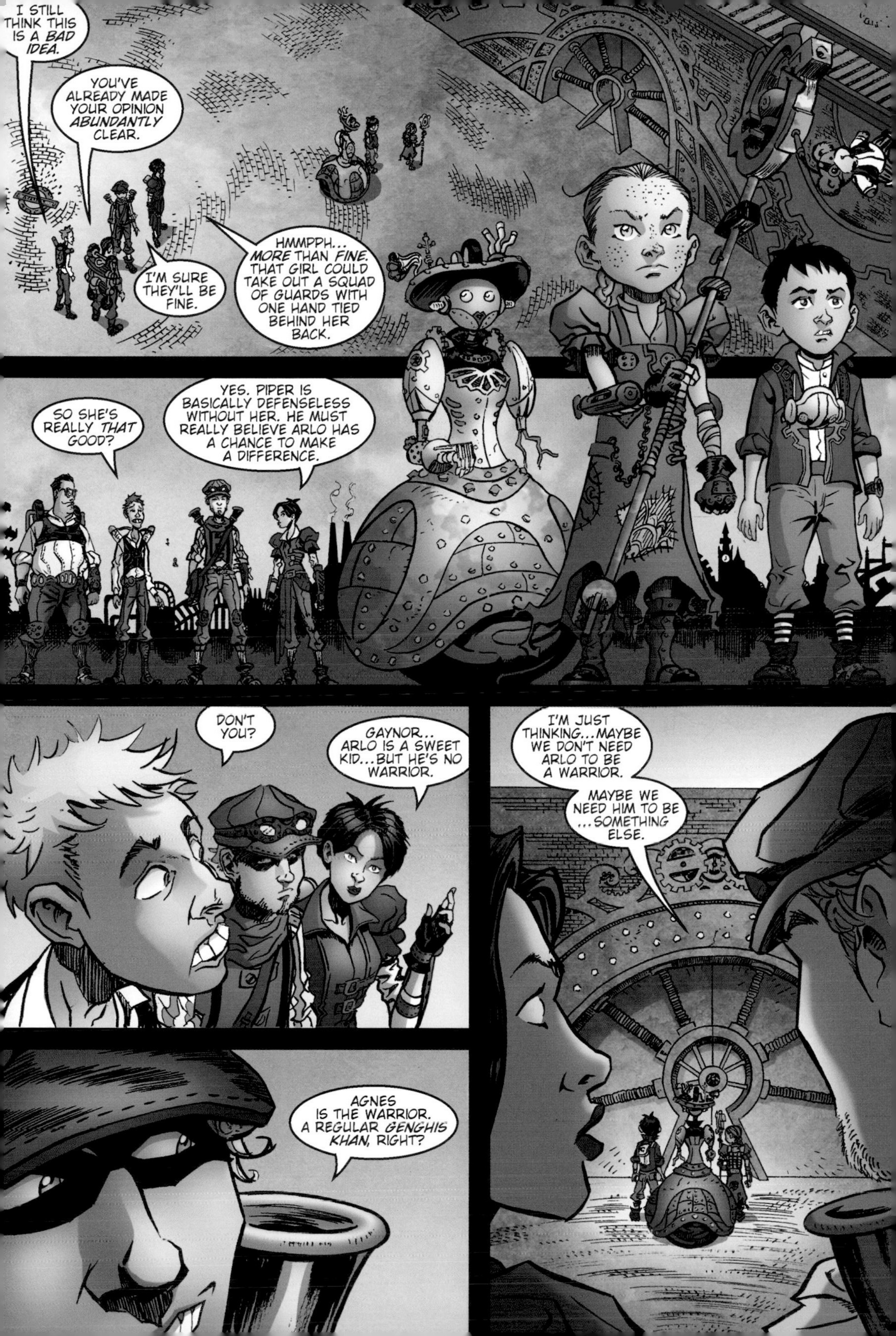
I STILL THINK THIS IS A BAD IDEA.
YOU'VE ALREADY MADE YOUR OPINION ABUNDANTLY CLEAR.
I'M SURE THEY'LL BE FINE.
HMMPPH... MORE THAN FINE. THAT GIRL COULD TAKE OUT A SQUAD OF GUARDS WITH ONE HAND TIED BEHIND HER BACK.
SO SHE'S REALLY THAT GOOD?
YES. PIPER IS BASICALLY DEFENSELESS WITHOUT HER. HE MUST REALLY BELIEVE ARLO HAS A CHANCE TO MAKE A DIFFERENCE.
DON'T YOU?
GAYNOR... ARLO IS A SWEET KID... BUT HE'S NO WARRIOR.
AGNES IS THE WARRIOR. A REGULAR GENGHIS KHAN, RIGHT?
I'M JUST THINKING... MAYBE WE DON'T NEED ARLO TO BE A WARRIOR.
MAYBE WE NEED HIM TO BE ...SOMETHING ELSE.

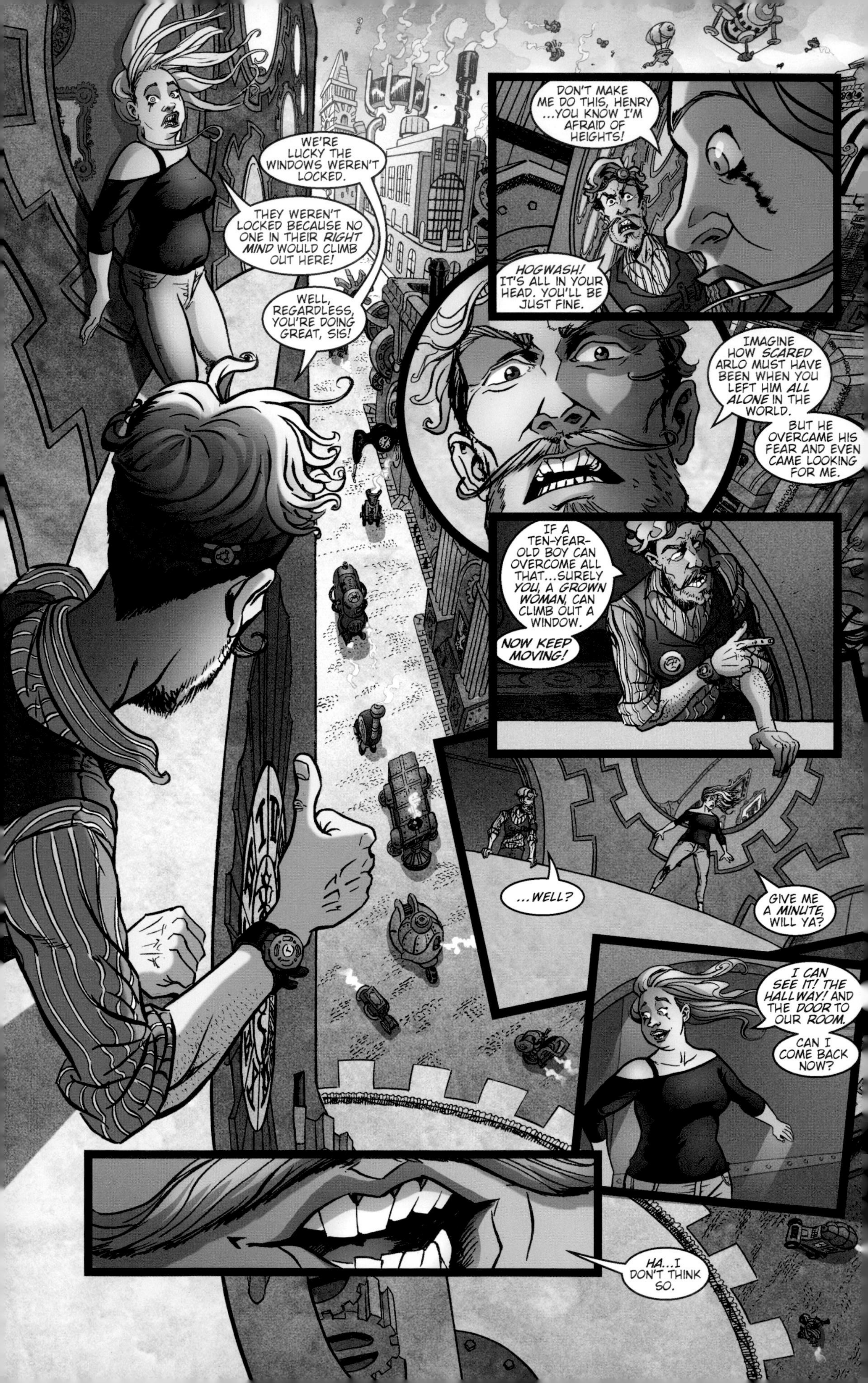
WE'RE LUCKY THE WINDOWS WEREN'T LOCKED.
THEY WEREN'T LOCKED BECAUSE NO ONE IN THEIR *RIGHT MIND* WOULD CLIMB OUT HERE!
WELL, REGARDLESS, YOU'RE DOING GREAT, SIS!
DON'T MAKE ME DO THIS, HENRY ...YOU KNOW I'M AFRAID OF HEIGHTS!
HOGWASH! IT'S ALL IN YOUR HEAD. YOU'LL BE JUST FINE.
IMAGINE HOW *SCARED* ARLO MUST HAVE BEEN WHEN YOU LEFT HIM *ALL ALONE* IN THE WORLD.
BUT HE OVERCAME HIS FEAR AND EVEN CAME LOOKING FOR ME.
IF A TEN-YEAR-OLD BOY CAN OVERCOME ALL THAT...SURELY *YOU*, A *GROWN WOMAN*, CAN CLIMB OUT A WINDOW.
NOW KEEP MOVING!
...WELL?
GIVE ME A *MINUTE*, WILL YA?
I CAN SEE IT! THE HALLWAY! AND THE *DOOR* TO OUR *ROOM*.
CAN I COME BACK NOW?
HA...I DON'T THINK SO.

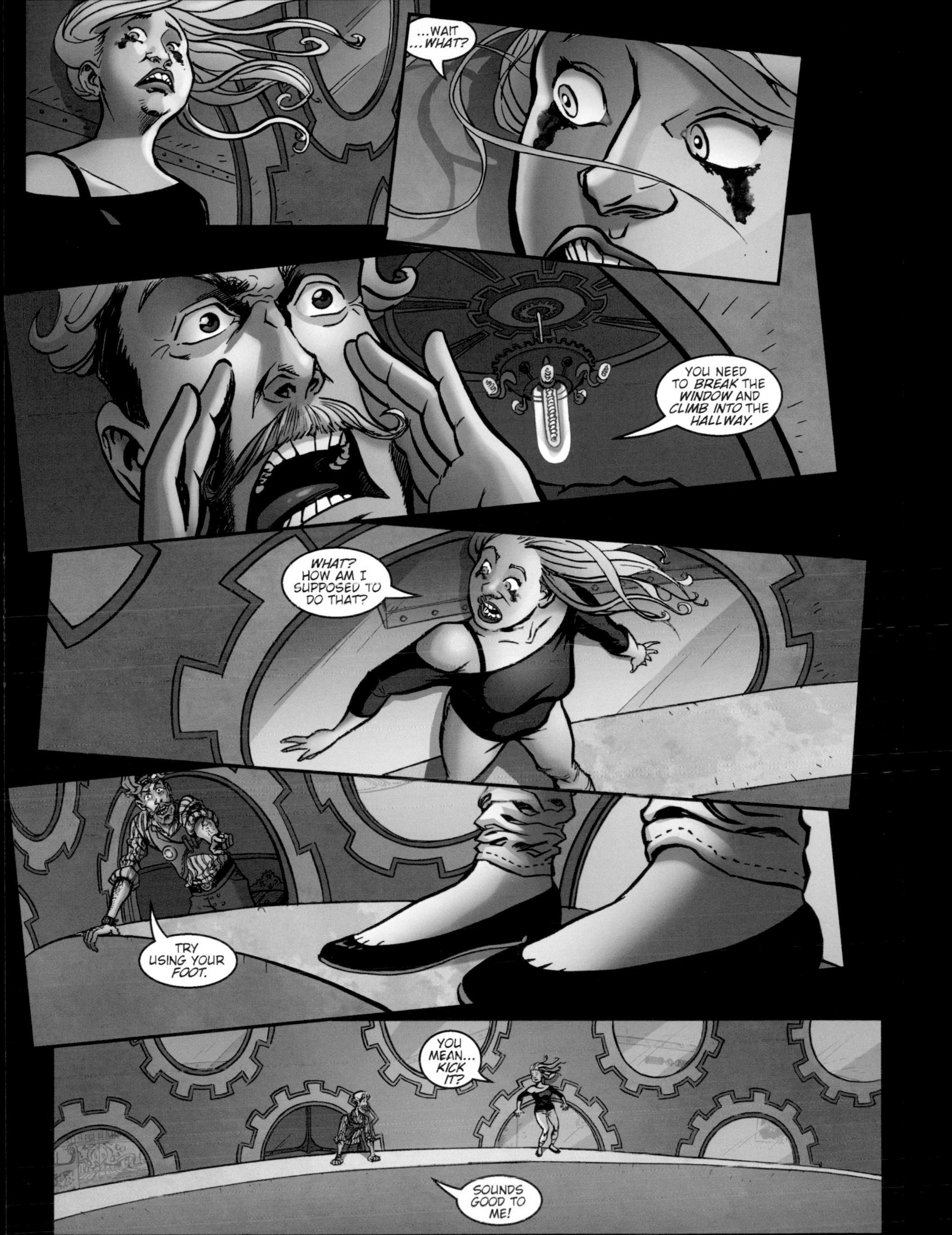
...WAIT ...WHAT?
YOU NEED TO BREAK THE WINDOW AND CLIMB INTO THE HALLWAY.
WHAT? HOW AM I SUPPOSED TO DO THAT?
TRY USING YOUR FOOT.
YOU MEAN... KICK IT?
SOUNDS GOOD TO ME!

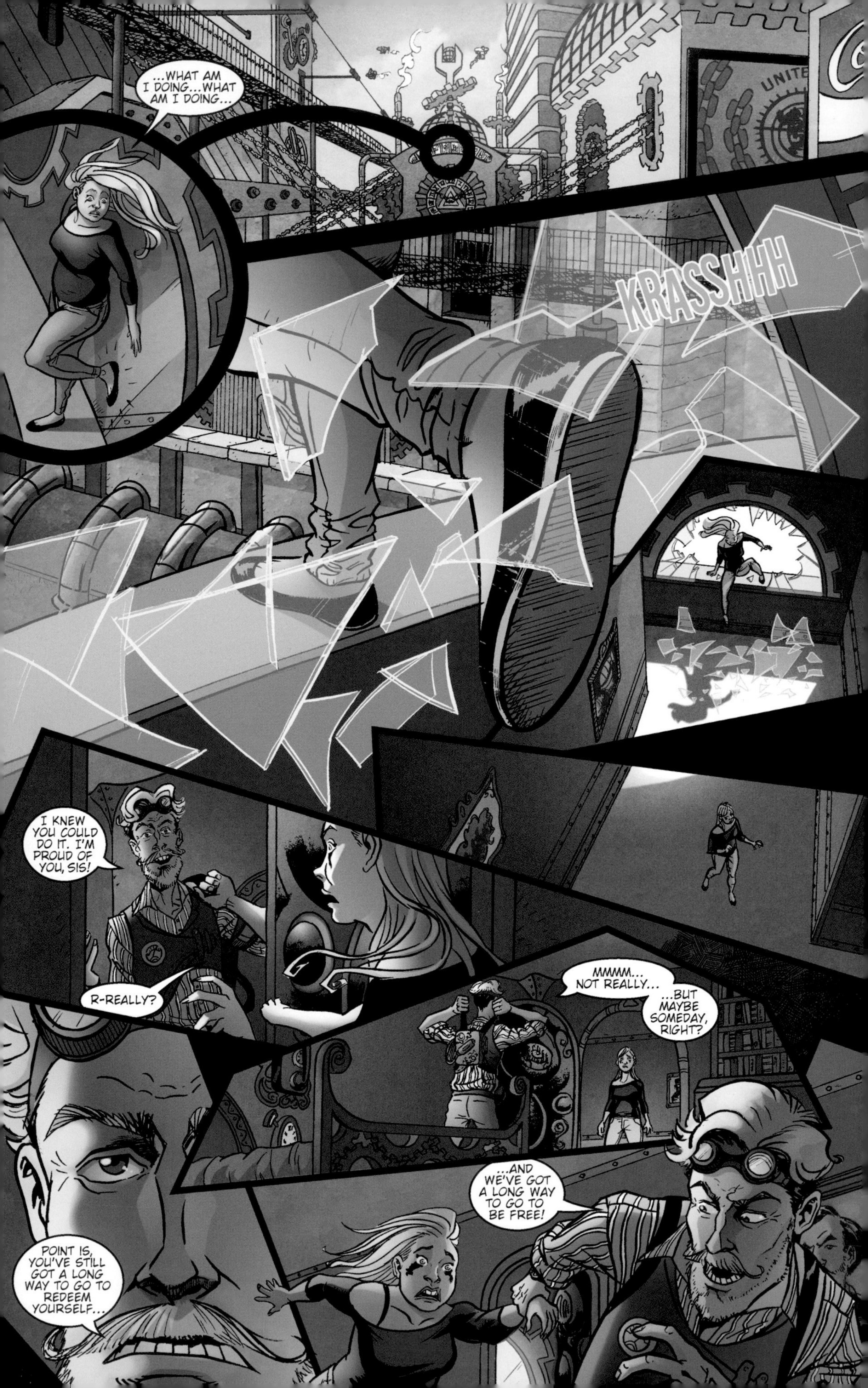
...WHAT AM I DOING...WHAT AM I DOING...
KRASSHHH
I KNEW YOU COULD DO IT. I'M PROUD OF YOU, SIS!
R-REALLY?
MMMM... NOT REALLY...
...BUT MAYBE SOMEDAY, RIGHT?
...AND WE'VE GOT A LONG WAY TO GO TO BE FREE!
POINT IS, YOU'VE STILL GOT A LONG WAY TO GO TO REDEEM YOURSELF...

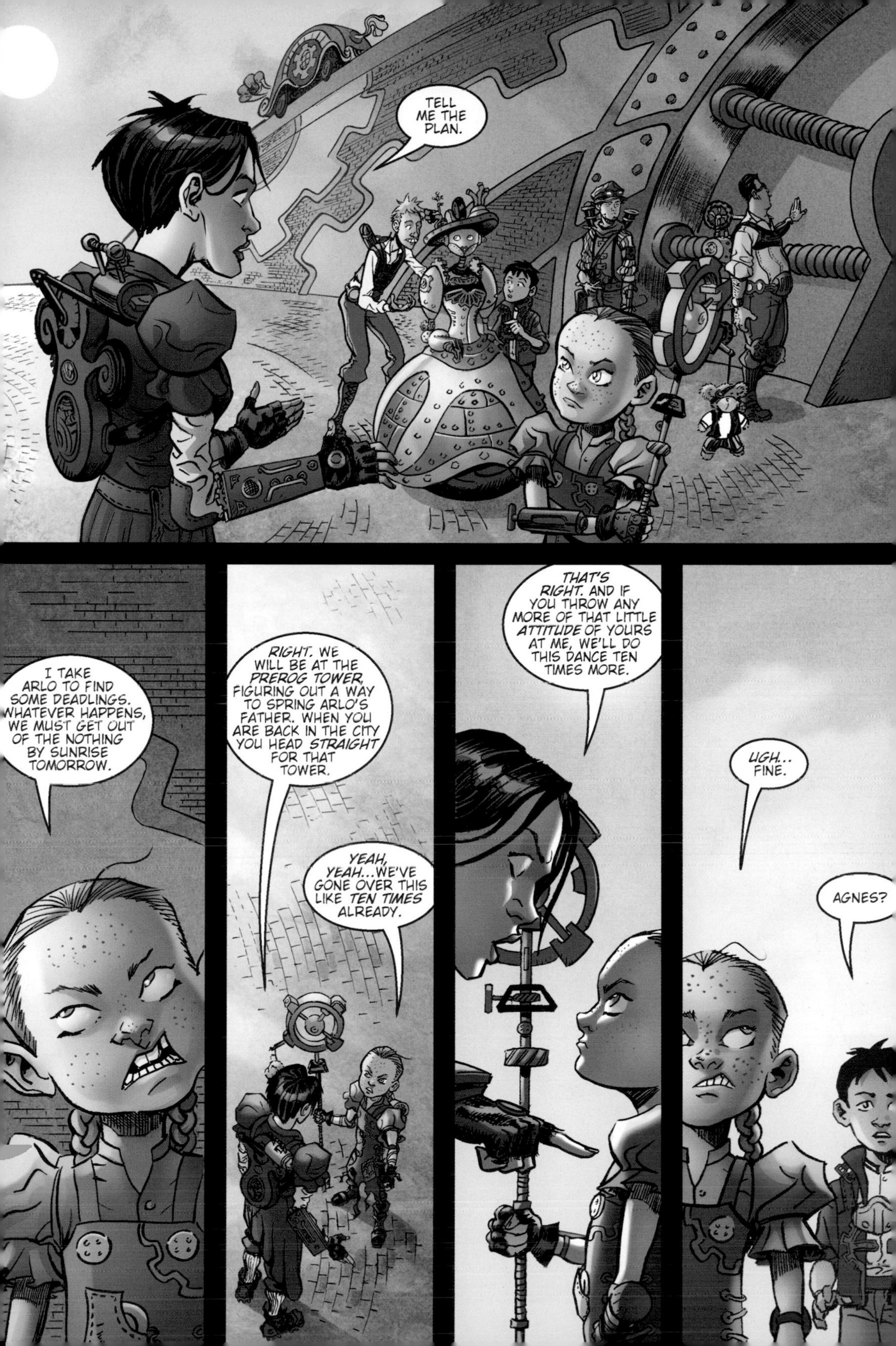
TELL ME THE PLAN.
I TAKE ARLO TO FIND SOME DEADLINGS. WHATEVER HAPPENS, WE MUST GET OUT OF THE NOTHING BY SUNRISE TOMORROW.
RIGHT. WE WILL BE AT THE PREROG TOWER, FIGURING OUT A WAY TO SPRING ARLO'S FATHER. WHEN YOU ARE BACK IN THE CITY YOU HEAD STRAIGHT FOR THAT TOWER.
YEAH, YEAH...WE'VE GONE OVER THIS LIKE TEN TIMES ALREADY.
THAT'S RIGHT. AND IF YOU THROW ANY MORE OF THAT LITTLE ATTITUDE OF YOURS AT ME, WE'LL DO THIS DANCE TEN TIMES MORE.
UGH... FINE.
AGNES?

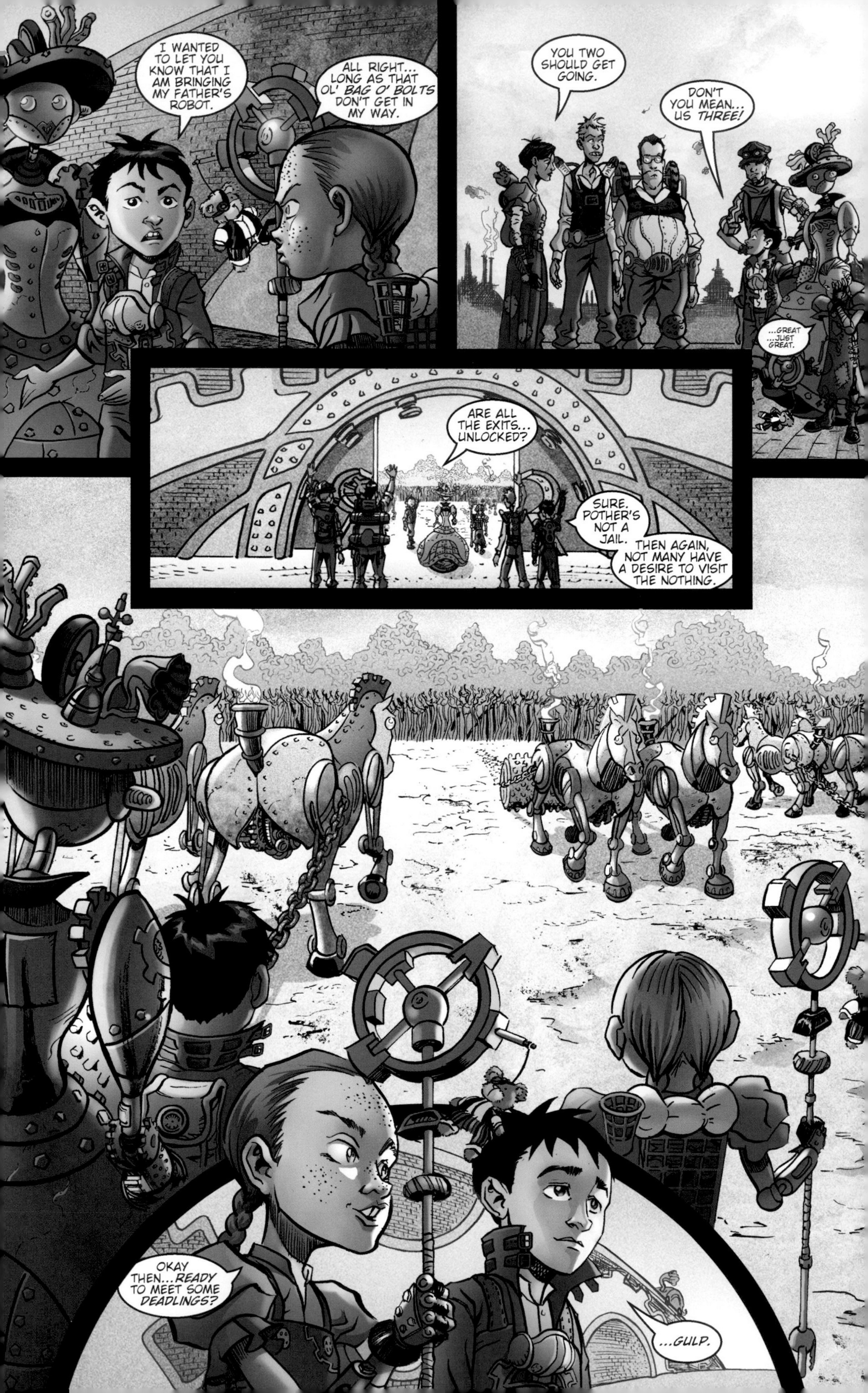
I WANTED TO LET YOU KNOW THAT I AM BRINGING MY FATHER'S ROBOT.
ALL RIGHT... LONG AS THAT OL' *BAG O' BOLTS* DON'T GET IN MY WAY.
YOU TWO SHOULD GET GOING.
DON'T YOU MEAN... US *THREE!*
...GREAT ...JUST GREAT.
ARE ALL THE EXITS... UNLOCKED?
SURE. POTHER'S NOT A JAIL.
THEN AGAIN, NOT MANY HAVE A DESIRE TO VISIT THE NOTHING.
OKAY THEN... *READY* TO MEET SOME *DEADLINGS?*
...*GULP.*

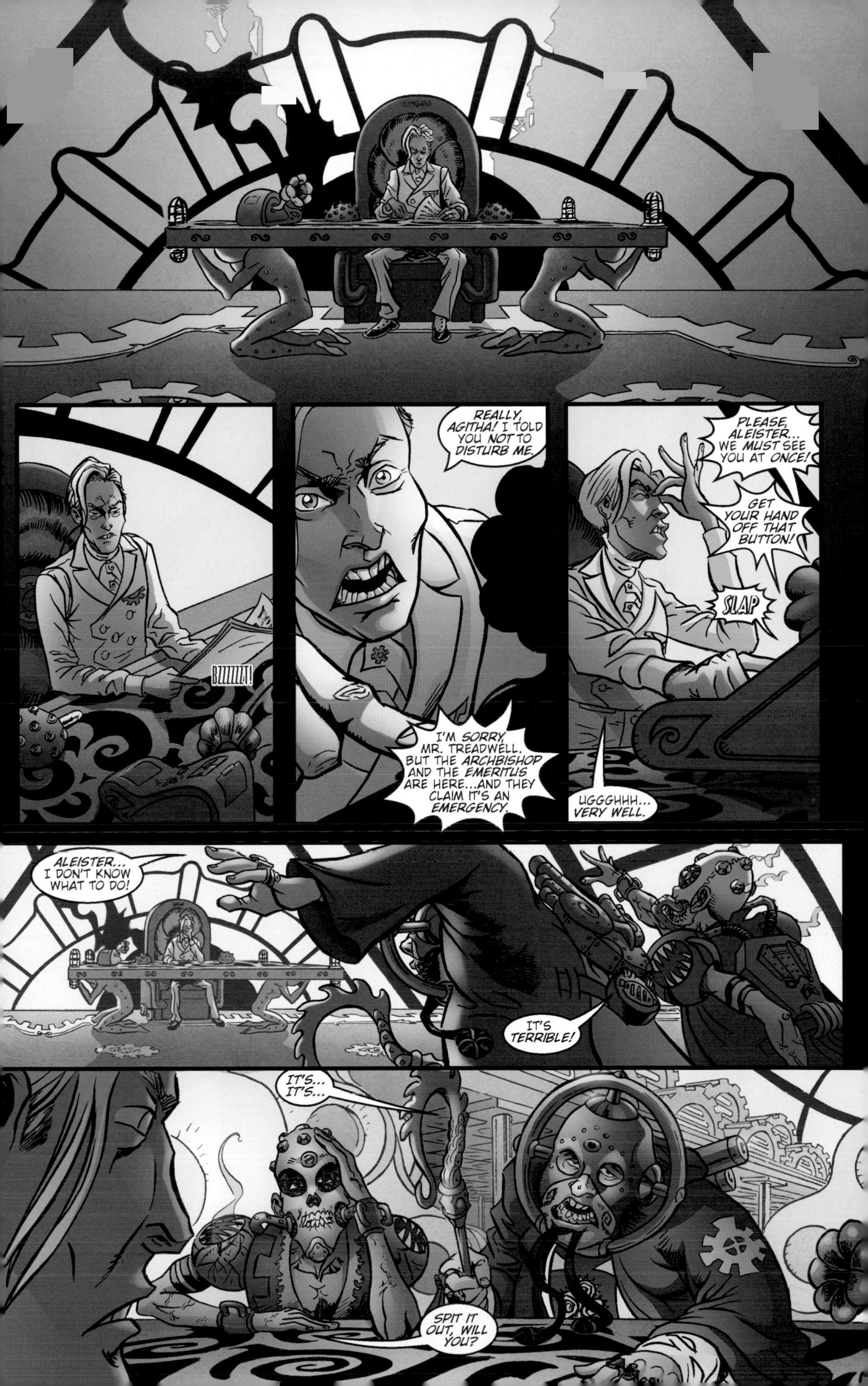
REALLY, AGITHA! I TOLD YOU NOT TO DISTURB ME.
BZZZZZZT!
I'M SORRY, MR. TREADWELL. BUT THE ARCHBISHOP AND THE EMERITUS ARE HERE...AND THEY CLAIM IT'S AN EMERGENCY.
PLEASE, ALEISTER... WE MUST SEE YOU AT ONCE!
GET YOUR HAND OFF THAT BUTTON!
SLAP
UGGGHHH... VERY WELL.
ALEISTER... I DON'T KNOW WHAT TO DO!
IT'S TERRIBLE!
IT'S... IT'S...
SPIT IT OUT, WILL YOU?

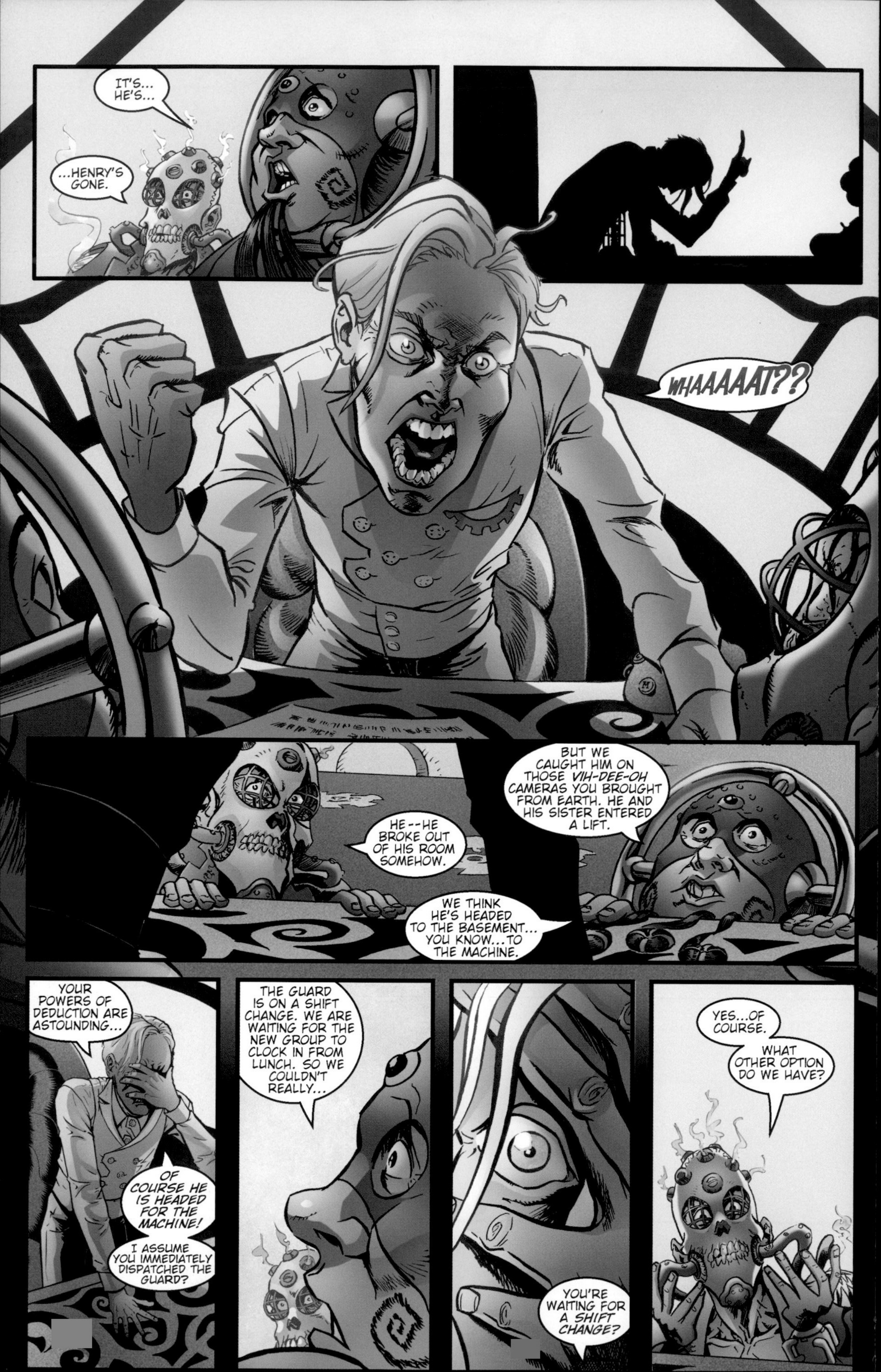
IT'S... HE'S...
...HENRY'S GONE.
WHAAAAAT??
BUT WE CAUGHT HIM ON THOSE VIH-DEE-OH CAMERAS YOU BROUGHT FROM EARTH. HE AND HIS SISTER ENTERED A LIFT.
HE--HE BROKE OUT OF HIS ROOM SOMEHOW.
WE THINK HE'S HEADED TO THE BASEMENT... YOU KNOW...TO THE MACHINE.
YOUR POWERS OF DEDUCTION ARE ASTOUNDING...
OF COURSE HE IS HEADED FOR THE MACHINE!
I ASSUME YOU IMMEDIATELY DISPATCHED THE GUARD?
THE GUARD IS ON A SHIFT CHANGE. WE ARE WAITING FOR THE NEW GROUP TO CLOCK IN FROM LUNCH. SO WE COULDN'T REALLY...
YOU'RE WAITING FOR A SHIFT CHANGE?
YES...OF COURSE.
WHAT OTHER OPTION DO WE HAVE?

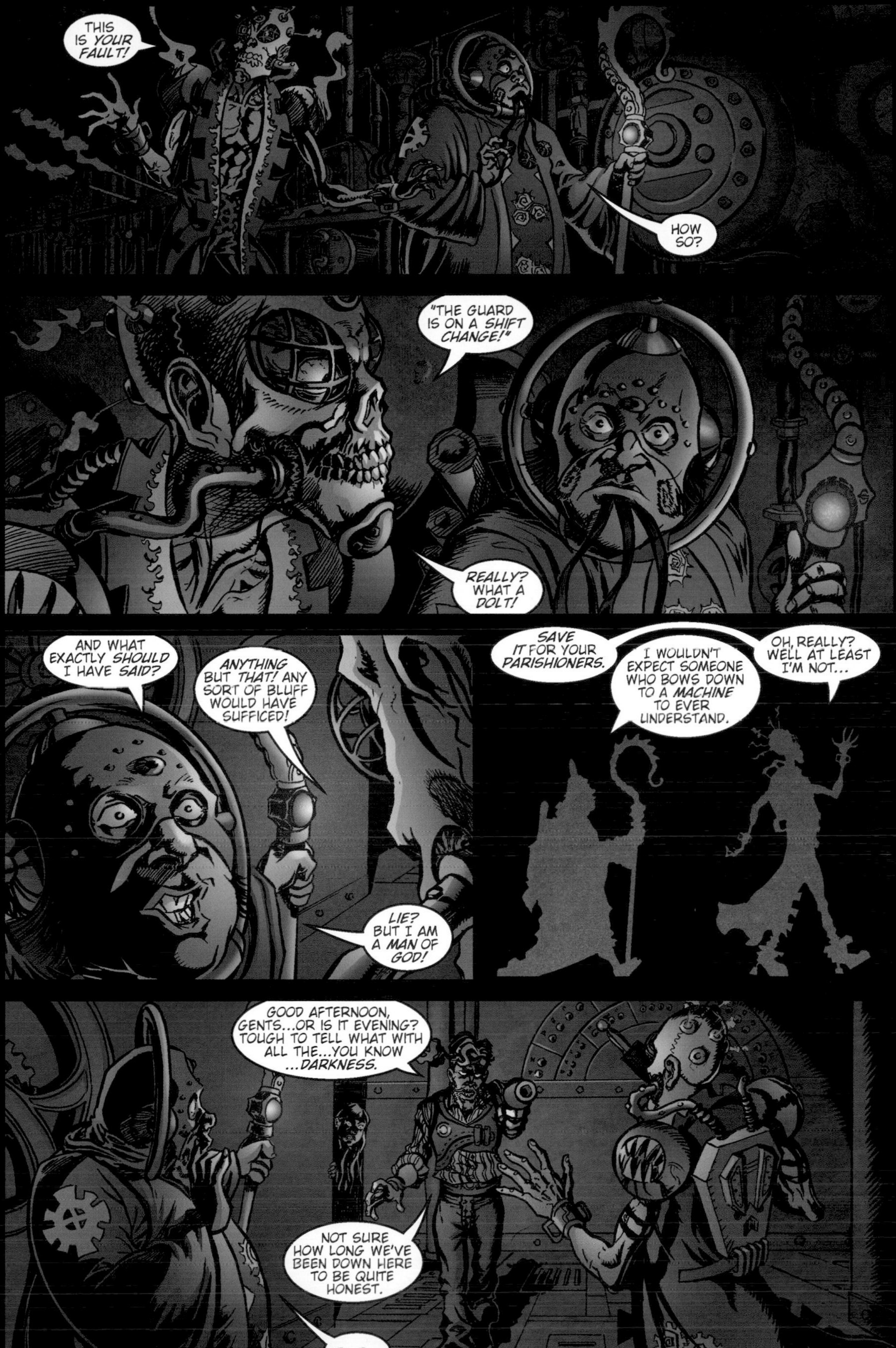
THIS IS YOUR FAULT!
HOW SO?
"THE GUARD IS ON A SHIFT CHANGE!"
REALLY? WHAT A DOLT!
AND WHAT EXACTLY SHOULD I HAVE SAID?
ANYTHING BUT THAT! ANY SORT OF BLUFF WOULD HAVE SUFFICED!
LIE? BUT I AM A MAN OF GOD!
SAVE IT FOR YOUR PARISHIONERS.
I WOULDN'T EXPECT SOMEONE WHO BOWS DOWN TO A MACHINE TO EVER UNDERSTAND.
OH, REALLY? WELL AT LEAST I'M NOT...
GOOD AFTERNOON, GENTS...OR IS IT EVENING? TOUGH TO TELL WHAT WITH ALL THE...YOU KNOW ...DARKNESS.
NOT SURE HOW LONG WE'VE BEEN DOWN HERE TO BE QUITE HONEST.
I...I...

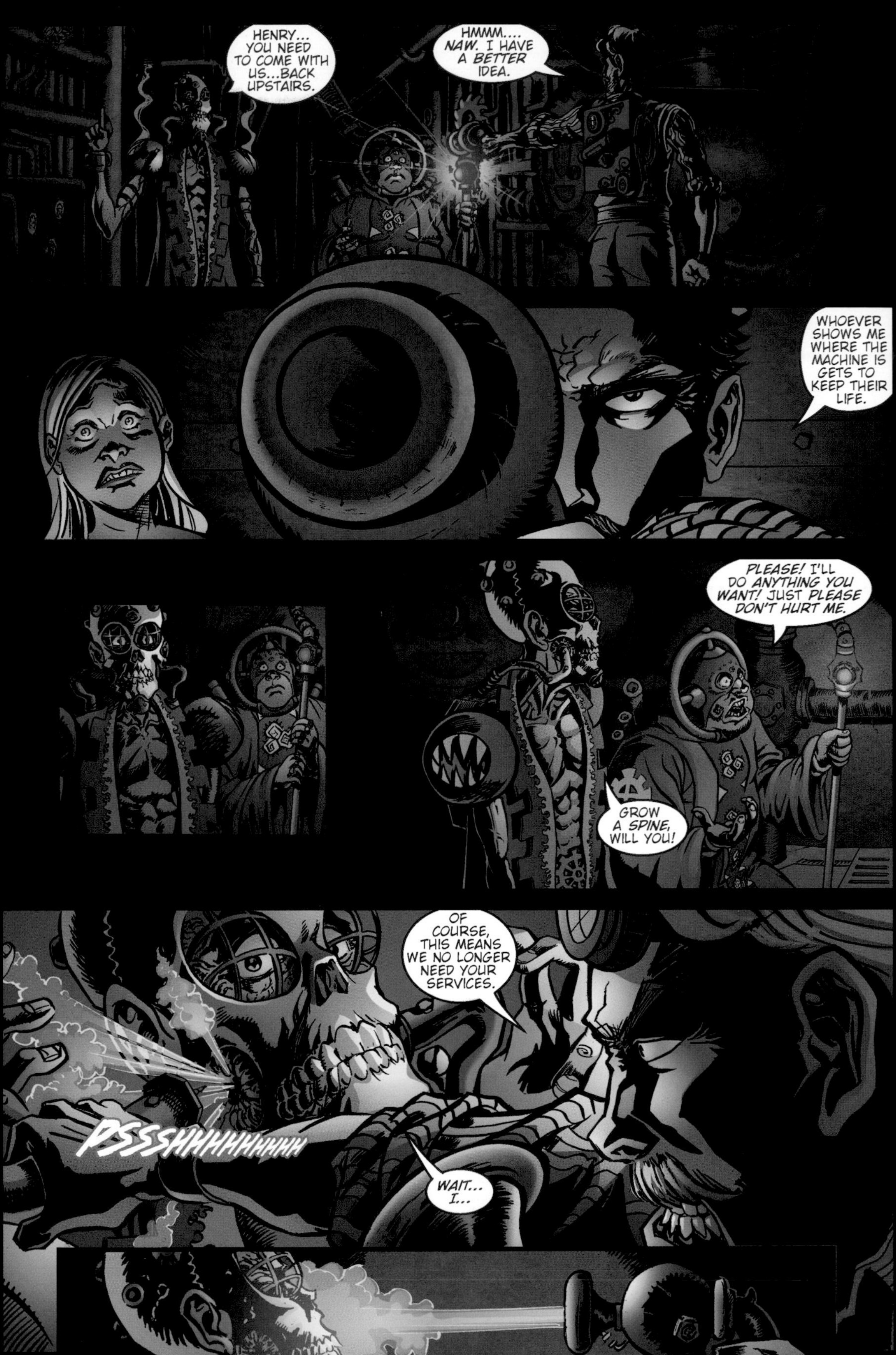
HENRY... YOU NEED TO COME WITH US...BACK UPSTAIRS.
HMMM.... NAW. I HAVE A BETTER IDEA.
WHOEVER SHOWS ME WHERE THE MACHINE IS GETS TO KEEP THEIR LIFE.
PLEASE! I'LL DO ANYTHING YOU WANT! JUST PLEASE DON'T HURT ME.
GROW A SPINE, WILL YOU!
OF COURSE, THIS MEANS WE NO LONGER NEED YOUR SERVICES.
PSSSHHHHHHHHH
WAIT... I...
SHHHHOOOOOOOOFFFF

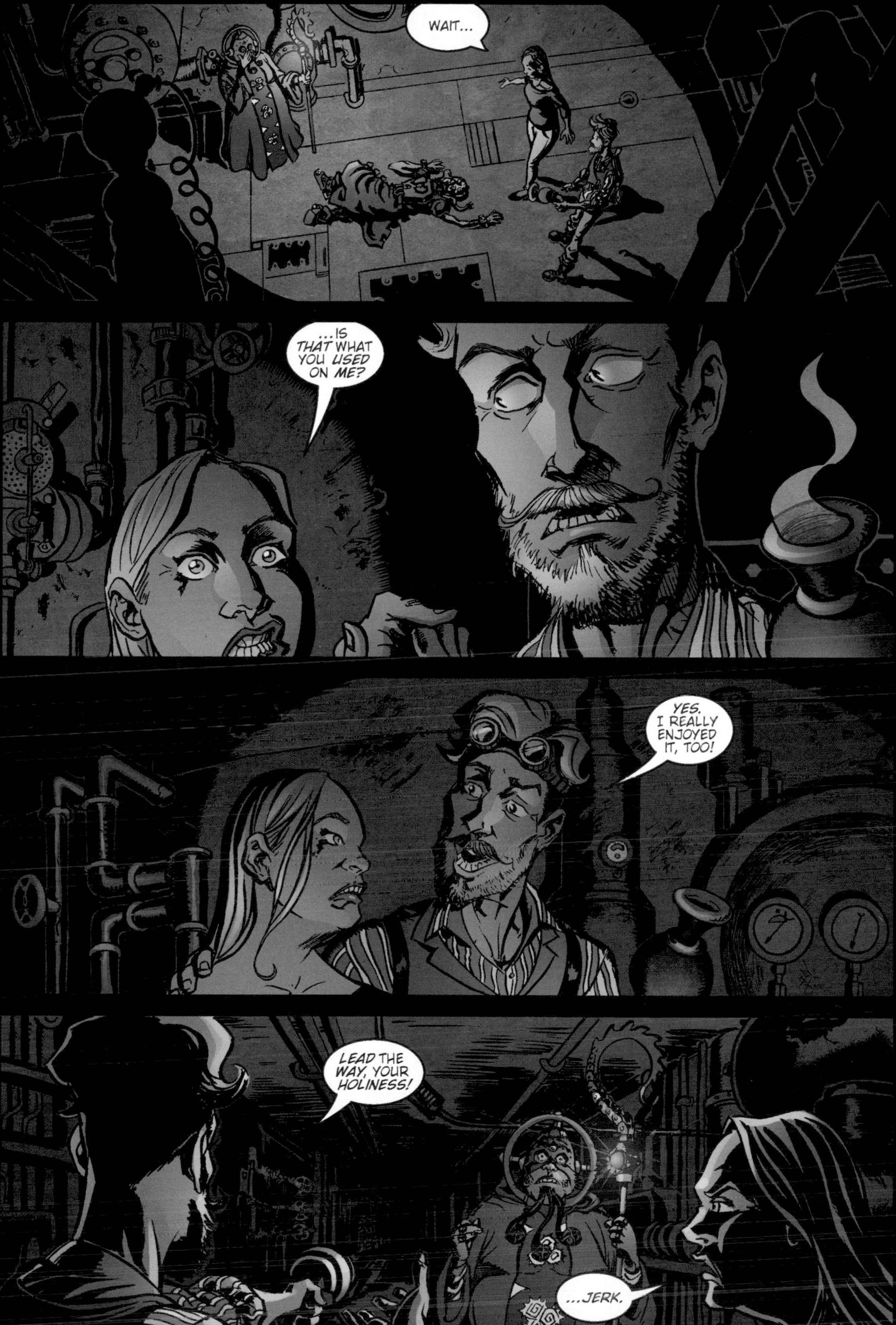
WAIT...
...IS THAT WHAT YOU USED ON ME?
YES. I REALLY ENJOYED IT, TOO!
LEAD THE WAY, YOUR HOLINESS!
...JERK.

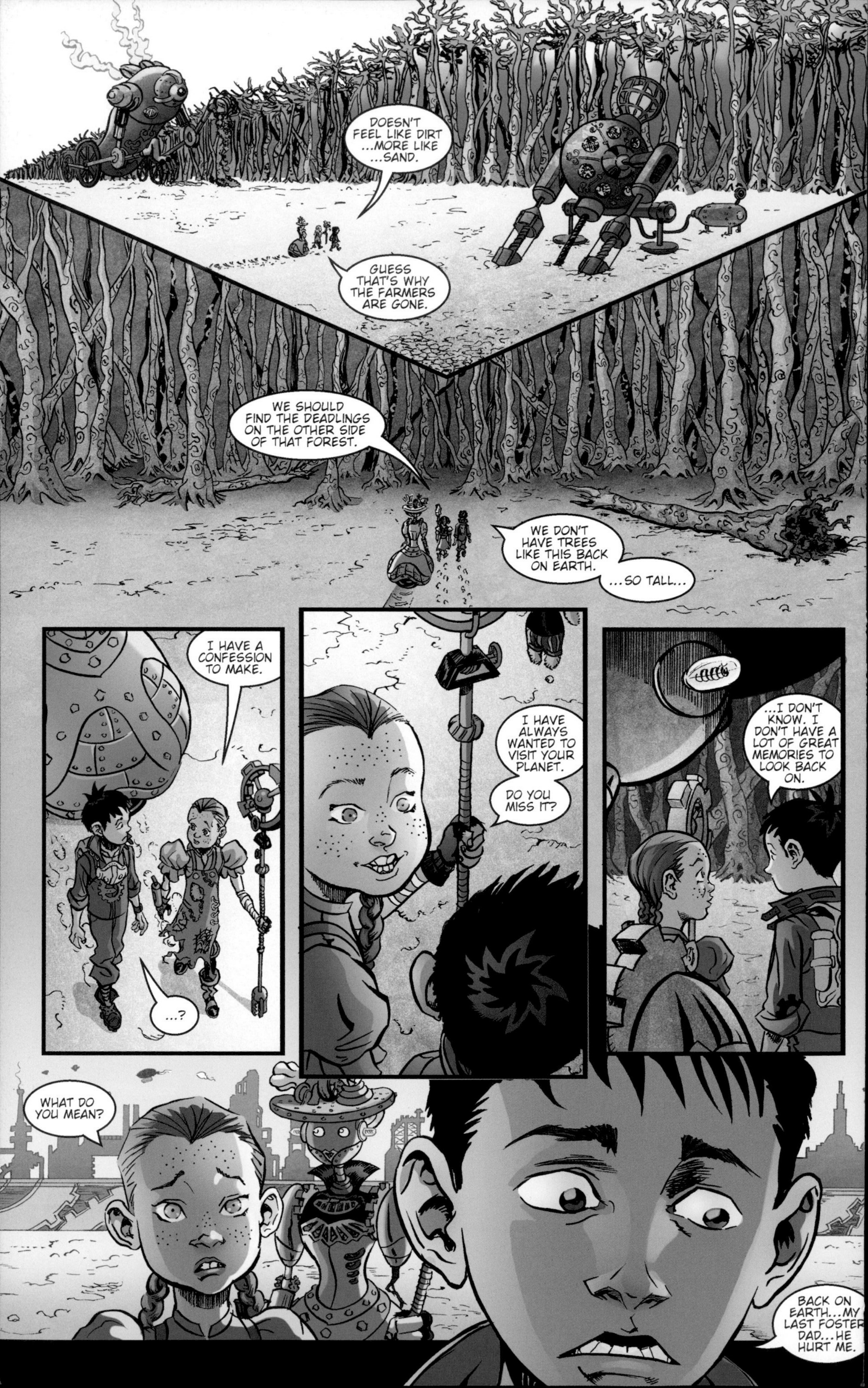
DOESN'T FEEL LIKE DIRT ...MORE LIKE ...SAND.
GUESS THAT'S WHY THE FARMERS ARE GONE.
WE SHOULD FIND THE DEADLINGS ON THE OTHER SIDE OF THAT FOREST.
WE DON'T HAVE TREES LIKE THIS BACK ON EARTH.
...SO TALL...
I HAVE A CONFESSION TO MAKE.
...?
I HAVE ALWAYS WANTED TO VISIT YOUR PLANET.
DO YOU MISS IT?
...I DON'T KNOW. I DON'T HAVE A LOT OF GREAT MEMORIES TO LOOK BACK ON.
WHAT DO YOU MEAN?
BACK ON EARTH...MY LAST FOSTER DAD...HE HURT ME.

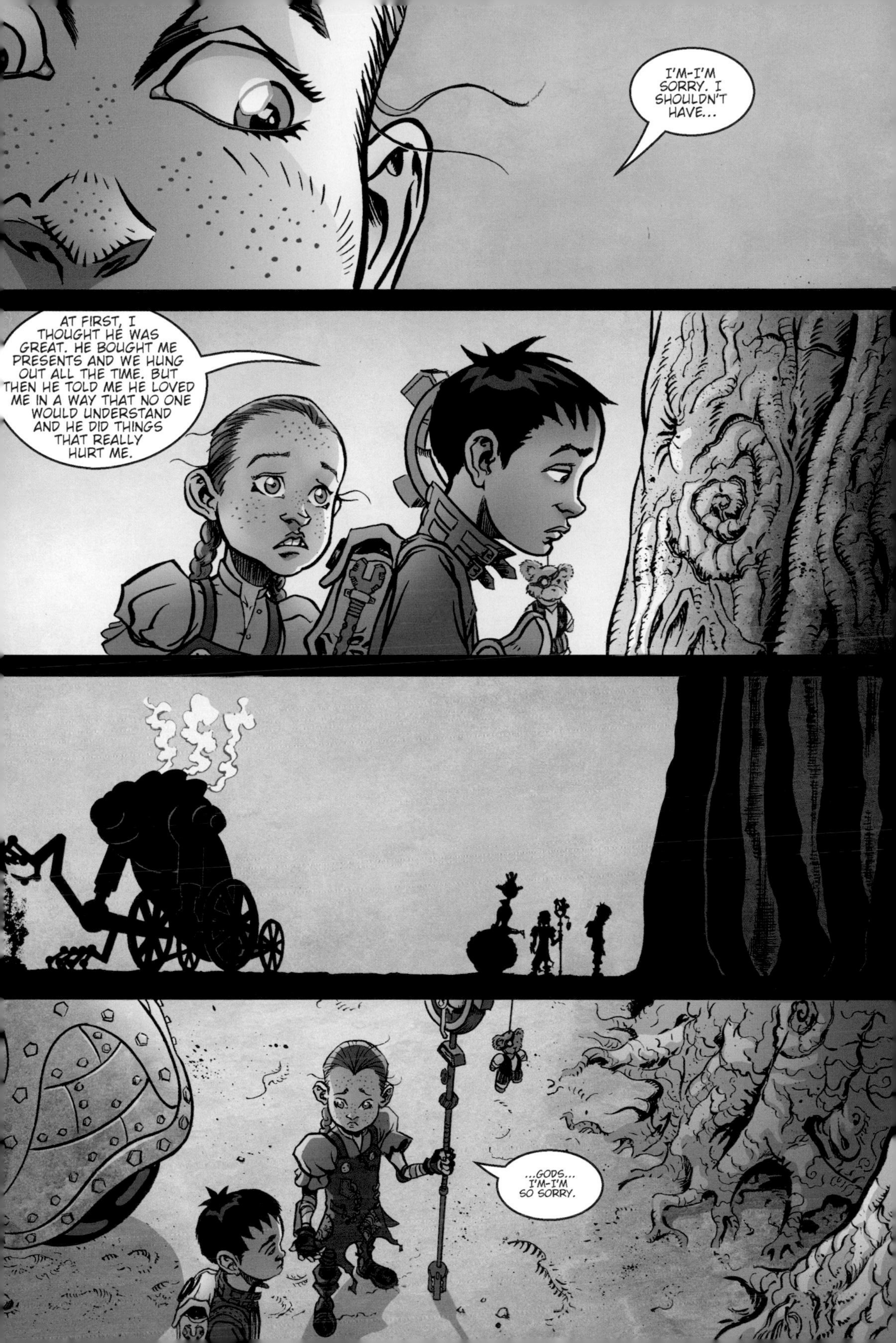
I'M-I'M SORRY. I SHOULDN'T HAVE...
AT FIRST, I THOUGHT HE WAS GREAT. HE BOUGHT ME PRESENTS AND WE HUNG OUT ALL THE TIME. BUT THEN HE TOLD ME HE LOVED ME IN A WAY THAT NO ONE WOULD UNDERSTAND AND HE DID THINGS THAT REALLY HURT ME.
...GODS... I'M-I'M SO SORRY.

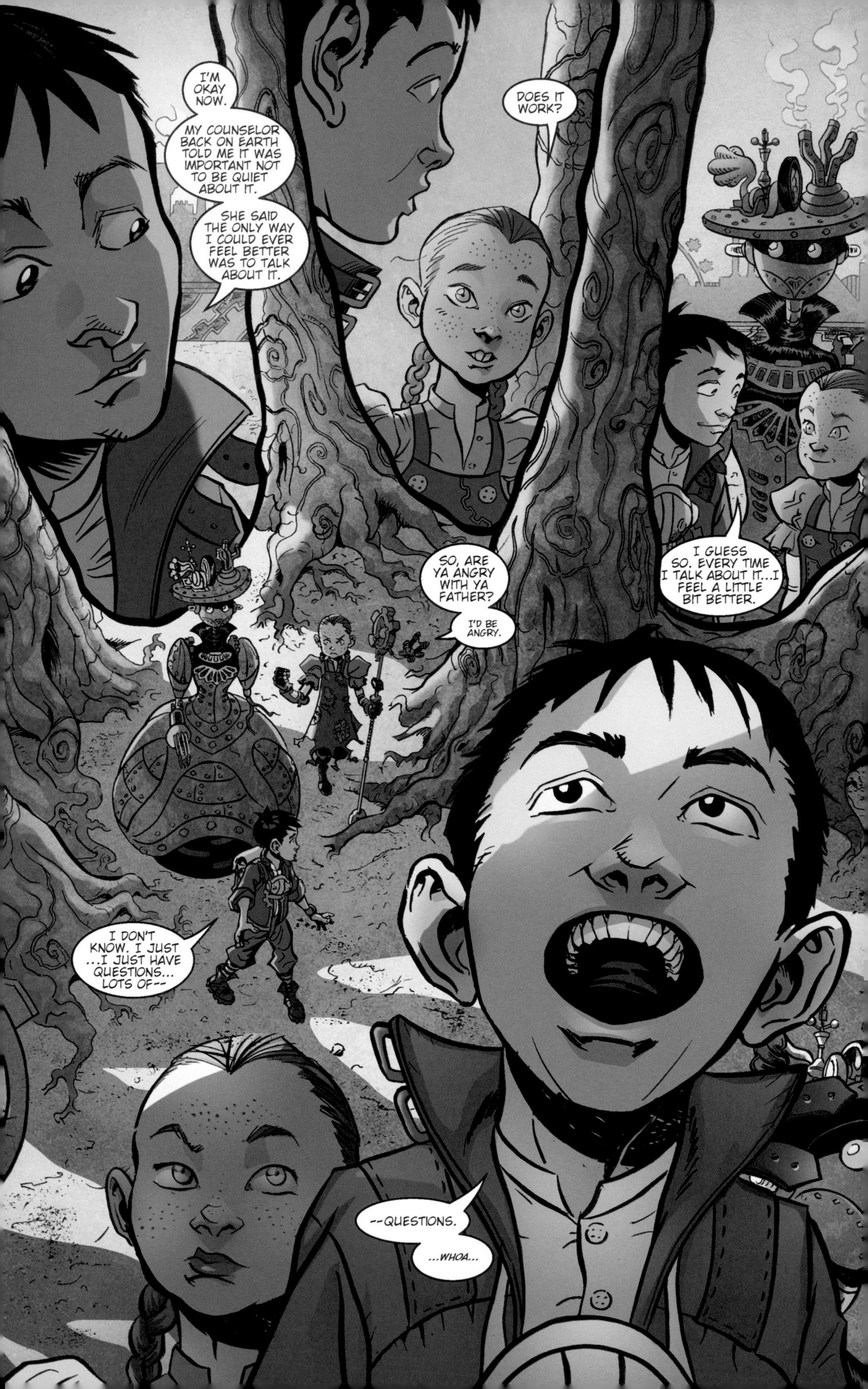
I'M OKAY NOW.
MY COUNSELOR BACK ON EARTH TOLD ME IT WAS IMPORTANT NOT TO BE QUIET ABOUT IT.
SHE SAID THE ONLY WAY I COULD EVER FEEL BETTER WAS TO TALK ABOUT IT.
DOES IT WORK?
I GUESS SO. EVERY TIME I TALK ABOUT IT...I FEEL A LITTLE BIT BETTER.
SO, ARE YA ANGRY WITH YA FATHER?
I'D BE ANGRY.
I DON'T KNOW. I JUST ...I JUST HAVE QUESTIONS... LOTS OF--
--QUESTIONS.
...WHOA...

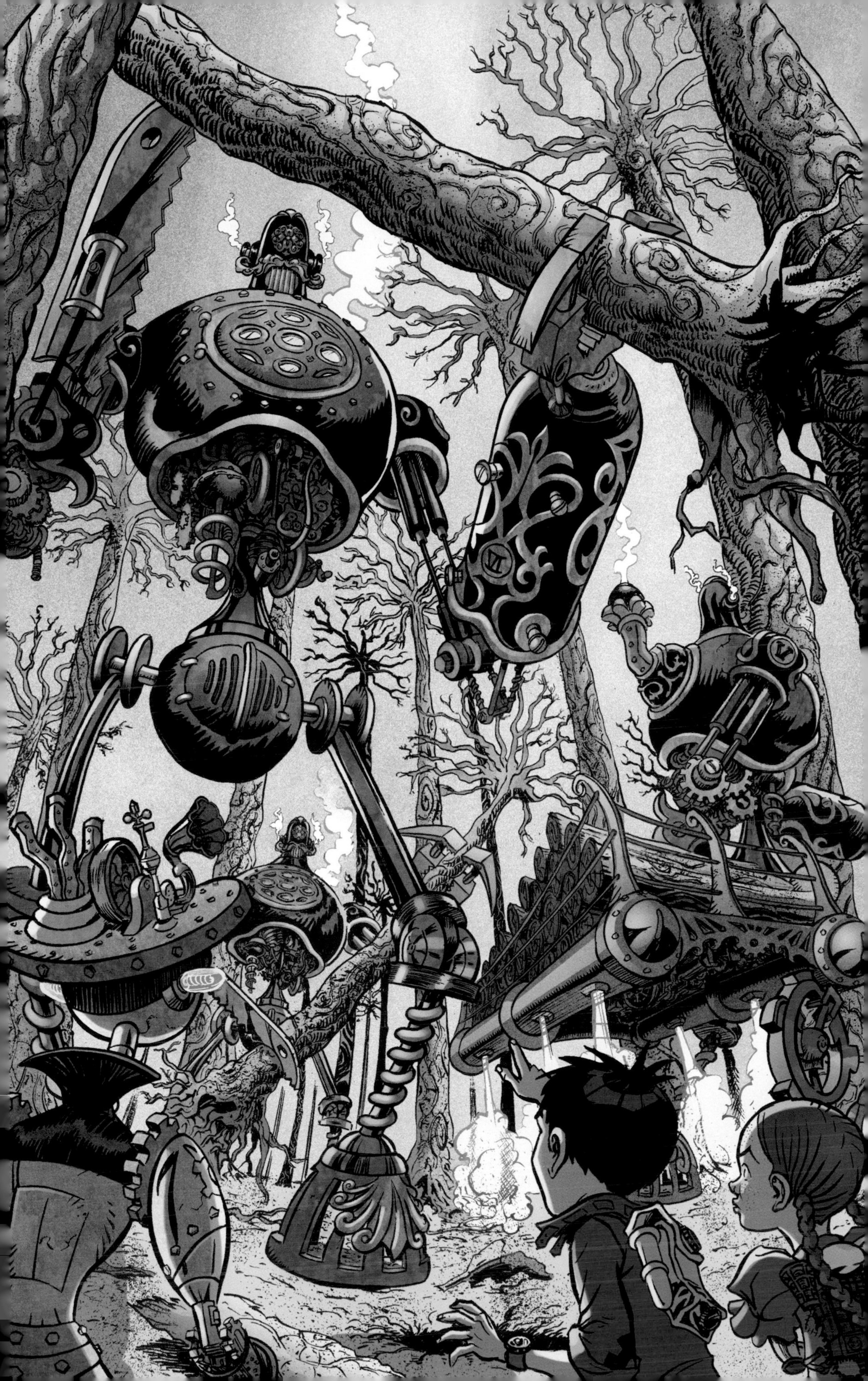

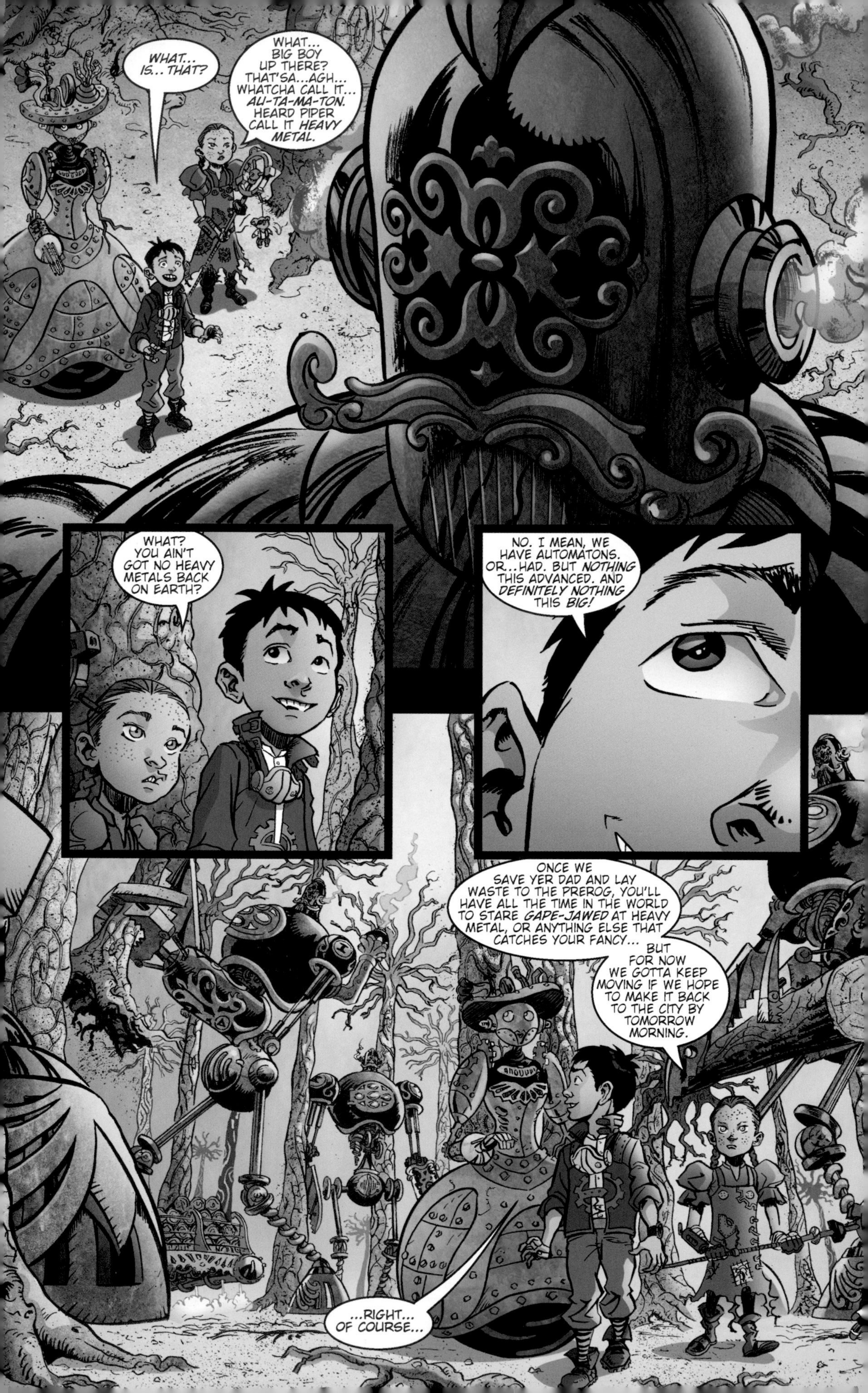
WHAT... IS... THAT?
WHAT... BIG BOY UP THERE? THAT'SA...AGH... WHATCHA CALL IT... *AU-TA-MA-TON.* HEARD PIPER CALL IT *HEAVY METAL.*
WHAT? YOU AIN'T GOT NO HEAVY METALS BACK ON EARTH?
NO. I MEAN, WE HAVE AUTOMATONS. OR...HAD. BUT *NOTHING* THIS ADVANCED. AND *DEFINITELY NOTHING* THIS *BIG!*
ONCE WE SAVE YER DAD AND LAY WASTE TO THE PREROG, YOU'LL HAVE ALL THE TIME IN THE WORLD TO STARE *GAPE-JAWED* AT HEAVY METAL, OR ANYTHING ELSE THAT CATCHES YOUR FANCY...
BUT FOR NOW WE GOTTA KEEP MOVING IF WE HOPE TO MAKE IT BACK TO THE CITY BY TOMORROW MORNING.
...RIGHT... OF COURSE...

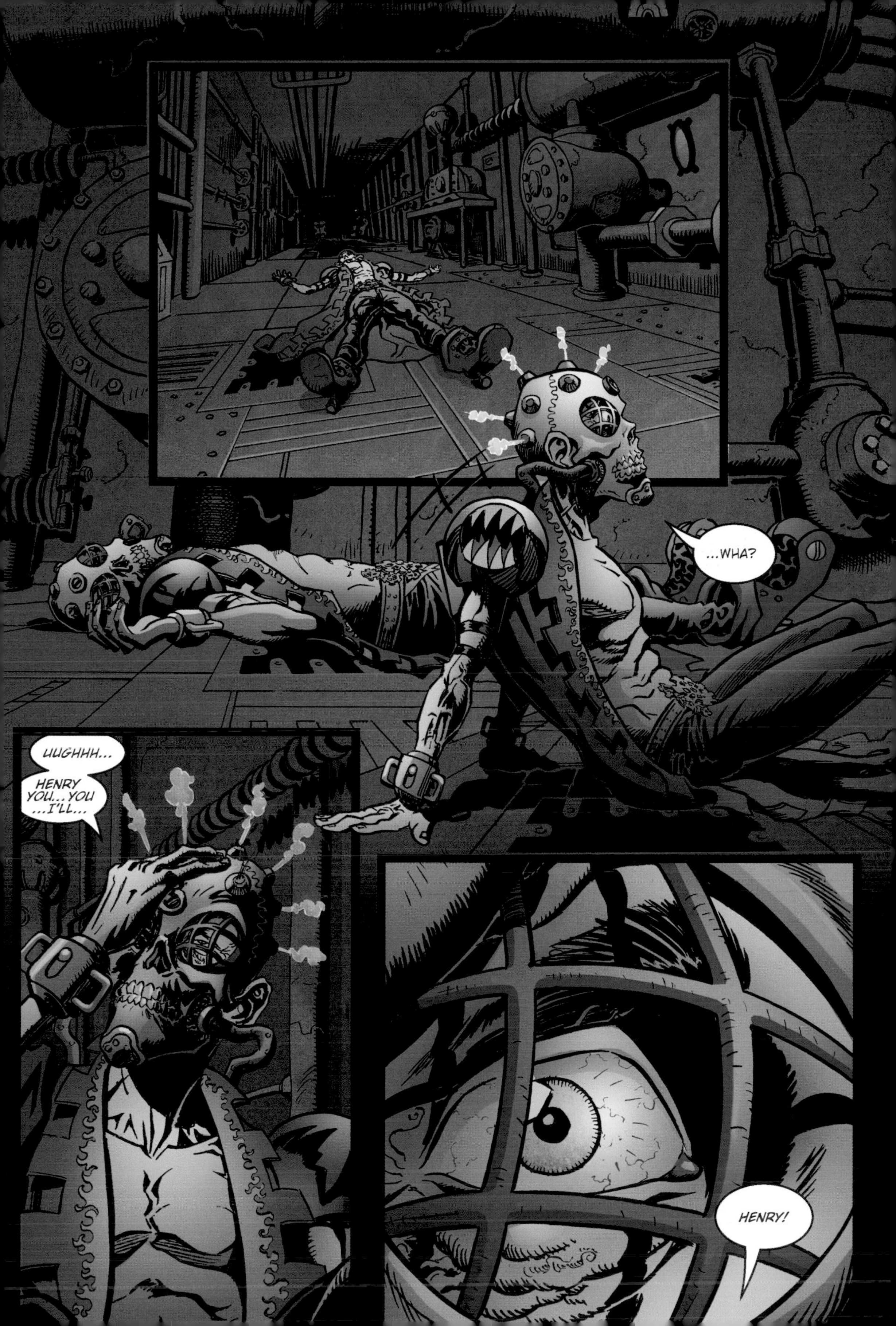
...WHA?
UUGHHH...
HENRY YOU...YOU ...I'LL...
HENRY!

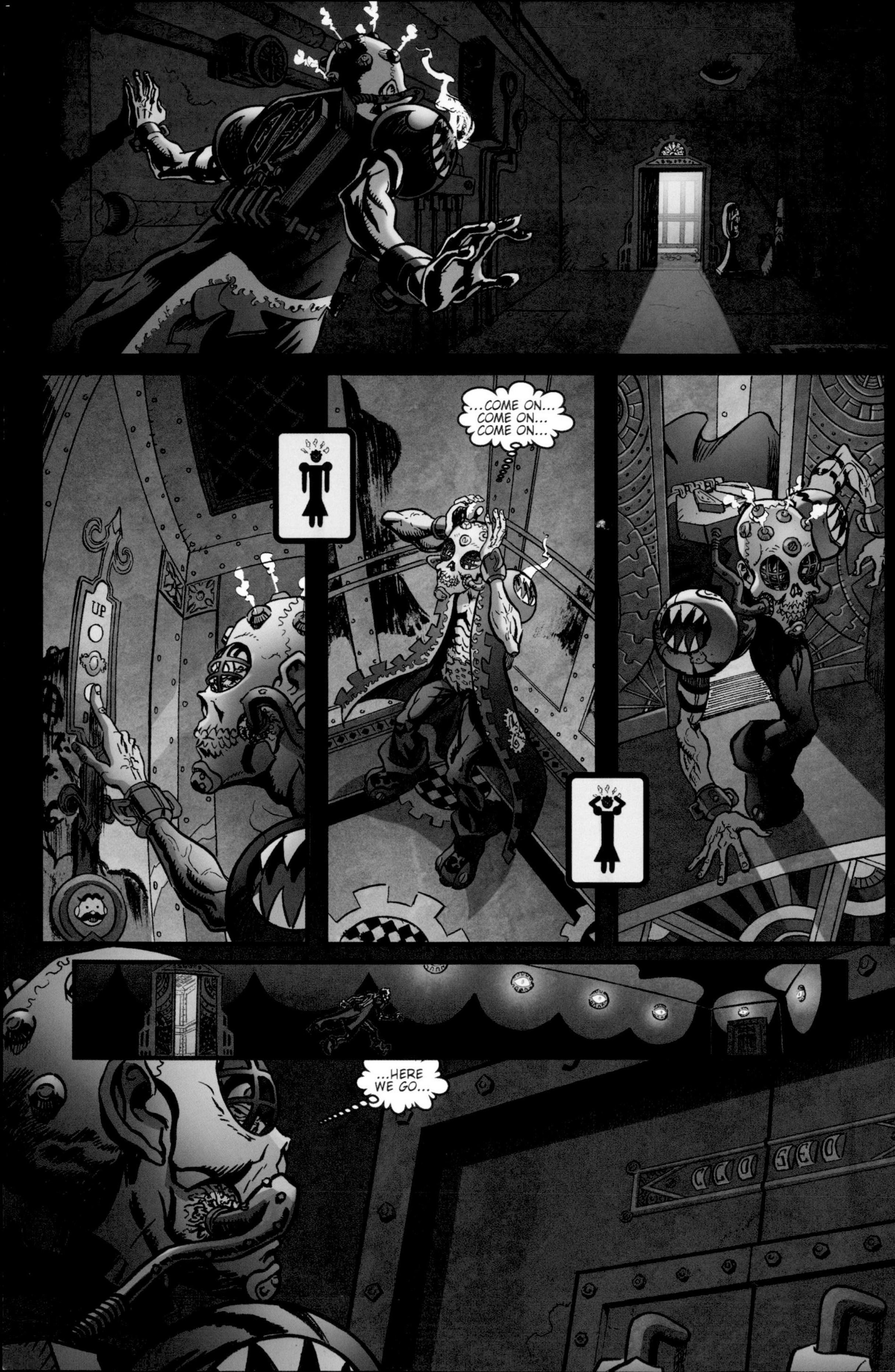
UP
...COME ON...
COME ON...
COME ON...
...HERE
WE GO...

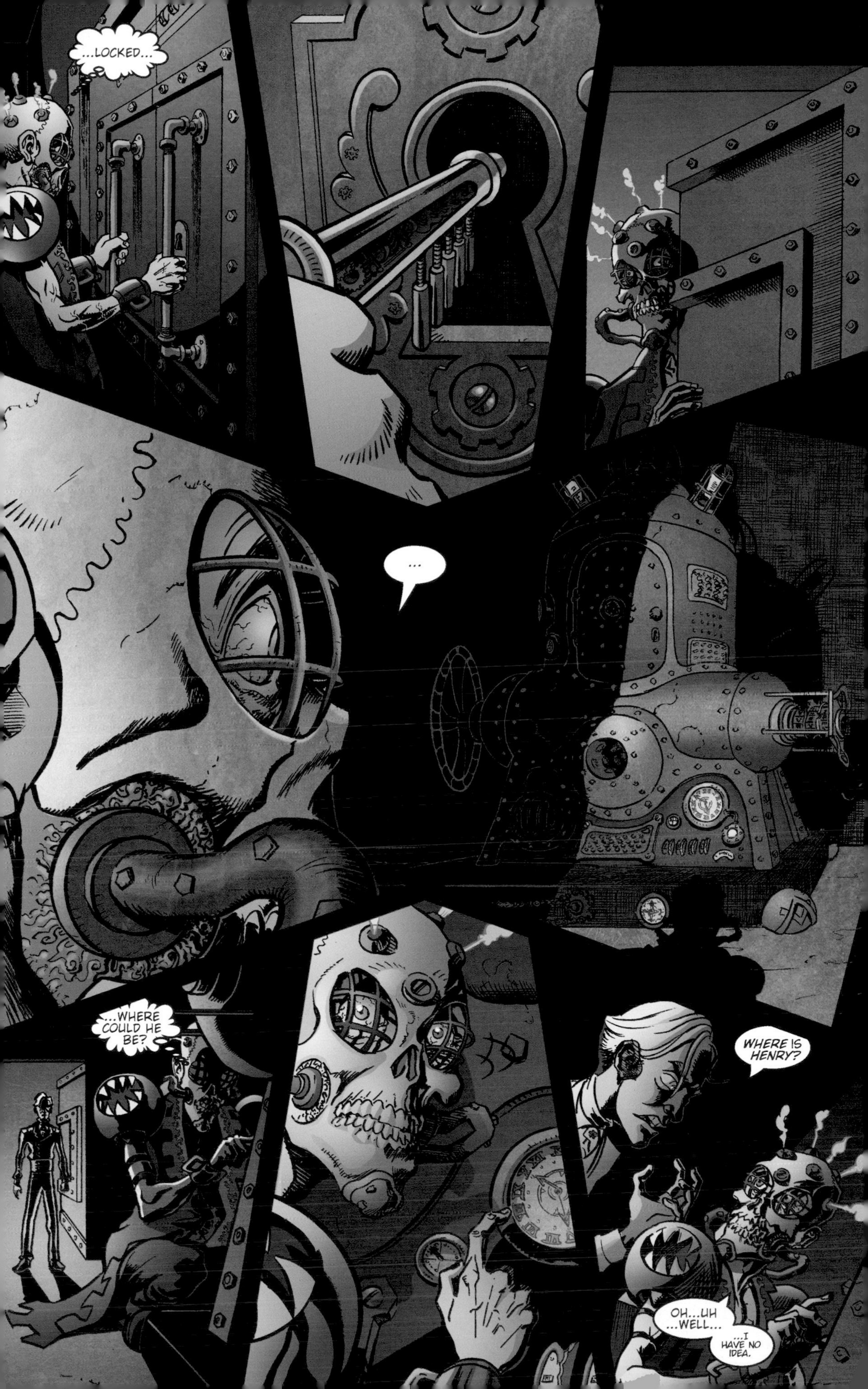
...LOCKED...
...
...WHERE COULD HE BE?
WHERE IS HENRY?
OH...UH ...WELL...
...I HAVE NO IDEA.

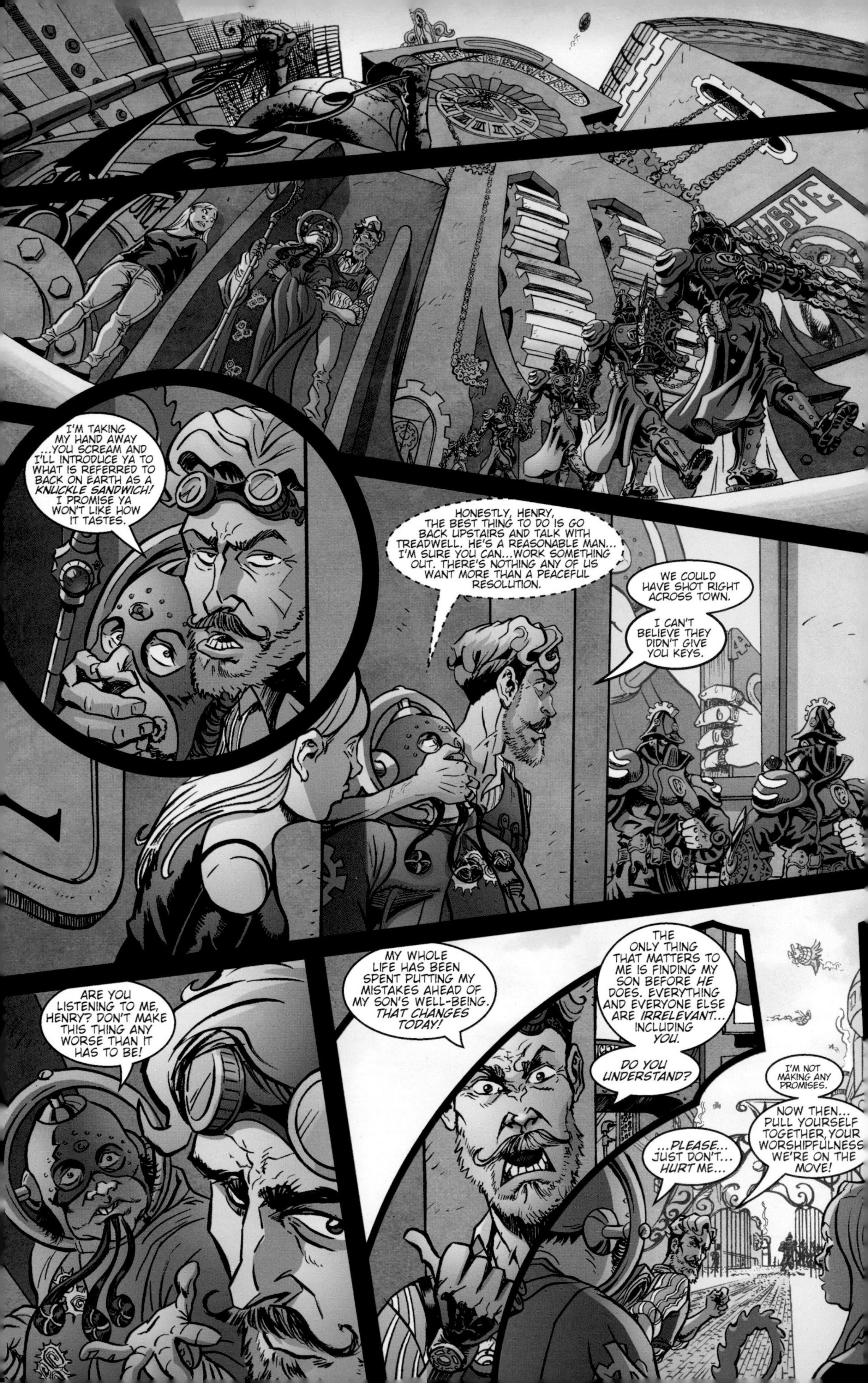

I'M TAKING MY HAND AWAY ...YOU SCREAM AND I'LL INTRODUCE YA TO WHAT IS REFERRED TO BACK ON EARTH AS A KNUCKLE SANDWICH! I PROMISE YA WON'T LIKE HOW IT TASTES.
HONESTLY, HENRY, THE BEST THING TO DO IS GO BACK UPSTAIRS AND TALK WITH TREADWELL. HE'S A REASONABLE MAN... I'M SURE YOU CAN...WORK SOMETHING OUT. THERE'S NOTHING ANY OF US WANT MORE THAN A PEACEFUL RESOLUTION.
WE COULD HAVE SHOT RIGHT ACROSS TOWN.
I CAN'T BELIEVE THEY DIDN'T GIVE YOU KEYS.
ARE YOU LISTENING TO ME, HENRY? DON'T MAKE THIS THING ANY WORSE THAN IT HAS TO BE!
MY WHOLE LIFE HAS BEEN SPENT PUTTING MY MISTAKES AHEAD OF MY SON'S WELL-BEING. THAT CHANGES TODAY!
THE ONLY THING THAT MATTERS TO ME IS FINDING MY SON BEFORE HE DOES. EVERYTHING AND EVERYONE ELSE ARE IRRELEVANT... INCLUDING YOU.
DO YOU UNDERSTAND?
...PLEASE... JUST DON'T... HURT ME...
I'M NOT MAKING ANY PROMISES.
NOW THEN... PULL YOURSELF TOGETHER, YOUR WORSHIPFULNESS WE'RE ON THE MOVE!

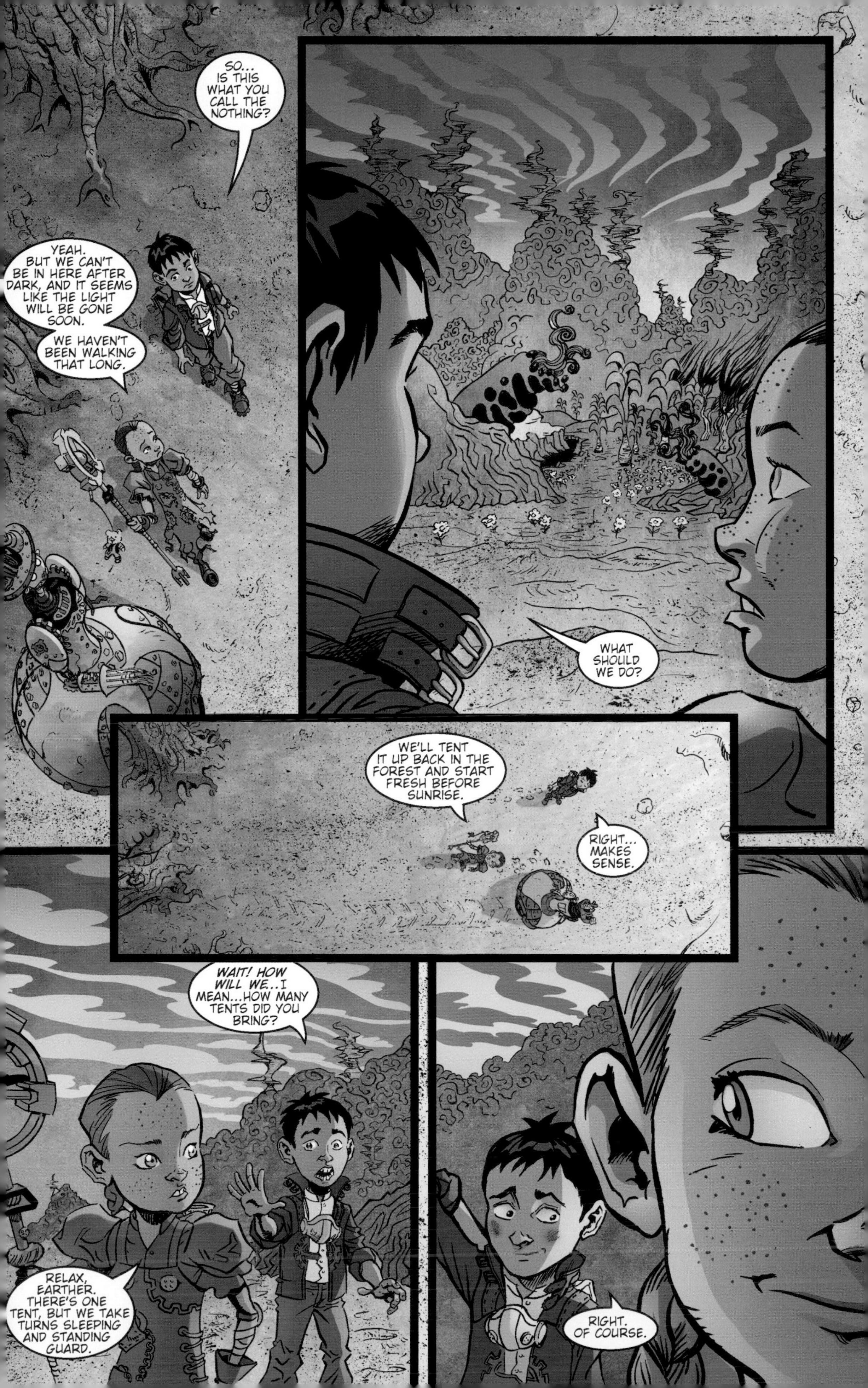
SO... IS THIS WHAT YOU CALL THE NOTHING?
YEAH. BUT WE CAN'T BE IN HERE AFTER DARK, AND IT SEEMS LIKE THE LIGHT WILL BE GONE SOON.
WE HAVEN'T BEEN WALKING THAT LONG.
WHAT SHOULD WE DO?
WE'LL TENT IT UP BACK IN THE FOREST AND START FRESH BEFORE SUNRISE.
RIGHT... MAKES SENSE.
WAIT! HOW WILL WE...I MEAN...HOW MANY TENTS DID YOU BRING?
RELAX, EARTHER. THERE'S ONE TENT, BUT WE TAKE TURNS SLEEPING AND STANDING GUARD.
RIGHT. OF COURSE.

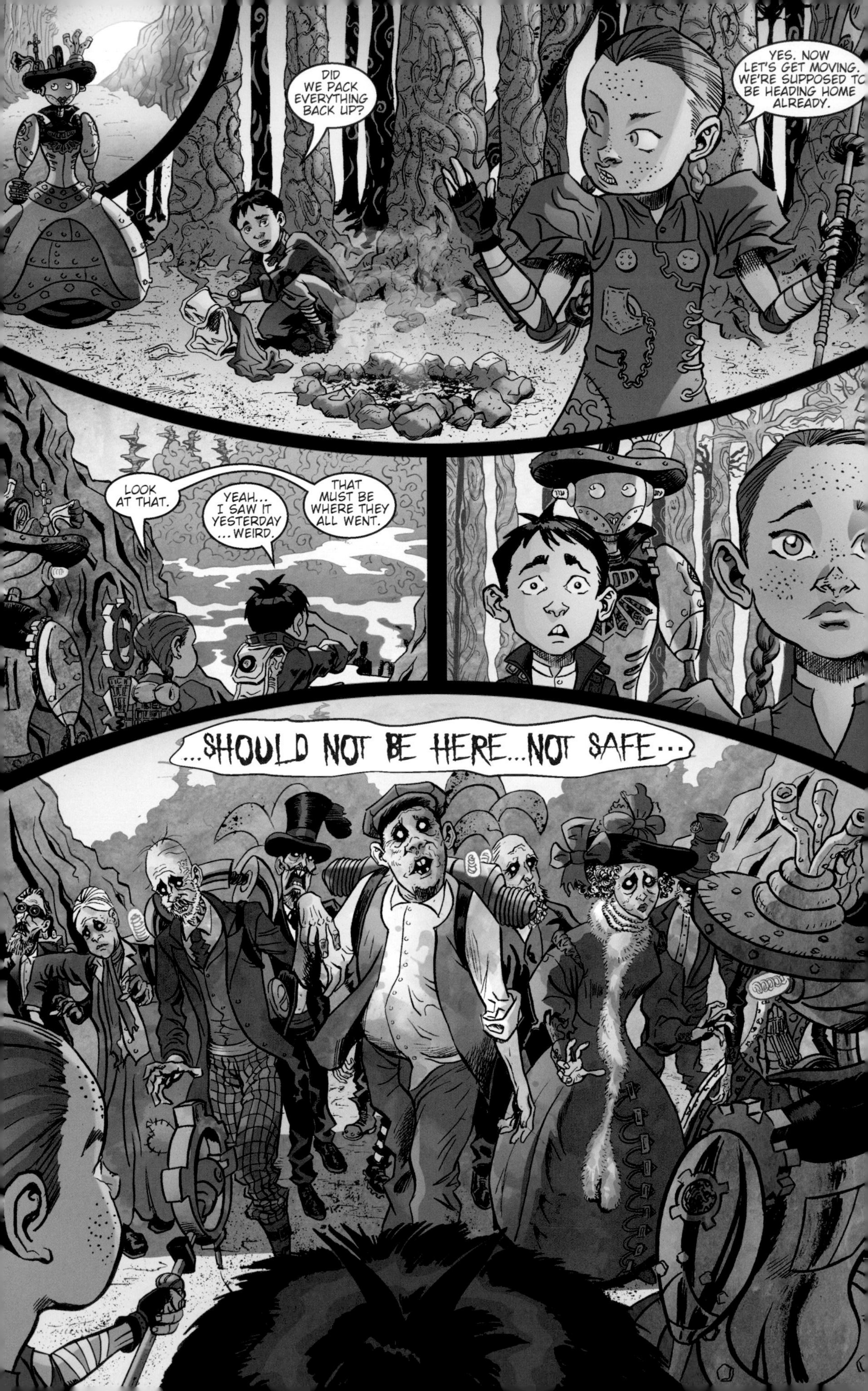
DID WE PACK EVERYTHING BACK UP?
YES. NOW LET'S GET MOVING. WE'RE SUPPOSED TO BE HEADING HOME ALREADY.
LOOK AT THAT.
YEAH... I SAW IT YESTERDAY ...WEIRD.
THAT MUST BE WHERE THEY ALL WENT.
...SHOULD NOT BE HERE...NOT SAFE...

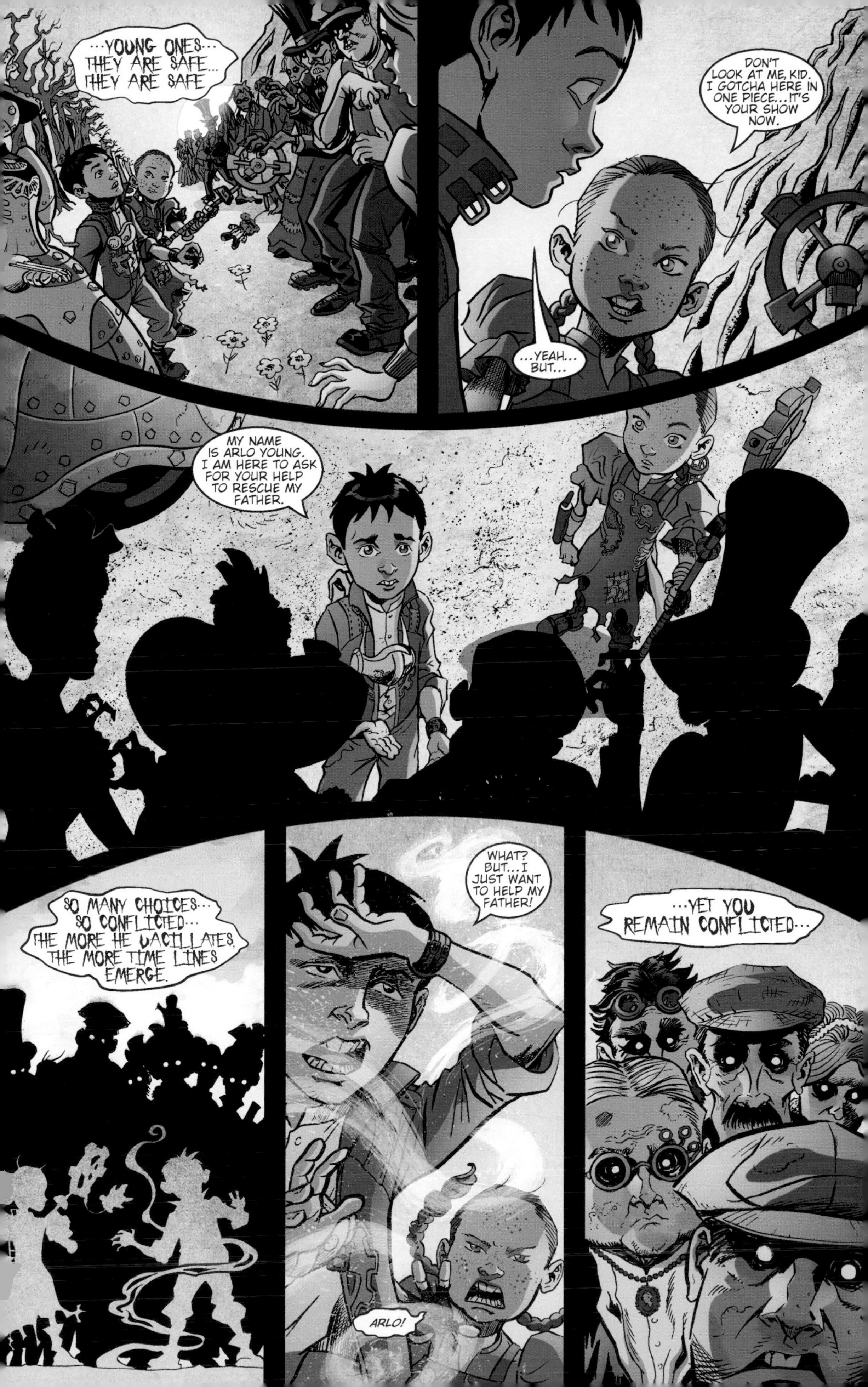
...YOUNG ONES... THEY ARE SAFE... THEY ARE SAFE
DON'T LOOK AT ME, KID. I GOTCHA HERE IN ONE PIECE... IT'S YOUR SHOW NOW.
...YEAH... BUT...
MY NAME IS ARLO YOUNG. I AM HERE TO ASK FOR YOUR HELP TO RESCUE MY FATHER.
SO MANY CHOICES... SO CONFLICTED... THE MORE HE VACILLATES, THE MORE TIME LINES EMERGE.
WHAT? BUT... I JUST WANT TO HELP MY FATHER!
ARLO!
...YET YOU REMAIN CONFLICTED...

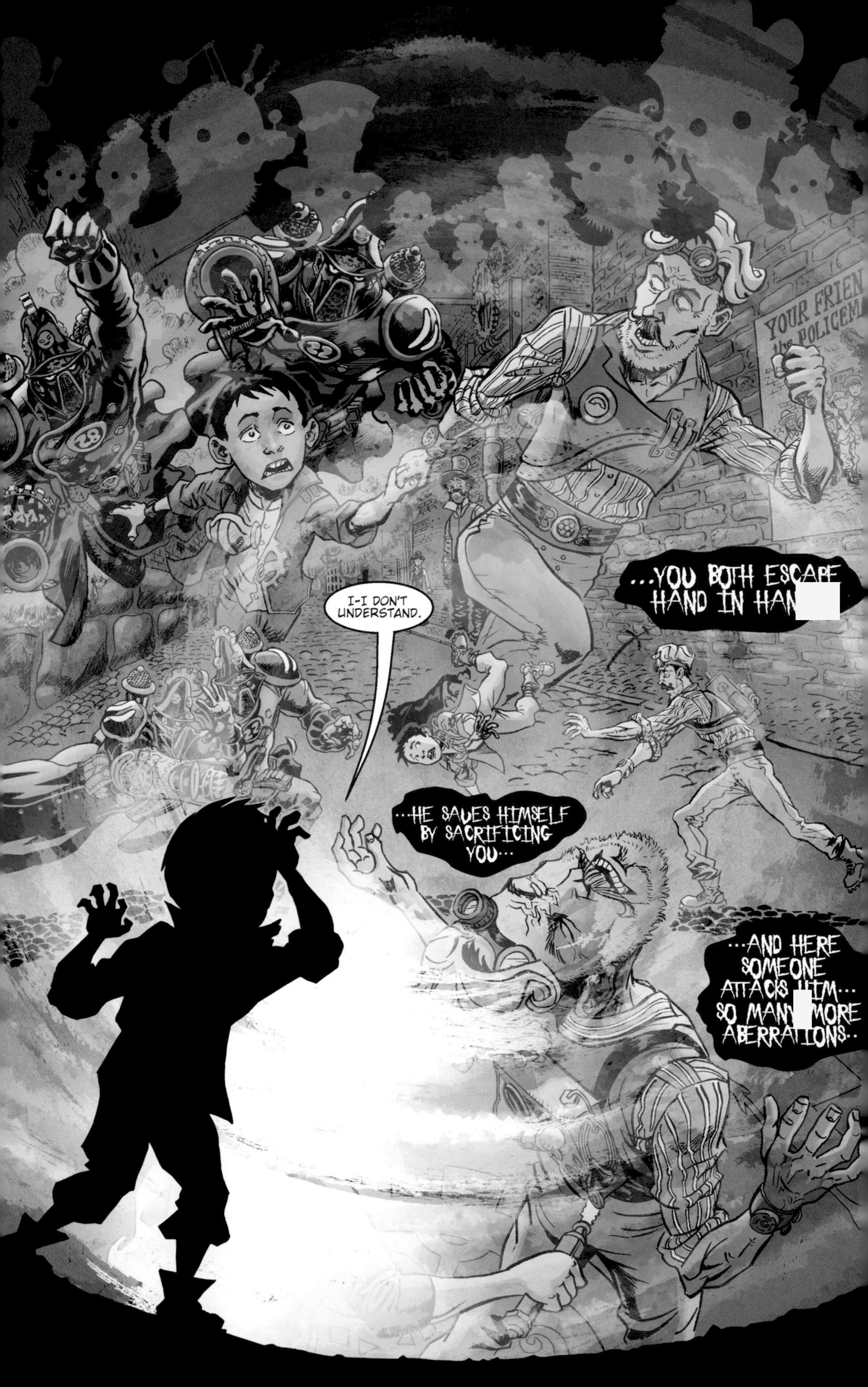
YOUR FRIEN
the POLICEM
...YOU BOTH ESCAPE
HAND IN HAN
I-I DON'T UNDERSTAND.
...HE SAVES HIMSELF BY SACRIFICING YOU...
...AND HERE SOMEONE ATTACKS HIM... SO MANY MORE ABERRATIONS...

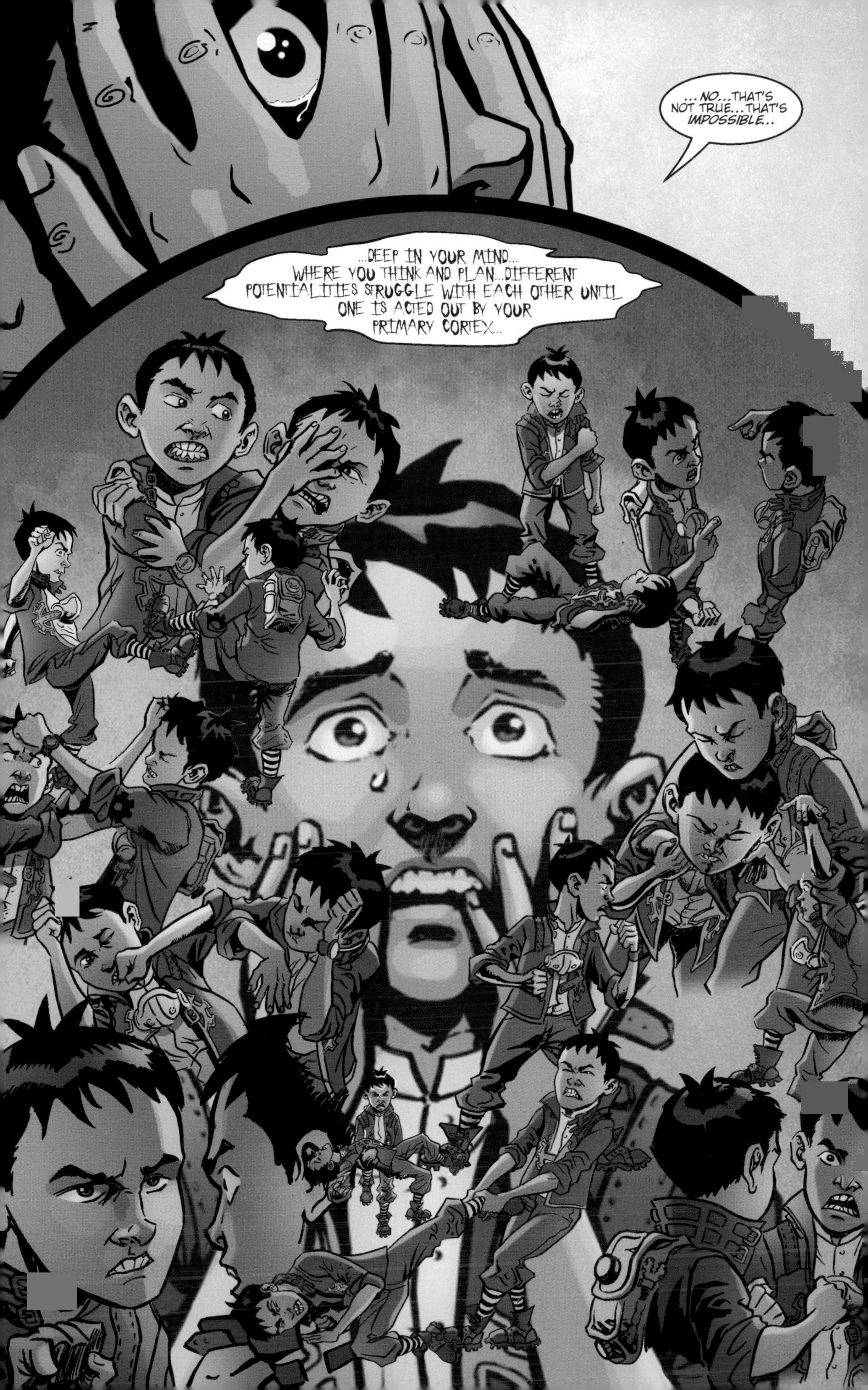
...NO...THAT'S NOT TRUE...THAT'S IMPOSSIBLE...
...DEEP IN YOUR MIND... WHERE YOU THINK AND PLAN...DIFFERENT POTENTIALITIES STRUGGLE WITH EACH OTHER UNTIL ONE IS ACTED OUT BY YOUR PRIMARY CORTEX...

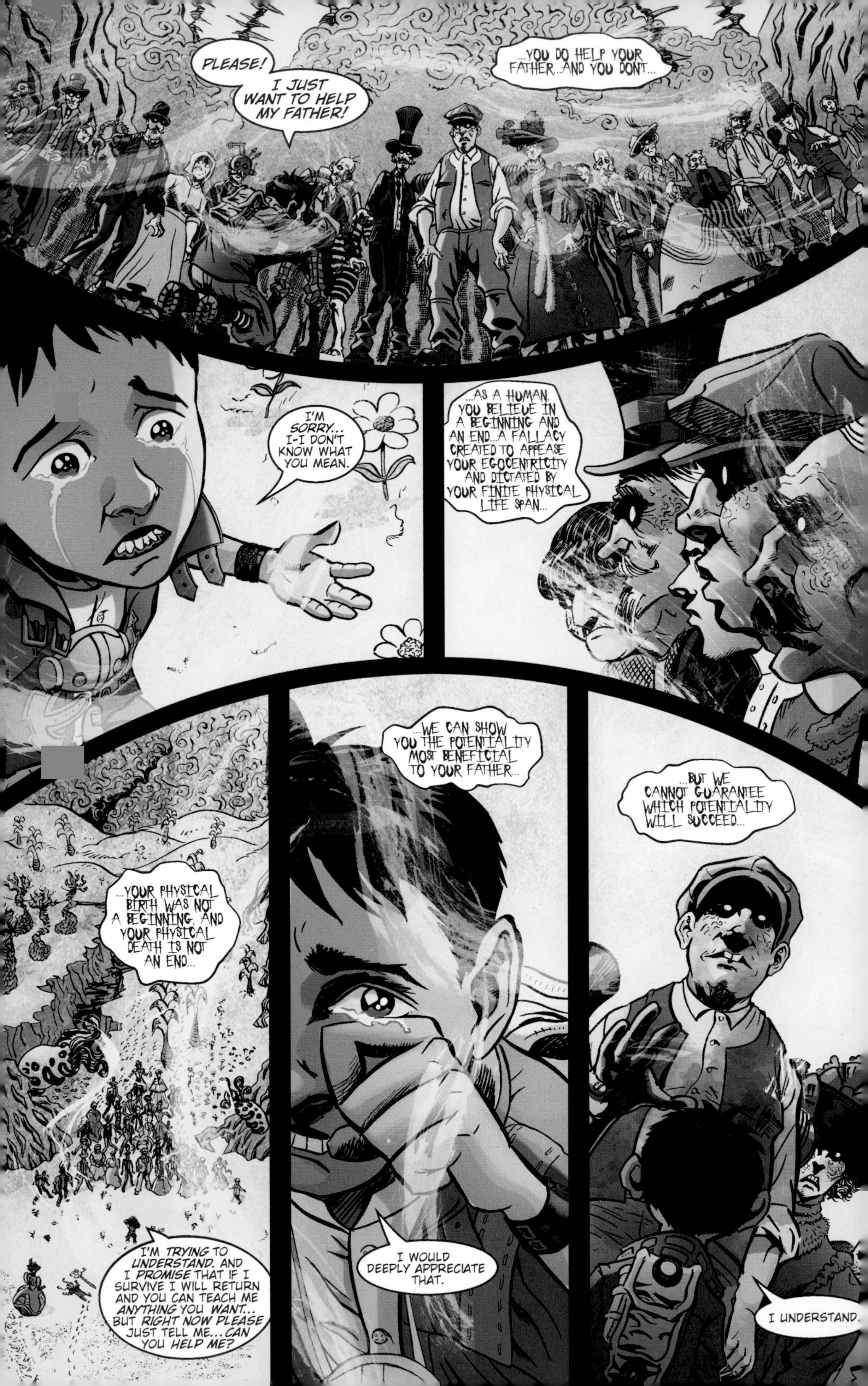
PLEASE! I JUST WANT TO HELP MY FATHER!
...YOU DO HELP YOUR FATHER...AND YOU DON'T...
I'M SORRY... I-I DON'T KNOW WHAT YOU MEAN.
...AS A HUMAN, YOU BELIEVE IN A BEGINNING AND AN END...A FALLACY CREATED TO APPEASE YOUR EGOCENTRICITY AND DICTATED BY YOUR FINITE PHYSICAL LIFE SPAN...
...YOUR PHYSICAL BIRTH WAS NOT A BEGINNING, AND YOUR PHYSICAL DEATH IS NOT AN END...
I'M TRYING TO UNDERSTAND. AND I PROMISE THAT IF I SURVIVE I WILL RETURN AND YOU CAN TEACH ME ANYTHING YOU WANT... BUT RIGHT NOW PLEASE JUST TELL ME... CAN YOU HELP ME?
...WE CAN SHOW YOU THE POTENTIALITY MOST BENEFICIAL TO YOUR FATHER...
I WOULD DEEPLY APPRECIATE THAT.
...BUT WE CANNOT GUARANTEE WHICH POTENTIALITY WILL SUCCEED...
I UNDERSTAND.

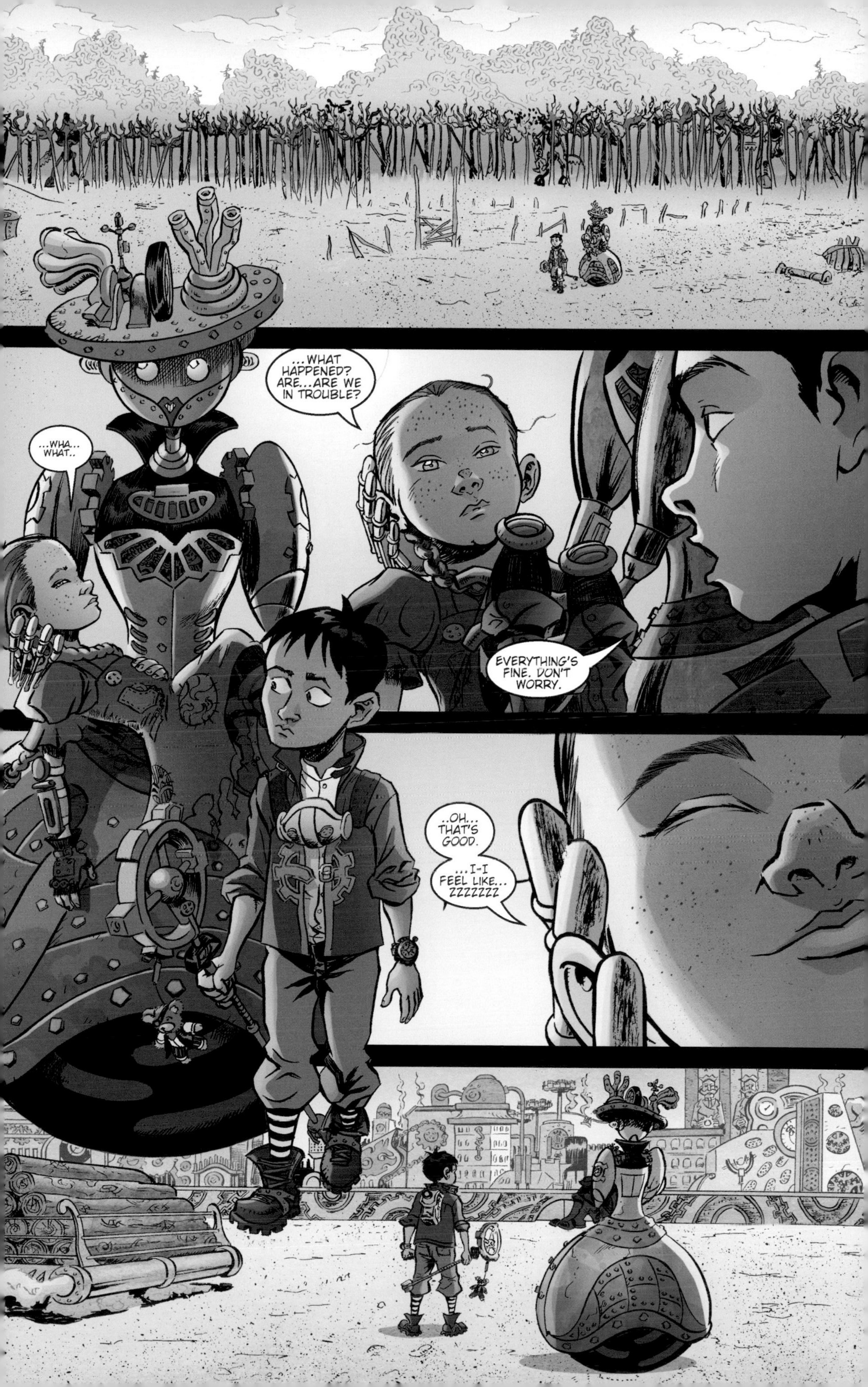
...WHA... WHAT..
...WHAT HAPPENED? ARE...ARE WE IN TROUBLE?
EVERYTHING'S FINE. DON'T WORRY.
..OH... THAT'S GOOD.
...I-I FEEL LIKE... ZZZZZZZ

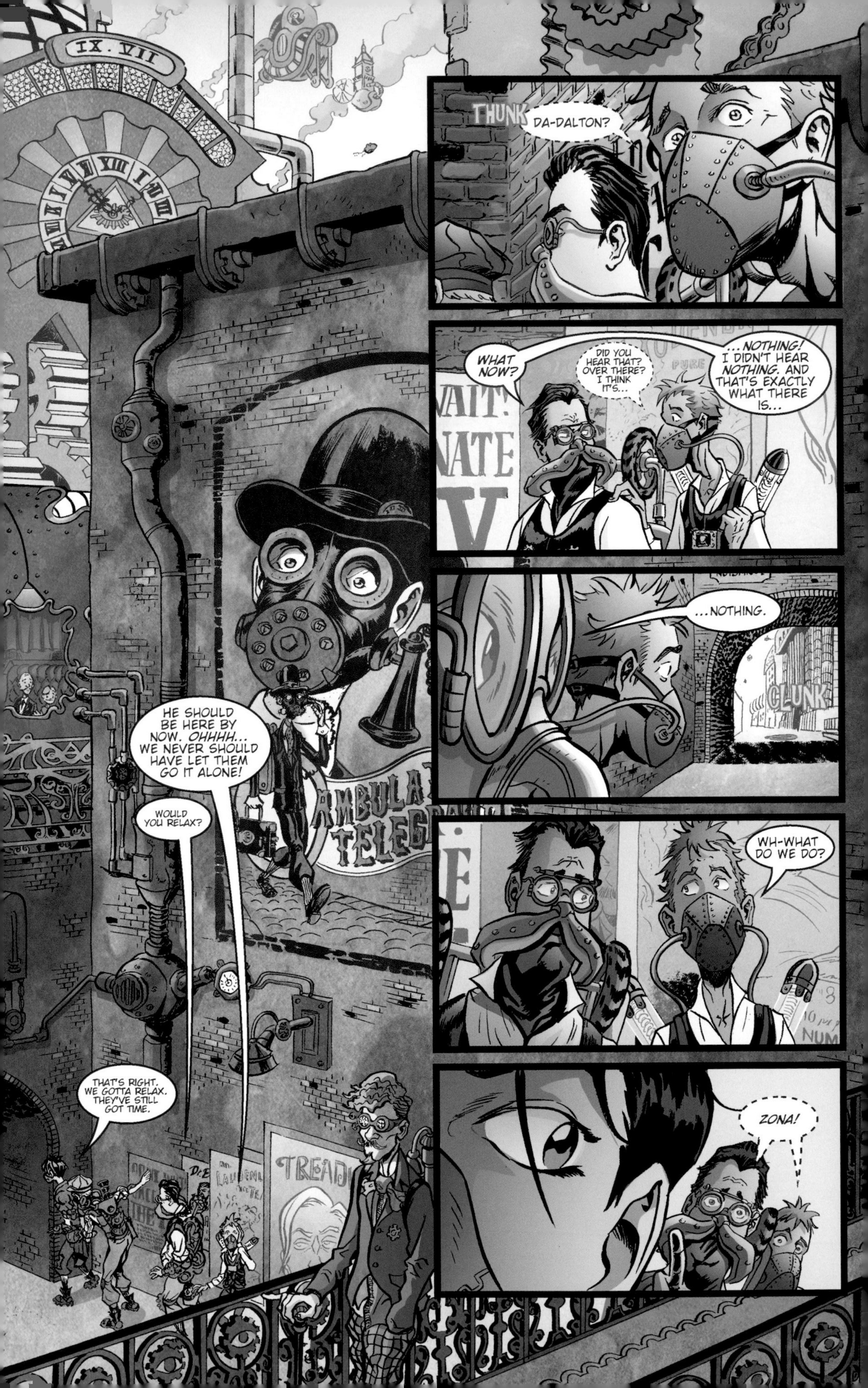
IX. VII
HE SHOULD BE HERE BY NOW. OHHHH... WE NEVER SHOULD HAVE LET THEM GO IT ALONE!
WOULD YOU RELAX?
THAT'S RIGHT. WE GOTTA RELAX. THEY'VE STILL GOT TIME.
THUNK
DA-DALTON?
WHAT NOW?
DID YOU HEAR THAT? OVER THERE? I THINK IT'S...
...NOTHING! I DIDN'T HEAR NOTHING. AND THAT'S EXACTLY WHAT THERE IS...
...NOTHING.
CLUNK
WH-WHAT DO WE DO?
ZONA!

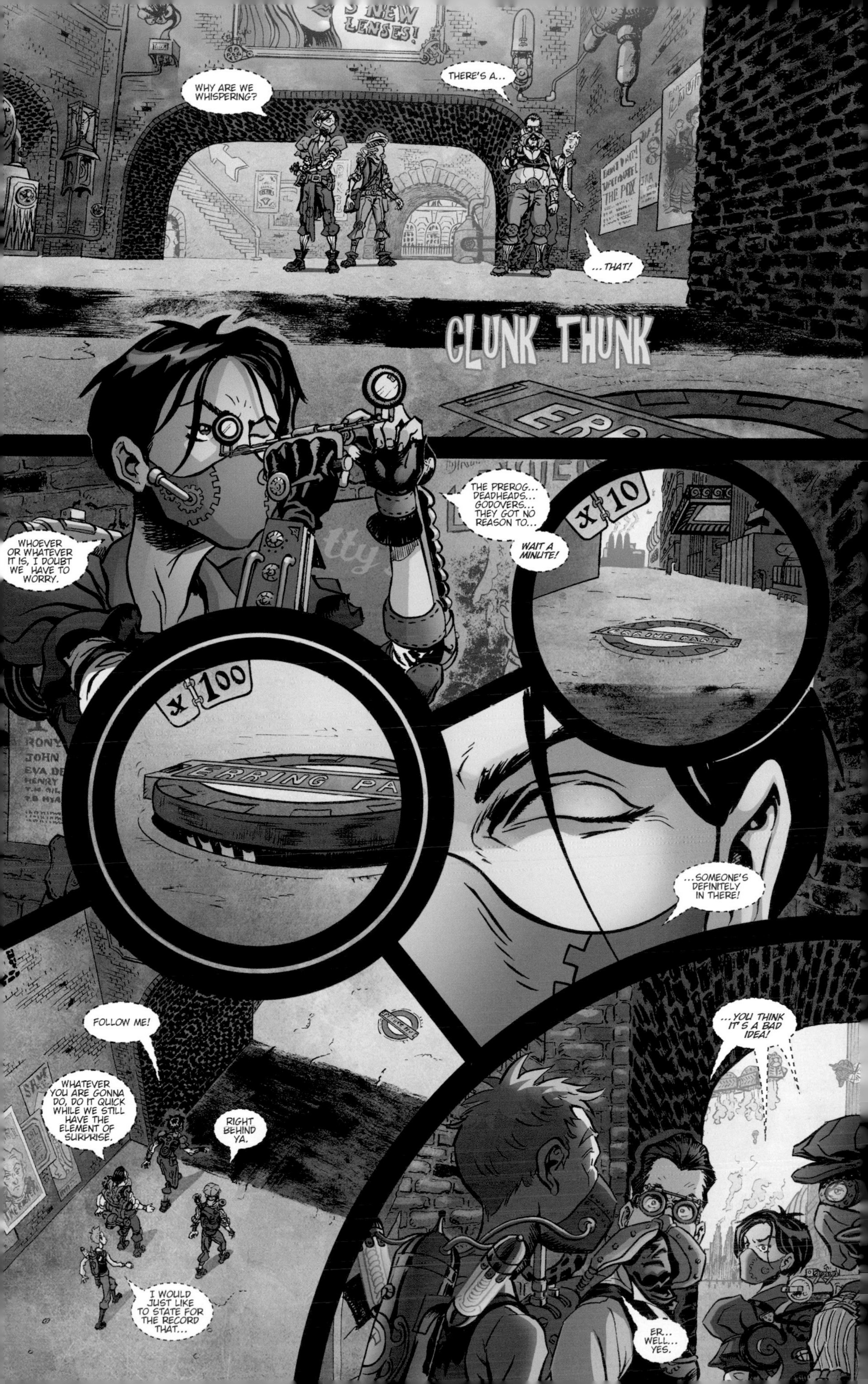
'S NEW LENSES!
WHY ARE WE WHISPERING?
THERE'S A...
...THAT!
CLUNK THUNK
WHOEVER OR WHATEVER IT IS, I DOUBT WE HAVE TO WORRY.
THE PREROG... DEADHEADS... GODOVERS... THEY GOT NO REASON TO...
WAIT A MINUTE!
x 10
x 100
ERRING PA
...SOMEONE'S DEFINITELY IN THERE!
FOLLOW ME!
WHATEVER YOU ARE GONNA DO, DO IT QUICK WHILE WE STILL HAVE THE ELEMENT OF SURPRISE.
RIGHT BEHIND YA.
I WOULD JUST LIKE TO STATE FOR THE RECORD THAT...
...YOU THINK IT'S A BAD IDEA!
ER... WELL... YES.

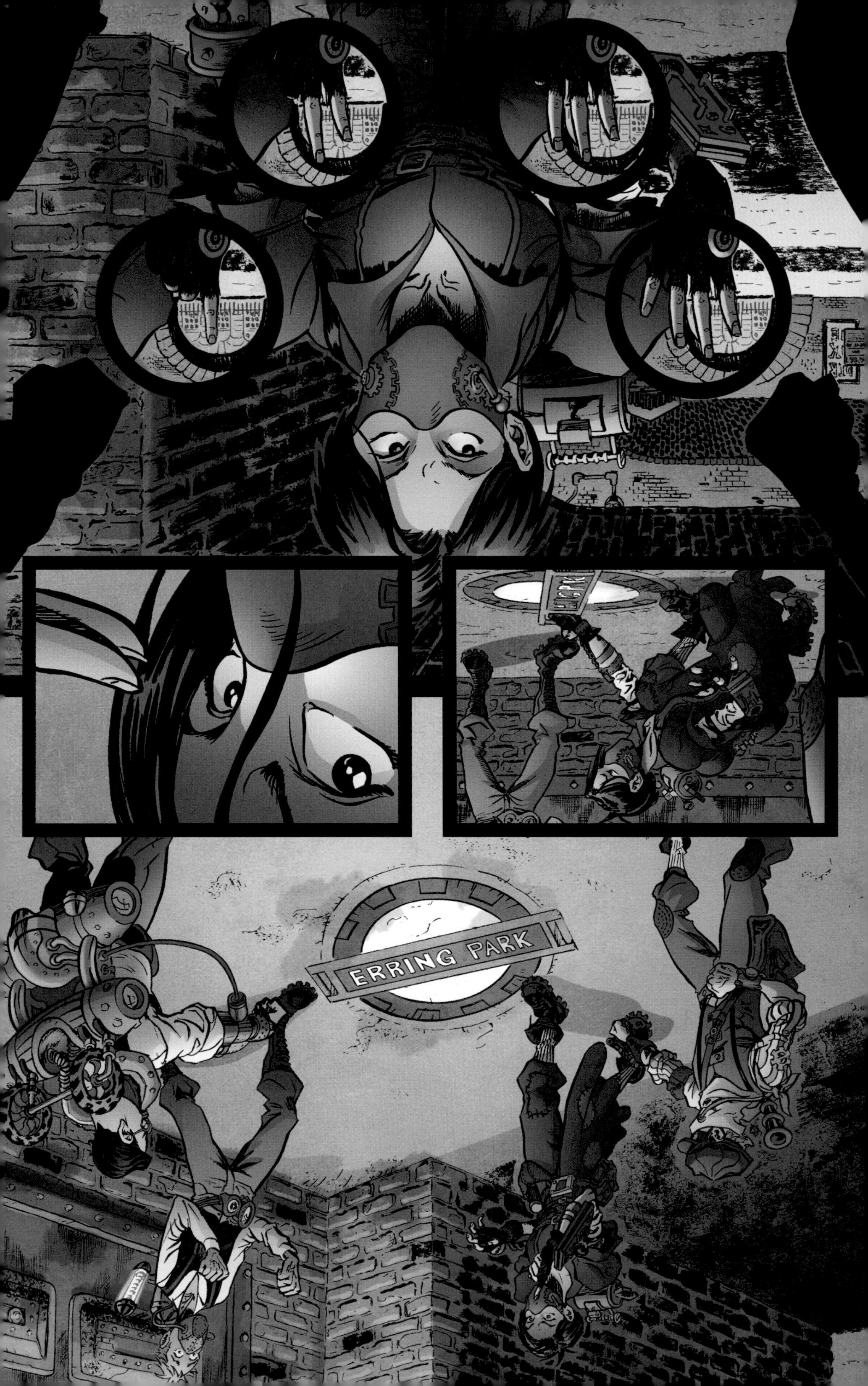
ERRING PARK

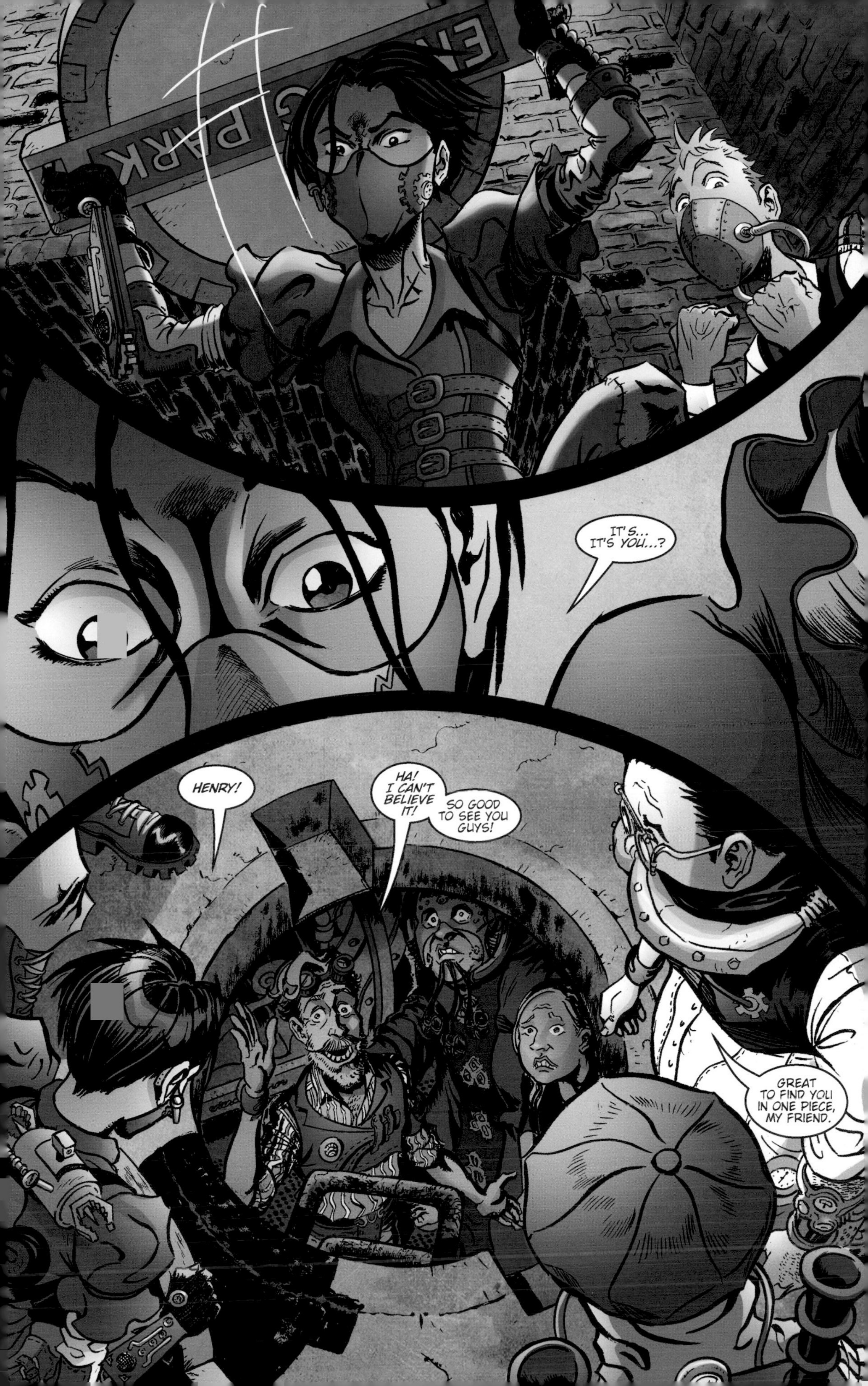
IT'S...
IT'S YOU...?
HENRY!
HA! I CAN'T BELIEVE IT!
SO GOOD TO SEE YOU GUYS!
GREAT TO FIND YOU IN ONE PIECE, MY FRIEND.

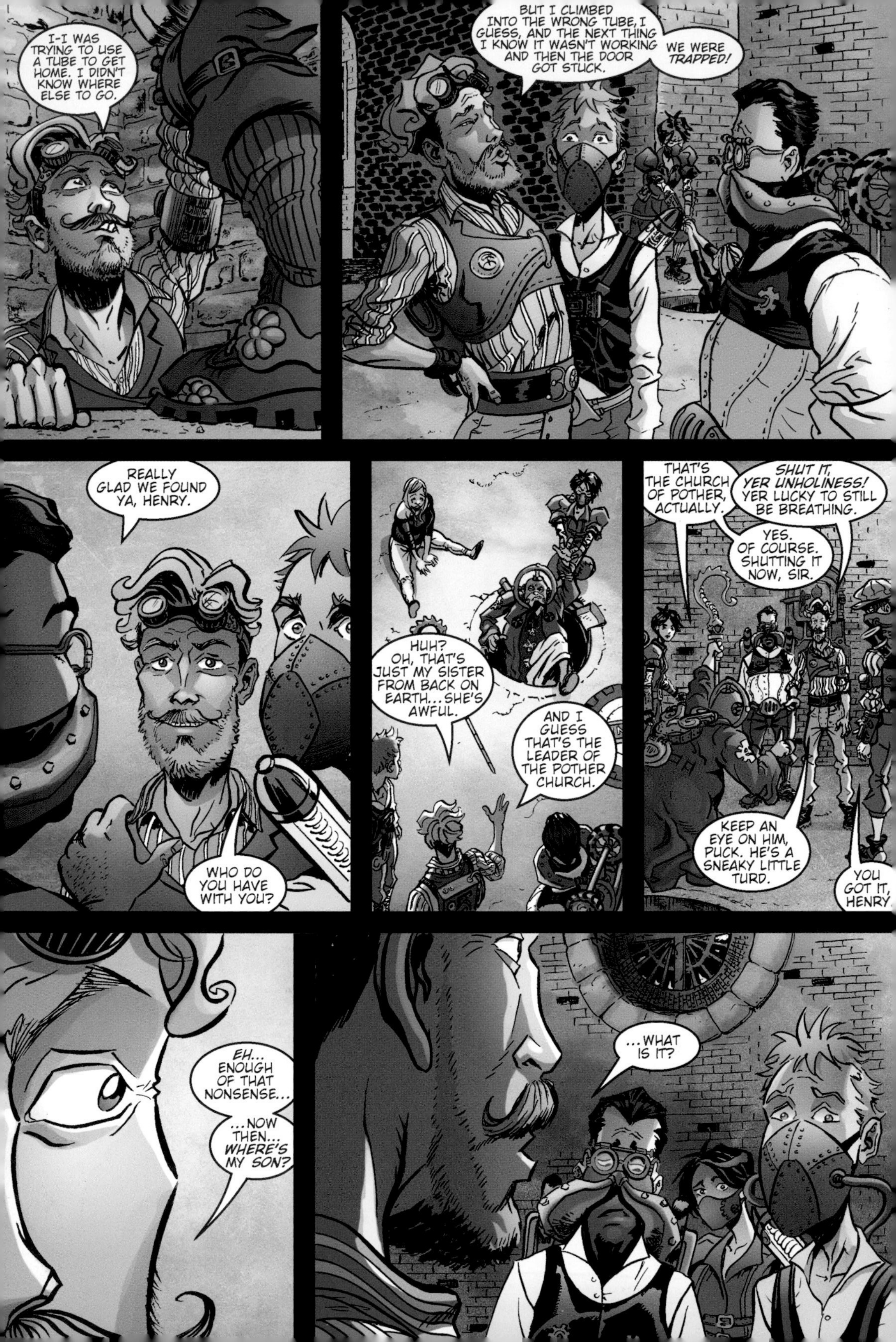
I-I WAS TRYING TO USE A TUBE TO GET HOME. I DIDN'T KNOW WHERE ELSE TO GO.
BUT I CLIMBED INTO THE WRONG TUBE, I GUESS, AND THE NEXT THING I KNOW IT WASN'T WORKING AND THEN THE DOOR GOT STUCK.
WE WERE *TRAPPED!*
REALLY GLAD WE FOUND YA, HENRY.
WHO DO YOU HAVE WITH YOU?
HUH? OH, THAT'S JUST MY SISTER FROM BACK ON EARTH... SHE'S AWFUL.
AND I GUESS THAT'S THE LEADER OF THE POTHER CHURCH.
THAT'S THE CHURCH OF POTHER, ACTUALLY.
SHUT IT, YER UNHOLINESS! YER LUCKY TO STILL BE BREATHING.
YES. OF COURSE. SHUTTING IT NOW, SIR.
KEEP AN EYE ON HIM, PUCK. HE'S A SNEAKY LITTLE TURD.
YOU GOT IT, HENRY.
EH... ENOUGH OF THAT NONSENSE...
...NOW THEN... *WHERE'S* MY SON?
...WHAT IS IT?

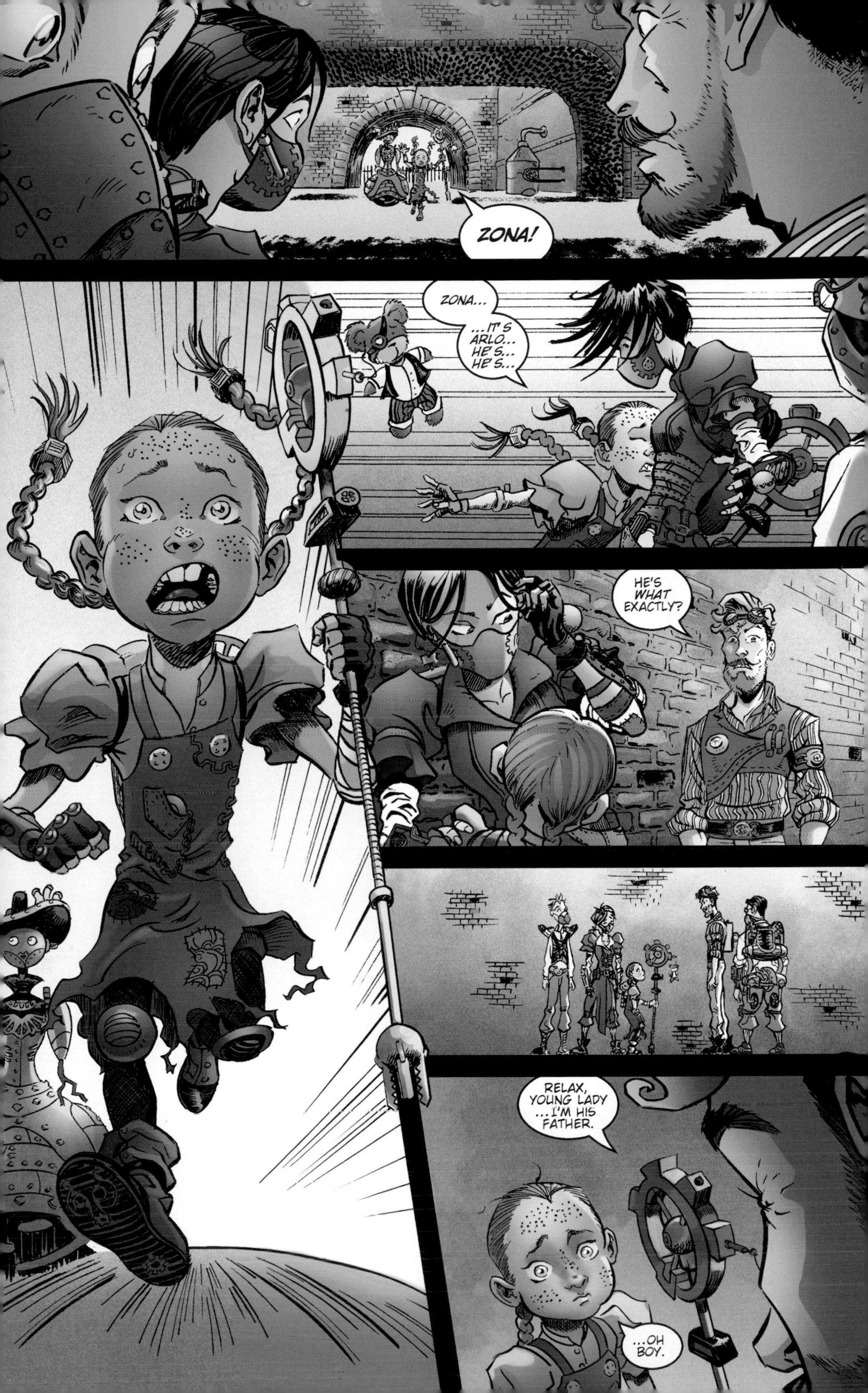
ZONA!
ZONA...
...IT'S ARLO... HE'S... HE'S...
HE'S WHAT EXACTLY?
RELAX, YOUNG LADY ...I'M HIS FATHER.
...OH BOY.

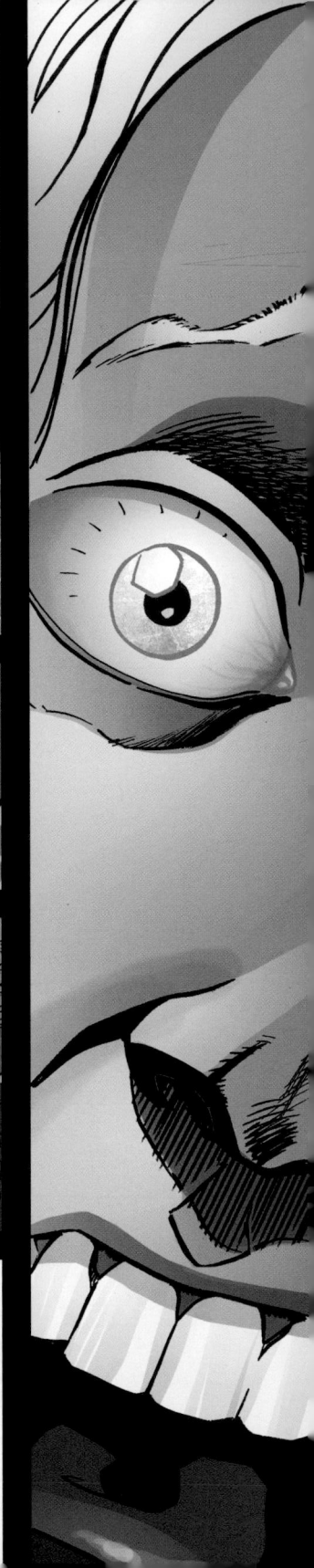

I DON'T WANT YOU TO CALL ANYONE! I DON'T WANT YOU TO DO *ANYTHING!*

YOU'VE DONE QUITE ENOUGH. YOU GOT THAT?

...MALFUNCTIONING MACHINE-LOVING MISFIT!

JUST KEEP YER TRAP SHUT.

SHOULDN'T WE BE TRYING TO FIND HIM? LET ME CALL MY--

I CAN'T THINK WITH ALL YOUR *JABBERING.*

NOW THEN...LET ME THINK...

I DON'T RECALL ASKING YOU TO SPEAK.

...UM... TREADWELL...

YOU CAN'T KEEP THOSE TIN LIPS SHUT, CAN YOU... NOT EVEN FOR A...

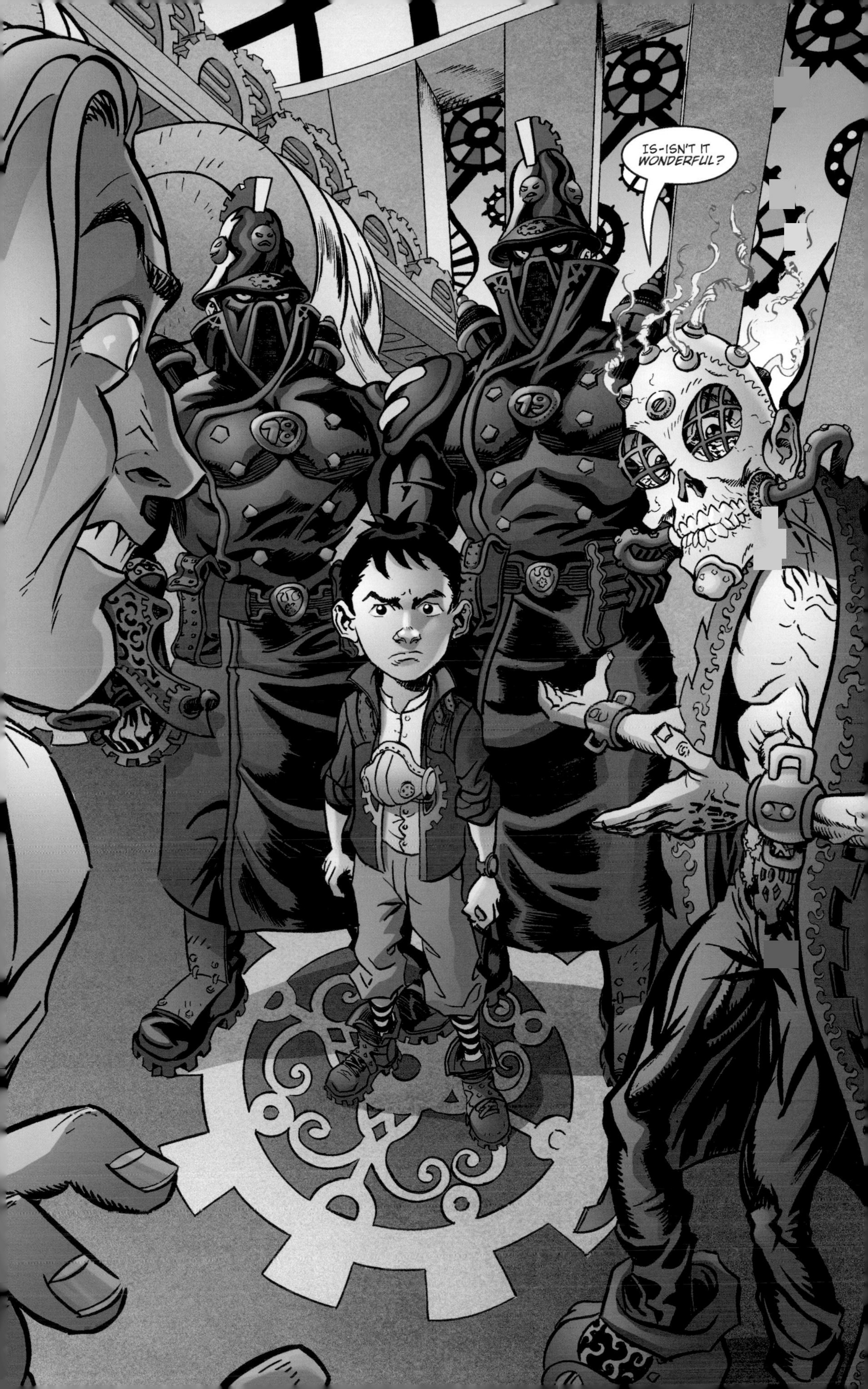
IS-ISN'T IT *WONDERFUL?*

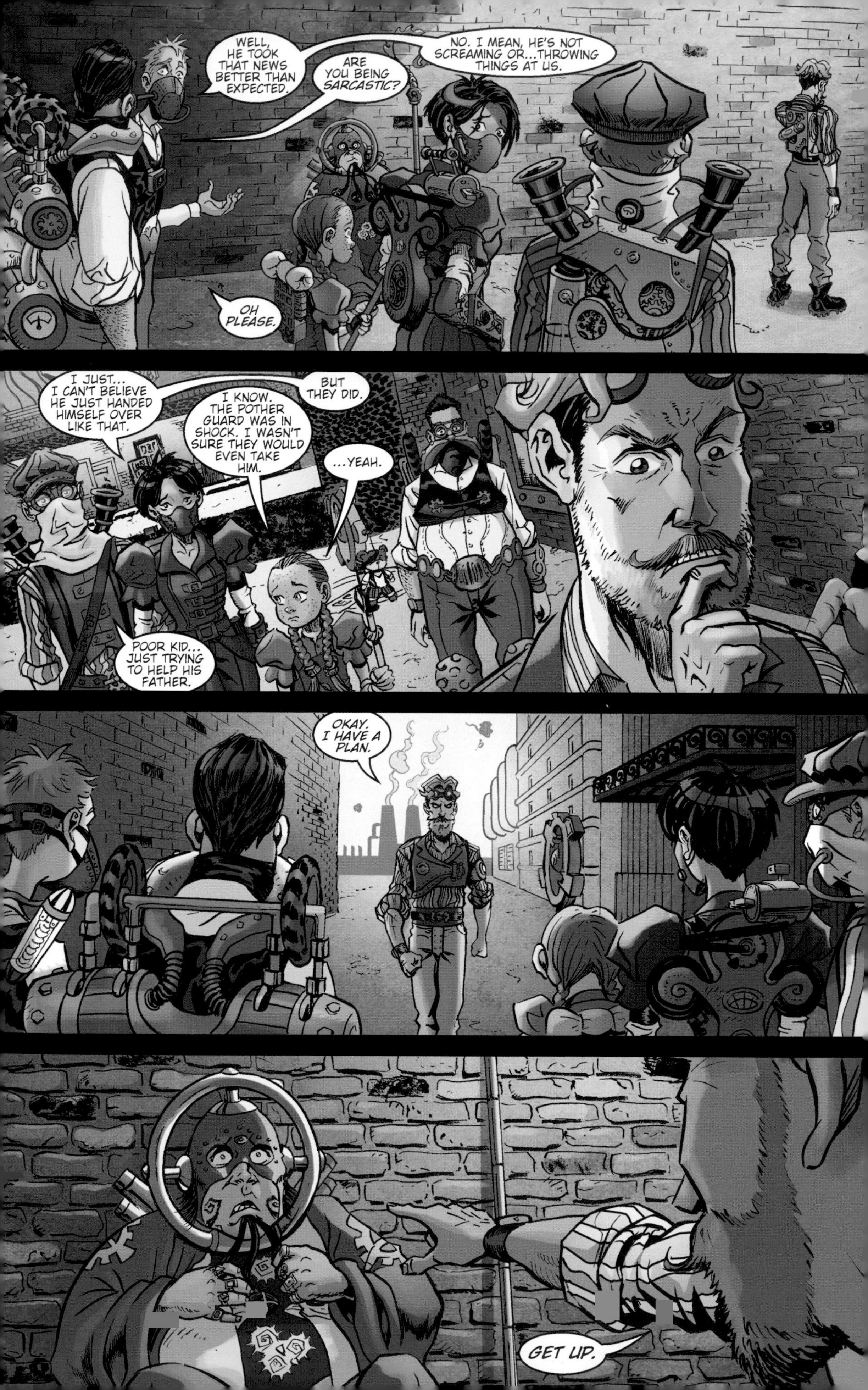
WELL, HE TOOK THAT NEWS BETTER THAN EXPECTED.
ARE YOU BEING SARCASTIC?
NO. I MEAN, HE'S NOT SCREAMING OR...THROWING THINGS AT US.
OH PLEASE.
I JUST... I CAN'T BELIEVE HE JUST HANDED HIMSELF OVER LIKE THAT.
I KNOW. THE POTHER GUARD WAS IN SHOCK. I WASN'T SURE THEY WOULD EVEN TAKE HIM.
BUT THEY DID.
...YEAH.
POOR KID... JUST TRYING TO HELP HIS FATHER.
OKAY. I HAVE A PLAN.
GET UP.

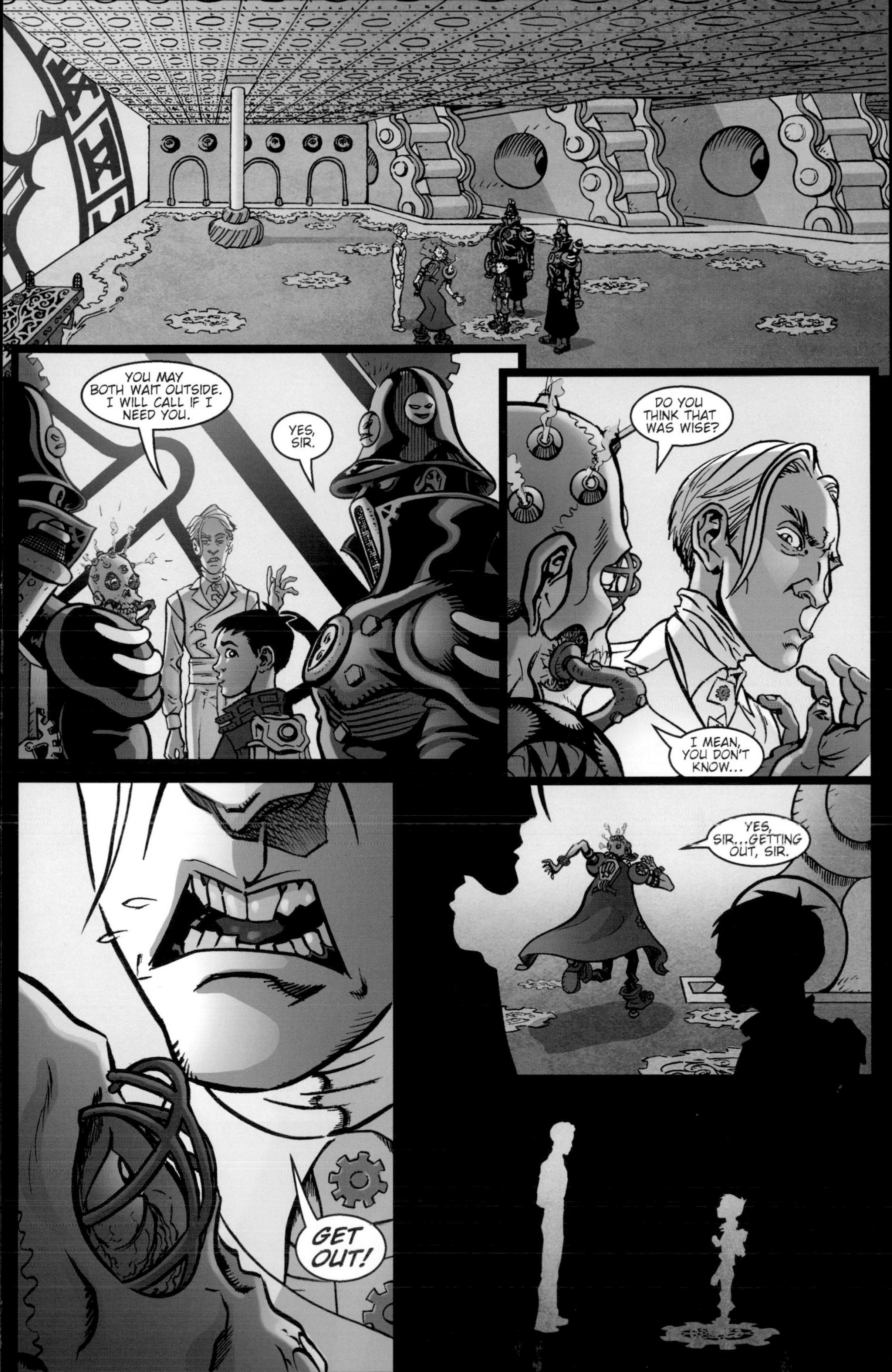
YOU MAY BOTH WAIT OUTSIDE. I WILL CALL IF I NEED YOU.
YES, SIR.
DO YOU THINK THAT WAS WISE?
I MEAN, YOU DON'T KNOW...
GET OUT!
YES, SIR...GETTING OUT, SIR.

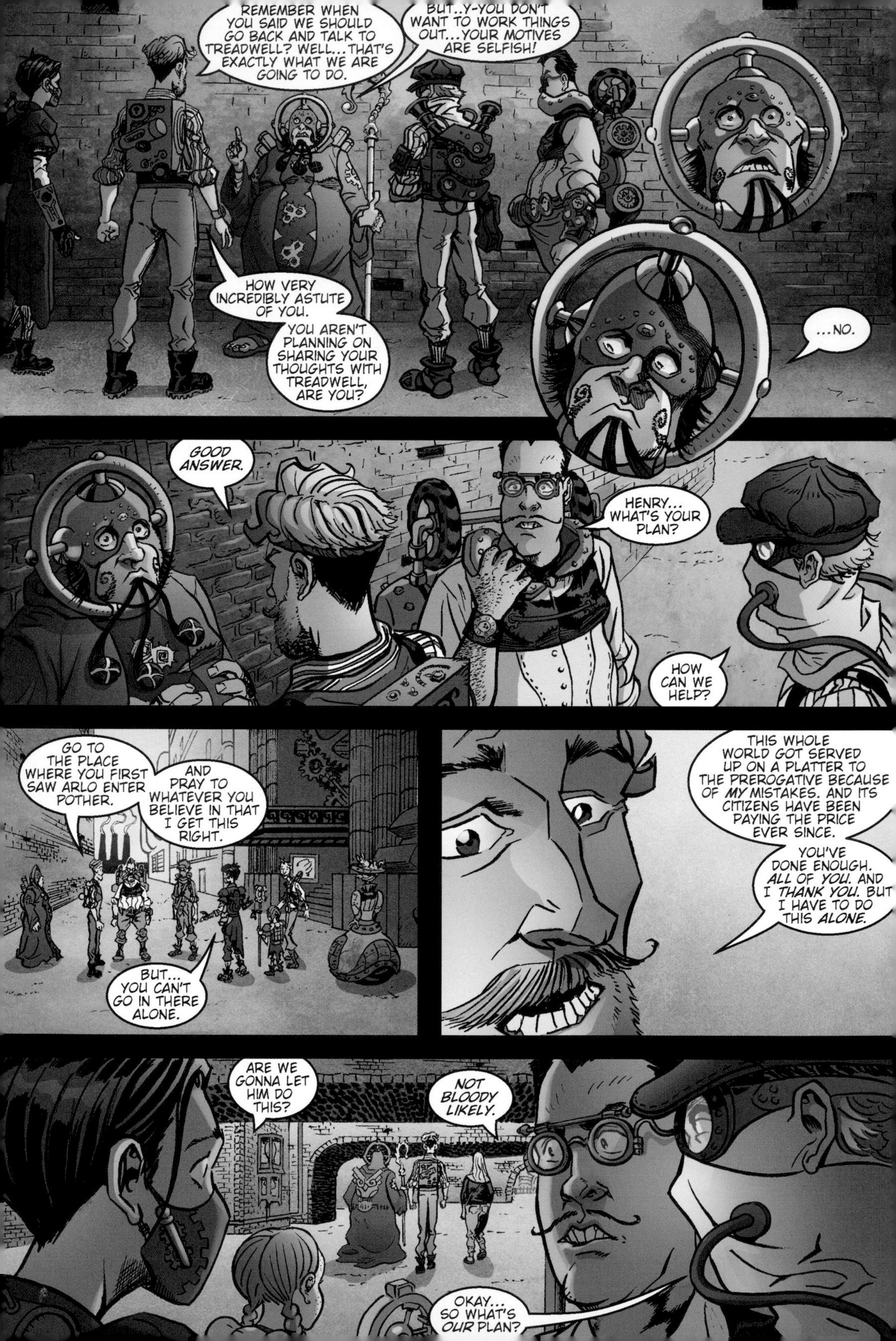
REMEMBER WHEN YOU SAID WE SHOULD GO BACK AND TALK TO TREADWELL? WELL...THAT'S EXACTLY WHAT WE ARE GOING TO DO.
BUT..Y-YOU DON'T WANT TO WORK THINGS OUT...YOUR MOTIVES ARE SELFISH!
HOW VERY INCREDIBLY ASTUTE OF YOU.
YOU AREN'T PLANNING ON SHARING YOUR THOUGHTS WITH TREADWELL, ARE YOU?
...NO.
GOOD ANSWER.
HENRY... WHAT'S YOUR PLAN?
HOW CAN WE HELP?
GO TO THE PLACE WHERE YOU FIRST SAW ARLO ENTER POTHER.
AND PRAY TO WHATEVER YOU BELIEVE IN THAT I GET THIS RIGHT.
BUT... YOU CAN'T GO IN THERE ALONE.
THIS WHOLE WORLD GOT SERVED UP ON A PLATTER TO THE PREROGATIVE BECAUSE OF MY MISTAKES. AND ITS CITIZENS HAVE BEEN PAYING THE PRICE EVER SINCE.
YOU'VE DONE ENOUGH. ALL OF YOU. AND I THANK YOU. BUT I HAVE TO DO THIS ALONE.
ARE WE GONNA LET HIM DO THIS?
NOT BLOODY LIKELY.
OKAY... SO WHAT'S OUR PLAN?

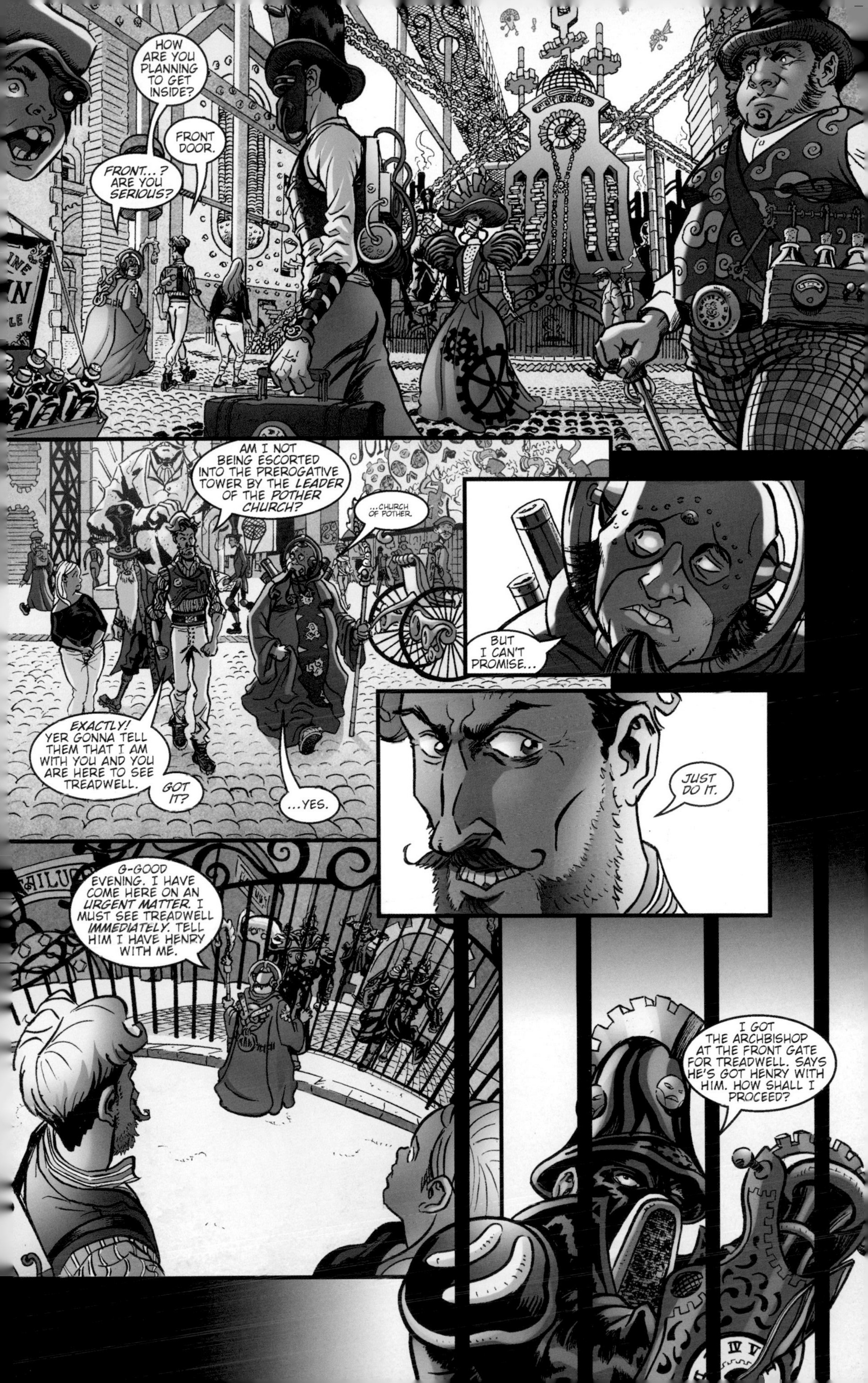
HOW ARE YOU PLANNING TO GET INSIDE?
FRONT DOOR.
FRONT...? ARE YOU SERIOUS?
AM I NOT BEING ESCORTED INTO THE PREROGATIVE TOWER BY THE LEADER OF THE POTHER CHURCH?
...CHURCH OF POTHER.
EXACTLY! YER GONNA TELL THEM THAT I AM WITH YOU AND YOU ARE HERE TO SEE TREADWELL.
GOT IT?
...YES.
BUT I CAN'T PROMISE...
JUST DO IT.
G-GOOD EVENING. I HAVE COME HERE ON AN URGENT MATTER. I MUST SEE TREADWELL IMMEDIATELY. TELL HIM I HAVE HENRY WITH ME.
I GOT THE ARCHBISHOP AT THE FRONT GATE FOR TREADWELL. SAYS HE'S GOT HENRY WITH HIM. HOW SHALL I PROCEED?

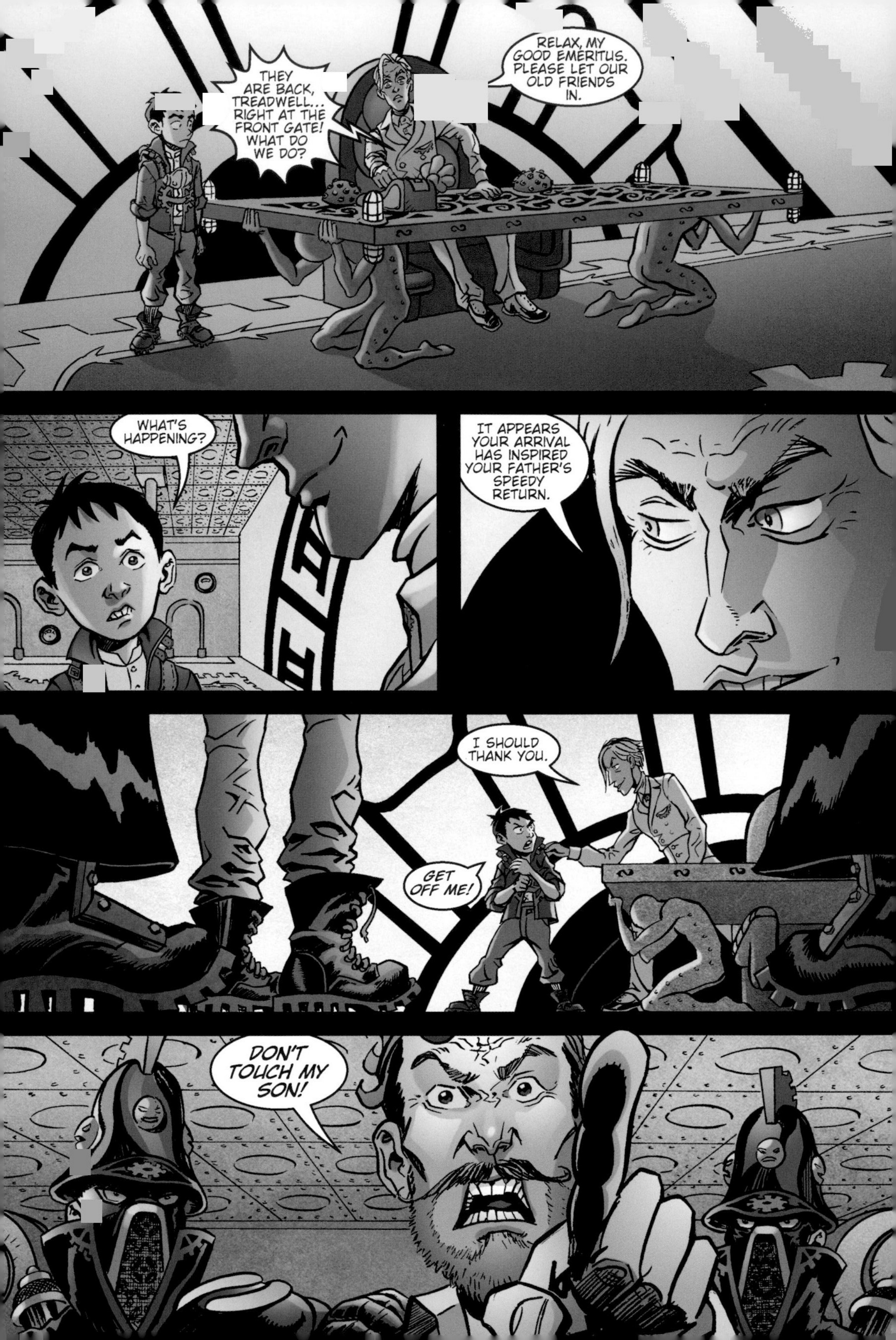
THEY ARE BACK, TREADWELL... RIGHT AT THE FRONT GATE! WHAT DO WE DO?
RELAX, MY GOOD EMERITUS. PLEASE LET OUR OLD FRIENDS IN.
WHAT'S HAPPENING?
IT APPEARS YOUR ARRIVAL HAS INSPIRED YOUR FATHER'S SPEEDY RETURN.
I SHOULD THANK YOU.
GET OFF ME!
DON'T TOUCH MY SON!

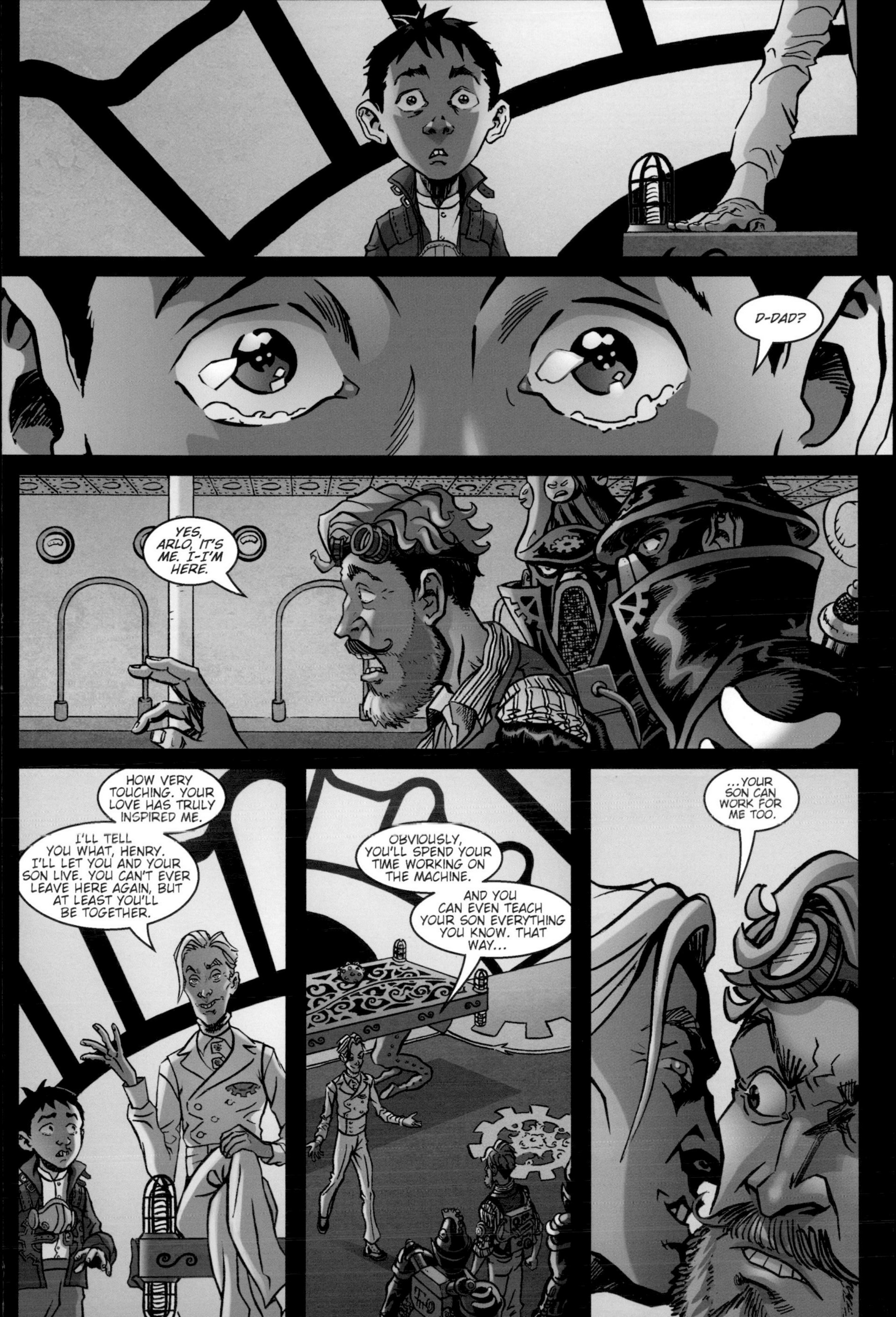
D-DAD?
YES, ARLO, IT'S ME. I-I'M HERE.
HOW VERY TOUCHING. YOUR LOVE HAS TRULY INSPIRED ME.
I'LL TELL YOU WHAT, HENRY. I'LL LET YOU AND YOUR SON LIVE. YOU CAN'T EVER LEAVE HERE AGAIN, BUT AT LEAST YOU'LL BE TOGETHER.
OBVIOUSLY, YOU'LL SPEND YOUR TIME WORKING ON THE MACHINE.
AND YOU CAN EVEN TEACH YOUR SON EVERYTHING YOU KNOW. THAT WAY...
...YOUR SON CAN WORK FOR ME TOO.

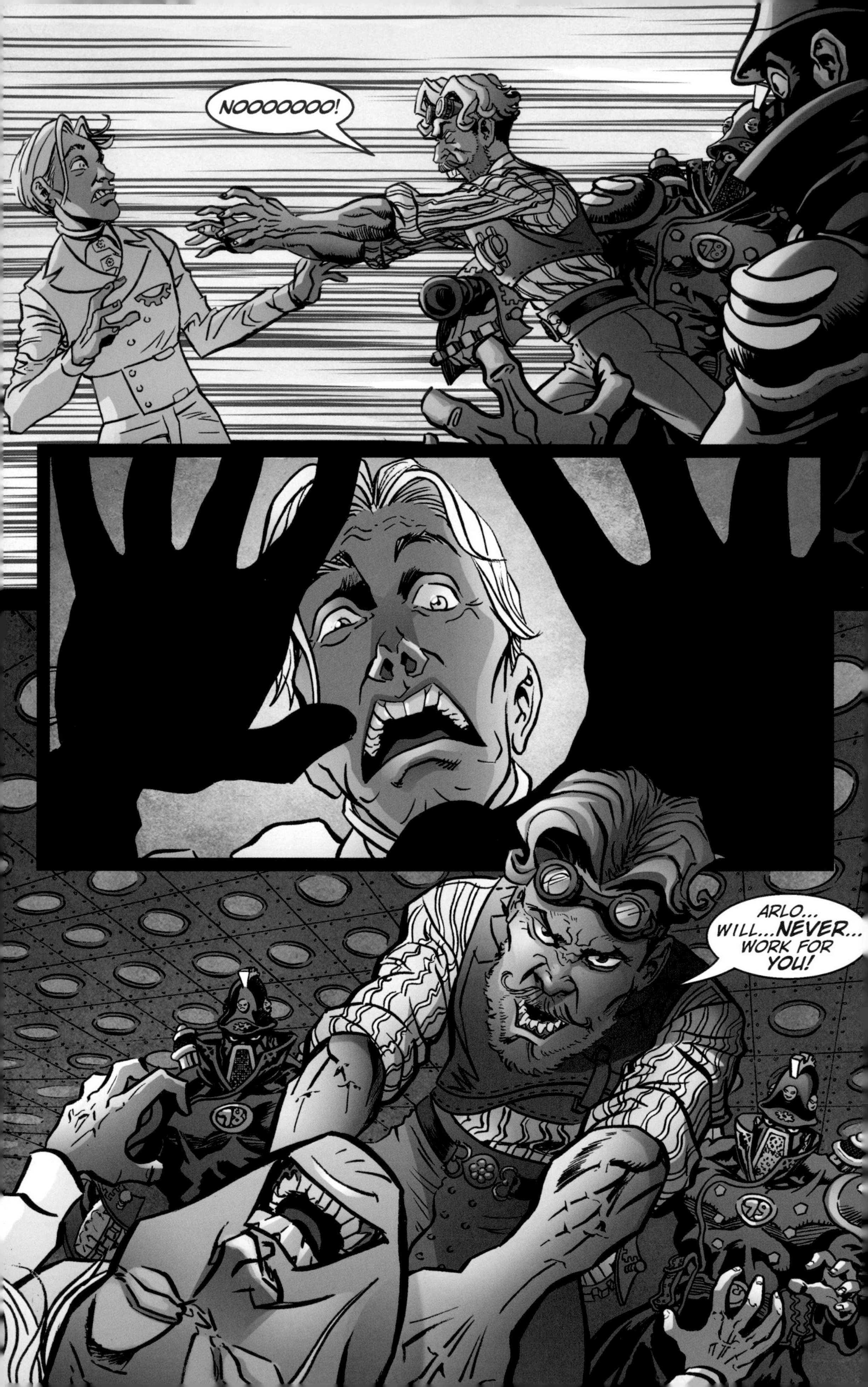
NOOOOOOO!
ARLO... WILL... NEVER... WORK FOR YOU!

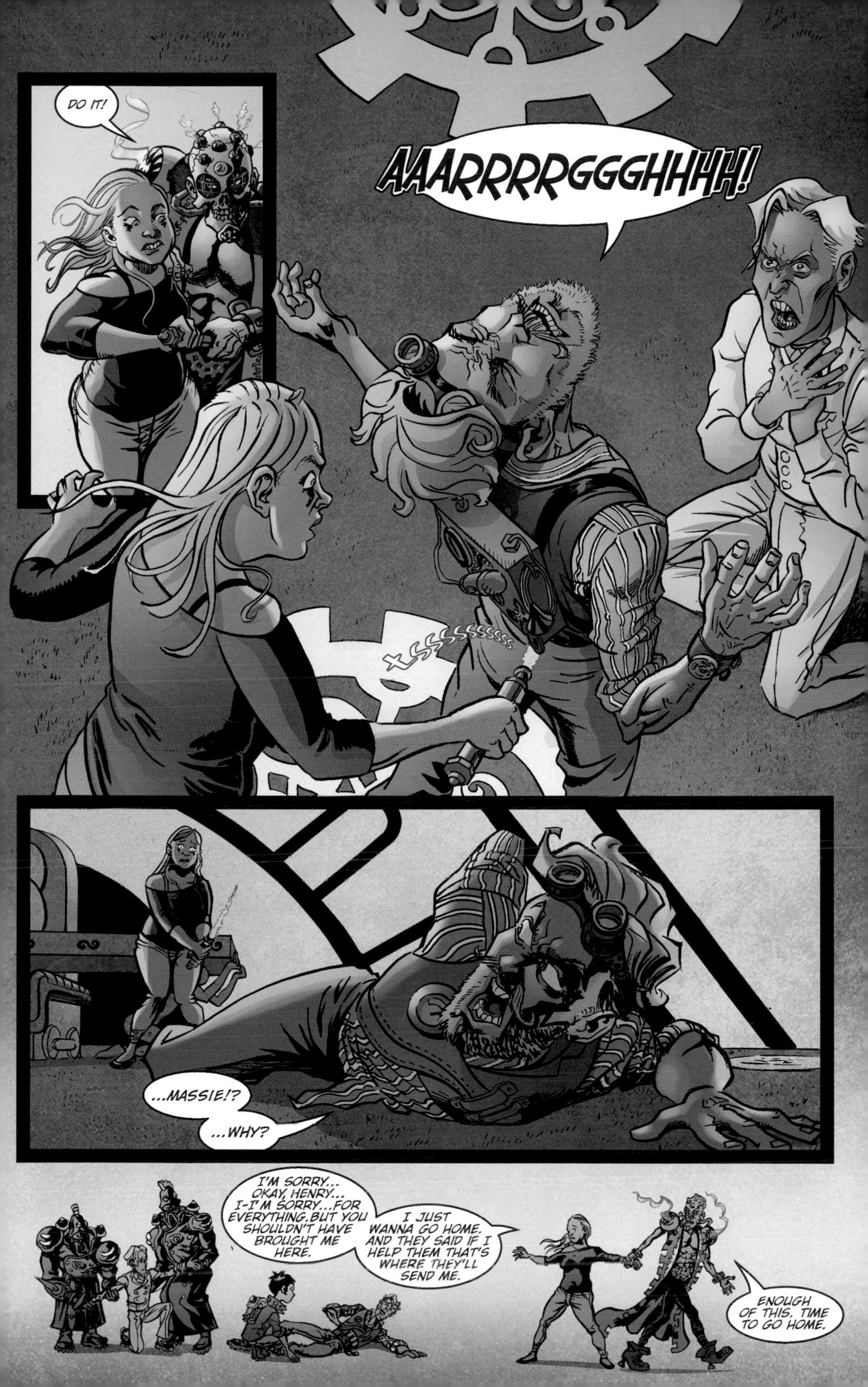
DO IT!
AAARRRRRGGGHHHH!
XSSSSSSSSSS
...MASSIE!?
...WHY?
I'M SORRY... OKAY, HENRY... I-I'M SORRY...FOR EVERYTHING.BUT YOU SHOULDN'T HAVE BROUGHT ME HERE.
I JUST WANNA GO HOME. AND THEY SAID IF I HELP THEM THAT'S WHERE THEY'LL SEND ME.
ENOUGH OF THIS. TIME TO GO HOME.

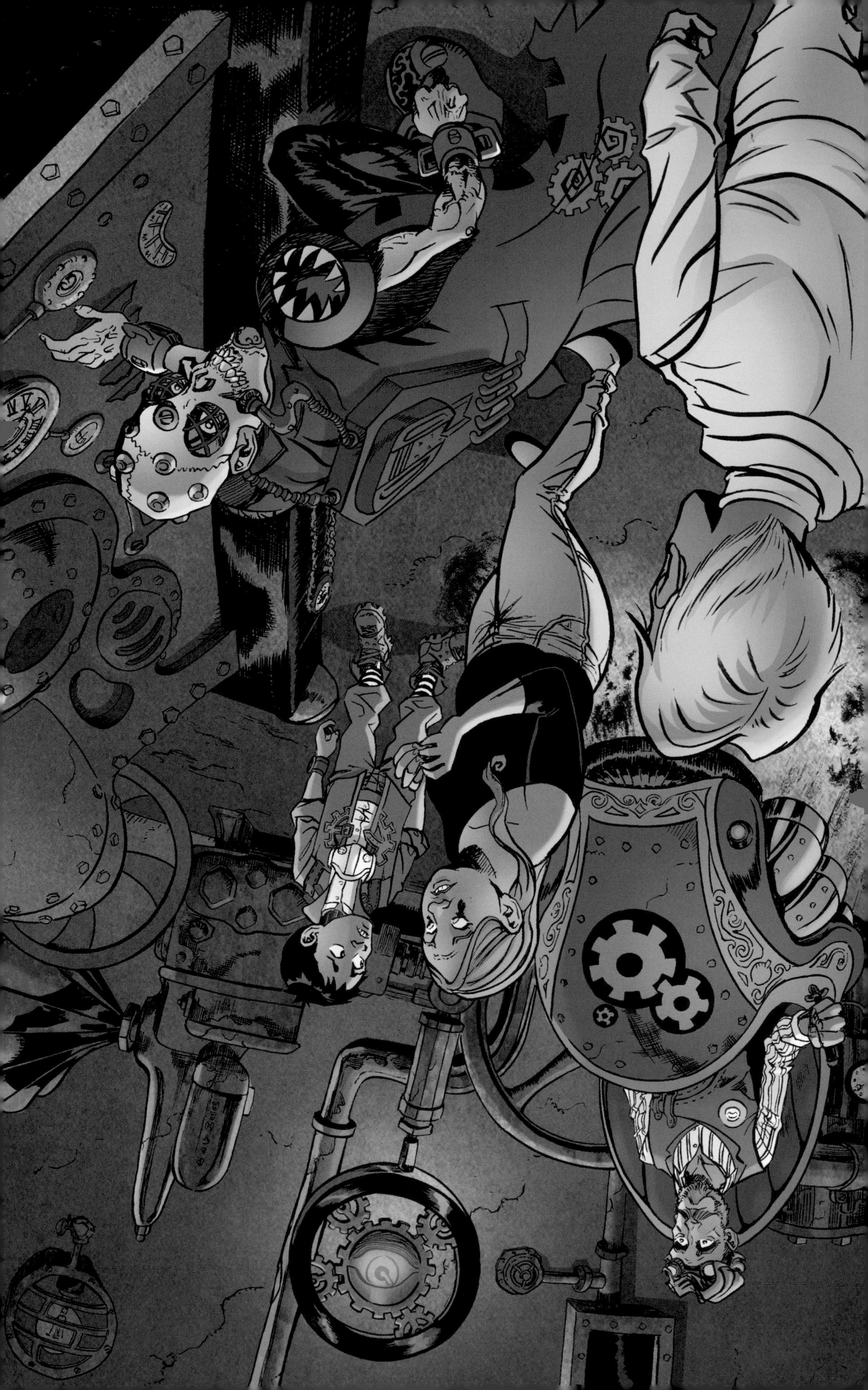

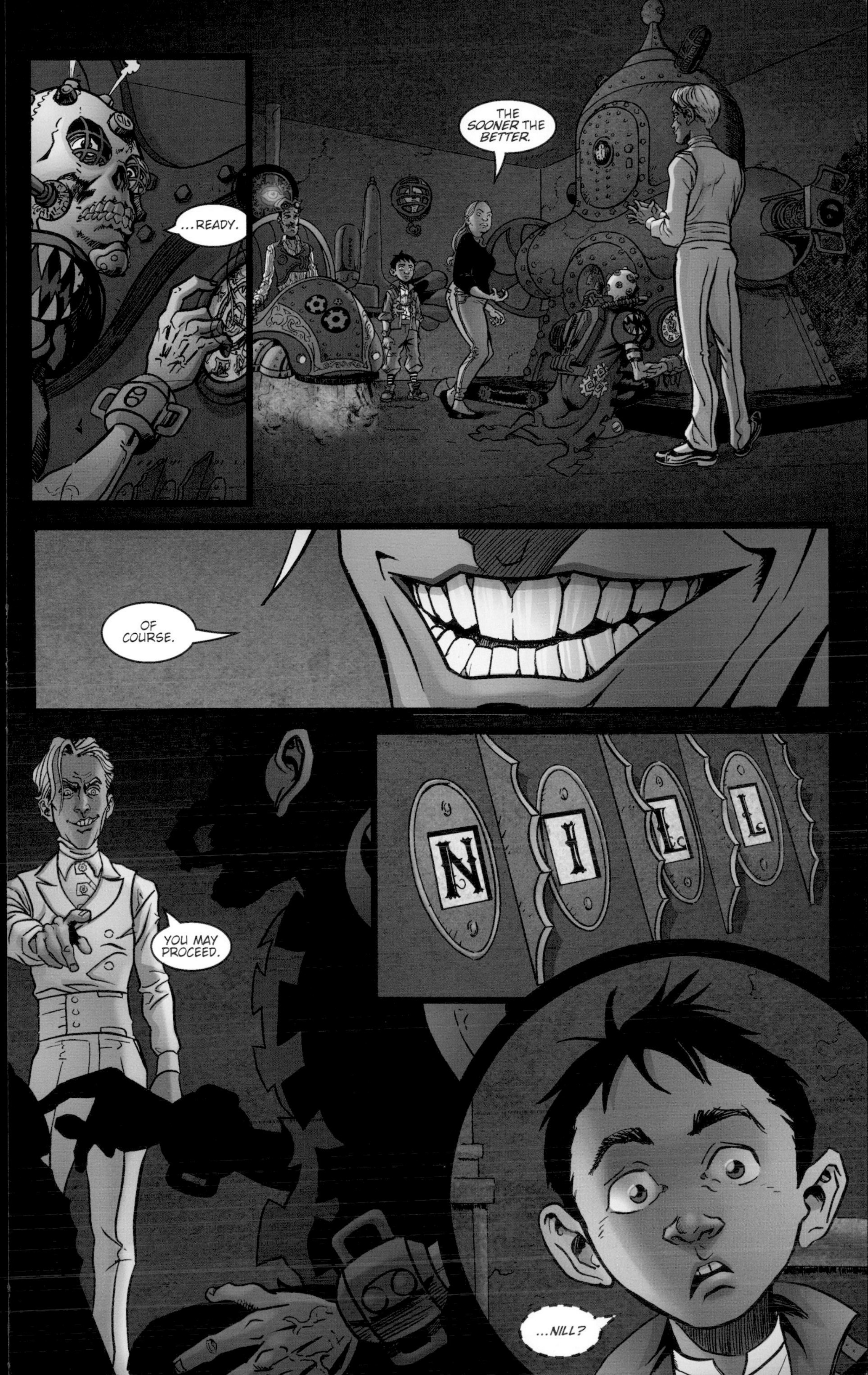
...READY.
THE SOONER THE BETTER.
OF COURSE.
YOU MAY PROCEED.
NILL
...NILL?

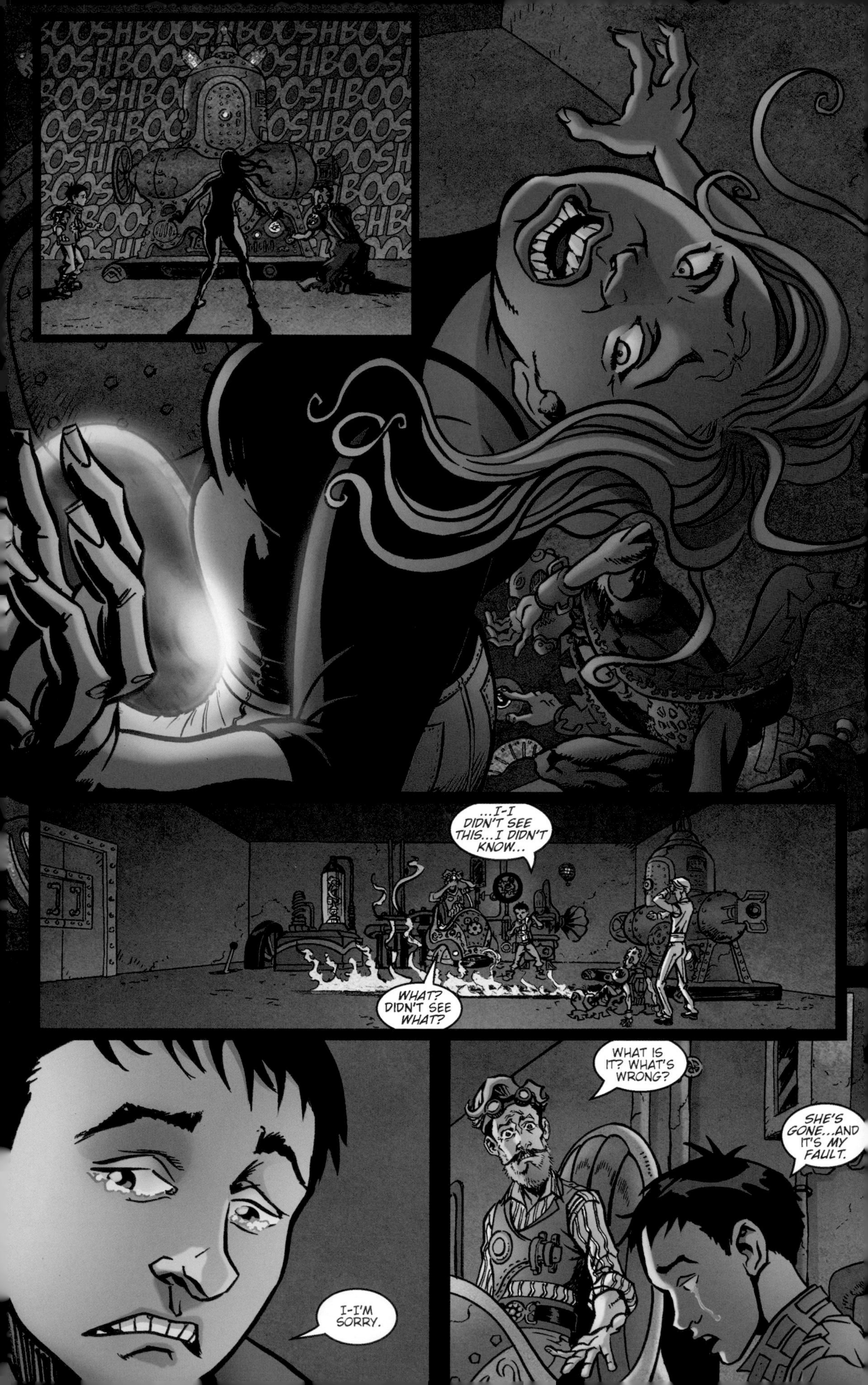
BOOSHBOOSHBOOSHBOOSH
...I-I DIDN'T SEE THIS...I DIDN'T KNOW...
WHAT? DIDN'T SEE WHAT?
I-I'M SORRY.
WHAT IS IT? WHAT'S WRONG?
SHE'S GONE...AND IT'S MY FAULT.

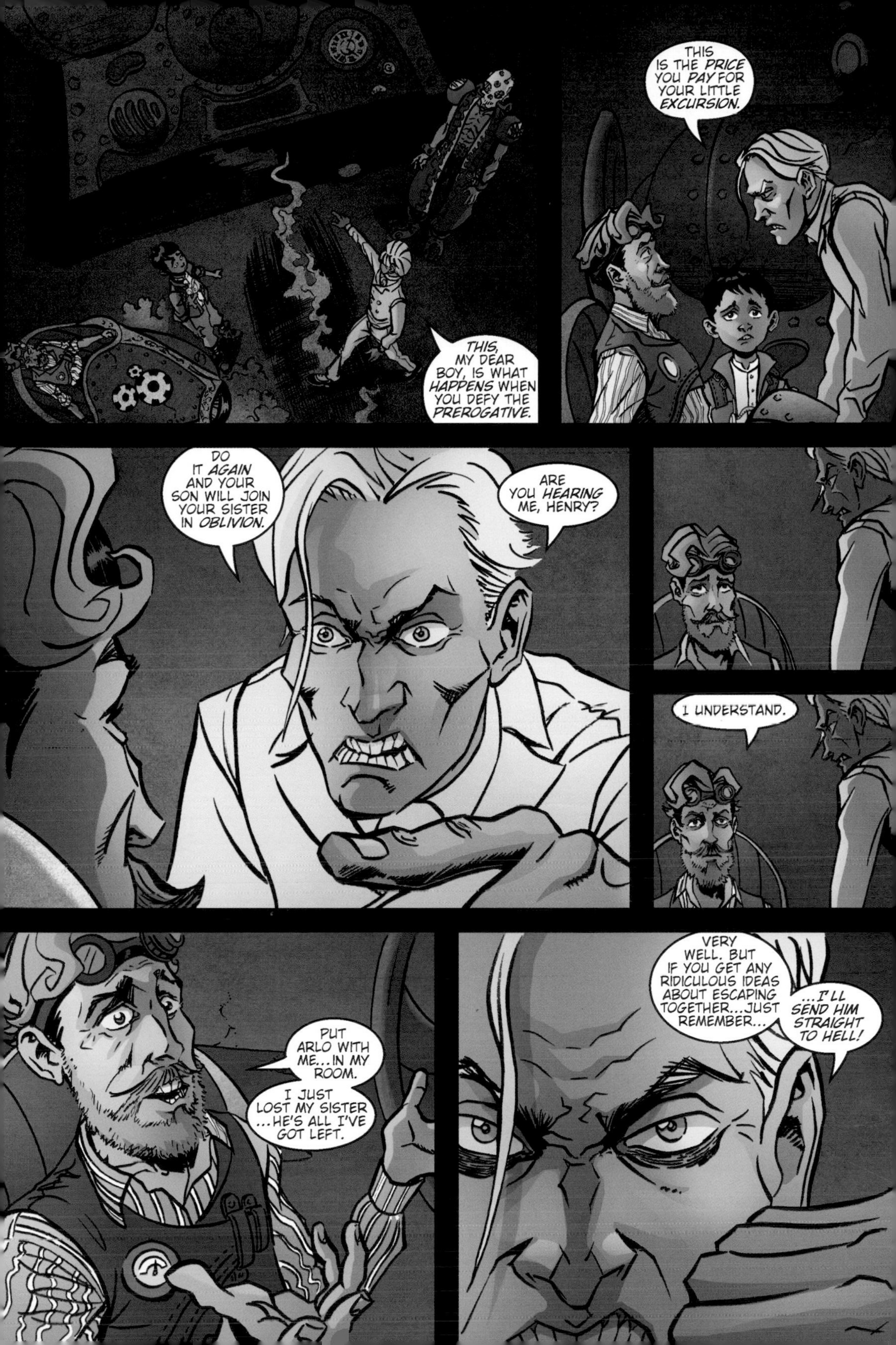
THIS, MY DEAR BOY, IS WHAT HAPPENS WHEN YOU DEFY THE PREROGATIVE.
THIS IS THE PRICE YOU PAY FOR YOUR LITTLE EXCURSION.
DO IT AGAIN AND YOUR SON WILL JOIN YOUR SISTER IN OBLIVION.
ARE YOU HEARING ME, HENRY?
I UNDERSTAND.
PUT ARLO WITH ME...IN MY ROOM.
I JUST LOST MY SISTER ...HE'S ALL I'VE GOT LEFT.
VERY WELL. BUT IF YOU GET ANY RIDICULOUS IDEAS ABOUT ESCAPING TOGETHER...JUST REMEMBER...
...I'LL SEND HIM STRAIGHT TO HELL!

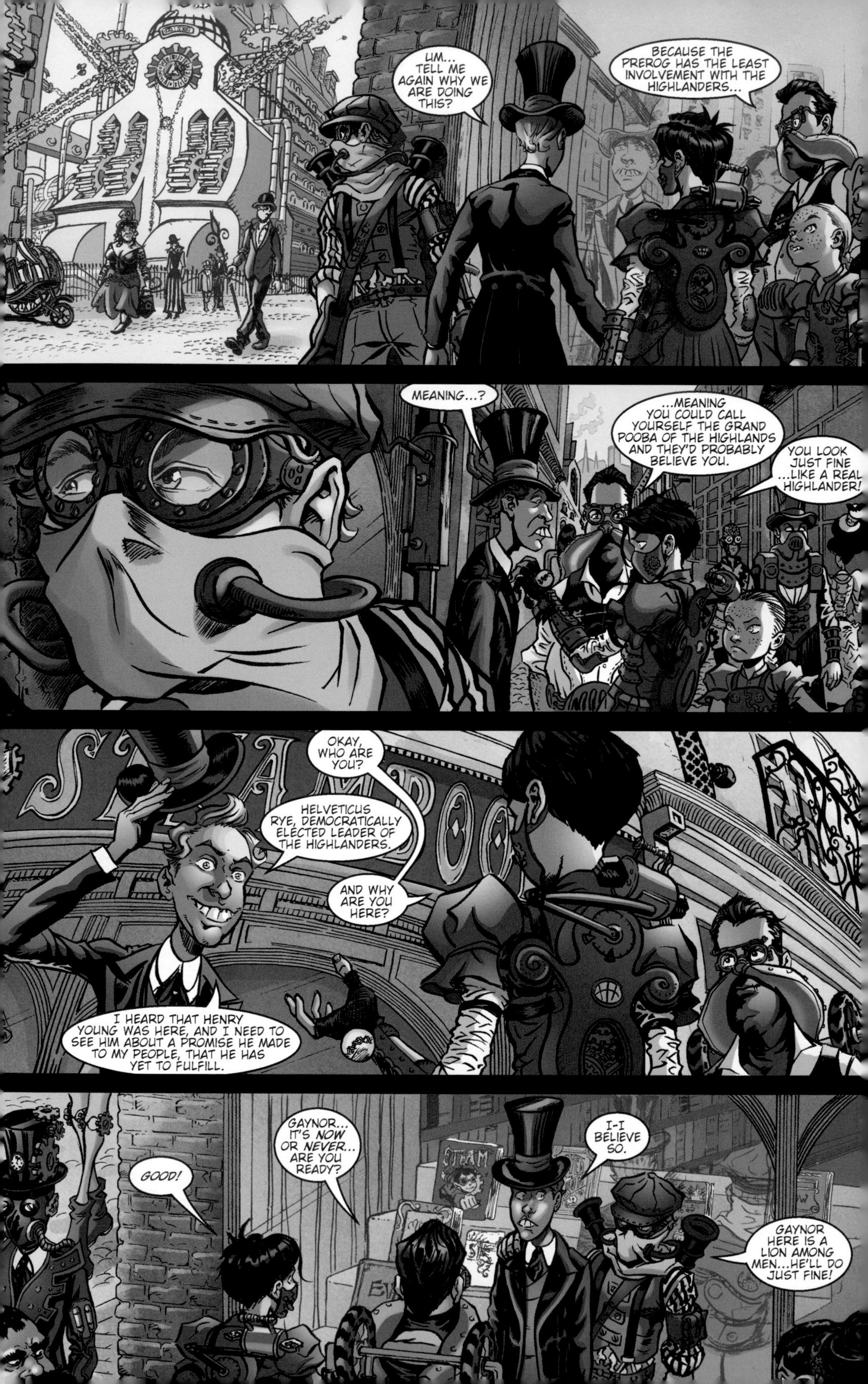
UM... TELL ME AGAIN WHY WE ARE DOING THIS?
BECAUSE THE PREROG HAS THE LEAST INVOLVEMENT WITH THE HIGHLANDERS...
MEANING...?
...MEANING YOU COULD CALL YOURSELF THE GRAND POOBA OF THE HIGHLANDS AND THEY'D PROBABLY BELIEVE YOU.
YOU LOOK JUST FINE ...LIKE A REAL HIGHLANDER!
OKAY, WHO ARE YOU?
HELVETICUS RYE, DEMOCRATICALLY ELECTED LEADER OF THE HIGHLANDERS.
AND WHY ARE YOU HERE?
I HEARD THAT HENRY YOUNG WAS HERE, AND I NEED TO SEE HIM ABOUT A PROMISE HE MADE TO MY PEOPLE, THAT HE HAS YET TO FULFILL.
GOOD!
GAYNOR... IT'S *NOW* OR *NEVER*... ARE YOU READY?
I-I BELIEVE SO.
GAYNOR HERE IS A LION AMONG MEN...HE'LL DO JUST FINE!

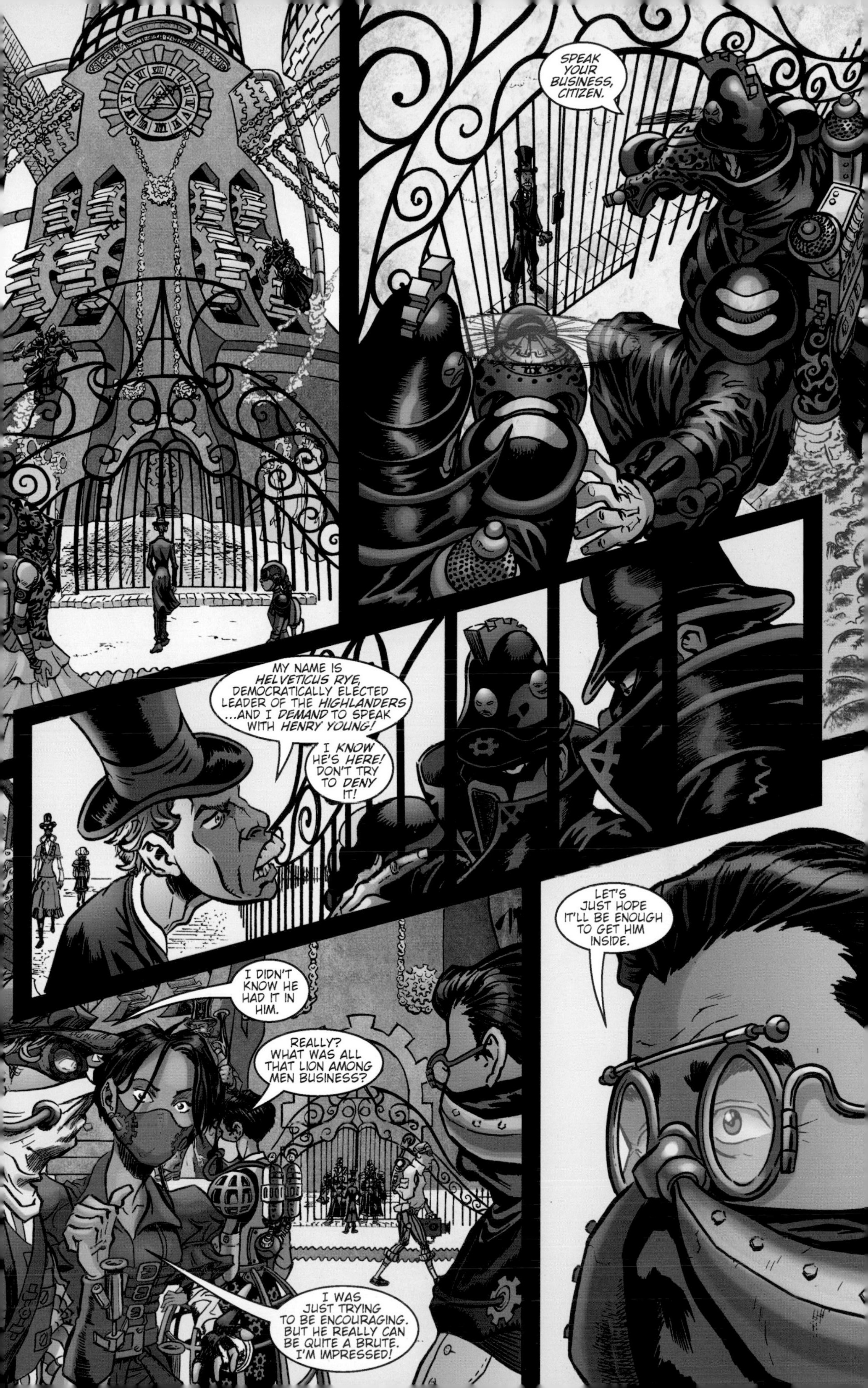
SPEAK YOUR BUSINESS, CITIZEN.
MY NAME IS HELVETICUS RYE, DEMOCRATICALLY ELECTED LEADER OF THE HIGHLANDERS ...AND I DEMAND TO SPEAK WITH HENRY YOUNG!
I KNOW HE'S HERE! DON'T TRY TO DENY IT!
LET'S JUST HOPE IT'LL BE ENOUGH TO GET HIM INSIDE.
I DIDN'T KNOW HE HAD IT IN HIM.
REALLY? WHAT WAS ALL THAT LION AMONG MEN BUSINESS?
I WAS JUST TRYING TO BE ENCOURAGING. BUT HE REALLY CAN BE QUITE A BRUTE. I'M IMPRESSED!

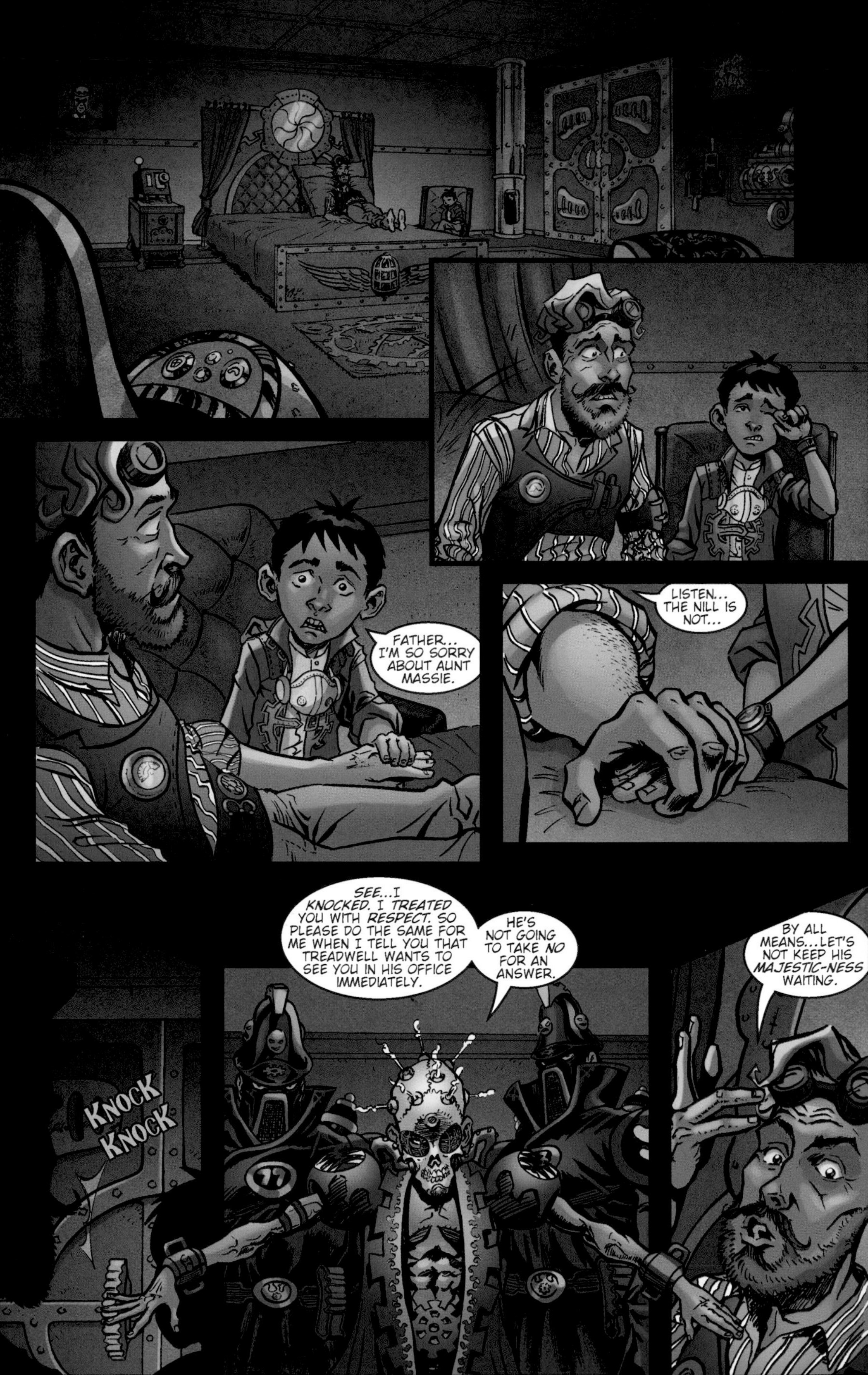
FATHER... I'M SO SORRY ABOUT AUNT MASSIE.
LISTEN... THE NILL IS NOT...
KNOCK KNOCK
SEE...I KNOCKED. I TREATED YOU WITH RESPECT. SO PLEASE DO THE SAME FOR ME WHEN I TELL YOU THAT TREADWELL WANTS TO SEE YOU IN HIS OFFICE IMMEDIATELY.
HE'S NOT GOING TO TAKE NO FOR AN ANSWER.
BY ALL MEANS...LET'S NOT KEEP HIS MAJESTIC-NESS WAITING.

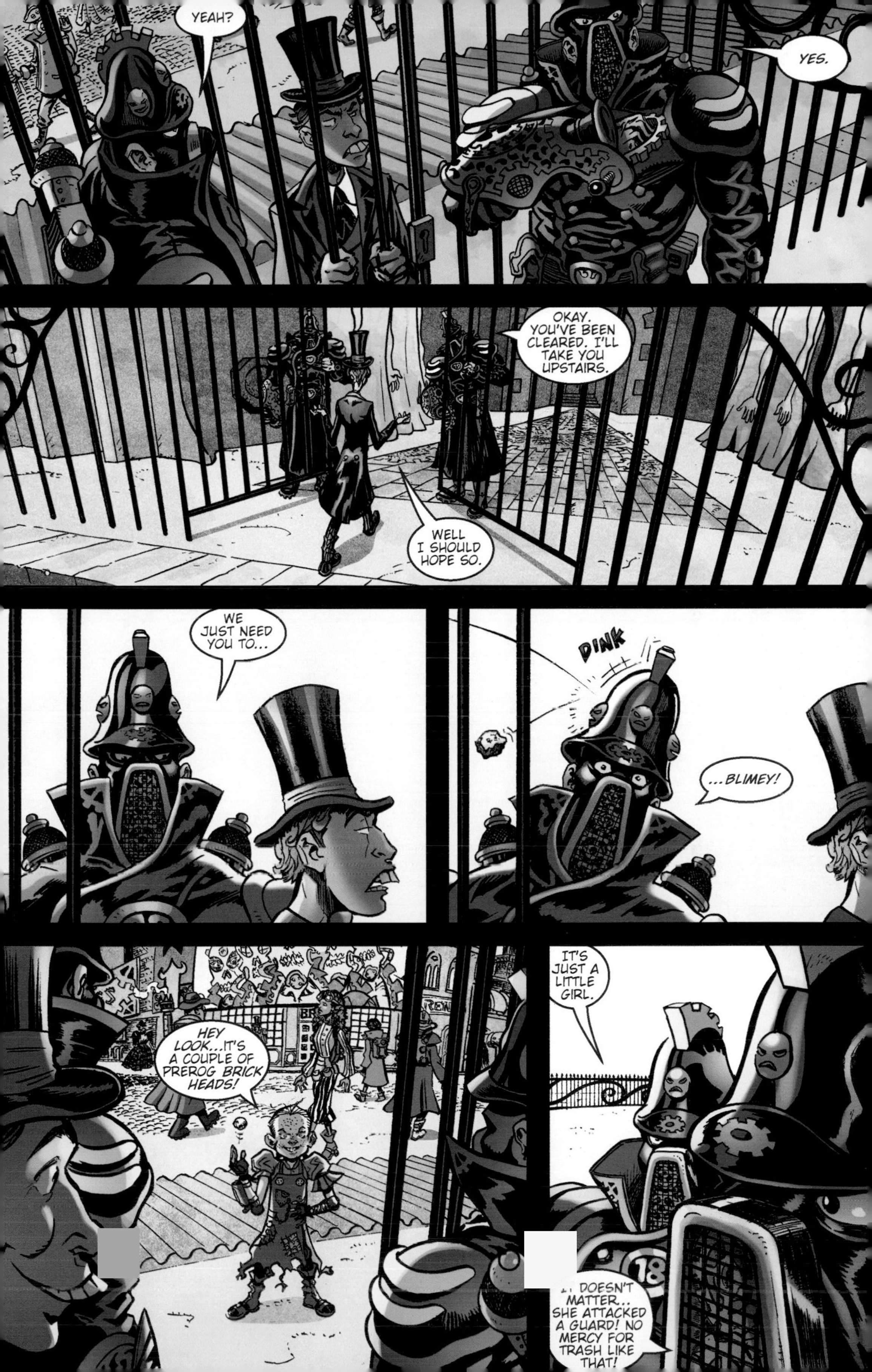
YEAH?
YES.
OKAY. YOU'VE BEEN CLEARED. I'LL TAKE YOU UPSTAIRS.
WELL I SHOULD HOPE SO.
WE JUST NEED YOU TO...
DINK
...BLIMEY!
HEY LOOK...IT'S A COUPLE OF PREROG BRICK HEADS!
IT'S JUST A LITTLE GIRL.
DOESN'T MATTER... SHE ATTACKED A GUARD! NO MERCY FOR TRASH LIKE THAT!

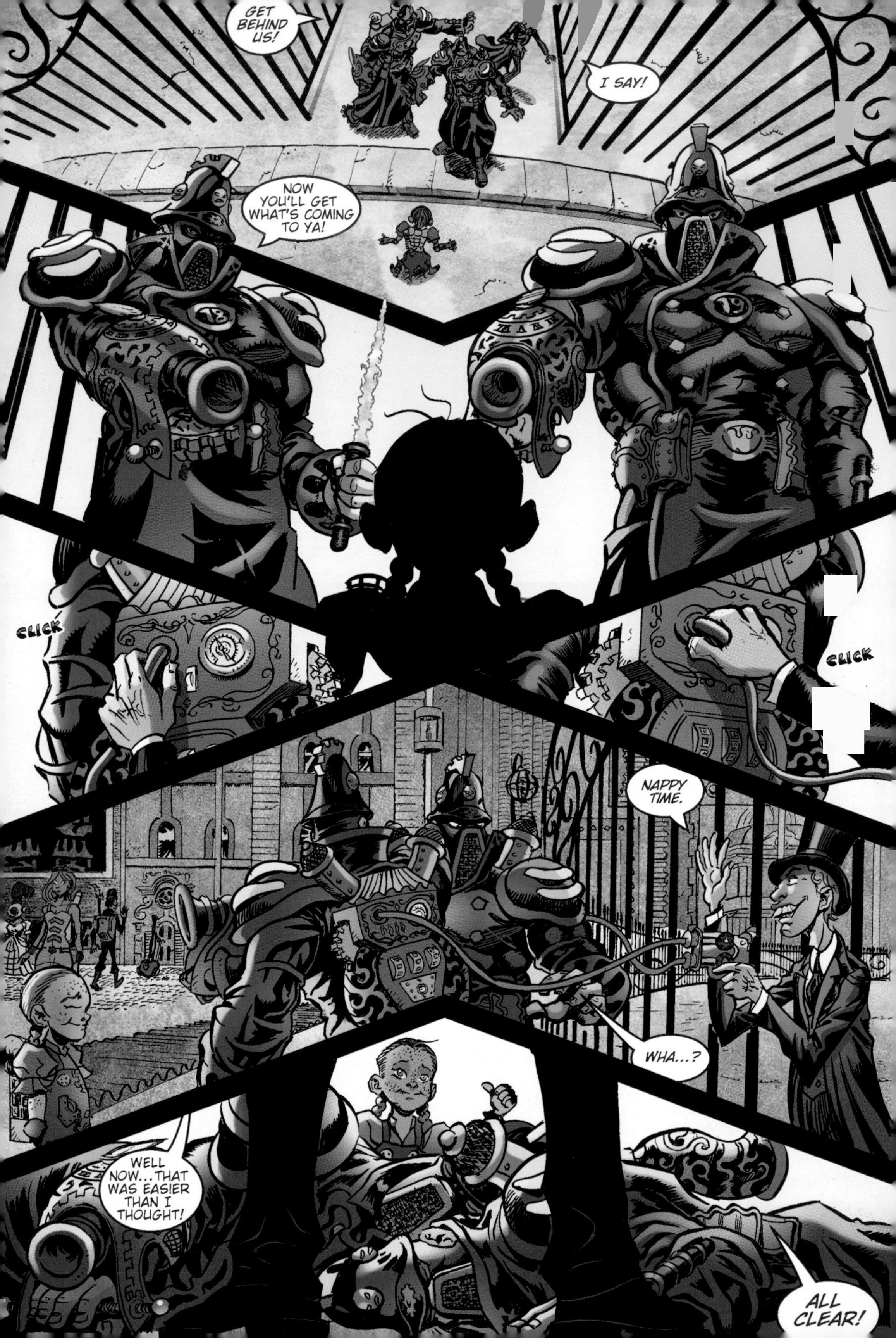
GET BEHIND US!
I SAY!
NOW YOU'LL GET WHAT'S COMING TO YA!
CLICK
CLICK
NAPPY TIME.
WHA...?
WELL NOW...THAT WAS EASIER THAN I THOUGHT!
ALL CLEAR!

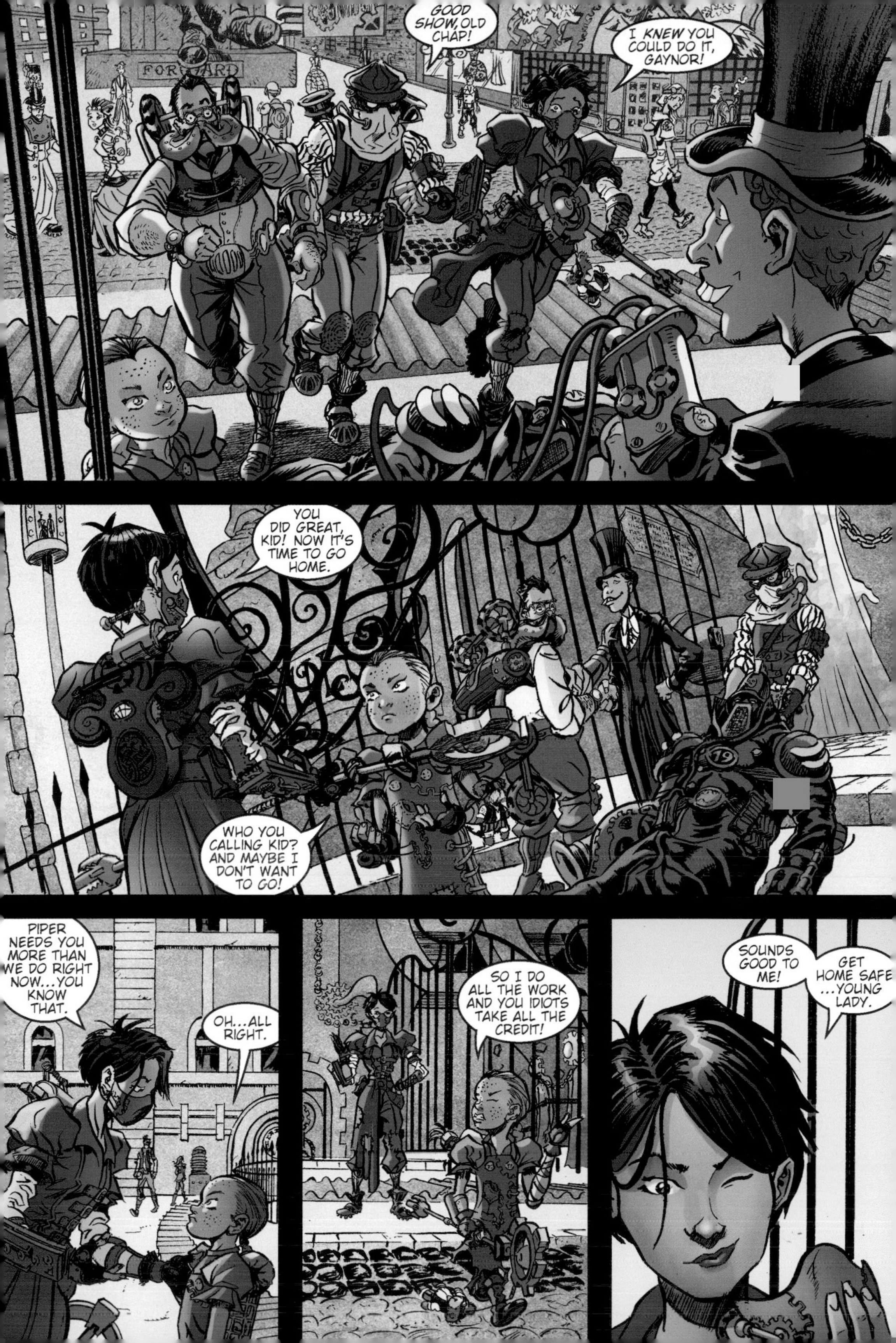
FORWARD
GOOD SHOW, OLD CHAP!
I KNEW YOU COULD DO IT, GAYNOR!
YOU DID GREAT, KID! NOW IT'S TIME TO GO HOME.
WHO YOU CALLING KID? AND MAYBE I DON'T WANT TO GO!
PIPER NEEDS YOU MORE THAN WE DO RIGHT NOW...YOU KNOW THAT.
OH...ALL RIGHT.
SO I DO ALL THE WORK AND YOU IDIOTS TAKE ALL THE CREDIT!
SOUNDS GOOD TO ME!
GET HOME SAFE ...YOUNG LADY.

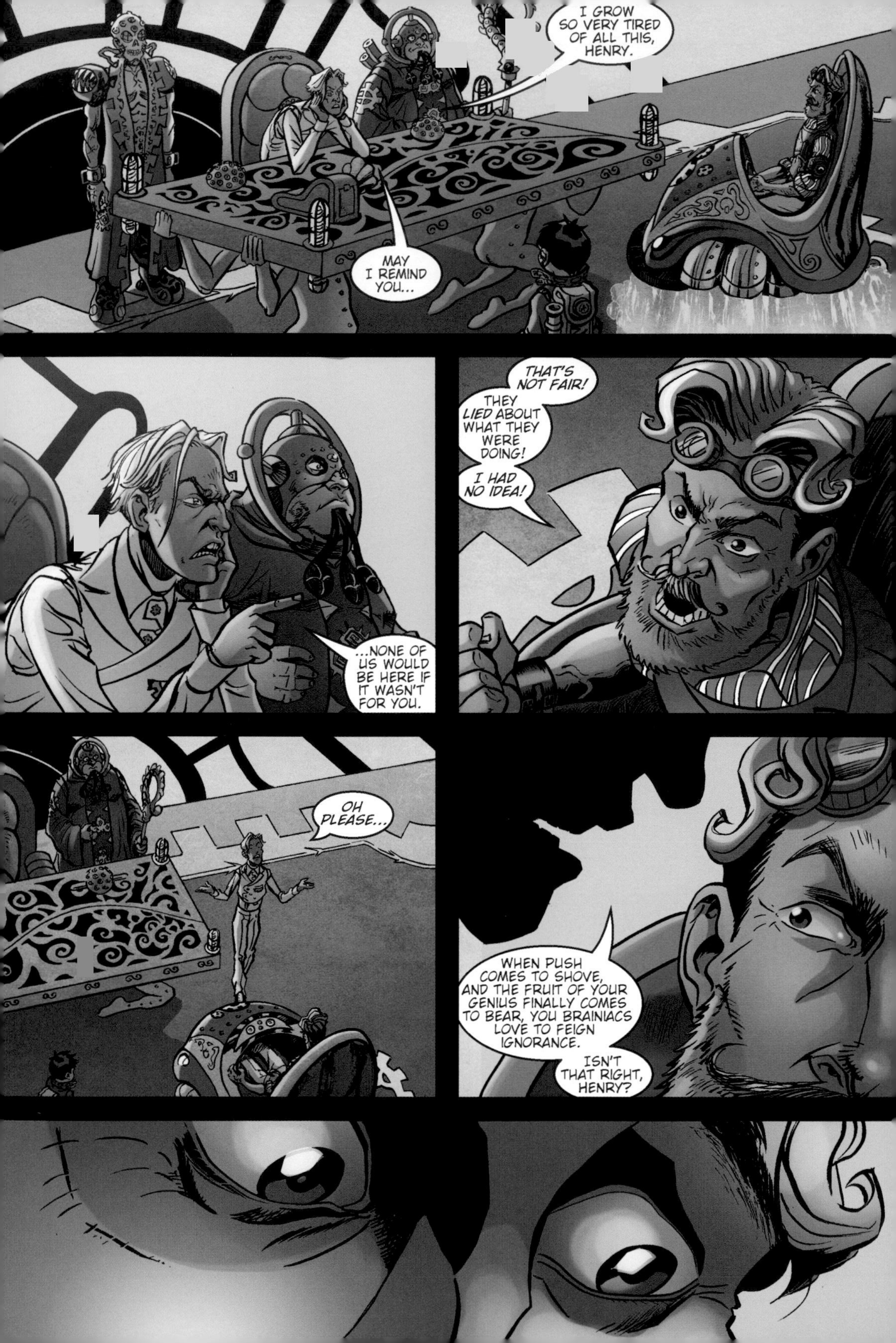
I GROW SO VERY TIRED OF ALL THIS, HENRY.
MAY I REMIND YOU...
THAT'S NOT FAIR!
THEY LIED ABOUT WHAT THEY WERE DOING!
I HAD NO IDEA!
...NONE OF US WOULD BE HERE IF IT WASN'T FOR YOU.
OH PLEASE...
WHEN PUSH COMES TO SHOVE, AND THE FRUIT OF YOUR GENIUS FINALLY COMES TO BEAR, YOU BRAINIACS LOVE TO FEIGN IGNORANCE.
ISN'T THAT RIGHT, HENRY?

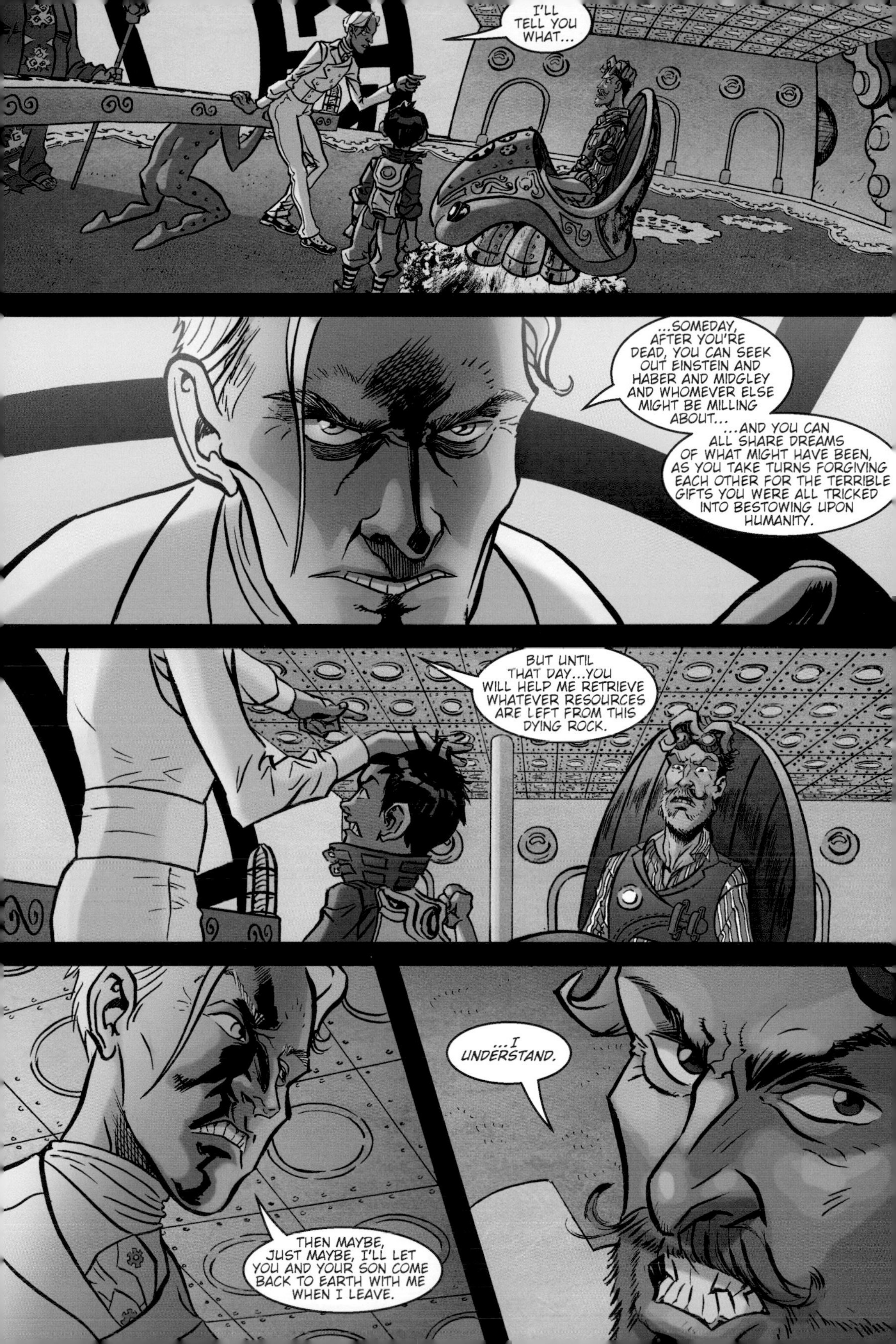
I'LL TELL YOU WHAT...
...SOMEDAY, AFTER YOU'RE DEAD, YOU CAN SEEK OUT EINSTEIN AND HABER AND MIDGLEY AND WHOMEVER ELSE MIGHT BE MILLING ABOUT...
...AND YOU CAN ALL SHARE DREAMS OF WHAT MIGHT HAVE BEEN, AS YOU TAKE TURNS FORGIVING EACH OTHER FOR THE TERRIBLE GIFTS YOU WERE ALL TRICKED INTO BESTOWING UPON HUMANITY.
BUT UNTIL THAT DAY...YOU WILL HELP ME RETRIEVE WHATEVER RESOURCES ARE LEFT FROM THIS DYING ROCK.
THEN MAYBE, JUST MAYBE, I'LL LET YOU AND YOUR SON COME BACK TO EARTH WITH ME WHEN I LEAVE.
...I UNDERSTAND.

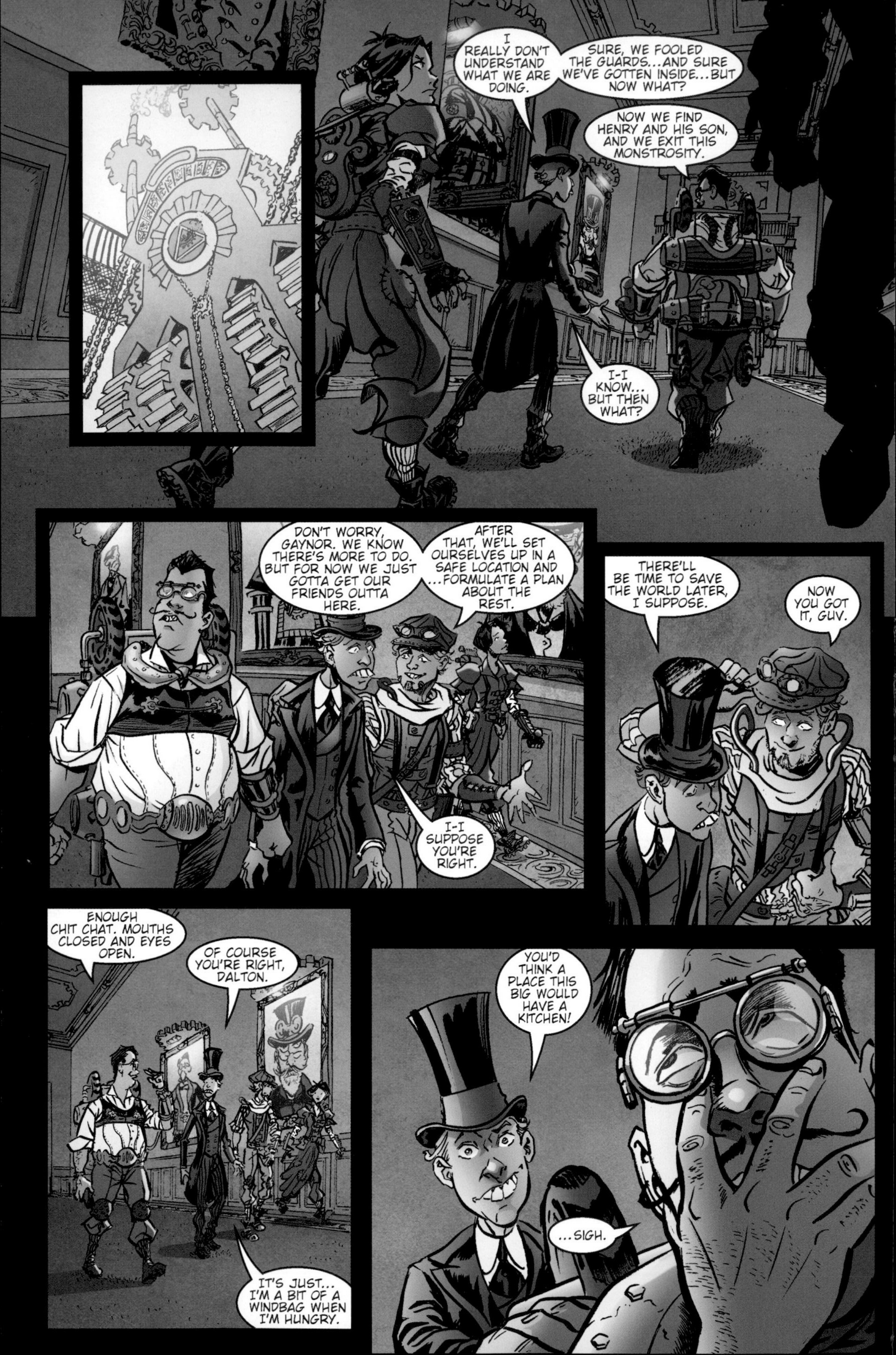
I REALLY DON'T UNDERSTAND WHAT WE ARE DOING.
SURE, WE FOOLED THE GUARDS...AND SURE WE'VE GOTTEN INSIDE...BUT NOW WHAT?
NOW WE FIND HENRY AND HIS SON, AND WE EXIT THIS MONSTROSITY.
I-I KNOW... BUT THEN WHAT?
DON'T WORRY, GAYNOR. WE KNOW THERE'S MORE TO DO. BUT FOR NOW WE JUST GOTTA GET OUR FRIENDS OUTTA HERE.
AFTER THAT, WE'LL SET OURSELVES UP IN A SAFE LOCATION AND ...FORMULATE A PLAN ABOUT THE REST.
I-I SUPPOSE YOU'RE RIGHT.
THERE'LL BE TIME TO SAVE THE WORLD LATER, I SUPPOSE.
NOW YOU GOT IT, GUV.
ENOUGH CHIT CHAT. MOUTHS CLOSED AND EYES OPEN.
OF COURSE YOU'RE RIGHT, DALTON.
IT'S JUST... I'M A BIT OF A WINDBAG WHEN I'M HUNGRY.
YOU'D THINK A PLACE THIS BIG WOULD HAVE A KITCHEN!
...SIGH.

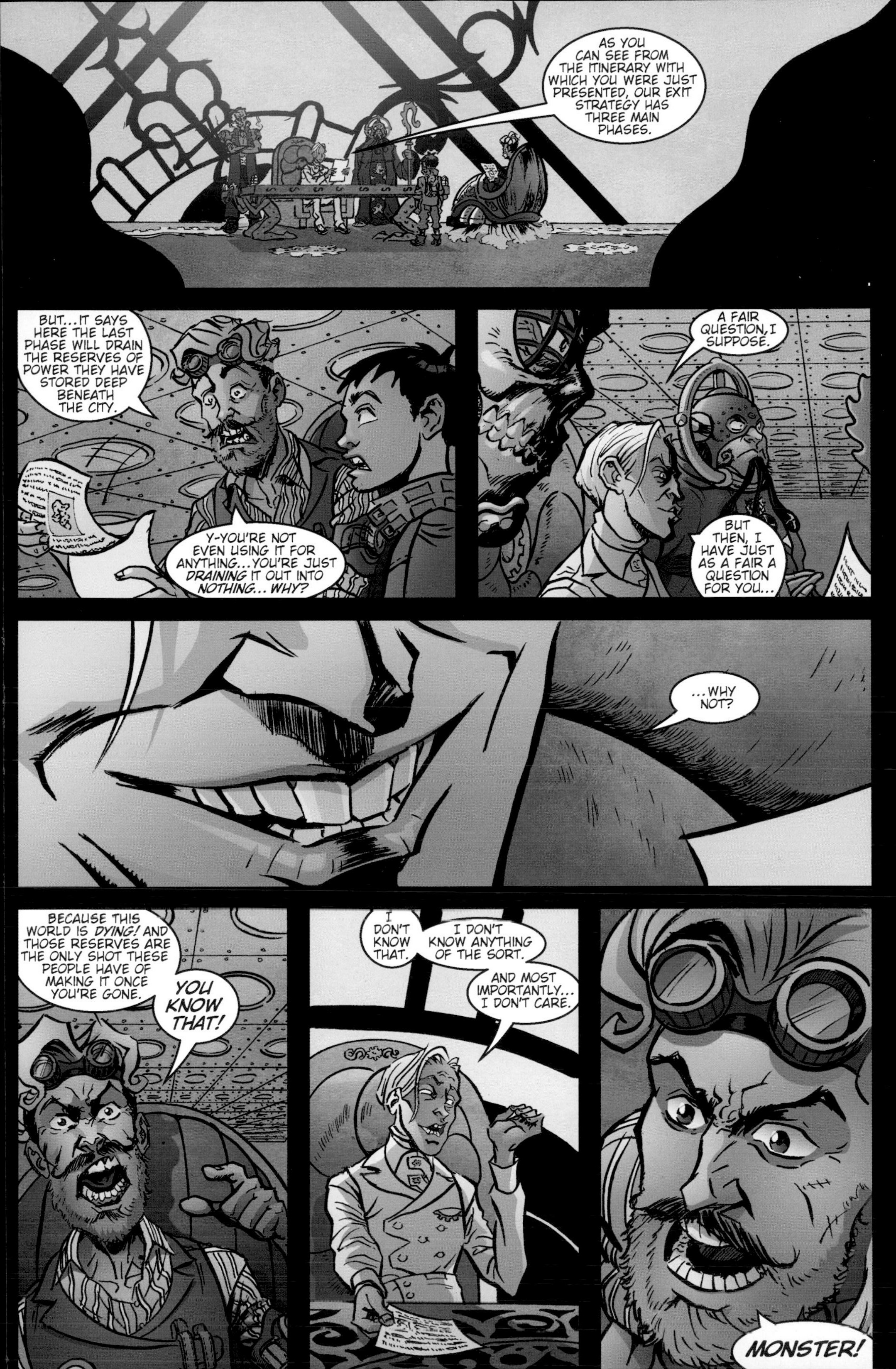
AS YOU CAN SEE FROM THE ITINERARY WITH WHICH YOU WERE JUST PRESENTED, OUR EXIT STRATEGY HAS THREE MAIN PHASES.
BUT...IT SAYS HERE THE LAST PHASE WILL DRAIN THE RESERVES OF POWER THEY HAVE STORED DEEP BENEATH THE CITY.
Y-YOU'RE NOT EVEN USING IT FOR ANYTHING...YOU'RE JUST *DRAINING* IT OUT INTO *NOTHING*... WHY?
A FAIR QUESTION, I SUPPOSE.
BUT THEN, I HAVE JUST AS A FAIR A QUESTION FOR YOU...
...WHY NOT?
BECAUSE THIS WORLD IS *DYING!* AND THOSE RESERVES ARE THE ONLY SHOT THESE PEOPLE HAVE OF MAKING IT ONCE YOU'RE GONE.
YOU KNOW THAT!
I DON'T KNOW THAT.
I DON'T KNOW ANYTHING OF THE SORT.
AND MOST IMPORTANTLY... I DON'T CARE.
MONSTER!

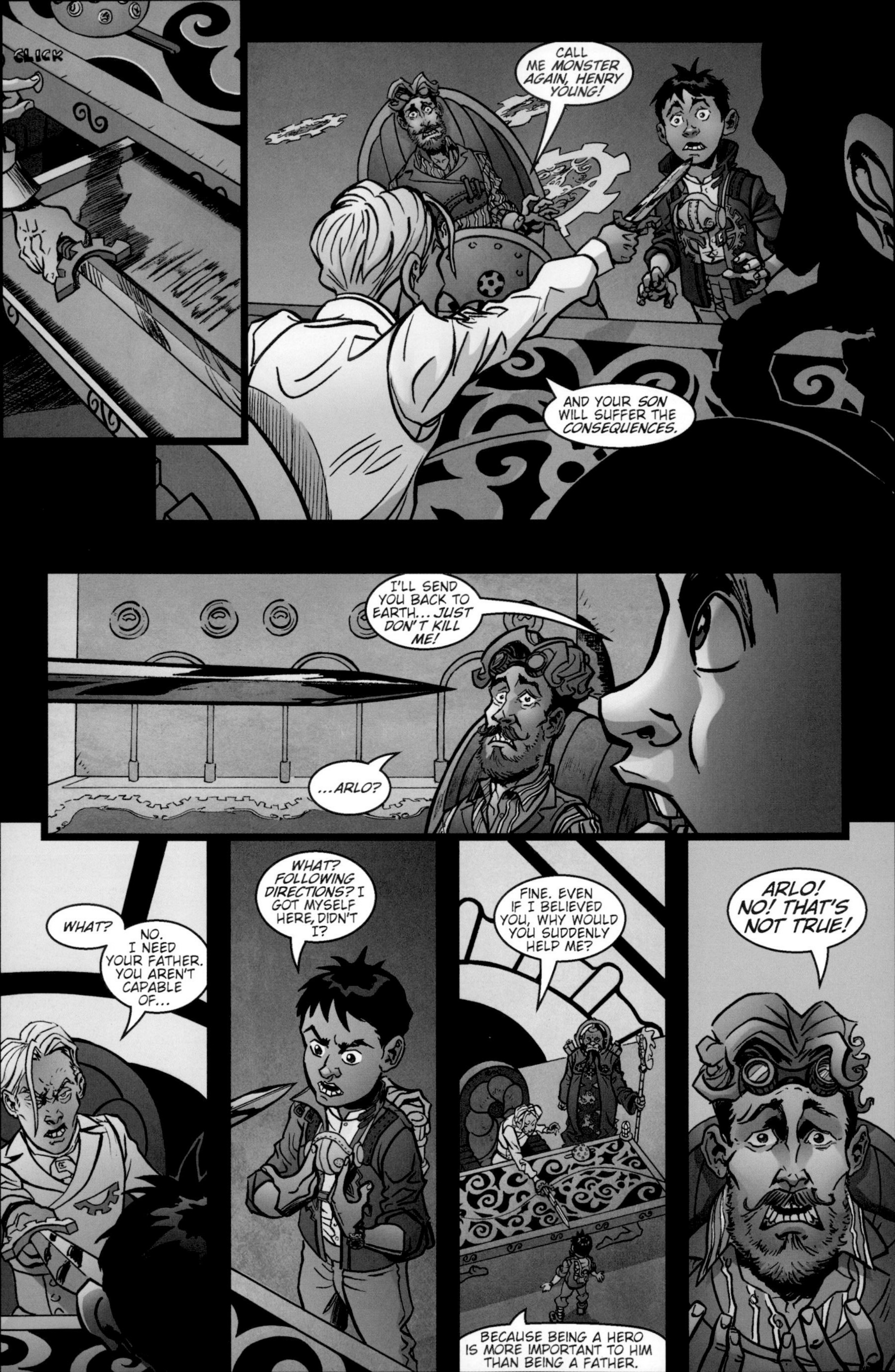
CLICK
CALL ME MONSTER AGAIN, HENRY YOUNG!
AND YOUR SON WILL SUFFER THE CONSEQUENCES.
I'LL SEND YOU BACK TO EARTH... JUST DON'T KILL ME!
...ARLO?
WHAT?
NO. I NEED YOUR FATHER. YOU AREN'T CAPABLE OF...
WHAT? FOLLOWING DIRECTIONS? I GOT MYSELF HERE, DIDN'T I?
FINE. EVEN IF I BELIEVED YOU, WHY WOULD YOU SUDDENLY HELP ME?
BECAUSE BEING A HERO IS MORE IMPORTANT TO HIM THAN BEING A FATHER.
ARLO! NO! THAT'S NOT TRUE!

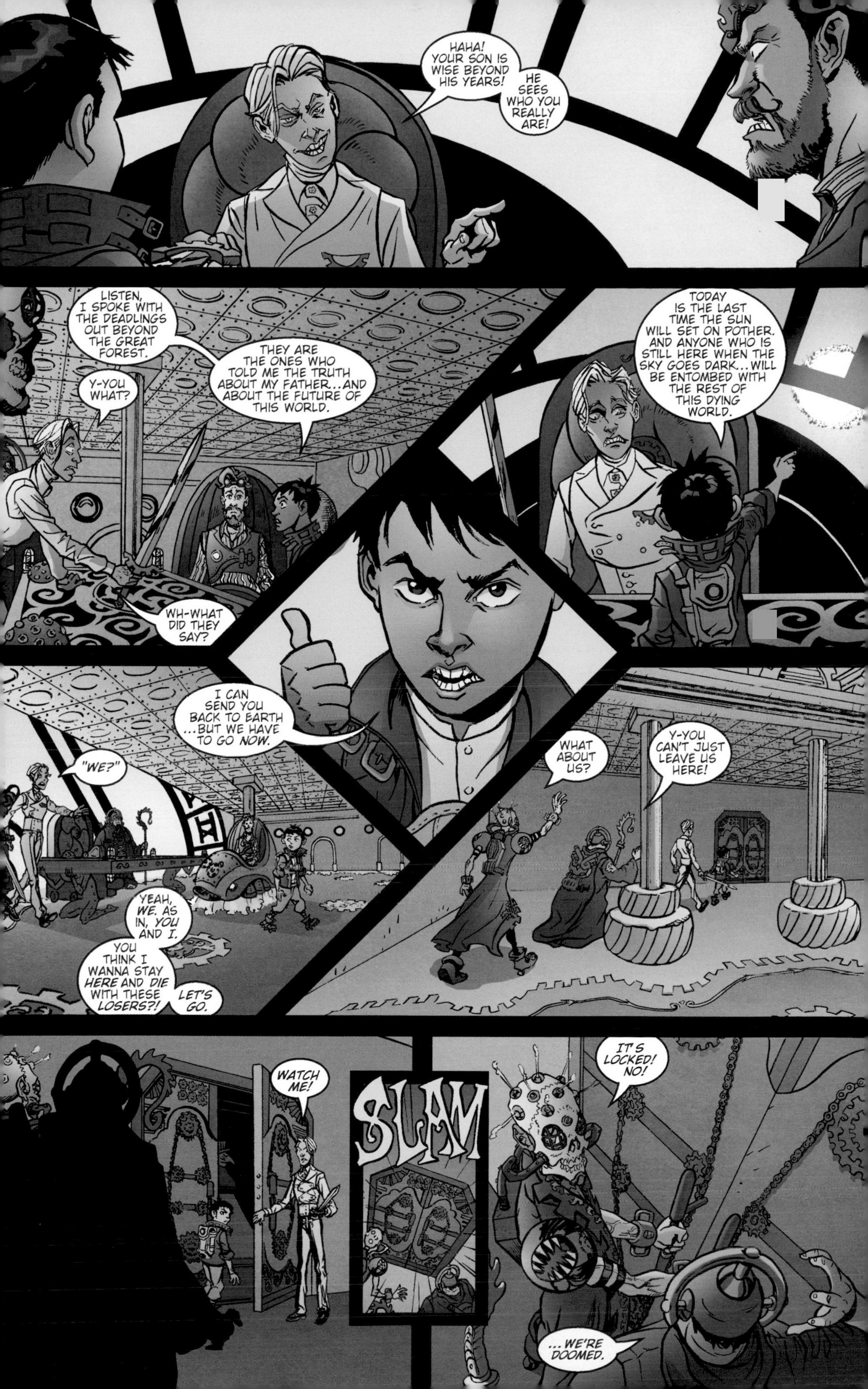
HAHA! YOUR SON IS WISE BEYOND HIS YEARS!
HE SEES WHO YOU REALLY ARE!
LISTEN, I SPOKE WITH THE DEADLINGS OUT BEYOND THE GREAT FOREST.
Y-YOU WHAT?
THEY ARE THE ONES WHO TOLD ME THE TRUTH ABOUT MY FATHER...AND ABOUT THE FUTURE OF THIS WORLD.
WH-WHAT DID THEY SAY?
TODAY IS THE LAST TIME THE SUN WILL SET ON POTHER. AND ANYONE WHO IS STILL HERE WHEN THE SKY GOES DARK...WILL BE ENTOMBED WITH THE REST OF THIS DYING WORLD.
I CAN SEND YOU BACK TO EARTH ...BUT WE HAVE TO GO NOW.
"WE?"
YEAH, WE. AS IN, YOU AND I.
YOU THINK I WANNA STAY HERE AND DIE WITH THESE LOSERS?!
LET'S GO.
WHAT ABOUT US?
Y-YOU CAN'T JUST LEAVE US HERE!
WATCH ME!
SLAM
IT'S LOCKED! NO!
...WE'RE DOOMED.

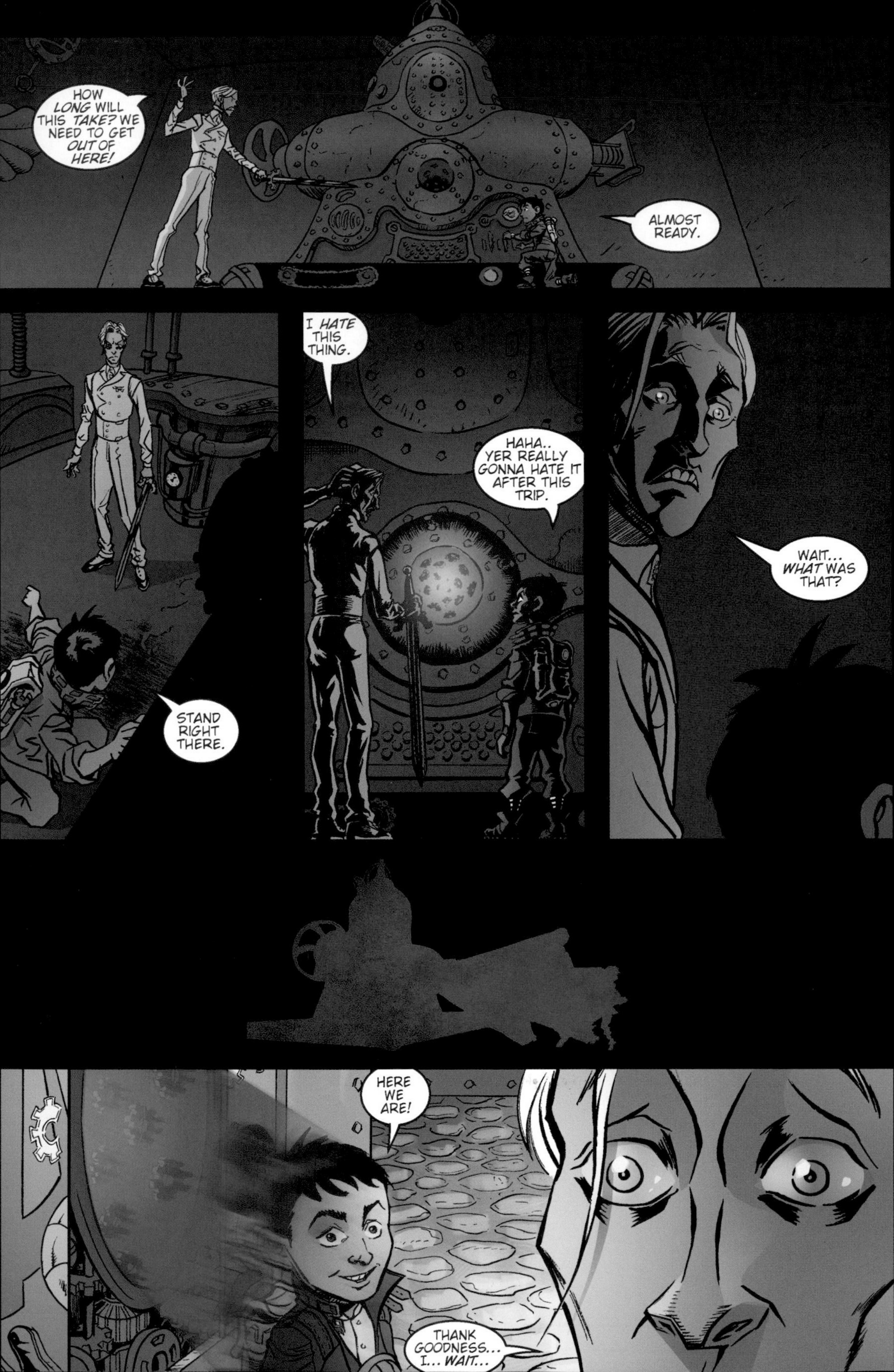
HOW *LONG* WILL THIS *TAKE?* WE NEED TO GET *OUT* OF *HERE!*
ALMOST READY.
STAND RIGHT THERE.
I *HATE* THIS THING.
HAHA.. YER REALLY GONNA HATE IT AFTER THIS TRIP.
WAIT... *WHAT* WAS THAT?
HERE WE ARE!
THANK GOODNESS... I... *WAIT...*

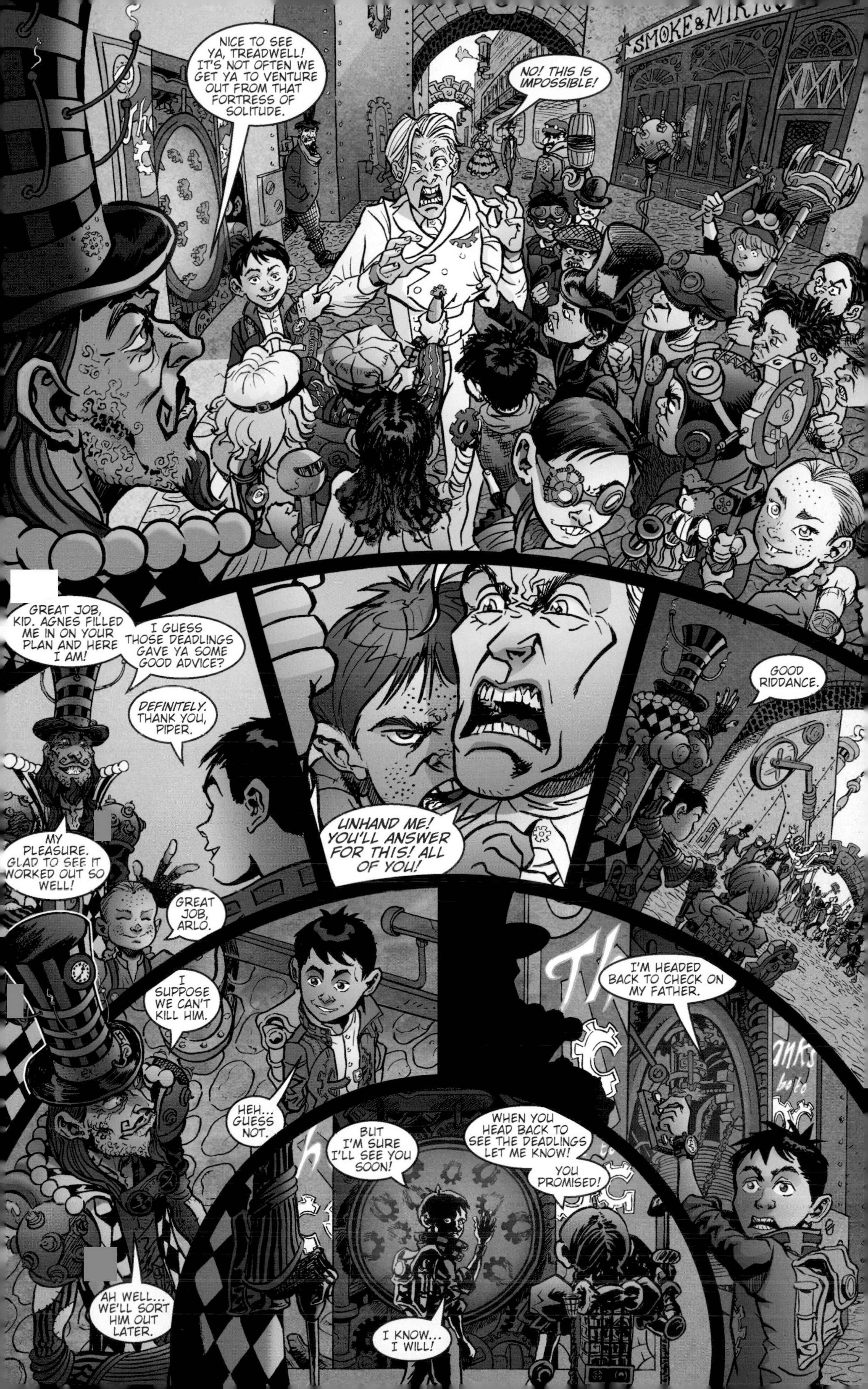
SMOKE & MIR
NICE TO SEE YA, TREADWELL! IT'S NOT OFTEN WE GET YA TO VENTURE OUT FROM THAT FORTRESS OF SOLITUDE.
NO! THIS IS IMPOSSIBLE!
GREAT JOB, KID. AGNES FILLED ME IN ON YOUR PLAN AND HERE I AM!
I GUESS THOSE DEADLINGS GAVE YA SOME GOOD ADVICE?
DEFINITELY. THANK YOU, PIPER.
MY PLEASURE. GLAD TO SEE IT WORKED OUT SO WELL!
GREAT JOB, ARLO.
UNHAND ME! YOU'LL ANSWER FOR THIS! ALL OF YOU!
GOOD RIDDANCE.
I SUPPOSE WE CAN'T KILL HIM.
HEH... GUESS NOT.
AH WELL... WE'LL SORT HIM OUT LATER.
I'M HEADED BACK TO CHECK ON MY FATHER.
BUT I'M SURE I'LL SEE YOU SOON!
WHEN YOU HEAD BACK TO SEE THE DEADLINGS LET ME KNOW!
YOU PROMISED!
I KNOW... I WILL!

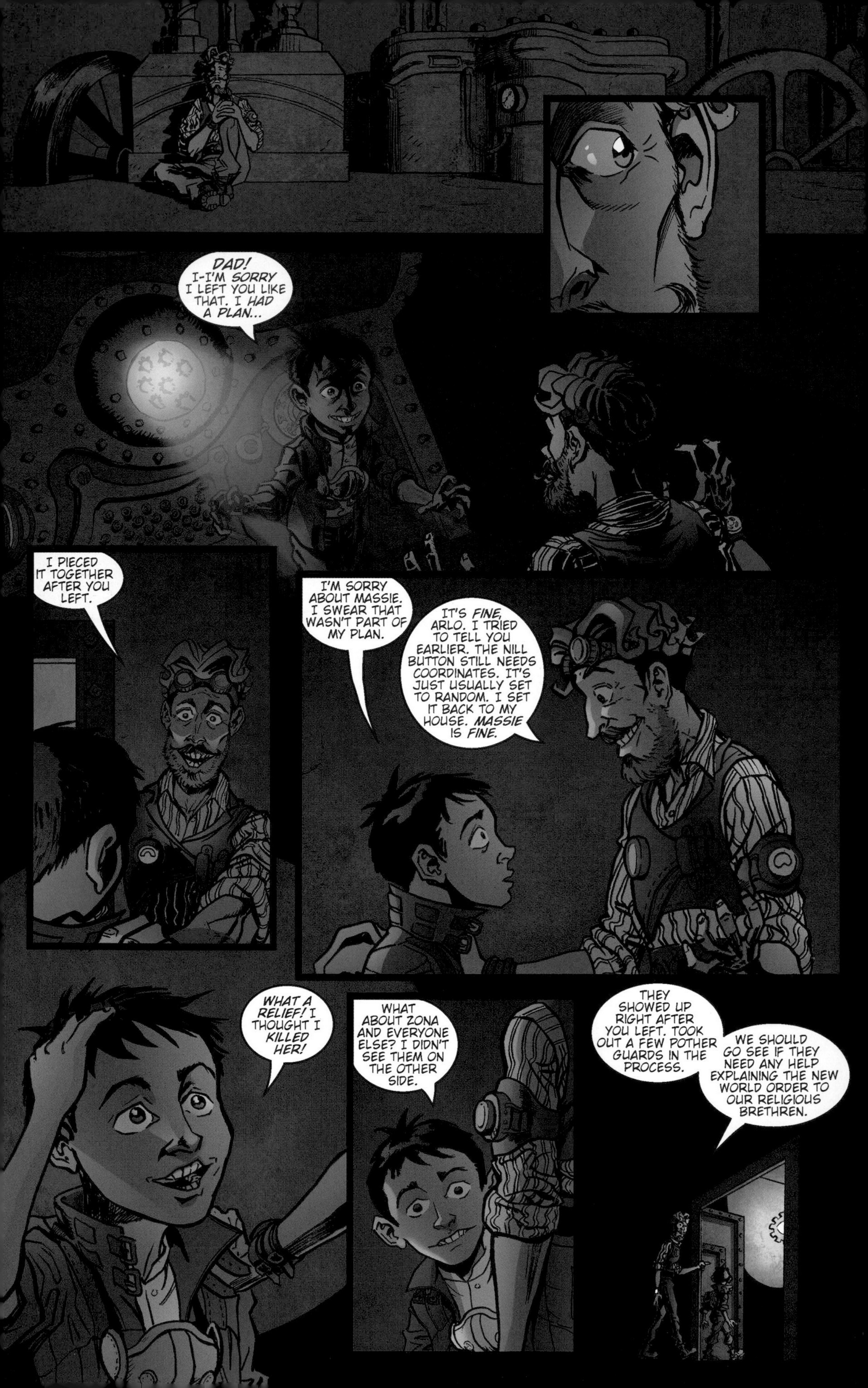
DAD! I-I'M SORRY I LEFT YOU LIKE THAT. I HAD A PLAN...
I PIECED IT TOGETHER AFTER YOU LEFT.
I'M SORRY ABOUT MASSIE. I SWEAR THAT WASN'T PART OF MY PLAN.
IT'S FINE, ARLO. I TRIED TO TELL YOU EARLIER. THE NILL BUTTON STILL NEEDS COORDINATES. IT'S JUST USUALLY SET TO RANDOM. I SET IT BACK TO MY HOUSE. MASSIE IS FINE.
WHAT A RELIEF! I THOUGHT I KILLED HER!
WHAT ABOUT ZONA AND EVERYONE ELSE? I DIDN'T SEE THEM ON THE OTHER SIDE.
THEY SHOWED UP RIGHT AFTER YOU LEFT. TOOK OUT A FEW POTHER GUARDS IN THE PROCESS.
WE SHOULD GO SEE IF THEY NEED ANY HELP EXPLAINING THE NEW WORLD ORDER TO OUR RELIGIOUS BRETHREN.

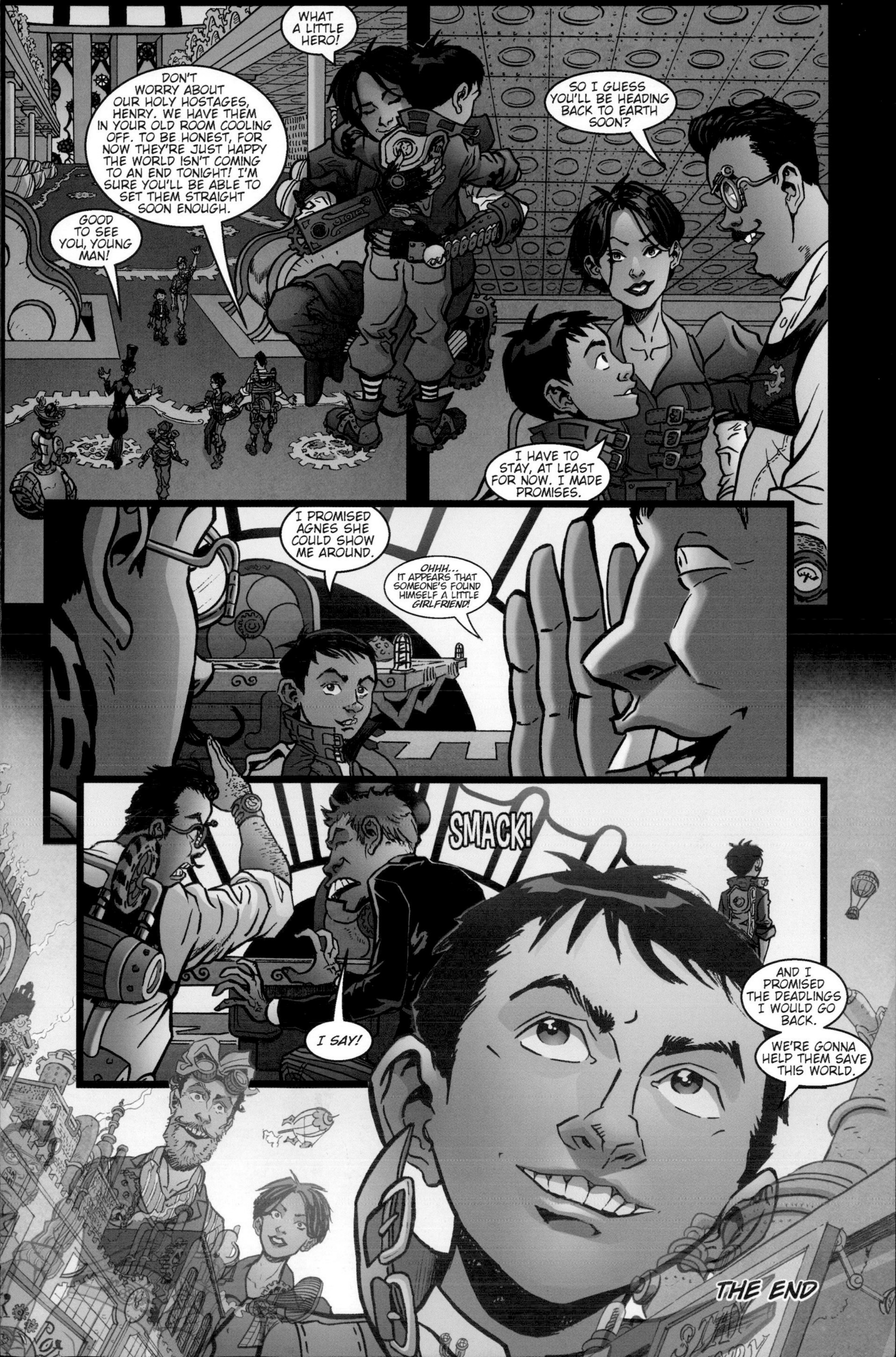
WHAT A LITTLE HERO!
DON'T WORRY ABOUT OUR HOLY HOSTAGES, HENRY. WE HAVE THEM IN YOUR OLD ROOM COOLING OFF. TO BE HONEST, FOR NOW THEY'RE JUST HAPPY THE WORLD ISN'T COMING TO AN END TONIGHT! I'M SURE YOU'LL BE ABLE TO SET THEM STRAIGHT SOON ENOUGH.
GOOD TO SEE YOU, YOUNG MAN!
SO I GUESS YOU'LL BE HEADING BACK TO EARTH SOON?
I HAVE TO STAY, AT LEAST FOR NOW. I MADE PROMISES.
I PROMISED AGNES SHE COULD SHOW ME AROUND.
OHHH... IT APPEARS THAT SOMEONE'S FOUND HIMSELF A LITTLE GIRLFRIEND!
SMACK!
I SAY!
AND I PROMISED THE DEADLINGS I WOULD GO BACK.
WE'RE GONNA HELP THEM SAVE THIS WORLD.
THE END

I named the steam-powered world Pother, because it means:
1. a heated discussion, debate, or argument; fuss; to-do (like the debate that splits the world's population).
2. a choking or suffocating cloud, as of smoke or dust (like a dirty form of steam).

—Drew Ford

Commentary by Duane Leslie.

This is an abandoned cover idea. I much prefer the elements and sensation of the cover version we eventually went with, so I was happy to see this one go to the *Steam* scrapyard. Good thing, too, because Arlo's coconut was ginormous in this picture!

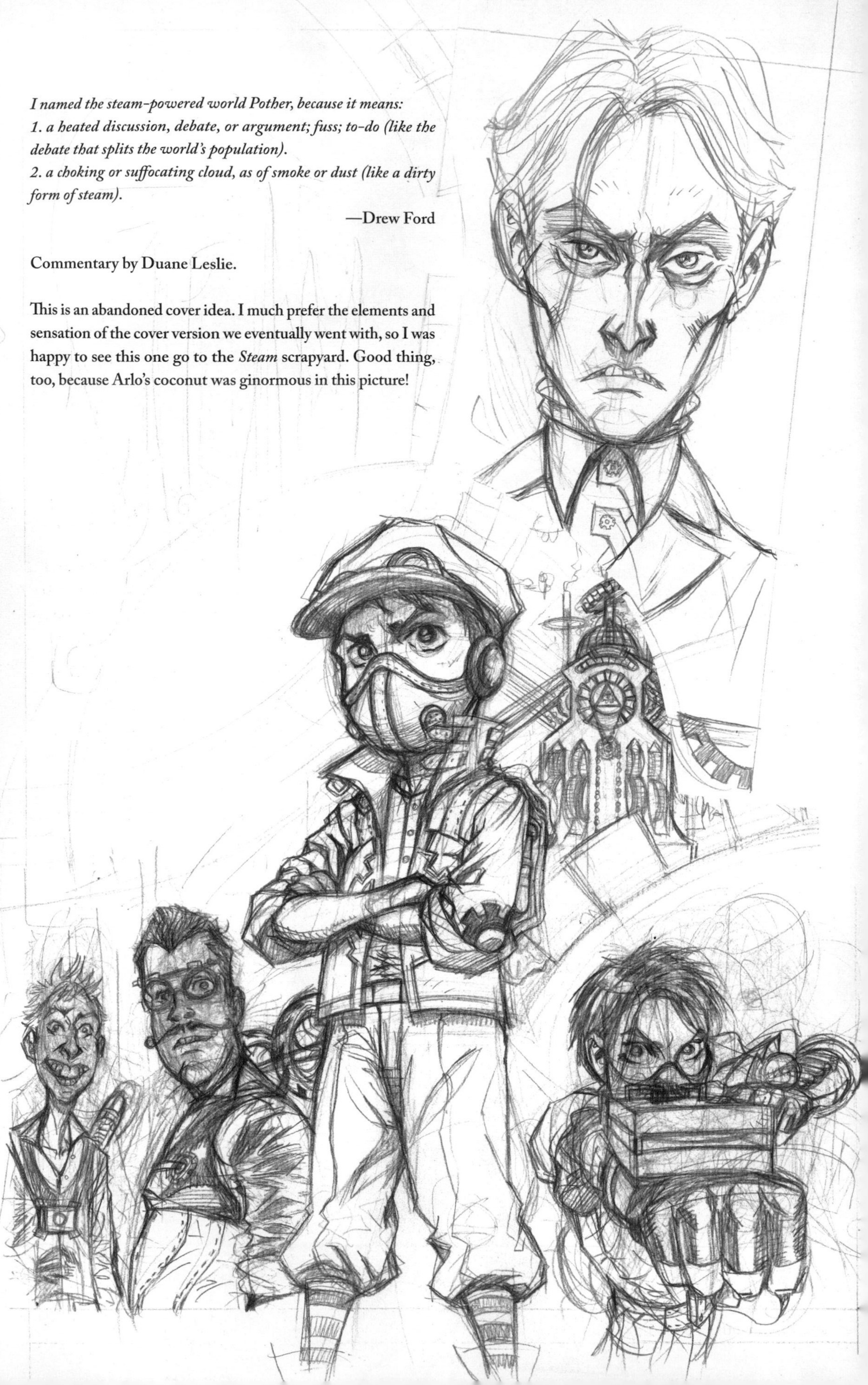

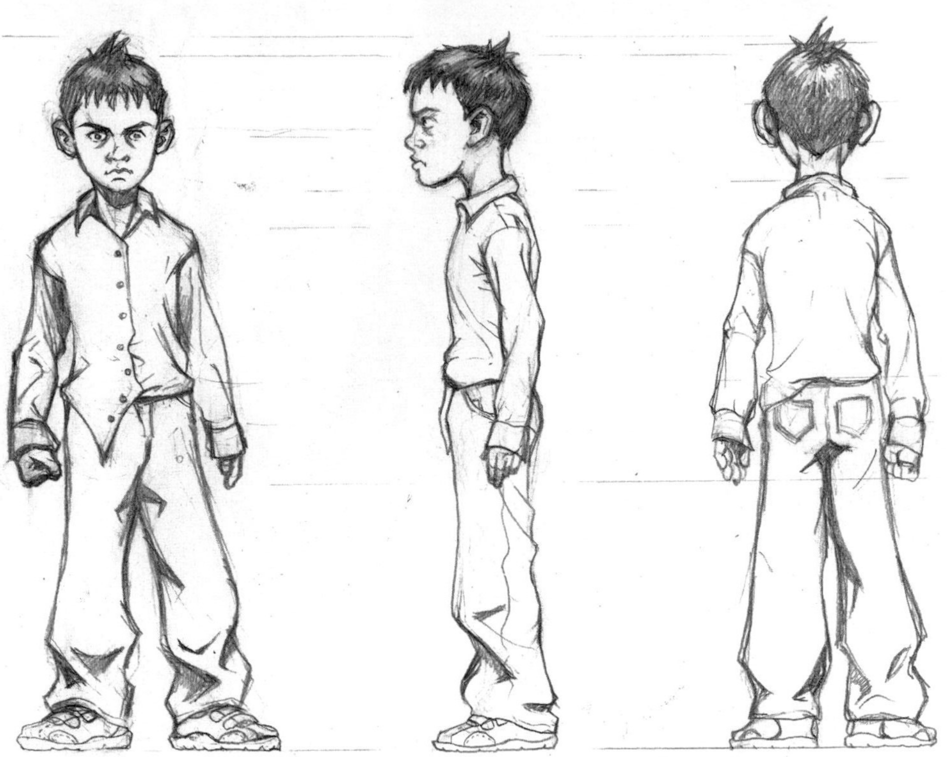

Arlo was based on a stock picture of an angry boy I came across online who looked like he could do with a Steampunk adventure himself. In this character design drawing I had his hair and clothing loose and dishevelled to reflect his inner state as we see him pre-Pother. For his trip and the start of his exciting adventure I decided to put him in a t-shirt so I could add the more distinct fiery design element to his chest.

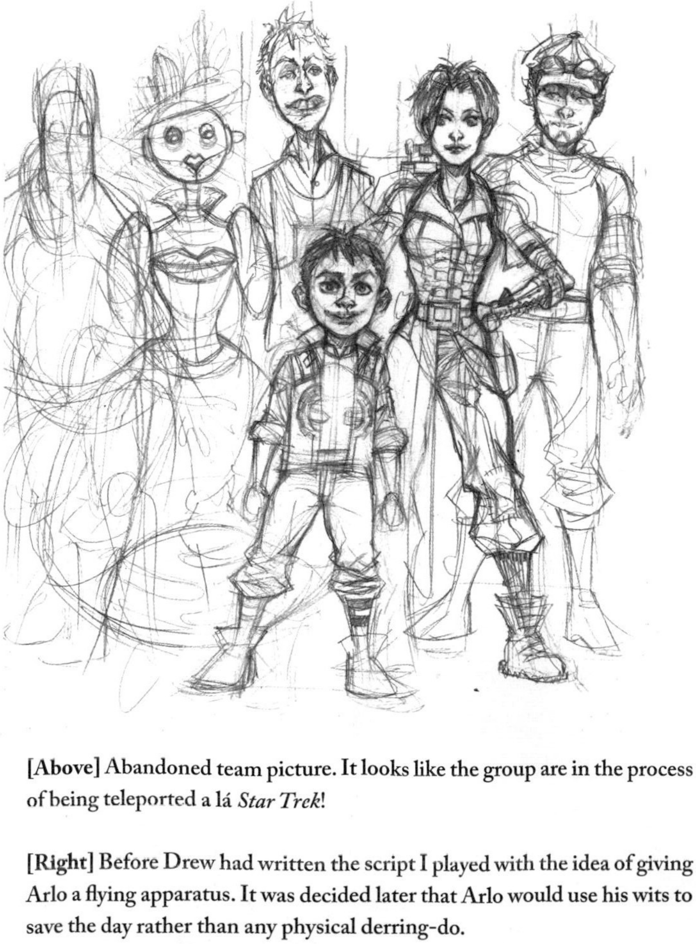

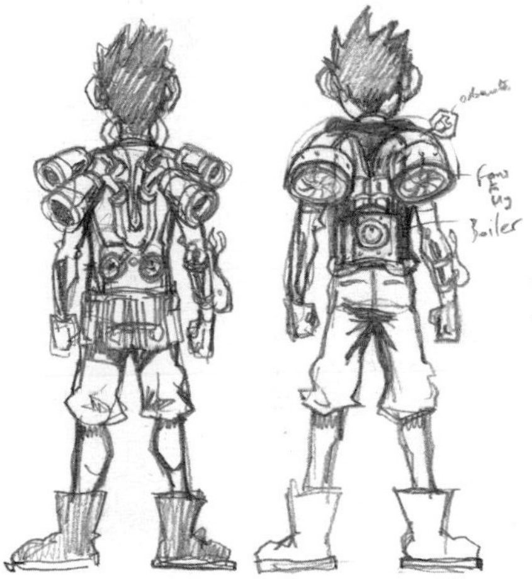
Boiler

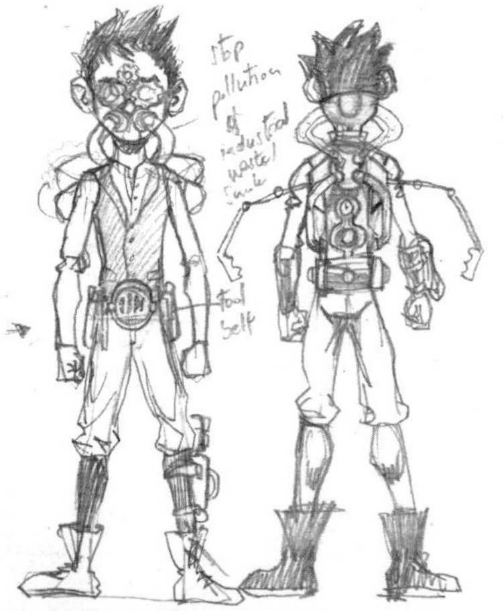
Stop
pollution
industrial

[Above] Abandoned team picture. It looks like the group are in the process of being teleported a lá *Star Trek*!

[Right] Before Drew had written the script I played with the idea of giving Arlo a flying apparatus. It was decided later that Arlo would use his wits to save the day rather than any physical derring-do.

Robot went through multiple iterations before I arrived at the final idea. She is special to Arlo because, well, she's a working robot, but also because he finds out she was made by his father. I wanted to make her look amiable and maternal as if his father somehow knew his son would one day arrive in Pother and would need her protection in his absence.

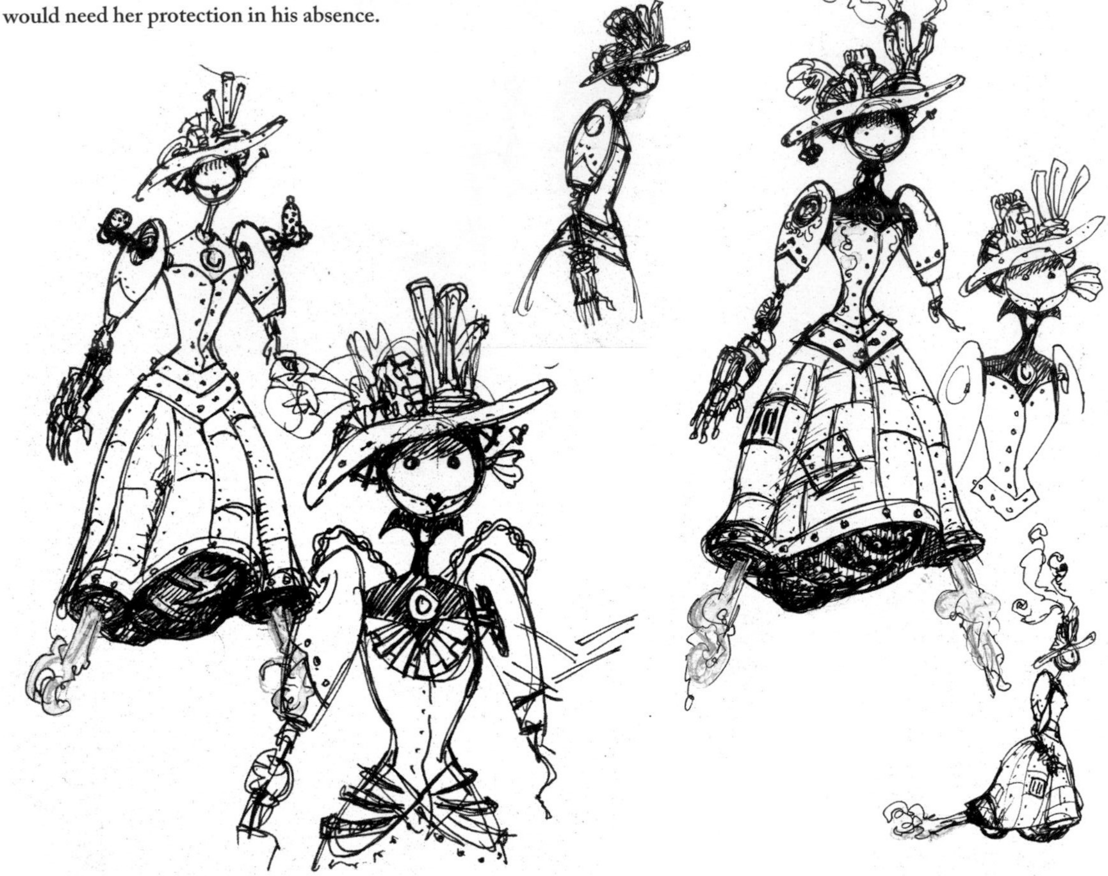

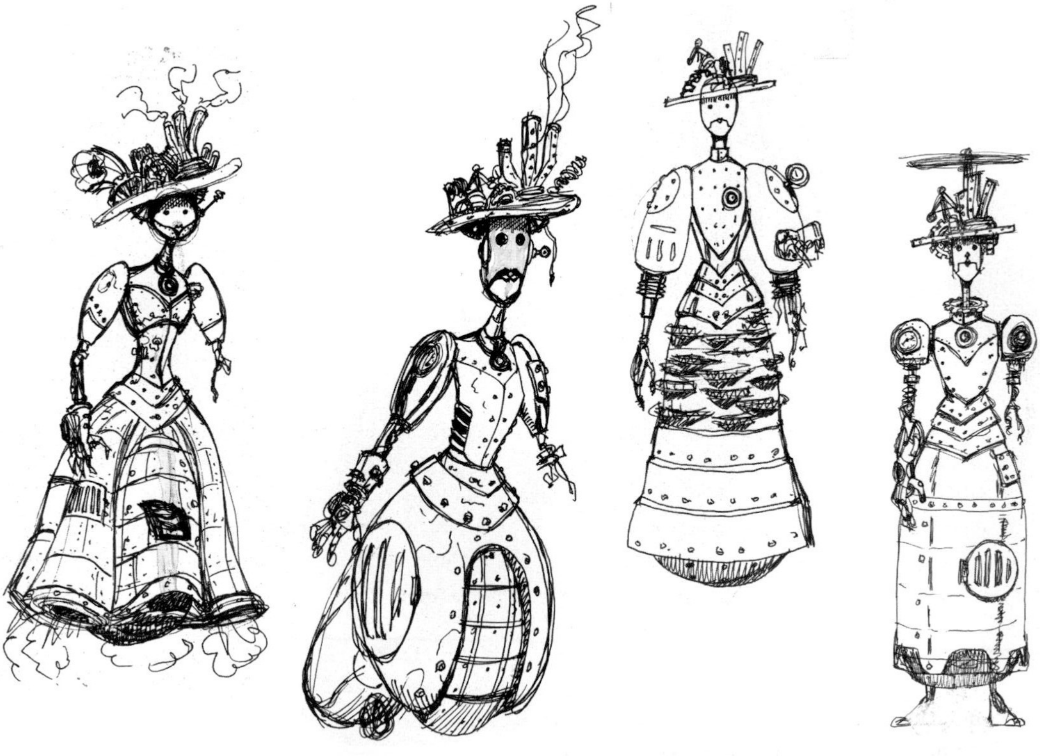

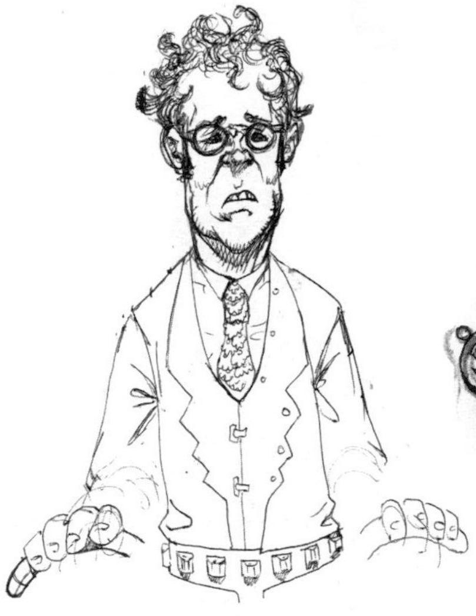
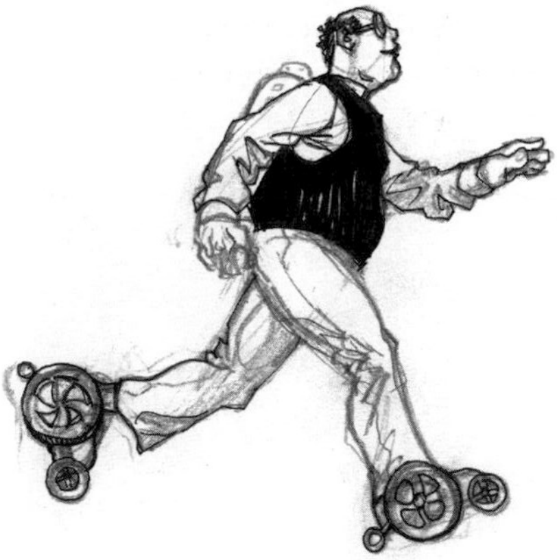
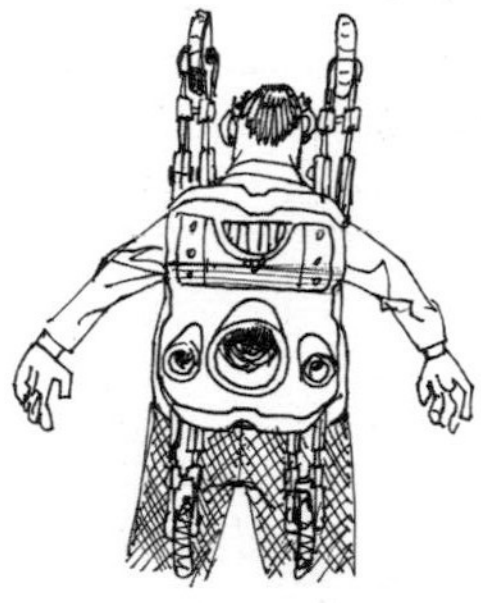
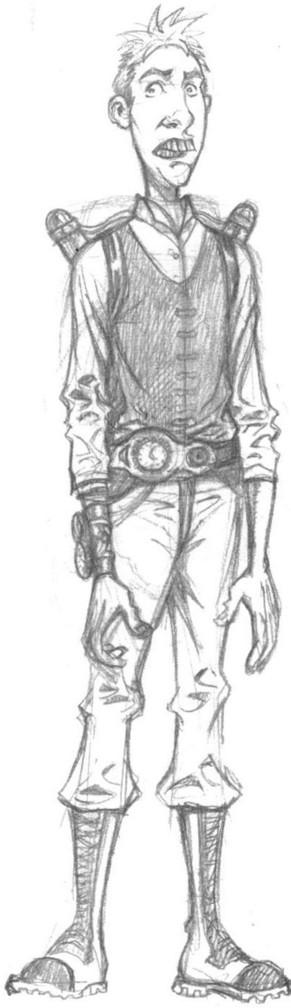
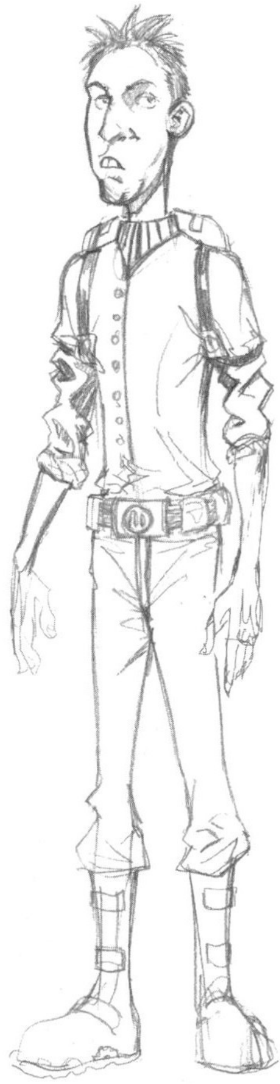
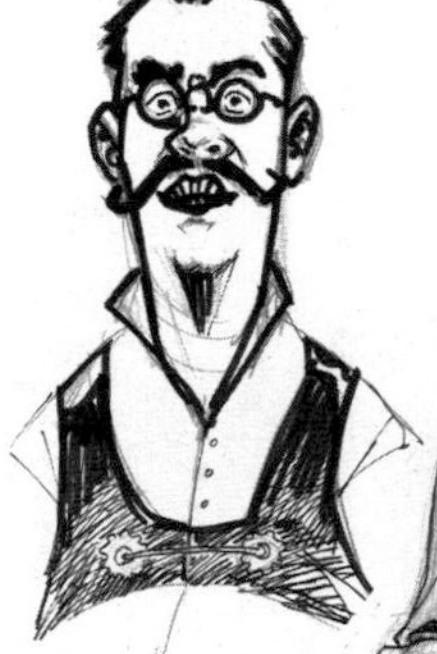
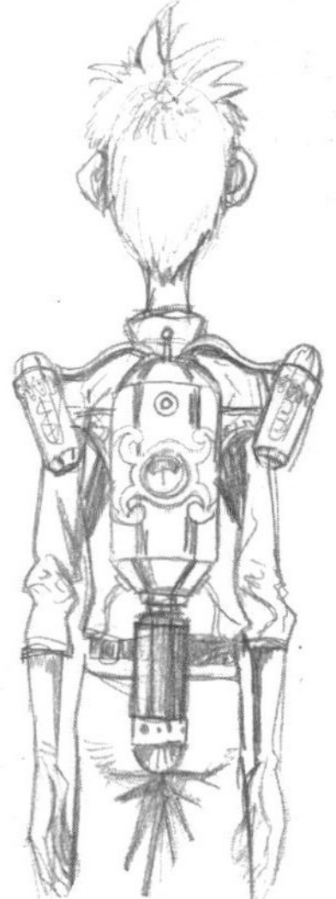
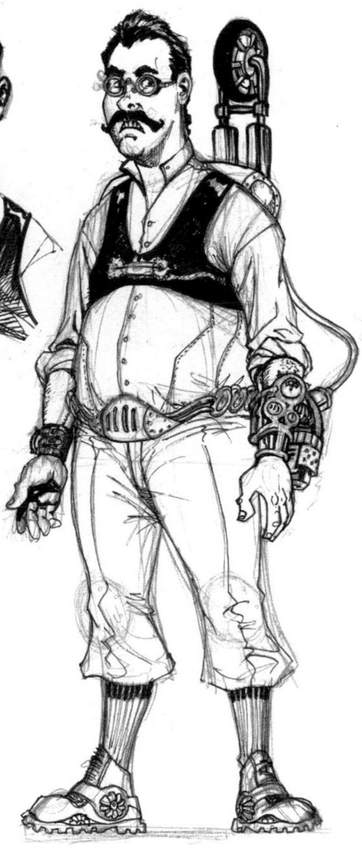

Drew made Dalton & Gaynor the quintessential double act and so in that tradition I wanted to make them distinctly different in appearance for maximum comic effect. Dalton was staid, bespectacled, portly, and dark-haired, while Gaynor was skinny, fair-haired, and goofy in both meanings of the word. Their backpacks were also designed to match their respective endomorphic and ectomorphic body types.

Drew liked the idea that in response to a dying polluted world, all Pother residents should carry backpacks which would hold a supply of needed oxygen, tools, and whatever else they wanted custom built into the packs. Originally, in the opening Pother Arlo rescue scene, Dalton was going to arrive in a steampunk chariot of some description but I thought it would be interesting if Dalton's backpack was the transport.

Unlike Dalton, Gaynor never had an opportunity to showcase his backpack which actually allows him to fly short distances.

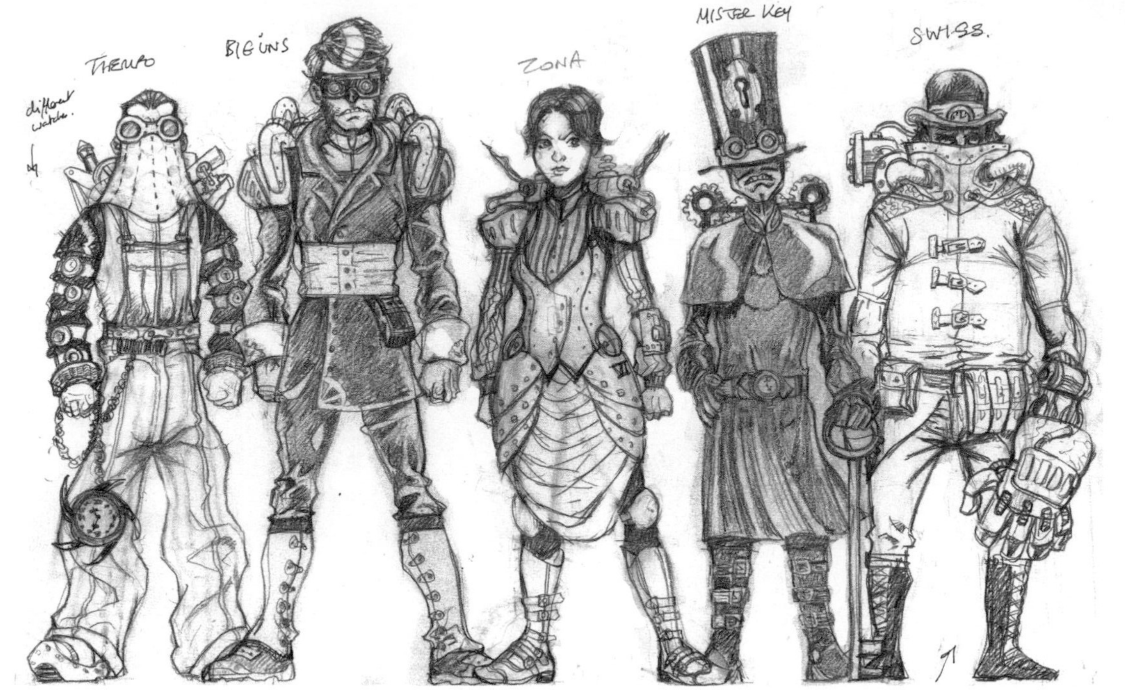
THEMPO
BIG'UNS
ZONA
MISTER KEY
SWISS.

An early version of the script had Zona as the leader of a fifth column rebel gang. I had fun coming up with this group of subversive teenage orphans but later script changes meant that only Zona made the cut.

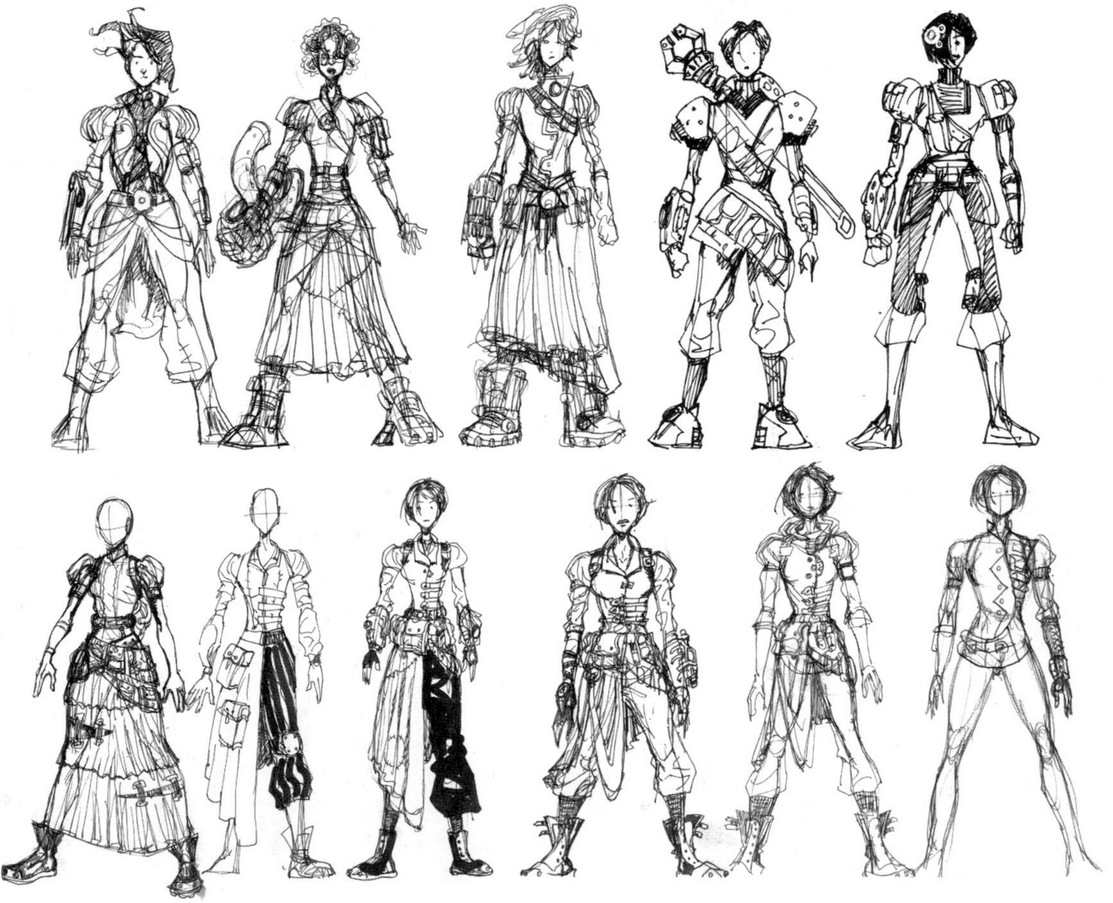

Zona's character was the most difficult design to achieve but for no good reason. Brought up by Piper in the roughest area of Pother among hardened boys meant she was never going to be seen in a Victorian hoop skirt or bustle but I wanted to intersperse traditional feminine elements of the era around her costume to represent the gentle emotional sensibility behind the tomboy persona.

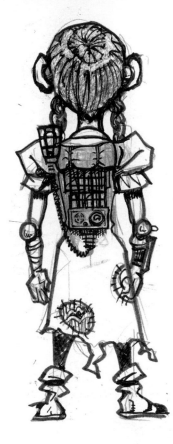

I laughed out loud when I read that Drew had a tiny creature like Agnes as Piper's fiercest warrior. My only task really was to make her cute so I gave her pigtails and freckles which are the last thing her enemies see before the world goes black!

Eva de la Cruz had the good sense to make her a fiery redhead which completed the character in my eyes. I ditched the forearm claw in this picture and gave her a staff just so I could hang a tiny teddy bear for further comic effect.

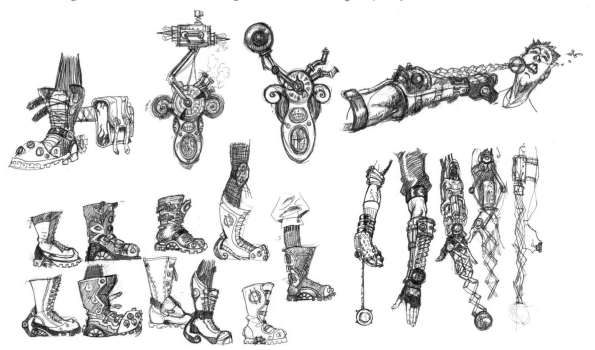

Zona's kit includes a wrist communicator, an extendable bean-bag basher gauntlet, and a two-way grappling-hook firing spear gun attached to a metal arm on her backpack. The latter was going to be used in a rooftop chase scene in

an earlier script but wasn't needed in the end. I liked the spear gun though so I kept it in for aesthetic purposes. Sorry, Zona . . . maybe next time you'll get to use all those neat gadgets.

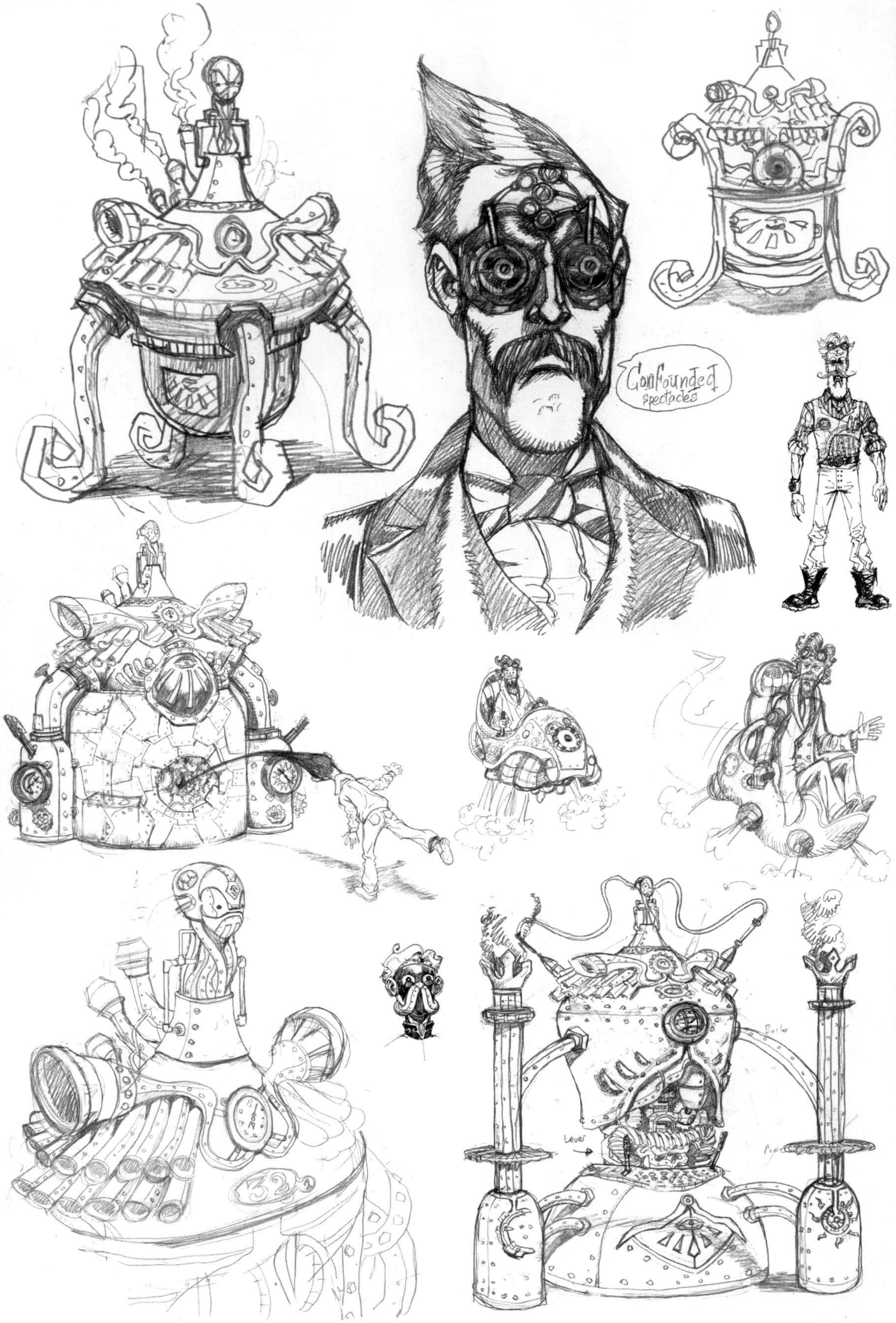
Confounded spectacles
Lever
Boiler

Arlo's father Henry was an exaggerated version of a slender bearded fellow I came across on the internet during my *Steam* research. The book couldn't be deemed a Steampunk work without one character wearing goggles so Henry took on the responsibility and it fit with his engineering/scientific profile. I added a weird waistcoat and armband with dials and gauges and the character was born.

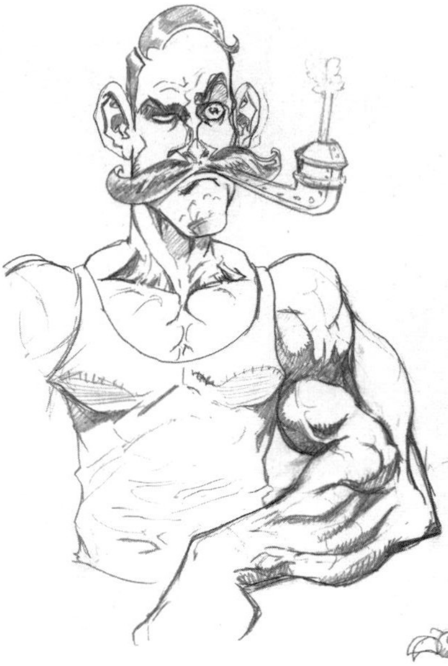

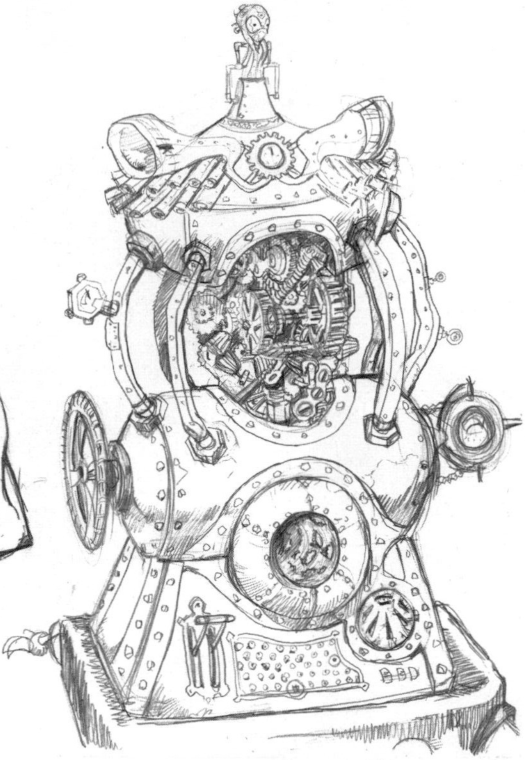

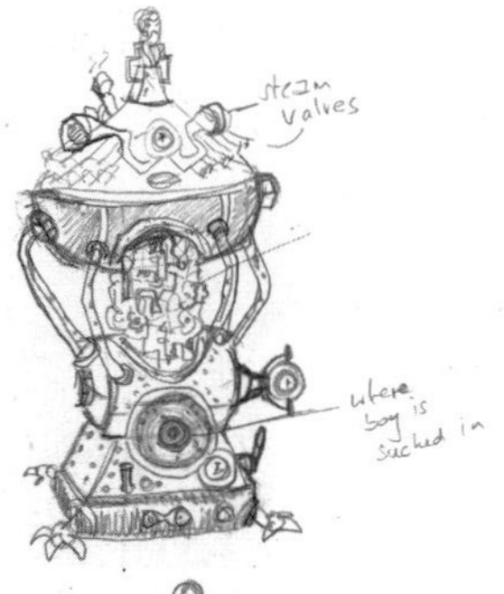
steam valves
where boy is sucked in

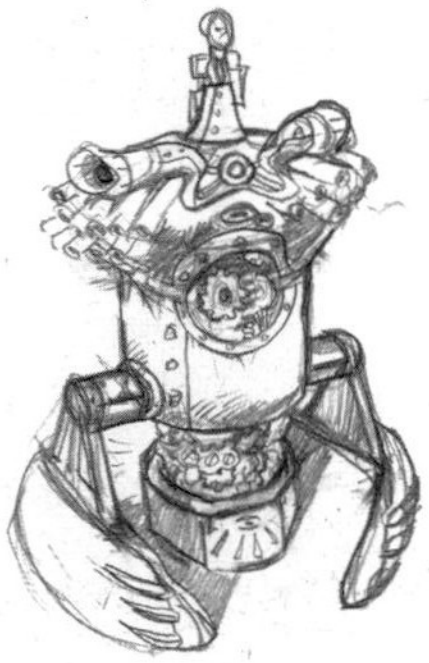

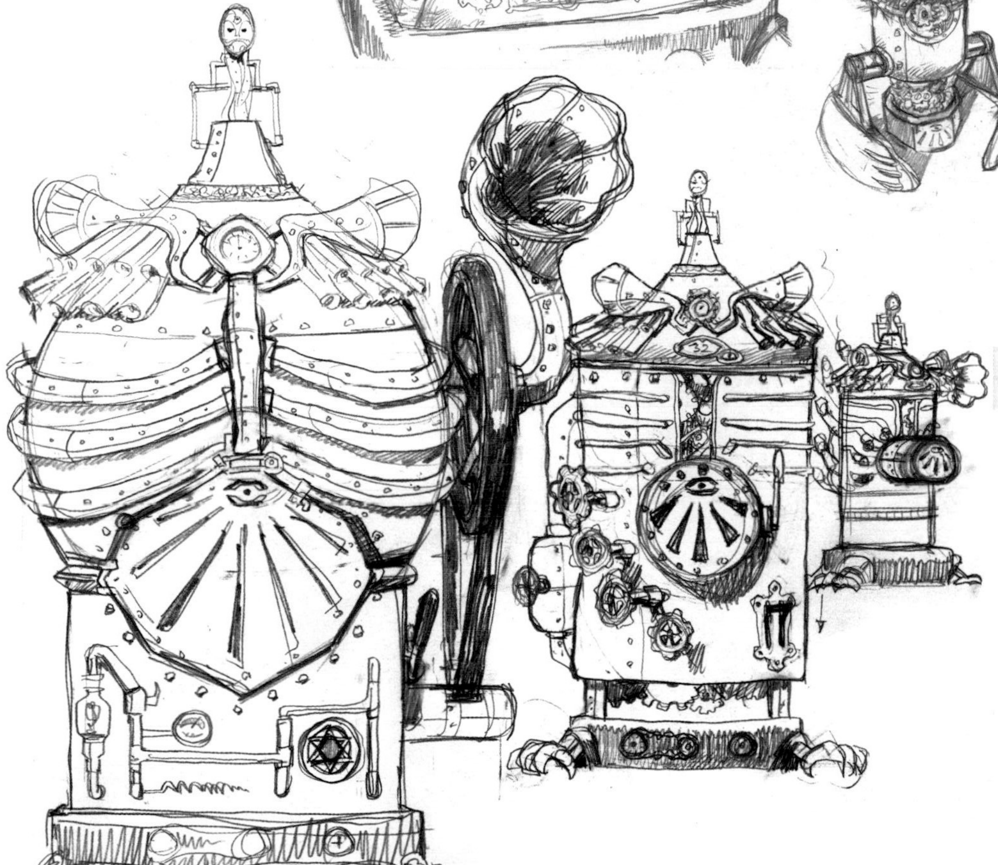

After a few failed tries I looked to Japanese animation for inspiration for the final version of the Steampunk machine that allows Arlo passage between worlds. After watching *Howl's Moving Castle*, *Steamboy*, and *Spirited Away* and then remembering a few other Steampunk bits and bobs I'd seen, my mind pieced together the design that ended up in the book. As a centerpiece for the whole adventure and the object that amazes Arlo upon first popping his head above the rafters of the attic, I felt it needed to look mysterious and magical so I threw some esoteric symbols in with the array of pipes, gauges, levers, nuts, bolts, and all-important cogs. I was pleased with the result and additionally pleased with Eva de la Cruz's wonderful color choices with it.

PULP ADVENTURES AROUND THE WORLD!

"THIS IS A FEEL-GOOD ADVENTURE LOADED WITH PERILOUS MOMENTS AND TENSION-FILLED SITUATIONS THAT KEEP THE PAGES FLYING BY."–GEEK DAD

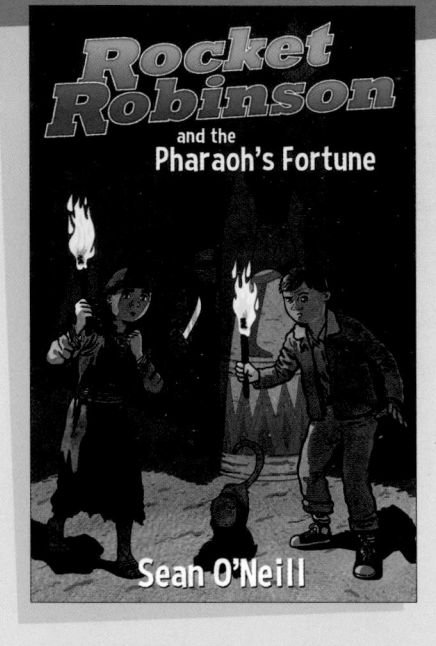

Rocket Robinson
and the
Pharaoh's Fortune
Sean O'Neill

ROCKET ROBINSON AND THE PHARAOH'S FORTUNE

The Egyptian capital is a buzzing hive of treasure-hunters, thrill-seekers, and adventurers, but to 12-year-old Ronald "Rocket" Robinson, it's just another sticker on his well-worn suitcase. But when Rocket finds a strange note written in Egyptian hieroglyphs, he stumbles into an adventure more incredible than anything he's ever dreamt of.

ISBN 978-1-50670-618-4 • $14.99

ROCKET ROBINSON AND THE SECRET OF THE SAINT

Rocket, Nuri, and Screech find themselves in the French capital, where a rare and mysterious painting from the middle ages has been stolen from the Louvre Museum! The young adventurers are soon hot on the trail and the secret contained within may lead all the way to the most mysterious and sought-after treasure in history.

ISBN 978-1-50670-679-5 • $14.99

Rocket Robinson
and the Secret
of the Saint
Sean O'Neill

AVAILABLE AT YOUR LOCAL COMICS SHOP OR BOOKSTORE! To find a comics shop in your area, visit comicshoplocator.com. For more information or to order direct: On the web: DarkHorse.com • Email: mailorder@darkhorse.com • Phone: 1-800-862-0052 Mon.–Fri. 9 AM to 5 PM Pacific Time

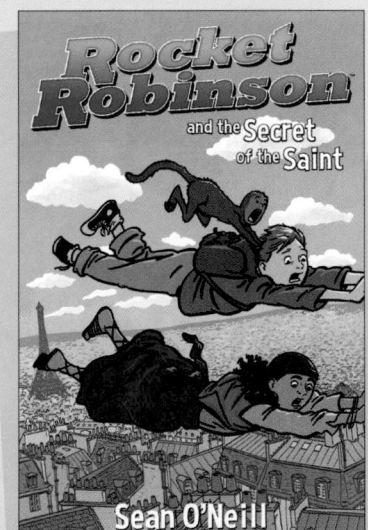

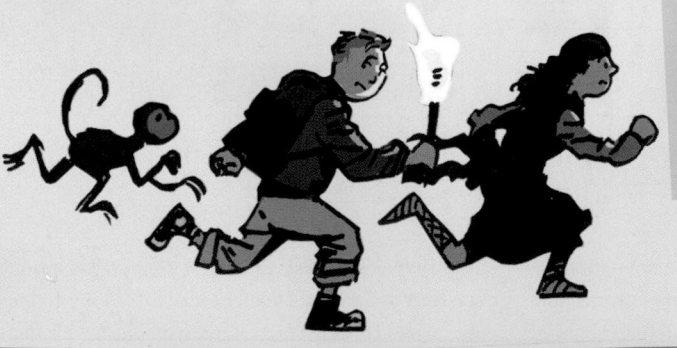

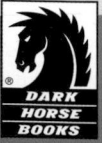

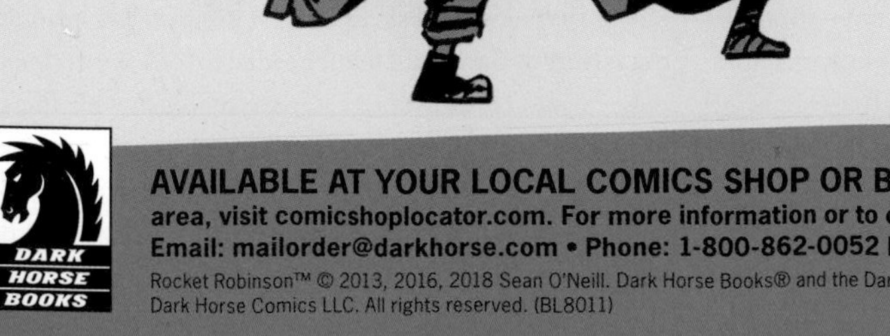